A TOUR OF THE NIGHT

18 original stories by today's most acclaimed dark fantasy authors.
From the New Orleans goth scene
to the deathpunk bars of gay Amsterdam—
from the Dark behind the lights of Vegas,
to the secret lovers who live in Lugosi's tomb—
platinum popstars, lascivious lap dancers, naughty necrophiles . . .
all with one uncommon thing in common.
For them, desire and hunger are one.

LOVE IN VEIN II

Vampiric Erotica from

Neil Gaiman • Randy Fox • Pat Califia • Jean-Daniel Brèque •
Janet Berliner and George Guthridge • Lucy Taylor •
Christopher Fowler •O'Neil De Noux • Thomas S. Roche •
Stephen Mark Rainey • David J. Schow •Richard Laymon •
Nicholas Royle • Roberta Lannes • David Niall Wilson • Brian Hodge •
Th. Metzger • Caitlín R. Kiernan

Also edited by Poppy Z. Brite

Love in Vein
Twenty Original Tales of Vampiric Erotica

Published by HarperPrism

LOVE IN VEIN II

EIGHTEEN MORE TALES OF
VAMPIRIC EROTICA

Selected and
Edited by
Poppy Z. Brite

HarperPrism
An Imprint of HarperPaperbacks

HarperPaperbacks
A Division of HarperCollins*Publishers*
10 East 53rd Street, New York, N.Y. 10022-5299

Printed in the United States of America

First printing: January 1997

Cover illustration by Mel Odom

Library of Congress Cataloging-in-Publication Data

Love in vein II: 18 more tales of vampiric erotica/edited by Poppy Z. Brite.
p. cm.
ISBN 0-06-105333-3 (TP)
1. —Vampires—Fiction. 2. Horror tales, American. 3. Erotic stories, American I. Brite, Poppy Z.
PS648.V35L683 1997
813'.0873808375--dc20 96-31082
CIP

96 97 98 99 ❖ 10 9 8 7 6 5 4 3 2 1

For Chuckie B.,
who lost six *fleurs du mal*

Table of Contents

Snow, Glass, Apples

Neil Gaiman

I do not know what manner of thing she is. None of us do. She killed her mother in the birthing, but that's never enough to account for it.

They call me wise, but I am far from wise, for all that I foresaw fragments of it, frozen moments caught in pools of water or in the cold glass of my mirror. If I were wise I would not have tried to change what I saw. If I were wise I would have killed myself before ever I encountered her, before ever I caught him.

Wise, and a witch, or so they said, and I'd seen his face in my dreams and in reflections for all my life: sixteen years of dreaming of him before he reined his horse by the bridge that day, and asked my name. He helped me onto his high horse and we rode together to my little cottage, my face buried in the gold of his hair. He asked for the best of what I had; a king's right, it was.

His beard was red-bronze in the morning light, and I knew him, not as a king, for I knew nothing of kings then, but as my love. He took all he wanted from me, the right of kings, but he returned to me on the following day, and on the night after that: his beard so red, his hair so gold, his eyes the blue of a summer sky, his skin tanned the gentle brown of ripe wheat.

His daughter was only a child: no more than five years of age when I came to the palace. A portrait of her dead mother hung in the princess's tower room; a tall woman, hair the colour of dark wood, eyes nut-brown. She was of a different blood to her pale daughter.

The girl would not eat with us.

I do not know where in the palace she ate.

I had my own chambers. My husband the king, he had his own rooms also. When he wanted me he would send for me, and I would go to him, and pleasure him, and take my pleasure with him.

One night, several months after I was brought to the palace, she came to my rooms. She was six. I was embroidering by lamplight, squinting my eyes against the lamp's smoke and fitful illumination. When I looked up, she was there.

"Princess?"

She said nothing. Her eyes were black as coal, black as her hair; her lips were redder than blood. She looked up at me and smiled. Her teeth seemed sharp, even then, in the lamplight.

"What are you doing away from your room?"

"I'm hungry," she said, like any child.

It was winter, when fresh food is a dream of warmth and sunlight; but I had strings of whole apples, cored and dried, hanging from the beams of my chamber, and I pulled an apple down for her.

"Here."

Autumn is the time of drying, of preserving, a time of picking apples, of rendering the goose-fat. Winter is the time of hunger, of snow, and of death; and it is the time of the midwinter feast, when we rub the goose-fat into the skin of a whole pig, stuffed with that autumn's apples; then we roast it or spit it, and we prepare to feast upon the crackling.

She took the dried apple from me and began to chew it with her sharp yellow teeth.

"Is it good?"

She nodded. I had always been scared of the little princess, but at that moment I warmed to her and, with my fingers, gently, I stroked her cheek. She looked at me and smiled—she smiled but rarely—then she sank her teeth into the base of my thumb, the Mound of Venus, and she drew blood.

I began to shriek, from pain and from surprise; but she looked at me and I fell silent.

The little princess fastened her mouth to my hand and licked and sucked and drank. When she was finished, she left my chamber. Beneath my gaze the cut that she had made began to close, to scab, and to heal. The next day it was an old scar: I might have cut my hand with a pocketknife in my childhood.

I had been frozen by her, owned and dominated. That scared me, more than the blood she had fed on. After that night I locked my chamber door at dusk, barring it with an oaken pole, and I had the smith forge iron bars, which he placed across my windows.

My husband, my love, my king, sent for me less and less, and when I came to him he was dizzy, listless, confused. He could no longer make love as a man makes love; and he would not permit me to pleasure him with my mouth: the one time I tried, he started, violently, and began to weep. I pulled my mouth away and held him tightly, until the sobbing had stopped, and he slept, like a child.

I ran my fingers across his skin as he slept. It was covered in a multitude of ancient scars. But I could recall no scars from the days of our courtship, save one, on his side, where a boar had gored him when he was a youth.

Soon he was a shadow of the man I had met and loved by the bridge. His bones showed, blue and white, beneath his skin. I was with him at the last: his hands were cold as stone, his eyes milky-blue, his hair and beard faded and lustreless and limp. He died unshriven, his skin nipped and pocked from head to toe with tiny, old scars.

He weighed near to nothing. The ground was frozen hard, and we could dig no grave for him, so we made a cairn of rocks and stones above his body, as a memorial only, for there was little enough of him left to protect from the hunger of the beasts and the birds.

So I was queen.

And I was foolish, and young—eighteen summers had come and gone since first I saw daylight—and I did not do what I would do, now.

If it were today, I would have her heart cut out, true. But then I would have her head and arms and legs cut off. I would have them disembowel her. And then I would watch, in the town square, as the hangman heated the fire to white-heat with bellows, watch unblinking as he consigned each part of her to the fire. I would have archers around the square, who would shoot any bird or animal who came close to the flames, any raven or dog or hawk or rat. And I would not close my eyes until the princess was ash, and a gentle wind could scatter her like snow.

I did not do this thing, and we pay for our mistakes.

They say I was fooled; that it was not her heart. That it was the heart of an animal—a stag, perhaps, or a boar. They say that, and they are wrong.

And some say (but it is *her* lie, not mine) that I was given the heart, and that I ate it. Lies and half-truths fall like snow, covering the things that I remember, the things I saw. A landscape, unrecognisable after a snowfall: that is what she has made of my life.

There were scars on my love, her father's thighs, and on his ballock-pouch, and on his male member, when he died.

I did not go with them. They took her in the day, while she slept, and was at her weakest. They took her to the heart of the forest, and there they opened her blouse, and they cut out her heart, and they left her dead, in a gully, for the forest to swallow.

The forest is a dark place, the border to many kingdoms; no one would be foolish enough to claim jurisdiction over it. Outlaws live in the forest. Robbers live in the forest, and so do wolves. You can ride through the forest for a dozen days and never see a soul; but there are eyes upon you the entire time.

They brought me her heart. I know it was hers—no sow's heart or doe's would have continued to beat and pulse after it had been cut out, as that one did.

I took it to my chamber.

I did not eat it: I hung it from the beams above my bed, placed it on a length of twine that I strung with rowan berries, orange-red as a robin's breast, and with bulbs of garlic.

Outside, the snow fell, covering the footprints of my huntsmen, covering her tiny body in the forest where it lay.

I had the smith remove the iron bars from my windows, and I would spend some time in my room each afternoon through the short winter days, gazing out over the forest, until darkness fell.

There were, as I have already stated, people in the forest. They would come out, some of them, for the Spring Fair: a greedy, feral, dangerous people; some were stunted—dwarfs and midgets and hunchbacks; others had the huge teeth and vacant gazes of idiots; some had fingers like flippers or crab-claws. They would creep out of the forest each year for the Spring Fair, held when the snows had melted.

As a young lass I had worked at the fair, and they had scared me then, the forest folk. I told fortunes for the fairgoers, scrying in a pool of still water; and, later, when I was older, in a disk of polished glass, its back all silvered—a gift from a merchant whose straying horse I had seen in a pool of ink.

The stallholders at the fair were afraid of the forest folk; they would nail their wares to the bare boards of their stalls—slabs of gingerbread or leather belts were nailed with great iron nails to the wood. If their wares were not nailed, they said, the forest folk would take them, and run away, chewing on the stolen gingerbread, flailing about them with the belts.

The forest folk had money, though: a coin here, another there, sometimes stained green by time or the earth, the face on the coin unknown to even the oldest of us. Also they had things to trade, and thus the fair continued, serving the outcasts and the dwarfs, serving the robbers (if they were circumspect) who preyed on the rare travellers from lands beyond the forest, or on gypsies, or on the deer. (This was robbery in the eyes of the law. The deer were the queen's.)

The years passed by slowly, and my people claimed that I ruled them with wisdom. The heart still hung above my bed, pulsing gently in the night. If there were any who mourned the child, I saw no evidence: she was a thing of terror, back then, and they believed themselves well rid of her.

Spring Fair followed Spring Fair: five of them, each sadder, poorer, shoddier than the one before. Fewer of the forest folk came out of the forest to buy. Those who did seemed subdued and listless. The stallholders stopped nailing their wares to the boards of their stalls. And by the fifth year but a handful of folk came from the forest—a fearful huddle of little hairy men, and no one else.

The Lord of the Fair, and his page, came to me when the fair was done. I had known him slightly, before I was queen.

"I do not come to you as my queen," he said.

I said nothing. I listened.

"I come to you because you are wise," he continued. "When you were a child you found a strayed foal by staring into a pool of ink; when you were a maiden you found a lost infant who had wandered far from her mother, by staring into that mirror of yours. You know secrets and you can seek out things hidden. My queen," he asked, "what is taking the forest folk? Next year there will be no Spring Fair. The travellers from other kingdoms have grown scarce and few, the folk of the forest are almost gone. Another year like the last, and we shall all starve."

I commanded my maidservant to bring me my looking glass. It was a simple thing, a silver-backed glass disk, which I kept wrapped in a doe-skin, in a chest, in my chamber.

They brought it to me, then, and I gazed into it:

She was twelve and she was no longer a little child. Her skin was still pale, her eyes and hair coal-black, her lips blood-red. She wore the clothes she had worn when she left the castle for the last time—the blouse, the skirt—although they were much let-out, much mended. Over them she wore a leather cloak, and instead of boots she had leather bags, tied with thongs, over her tiny feet.

She was standing in the forest, beside a tree.

As I watched, in the eye of my mind, I saw her edge and step and flitter and pad from tree to tree, like an animal: a bat or a wolf. She was following someone.

He was a monk. He wore sackcloth, and his feet were bare, and scabbed and hard. His beard and tonsure were of a length, overgrown, unshaven.

She watched him from behind the trees. Eventually he paused for the night, and began to make a fire, laying twigs down, breaking up a robin's nest as kindling. He had a tinderbox in his robe, and he knocked the flint against the steel until the sparks caught the tinder and the fire flamed. There had been two eggs in the nest he had found, and these he ate, raw. They cannot have been much of a meal for so big a man.

He sat there in the firelight, and she came out from her hiding place. She crouched down on the other side of the fire, and stared at him. He grinned, as if it were a long time since he had seen another human, and beckoned her over to him.

She stood up and walked around the fire, and waited, an arm's length away. He pulled in his robe until he found a coin—a tiny, copper penny—and tossed it to her. She caught it, and nodded, and went to him. He pulled at the robe around his waist, and his robe swung open. His body was as hairy as a bear's. She pushed him back onto the moss. One hand crept, spiderlike, through the tangle of hair, until it closed on his manhood; the other hand traced a circle on his left nipple. He closed his eyes, and fumbled one huge hand under her skirt. She lowered her mouth to the nipple she had been teasing, her smooth skin white on the furry brown body of him.

She sank her teeth deep into his breast. His eyes opened, then they closed again, and she drank.

She straddled him, and she fed. As she did so a thin blackish liquid began to dribble from between her legs. . . .

"Do you know what is keeping the travellers from our town? What is happening to the forest people?" asked the Head of the Fair.

I covered the mirror in doeskin, and told him that I would personally take it upon myself to make the forest safe once more.

I had to, although she terrified me. I was the queen.

A foolish woman would have gone then into the forest and tried to capture the creature; but I had been foolish once and had no wish to be so a second time.

I spent time with old books. I spent time with the gypsy women (who passed through our country across the mountains to the south, rather than cross the forest to the north and the west).

I prepared myself, and obtained those things I would need, and when the first snows began to fall, I was ready.

Naked, I was, and alone in the highest tower of the palace, a place open to the sky. The winds chilled my body; goose pimples crept across my arms and thighs and breasts. I carried a silver basin, and a basket in which I had placed a silver knife, a silver pin, some tongs, a grey robe and three green apples.

I put them down and stood there, unclothed, on the tower, humble before the night sky and the wind. Had any man seen me standing there, I would have had his eyes; but there was no one to spy. Clouds scudded across the sky, hiding and uncovering the waning moon.

I took the silver knife and slashed my left arm—once, twice, three times. The blood dripped into the basin, scarlet seeming black in the moonlight.

I added the powder from the vial that hung around my neck. It was a brown dust, made of dried herbs and the skin of a particular toad, and from certain other things. It thickened the blood, while preventing it from clotting.

I took the three apples, one by one, and pricked their skins gently with my silver pin. Then I placed the apples in the silver bowl, and let them sit there while the first tiny flakes of snow of the year fell slowly onto my skin, and onto the apples, and onto the blood.

When dawn began to brighten the sky I covered myself with the grey cloak, and took the red apples from the silver bowl, one by one, lifting each into my basket with silver tongs, taking care not to touch it. There was nothing left of my blood or of the brown powder in the silver bowl, nothing save a black residue, like a verdigris, on the inside.

I buried the bowl in the earth. Then I cast a glamour on the apples (as once, years before, by a bridge, I had cast a glamour on myself), that they were, beyond any doubt, the most wonderful apples in the world, and the crimson blush of their skins was the warm colour of fresh blood.

I pulled the hood of my cloak low over my face, and I took ribbons and pretty hair ornaments with me, placed them above the apples in the reed basket, and I walked alone into the forest, until I came to her dwelling: a high, sandstone cliff, laced with deep caves going back a way into the rock wall.

There were trees and boulders around the cliff-face, and I walked quietly and gently from tree to tree, without disturbing a twig or a fallen leaf. Eventually I found my place to hide, and I waited, and I watched.

After some hours a clutch of dwarfs crawled out of the hole in the cavefront—ugly, misshapen, hairy little men, the old inhabitants of this country. You saw them seldom now.

They vanished into the wood, and none of them espied me, though one of them stopped to piss against the rock I hid behind.

I waited. No more came out.

I went to the cave entrance and hallooed into it, in a cracked old voice.

The scar on my Mound of Venus throbbed and pulsed as she came toward me, out of the darkness, naked and alone.

She was thirteen years of age, my stepdaughter, and nothing marred the perfect whiteness of her skin save for the livid scar on her left breast, where her heart had been cut from her long since.

The insides of her thighs were stained with wet black filth.

She peered at me, hidden, as I was, in my cloak. She looked at me hungrily. "Ribbons, goodwife," I croaked. "Pretty ribbons for your hair . . . "

She smiled and beckoned to me. A tug; the scar on my hand was pulling me toward her. I did what I had planned to do, but I did it more readily than I had planned: I dropped my basket, and screeched like the bloodless old peddler woman I was pretending to be, and I ran.

My grey cloak was the colour of the forest, and I was fast; she did not catch me.

I made my way back to the palace.

I did not see it. Let us imagine though, the girl returning, frustrated and hungry, to her cave, and finding my fallen basket on the ground.

What did she do?

I like to think she played first with the ribbons, twined them into her raven hair, looped them around her pale neck or her tiny waist.

And then, curious, she moved the cloth to see what else was in the basket; and she saw the red, red apples.

They smelled like fresh apples, of course; and they also smelled of blood. And she was hungry. I imagine her picking up an apple, pressing it against her cheek, feeling the cold smoothness of it against her skin.

And she opened her mouth and bit deep into it. . . .

By the time I reached my chambers, the heart that hung from the roofbeam, with the apples and hams and the dried sausages, had ceased to beat. It hung there, quietly, without motion or life, and I felt safe once more.

That winter the snows were high and deep, and were late melting. We were all hungry come the spring.

The Spring Fair was slightly improved that year. The forest folk were few, but they were there, and there were travellers from the lands beyond the forest.

I saw the little hairy men of the forest-cave buying and bargaining for pieces of glass, and lumps of crystal and of quartz-rock. They paid for the glass with silver coins—the spoils of my stepdaughter's depredations, I had no doubt. When it got about what they were buying, townsfolk rushed back to their homes, came back with their lucky crystals, and, in a few cases, with whole sheets of glass.

I thought, briefly, about having the little men killed, but I did not. As long as the heart hung, silent and immobile and cold, from the beam of my chamber, I was safe, and so were the folk of the forest, and, thus, eventually, the folk of the town.

My twenty-fifth year came, and my stepdaughter had eaten the poisoned fruit two winters back, when the prince came to my palace. He was tall, very tall, with cold green eyes and the swarthy skin of those from beyond the mountains.

He rode with a small retinue: large enough to defend him, small enough that another monarch—myself, for instance—would not view him as a potential threat.

I was practical: I thought of the alliance of our lands, thought of the kingdom running from the forests all the way south to the sea; I thought of my golden-haired bearded love, dead these eight years; and, in the night, I went to the prince's room.

I am no innocent, although my late husband, who was once my king, was truly my first lover, no matter what they say.

At first the prince seemed excited. He bade me remove my shift, and made me stand in front of the opened window, far from the fire, until my skin was chilled stone-cold. Then he asked me to lie upon my back, with my hands folded across my breasts, my eyes wide open—but staring only at the beams above. He told me not to move, and to breathe as little as possible. He implored me to say nothing. He spread my legs apart.

It was then that he entered me.

As he began to thrust inside me, I felt my hips raise, felt myself begin to match him, grind for grind, push for push. I moaned. I could not help myself.

His manhood slid out of me. I reached out and touched it, a tiny, slippery thing.

"Please," he said, softly. "You must neither move nor speak. Just lie there on the stones, so cold and so fair."

I tried, but he had lost whatever force it was that had made him virile; and, some short while later, I left the prince's room, his curses and tears still resounding in my ears.

He left early the next morning, with all his men, and they rode off into the forest.

I imagine his loins, now, as he rode, a knot of frustration at the base of his manhood. I imagine his pale lips pressed so tightly together. Then I imagine his little troupe riding through the forest, finally coming upon the glass-and-crystal cairn of my stepdaughter. So pale. So cold. Naked, beneath the glass, and little more than a girl, and dead.

In my fancy, I can almost feel the sudden hardness of his manhood inside his britches, envision the lust that took him then, the prayers he muttered beneath his breath in thanks for his good fortune. I imagine him negotiating with the little hairy men—offering them gold and spices for the lovely corpse under the crystal mound.

Did they take his gold willingly? Or did they look up to see his men on their horses, with their sharp swords and their spears, and realize they had no alternative?

I do not know. I was not there; I was not scrying. I can only imagine. . . .

Hands, pulling off the lumps of glass and quartz from her cold body. Hands, gently caressing her cold cheek, moving her cold arm, rejoicing to find the corpse still fresh and pliable.

Did he take her there, in front of them all? Or did he have her carried to a secluded nook before he mounted her?

I cannot say.

Did he shake the apple from her throat? Or did her eyes slowly open as he pounded into her cold body; did her mouth open, those red lips part, those sharp yellow teeth close on his swarthy neck, as the blood, which is the life, trickled down her throat, washing down and away the lump of apple, my own, my poison?

I imagine; I do not know.

This I do know: I was woken in the night by her heart pulsing and beating once more. Salt blood dripped onto my face from above. I sat up. My hand burned and pounded as if I had hit the base of my thumb with a rock.

There was a hammering on the door. I felt afraid, but I am a queen, and I would not show fear. I opened the door.

First his men walked into my chamber and stood around me, with their sharp swords, and their long spears.

Then he came in; and he spat in my face.

Finally, she walked into my chamber, as she had when I was first a queen, and she was a child of six. She had not changed. Not really.

She pulled down the twine on which her heart was hanging. She pulled off the rowan berries, one by one; pulled off the garlic bulb—now a dried thing, after all these years; then she took up her own, her pumping heart—a small thing, no larger than that of a nanny goat or a she-bear—as it brimmed and pumped its blood into her hand.

Her fingernails must have been as sharp as glass: she opened her breast with them, running them over the purple scar. Her chest gaped, suddenly, open and bloodless. She licked her heart, once, as the blood ran over her hands, and she pushed the heart deep into her breast.

I saw her do it. I saw her close the flesh of her breast once more. I saw the purple scar begin to fade.

Her prince looked briefly concerned, but he put his arm around her nonetheless, and they stood, side by side, and they waited.

And she stayed cold, and the bloom of death remained on her lips, and his lust was not diminished in any way.

They told me they would marry, and the kingdoms would indeed be joined. They told me that I would be with them on their wedding day.

It is starting to get hot in here.

They have told the people bad things about me; a little truth to add savour to the dish, but mixed with many lies.

I was bound and kept in a tiny stone cell beneath the palace, and I remained there through the autumn. Today they fetched me out of the cell; they stripped the rags from me, and washed the filth from me, and then they shaved my head and my loins, and they rubbed my skin with goose-grease.

The snow was falling as they carried me—two men at each hand, two men at each leg—utterly exposed, and spread-eagled and cold, through the midwinter crowds, and brought me to this kiln.

My stepdaughter stood there with her prince. She watched me, in my indignity, but she said nothing.

As they thrust me inside, jeering and chaffing as they did so, I saw one snowflake land upon her white cheek, and remain there without melting.

They closed the kiln door behind me. It is getting hotter in here, and outside they are singing and cheering and banging on the sides of the kiln.

She was not laughing, or jeering, or talking. She did not sneer at me or turn away. She looked at me, though; and for a moment I saw myself reflected in her eyes.

I will not scream. I will not give them that satisfaction. They will have my body, but my soul and my story are my own, and will die with me.

The goose-grease begins to melt and glisten upon my skin. I shall make no sound at all. I shall think no more on this.

I shall think instead of the snowflake on her cheek.

I think of her hair as black as coal, her lips, redder than blood, her skin, snow-white.

Bela's Plot

Caitlín R. Kiernan

Hollywood is a vampire, Magwitch thinks again and sips at his sweet, iced coffee, coffee milkfaded the muddy color of rainwater. He stares out at the heat shimmering up from the four o'clock street, the asphalt that looks wet, that looks like a perfect stream of melted licorice beneath the too-blue sky. Stares out through his dime store shades and the diner's smudge-tinted plate glass and wishes his nerves would stop jangling, humming live-wire from the ecstasy he dropped with Lark and Crispin the night before.

A very bedraggled hooker crosses Vine, limping slow on a broken heel, squinting at the ripening afternoon. Magwitch watches her, and wonders that she doesn't simply burst into white flame, doesn't dance a fiery jig past the diner window until there's only a little ash and singed wig scraps floating on the liquid blacktop. He closed his eyes and she's still there, and all the wriggling electric lines of static from his head.

When he opens them again, Tam's walking toward him between the tangerine booths, her long-legged, confident stride and layers of lace and ragged fishnet beneath the black vinyl jacket she almost always wears. He smiles and stirs at his coffee, rearranges ice cubes, and Tam draws attention from the fat waitress and the two old men at the counter as she comes. She sits down across from him, and he smells sweat and roses.

"Where's Lark?" she asks, and he hears the impatience rising in her voice, the crackling restlessness she wears more often even than the jacket.

"I told Crispin they could meet us at Holy Cross later on," and he watches her eyes, her gray-green eyes painted in bold Egyptian strokes of mascara and shadow, looks for some hint of reproach that her instructions have not been followed, that anything is different than she planned.

But Tam only nods her head, drums nervous insect sounds against the table with her sharp, black nails and then the fat waitress sets a tumbler of ice water down in front of her and Tam orders nothing. They wait until the woman leaves them alone again, wait until the two old men stop looking and go back to their pie wedges and folded-newspaper browsing.

Tam takes a pink packet of saccharin, tears it open, and pours the coke-fine powder into her water. It sifts down between the crushed ice, dissolves, and she stirs it hard with her spoon.

"*Well?*" and she tests the water with the tip of her tongue, frowns, and dumps in another packet of Sweet'n Low. "Am I supposed to fucking guess, Maggie?"

"These guys are bad," he says, and he looks away from her mossy eyes, looks back out at the street, into the glare and broil; the prostitute has gone, vaporized, or maybe just limped away toward Hollywood Boulevard.

"These guys are bad motherfuckers," but Magwitch knows there's nothing he can say, and no point in trying, now that she's made up her mind.

You might have lied. You might have tried telling her you never found them, or that they laughed at you and threatened to kick your skinny ass if you ever came poking around again.

"And you're beginning to sound like a real pussy, Maggie." Tam raises the tumbler to her red lips, razored pout, and he watches her marble throat as she swallows. She leaves behind a lipsticky crescent on the clear plastic.

Magwitch sighs, brushes his long, inky bangs back from his face.

You might have told her to go to hell this time.

"Friday night, they'll be at Stigmata," he says, "and they said to bring the money with us if we want to talk."

"Then we're in," she says, and of course it's not a question; the certainty in her voice, the guarded hint of satisfaction at the corners of her painted mouth, make him cringe, down inside where Tam won't see.

And if he feels like a pussy it's only because he's the one that's done more than talk the talk, he's the one that sat very still and kept his eyes on the shit-stained men's room floor while Jimmy DeSade and the Gristle Twins laid down their gospel, the slippery rules that Tam had sent him off to learn.

"Did you drive?" she asks, and he knows that she's seen his rust-cruddy car parked on the street, baking beneath the July sun and gathering parking tickets like bright paper flies. Proves the point by not bothering to wait for his answer. "Christ, Maggie, I hope to fuck you got your AC fixed. I need to make some stops on the way."

Magwitch finishes his coffee, swallows a mouthful of creamslick ice, before he lays two dollars on the table and follows Tam out into the sun.

By the time they reach Slauson Avenue, twilight's gone and all the long shadows have run together into another sticky L.A. night. The gates of Holy Cross Cemetery are closed and locked, keeping the dead and living apart until dawn, but Tam slips the rent-a-cop at the gate twenty bucks and he lets them through on foot. Tam doesn't climb fences or walls, doesn't squeeze herself through chain link or risk glass-studded masonry, and he's seen her talk and bribe and blow her way into every boneyard in the valley.

Magwitch walks three steps behind her, and their Doc Marten boots clock softly against the paved drive, not quite in step with one another and keeping unsteady time with the fading traffic sounds. A little way more and they leave the drive and start up the sloping lawn, the perfect grass muzzling their footsteps as they pass reflecting pools like mirrors in darkened rooms and the phony grotto and its marble virgin, the stone woman in her stone shawl who kneels forever before the virgin's downcast eyes.

The markers are laid out in tuxedo-neat rows of black and white, one after the next like fallen dominos, and they step past the Tin Man's grave, over the fallen Father of Dixieland Jazz and Mr. Bing Crosby, and there are Lark and Crispin, nervous eyesores, waiting alone with Bela.

They could be twins, Magwitch thinks, fingers this old and well-worn observation. And he remembers how much he loves them, beautiful and interchangeable brothers or sisters in their spider threads and white faces, realizes how afraid he is for them now.

Neither of them say anything, wait to hear in their silk-silent anxiety, and Magwitch steps forward to stand beside Tam. The toes of her boots almost touch the flat headstone and it's much too dark to read the few words cut deep into granite, "Beloved Father," dates of birth and death.

There should be candles, he thinks, because there have always been candles, cinnamon or rose or the warm scent of mystery spices and their faces in the soft amber flicker. Sometimes so many candles at once that he was afraid the cops would see and make the guards run them out. Enough candles that they could sit with Bela and read aloud, taking turns with Mary Shelley or Anne Rice or *The Lair of the White Worm.*

"It's all been arranged," Tam says, her voice big and cavalier in the dark. "Friday night we'll meet them at Stigmata and work out the details."

"Oh," Lark says, and this one syllable seems to drift from somewhere far away; Crispin breathes in loudly and stares down at his feet.

"Jesus, you are *all* a bunch of pussies, aren't you?"

Crispin does not raise his head, does not risk her eyes, and when he speaks, it's barely a hoarse whisper.

"Tam, how do you even know that Jimmy DeSade is telling the truth about the cape?"

And Magwitch feels her tense, then, feels the anger gathering itself inside her, sleek anger and insult taut as jungle cat muscles and "She doesn't," he answers, and a heartbeat later, "Neither do I."

"Jesus Christ," Tam hisses and lights one of the pungent brown Indonesian cigarettes she smokes. For an instant, her high cheekbones and pouty lips are nailed in the glow of her lighter and then the night rushes back over them.

"If you guys fuck this up," but her voice trails away into a ghost cloud of smoke and they stand together at the old man's grave, junkie old man cold and in his final casket almost twenty years before Magwitch was born. And there is no thunder and forked lightning, no wolf-howling wind, only sirens and the raw squeal of tires on the cooling city streets.

Magwitch sits, smoking, on one rumpled corner of Tam's bed in the apartment he could never dream of affording, that she could never afford either if it was only her part-time at Retail Slut paying the rent. If it weren't for the checks from her mother and father that she pretends she doesn't get once a month, faithful as her period. The sun's coming up outside, the earth rolling around to burn again, and he can see the faintest graying blue rind around the edges of Tam's thick velvet drapes. The only other light comes from her big television, sleek black box and the sound down all the way, Catherine Deneuve and David Bowie at piano and cello.

"I wouldn't even have *thought* of suggesting it," she says, and it takes him a moment to find his place in the conversation, his place between her words. "Not if they weren't acting that way. If they weren't both scared totally shitless."

"It should be their call," he says softly, stubs out his cigarette. He doesn't want the twins along either, wants them clear of this so bad that he's almost willing to hurt them. But almost isn't ever enough, and no matter what Tam might say, he knows that she'll have them there, lovely china pawns by her side, lovelier for the fear just beneath their skin.

"Oh," she says. "Absolutely. I just won't have them going tharn and fucking everything up, Maggie. This is for real, not cemetery games, not trick or fucking treat."

Magwitch lies back on the cool sheets, satin like slippery midnight skin, and tries not to think about the twins or Jimmy DeSade. Watches Tam at her cluttered antique dressing table, the back of her head, hair blacker than the sheets and her face reflected stark in the art deco mirror. Knowing he could hate her if only he were a little bit stronger, if he'd never let himself love her. She selects a small brush and retraces the cupid's bow of her upper lip, her perfect pout, and he looks away, stares up at the ceiling, the dangling forest of dolls hanging there, dolls and parts of dolls, ripe and rotting Barbie fruit strung on wire and twine. The breeze from the air conditioner stirs them, makes them sway, some close enough to bump into others, a leg against an arm, an arm against a plastic torso.

And then Tam comes teasing slow to him, crosses the room in nothing but white, white skin and crimson panties. She crouches on the foot of the bed, just out of reach, a living gargoyle down from Notre Dame, stone made flesh by some unlikely and unforgiving alchemy. Her eyes sparkle in the TV's electric glare, more hungry than John and Miriam Blaylock ever imagined; as she speaks, her left hand drifts absently to the tattoo that entirely covers her heart, the maroon and ebony petals that hide her nipple and areola, thorns that twine themselves tight around her breast and draw inky drops of blood.

"I'm sure Lark and Crispin won't disappoint me," she says and smiles like a wound. "They never do."

And of course she's holding the razor clutched in her right hand, the straight and silver razor with its mother-of-pearl handle, bottomless green and blue iridescence.

"And you won't ever disappoint me, sweet Maggie."

He sits up, no need for her to have to ask, turns his back and grips the iron headboard, palms around cold metal like prison bars. The old springs creak and groan gentle protests as she slips across the bed to him, and Magwitch feels her fingertips, Braille reading the scars on his shoulders, down the length of his spine, one for every night he's spent with her.

"You love me," she says and he closes his eyes and waits for the release of the blade.

Friday night, very nearly Saturday morning now, and Magwitch is waiting with Lark and Crispin at their wobbly corner table on one edge of the matte black circus. Through the weave and writhe of dancers he catches occasional half-glimpses of Tam at the bar, Tam talking excitedly with the two pretty boys in taffeta and shiny midnight latex, the boys who have posed for *Propaganda* and *Re/Search* but whose names he can't remember. Lark sips uneasily at her second White Russian and Crispin's eyes never leave the crimson door at the other end of the dance floor. The Sisters of Mercy song ends, bleeds almost imperceptibly into a crashing remix of Fields of the Nephilim's "Preacher Man."

It has been more than a year since the first rumors, the tangled bits of hearsay and contradiction that surfaced in the shell shock still after the riots. A year since Tam sat across this same wobbly table and repeated every unlikely detail, her sage-green eyes sparking like flints and she whispered to him, "They have the cape, Maggie. They have the fucking *cape.*"

He doesn't remember exactly what he said, remembers her leaning close and the glinting scalpel of her voice.

"Hell, Maggie, there was so much going on they didn't even *care* if the cops saw them. They just walked right in and started digging. I mean, Christ, who's gonna give two shits if someone's out digging up dead guys when half the city's burning down?"

He didn't believe it then, still doesn't believe it, but Magwitch knows that playing these head games with the likes of Jimmy DeSade is worse than stupid or crazy. He fishes another Percodan from the inside pocket of his velvet frock coat and washes it down with a warm mouthful of bourbon.

"I don't think he's going to show," Crispin says, and there's just the faintest trace of relief, the slimmest wishful crust around his words. And then the crimson door opens on cue, opens wide and Jimmy DeSade, black leather and silver chains from head to toe, steps into the throb and wail of Stigmata.

And even over the music, the sound of Lark's glass hitting the floor is very, very loud.

Together, they are herded out of the smoky, blacklight pit of the club, up narrow stairs and down the long hall, past the husky old tattoo queen who checks IDs and halfheartedly searches everyone for dope and weapons, out into the night. Jimmy DeSade walks in front and one of the Gristle Twins drives them from behind, and as they leave the sidewalk and slip between abandoned warehouses, an alley like an asphalt paper cut, Magwitch wants to run, *would* run if it weren't for Crispin and Lark. Would leave Tam to play out this pretty little horror show on her own; he looks at Crispin and Lark, who hold white-knuckled hands, and there's nothing but the purest silver terror in their eyes.

Jimmy DeSade's junkheap car waits for them in the alley, rumbling hulk of a Lincoln, rust bleeding from a thousand dents and scrapes in its puke-green skin, one eye blazing, the other dangling blind. Its front fender hangs crooked loose beneath shattered grille teeth, truculent chrome held on with duct tape and wire. Jimmy DeSade opens a door and shoves them all into the backseat. And the car smells like its own shitty exhaust and stale cigarettes and pot smoke and spilled alcohol, but more than anything else, the sweet, clinging perfume of rot. Magwitch gags, covers his mouth with his hand, and then Tam is screaming.

"Don't mind Fido," Jimmy DeSade says in the Brit accent that no one has ever for a minute believed is real, and then the twisted thing stuffed into the corner with Tam tips over, all blood-crusty fur and legs bent in the wrong places, and lies stiff across their laps. Its ruined maroon coat is alive, maggot seethe, and parts that belong inside are slipping out between shattered ribs.

"Manny here ran into the poor thing the other day and shit, man, I always wanted a doggy."

Tam screams again and Crispin and Lark vomit in perfect, twinly unison, spray booze and the pork-flavored Ramen noodles they ate before leaving Magwitch's apartment onto the roadkill tangle. Magwitch swallows hard, turns his head to the window as Manny pulls out of the alley into traffic.

"You stupid, sick fuck . . . ," he says, and the Gristle Twins laugh and Jimmy DeSade grins his wide, yellow-toothed hyena-face, winks.

"Oh god," Tam whispers, "Oh god, oh god," and she dumps the mess into the floorboard, leaving their laps glazed with dog and vomit, velvet and satin and silk stained and gore-slicked.

When Jimmy DeSade laughs, it sounds like bricks and broken bottles tumbling in a clothes dryer.

"Man, I love you prissy little goth-geek motherfuckers," he says and thumbs through the stack of twenty- and fifty-dollar bills Tam gave him back at Stigmata, three hundred dollars all together, and he sniffs at the money before it's tucked inside his leather jacket.

"You dumb buggers wear that funeral drag and paint your eyes and think you're fucking around with death, think you're the reaper's own harem, don't you?"

"Fuck you," Tam says, whimpers, and "Yeah."

Jimmy DeSade says, "Yeah, well, we'll see, babe."

The city rushes past the Lincoln's windows and Magwitch tries to keep track, but nothing out there looks familiar, and he doesn't know if they're driving west, toward the ocean, or east, toward the desert.

"You better have it," Tam says. "I paid you your goddamned money and you better have it."

Jimmy DeSade watches her a moment silently, feral chalk-blue eyes, Nazi eyes, and he smiles again slow and flashes his porcelain fangs.

"You got yourself an unhealthy obsession there, little girl," he says, oozes the words across his lips like greasy pearls and the middle Gristle Twin, the one whose name isn't Manny, snickers.

"We made a deal," Tam says, and Magwitch has to stop himself from laughing.

"Don't you worry, Tammy. I got it all right. And *oh, Tammy,* you shoulda *seen 'im,* the shriveled old hunky fuck," and Jimmy DeSade's eyes sparkle, lightless shine, and he bites at his lower lip with one long canine. "Lying there so bloody peaceful in his penguin suit, the dirt just dribbling down into his face. And that cape, that cape still draped around his bony shoulders right where it was when they closed the casket on him."

Jimmy DeSade sniffles his cokehead's chronic sniffle and wipes his nose, grime-cracked nails and the one on his little finger elegant-long and polished candy-apple red.

"Nineteen hundred and fifty-six," he purls, "Terrible long time to go without one sweet breath of night air. That was Elvis's big year, did you know that, Tammy dear? Too damn bad it wasn't poor old Bela's."

The nameless Gristle Twin pops a cassette into the Lincoln's tape deck and a speed-metal blur screeches from the expensive, bass-heavy speakers behind their heads. Magwitch tries to ignore the music, tries desperately to concentrate on the buildings and street signs flashing past, as the car leaves Hollywood behind and rolls along through the hungry California night.

In the catacombs beneath downtown, the old tunnels dug a century before for smugglers and Chinese opium dens, the air is not warm here and smells like mold and standing water. Magwitch sits on his bare ass on the stone floor; his black jeans are a shapeless wad nearby, but when he reaches for them it wakes up the pain in his ribs and shoulder and he gasps, slumps back against the seeping wall. There is light, row after row of the stark and soulless fluorescent bulbs and so he can see Crispin and Lark, naked and filthy, huddled together on the other side of the chamber.

Tam, wrapped in muddy vinyl and torn pantyhose, stands with her back to them near the door.

There are chains like rusty intestine loops, chains that end in meathook claws, dangling worse things than the road dog in Jimmy DeSade's car.

And Jimmy DeSade sits on the high-backed wooden chair in the center of the room, smoking, watching them. The others have all gone, the Gristle Twins and the woman with teeth filed to sharp piranha points, the man without ears and only a pink, scar-puckered hole where his nose should have been.

"Are you finished?" Tam asks, "Are you satisfied?" and it frightens Magwitch how little her voice has changed, how ice-calm she still sounds.

"Will you show me the Dracula cape now?"

Jimmy DeSade chuckles low, shakes his shaggy head, and Magwitch hears a whole Laundromat full of dryers, each churning with its load of bricks and shattered soda bottles.

"I'd like to," he says and crushes his cigarette out on the floor, grinds the butt flat with the snakeskin toe of his boot. "I would, Tammy, I really would. But I'm afraid that's no longer something I can do."

Tam turns around slowly, arms crossed and the jacket pulled closed to hide her small breasts. Her face is streaked with blood and makeup smears, and livid bite marks, the welts and clotting punctures, dapple her throat and the backs of her hands. The flesh around her left eye looks pulpy and is swollen almost shut.

"Yeah, well, you see, I let it go last week to a Lugosi freak from Mexico City. This crazy fucker paid me ten Gs for the thing, can you believe that shit?"

For a moment, Tam's old mask holds, indomitable frost and those eyes that betray nothing, show nothing more or less than she wishes. But the moment passes and the mask splinters, falls away, revealing the roil beneath, shifting kaleidoscope of bone and skin, tumbling bright flecks of rage and violation. And Magwitch is almost afraid for Jimmy DeSade.

"Hey, Tammy. It's just biz, right?" And he holds out his hand to her. "These things happen. No bad feelings?"

Her lips part, wet, salmon hint of tongue between teeth before the cascade of emotion drains away and there's nothing left in its place, and she falls, collapses into herself and gravity's will, crumples like ash to her knees and the uneven cobblestones.

"Sure," Jimmy DeSade says, "I understand," and he stands, pushes the chair aside. "When you guys are done in here, turn off the lights, okay, and close the door behind you?" He points to a switch plate rigged on one wall, a bundle of exposed red and yellow wires.

And they're alone, then, except for the things without eyes, the careless hanging sculptures of muscle and barbed wire, and Magwitch drags himself the seven or eight feet to Tam. The pain in his side strobes violet and he has to stop twice, stop and wait for his head to clear, for the crooning promise of numb and quiet and cool oblivion pressing at his temples to fade.

They do not come here much anymore, visit the old man less and less as summer slips unnoticed into fall. Without Tam, the guards are less agreeable, and they've been caught once already sneaking in, have been warned and threatened with jail. Tonight there is a cough-dry wind and Magwitch has heard on the radio that there are wildfires burning somewhere in the mountains.

Lark finishes the chapter, Mina's account of the sea captain's funeral and the terrified dog, somnambulant Lucy, and Crispin blows out the single votive candle he's held up to the pages while she read. Even such a small flame is a comfort and Magwitch knows they share the same sudden uneasiness when there's only its afterimage floating in their eyes, the baby-aspirin orange blot accenting the night.

Lark closes her paperback and lays it on the headstone, sets it neatly between the three white roses and the photocopied snapshot in its cheap drugstore frame. A dashing, impossibly young Lugosi, 1914 and the shadow of his fedora soft across eyes still clear with youth and ignorance of the future. In the morning, the groundskeeper will clear it all away, will grumble and hastily restore the sterile symmetry of his ghostless, modern cemetery.

"I saw Daniel Mosquera last night," Lark says, and it takes Magwitch a second to place the name with a face. "He said someone saw Tam in San Francisco last week, and she's dancing at the House of Usher now."

And then she pauses and the traffic murmurs through the wordless space she's left; Magwitch imagines he can smell wood smoke on the breeze.

"This is the last time I can come here, Maggie."

"Yeah," he says, "I know," and Crispin nods and puts the stub end of his candle down with everything else.

"But we'll still see each other, right? At DDT, and next month Shadow Project's playing the Roxy and we'll see you then."

"Sure," Magwitch says. He knows better but is careful to sound like he doesn't.

"You sleep tight," Lark whispers and kisses her fingertips, then touches them to the grass.

When they've gone, Magwitch lights a cigarette and sits with Bela another hour more.

For Concrete Blonde, with thanks to Garland.

Armies of the Heart

Christopher Fowler

Looking down at the child, he realized he had surprised himself with his own strength. The boy lay face-down in the litter-strewn grass, his hands twisted behind his back with the palms up, as if he had fallen to earth while skydiving. His jeans were torn down around his thin ankles, his pants and buttocks stained carmine. His baseball cap had been caught by the thorns of the gorse bush that hid them both from the road.

His attacker rose and wiped the sweat from his face. It was getting dark. He would soon be missed at home. He had not meant to be so rough. At his feet the boy lay motionless, the focus of his eyes lost in a far-off place. Thin strands of blood leaked from his oval mouth to the ground like hungry roots. An arc of purple bites scarred the pale flesh below his shoulder blades where the cheap cotton T-shirt he wore had been wrenched up. His life had been extinguished four days before his eleventh birthday.

There was nothing to be done for the lad. Readjusting the belt of his trousers and shaking out the pain from his bitten hand, the man stepped away from the cooling body and walked back toward the path that bisected the wasteground. His main concern now was relocating the Volvo and getting home to his wife and children before they started to ask where he had been.

"You won't."

"I will."

"You won't."

"I *will*."

"You bloody won't."

"I bloody will."

"Wait, I forgot what you two are arguing about."

"She says she'll get in, and I say she won't."

"Well, we'll just have to see, won't we?"

The venue was five hundred yards ahead of them, a large Victorian pub standing by itself at the junction of two roads. It appeared derelict; the windows were covered with sheets of steel and wood, painted matte black. No lights showed. The tenebrous building reared against the stars like a great abandoned ship. On either side of it apartment blocks curved endlessly off into darkness.

"We should get off the street, man," said Bax. "This is not a good area to be seen in." There were three of them: Bax, Jack, and Woody, whose real name was Claire Woodson. There was no one else around.

"It's okay for you," Woody complained. "We're white. We stick out like neon bulbs."

"Fuck you, Woody. You wanna know something? There's as many white people living here as black. You're just scared of being around poor folks. You wanna hang out with your lowlife friends so you can piss off your mummy and daddy. They ain't gonna let you inside, anyway."

"If they don't," said Jack, "Bax and I are still gonna go in, okay? That was the deal."

"I know. I agreed, didn't I? Well, you don't have to worry about me. I'll just head somewhere else. There must be plenty of other places."

"Around here?" Bax released a guffaw. "Right. Gangsta bars full of guys with spiderwebs tattooed on their elbows. I don't know why you have to do this, Woody, it's like you got something to prove. You just hanging out with us 'cause it makes a change from shopping. You need to get something goin' for yourself, girlfriend."

"Hey, this is a new experience," said Woody as they reached the side entrance of the pub. "Something I haven't tried yet."

"Yeah? So's having a kidney removed; don't mean you gotta do it."

Jack reached over their heads and rang the doorbell. They waited outside the dingy crimson doors, their breath distilling in the chill November air. Bax and Woody were dressed in padded jackets, track-suit bottoms and Caterpillars. Jack hitched up a pair of baggy combat trousers. All three wore black hats over shaved heads. There was a specific reason for their loose clothing. From inside came the sound of a bolt being drawn back. Heat and thumping techno ballooned out at them as the door opened and the knuckle-dragger on the ticket stand stepped back to allow them entry.

"That's five quid each." His gimlet gaze shifted from one to the next. His eyes lingered on Woody, who lowered her head as she pretended to have trouble unbuttoning her jacket. The other two held their breath. The doorman accepted fifteen pounds from Jack, who held all the cash, and pointed them to a stack of green plastic bags on the floor.

"Okay, in you go; bags are over there." Jack scooped up three and passed the other two back as they walked on along the corridor.

"What are these for?"

"To put your clothes in," Bax explained. "Check 'em behind the counter in the corner."

"Where are you putting your wallet?"

"Down the side of my boot."

The corridor had opened out into a large bar area. Beyond this were the flashing greens and violets of a dance floor. The interior was also painted black. As Woody's eyes adjusted, she could see men in their underwear lounging around the bar drinking, smoking and talking just as if they were fully dressed. Some wore jockstraps, but most sported white designer-label pants and boots. Men were undressing beside powerful radiators in the gloomier corners. Jack stopped and turned to watch Woody. "This I've got to see," he said, grinning. "You know they'll go nuts if they find out there's a girl in here."

"Well, they're not going to find out." Woody removed her jacket to reveal a tight-fitting khaki combat vest.

"What did you do with your tits?" Bax was amazed.

"I strapped them down with tape." She pulled down her track-suit bottoms to reveal a pair of men's Calvin Klein Y-fronts. Her breasts were small, and suppressing them gave her the appearance of having developed pectoral muscles. She bundled her discarded clothes into the bag and stepped back, her hands resting lightly at her hips. "So—do I look okay?"

"You look like Valdez in *Aliens.*"

"But do I pass as a man?"

Jack pulled off his nylon cap and carefully stuffed it into the front of Woody's pants. "You do now."

"You wish."

"I *know.*" He and Bax stripped down to their underwear and headed for the bag-check. The bag-man handed them three reclaim tickets and took their clothing out into the small annex behind the bar that housed the cloakroom. Jack wasn't entirely sure how he had been persuaded to smuggle a girl into a men-only club on Underwear Night of all nights, but now they were inside together he decided to make the best of it. She had been nagging them to take her for weeks, ever since she'd heard about the place. Jack and Bax were her best friends, and the fact that they happened to be lovers never deterred her from hanging out with them wherever they went.

The club was called The Outlook, and attracted men who were prepared to take a walk on the wilder side of life, partly because the activities that took place beyond the dance floor were apt to get a little raunchy, and partly because the pub was situated at the edge of south London's largest and most trouble-ridden public housing estate. In the mid-1850s the Skinner's Arms had been a boxing pub with a glass cupola above a sweat-stained ring, where workers gathered to cheer and bet on the neighborhood's finest fighters. The matches had been halted by an unavailability of suitable pugilists during the Great War, and the old glass roof had been demolished by a stray bomb in the next. In the seventies the ground floor had been cleared of its separate Snug and Saloon bars to become a disco, and in the late eighties it had turned into a crack den. No matter how many times the police held raids, the local hoods continued to trade drugs both inside and on the street. By the time it was turned into a gay club the exhausted police and desperate residents of the estate were happy to leave it alone because, in their eyes, anything was better than pushers, even queers. Just so long as no one could see or hear what was going on inside it remained under a flag of uneasy truce, on the front line of a no-go area. People entered and vacated the building quietly, and the smart cars that parked outside were left alone, because even the local kids could figure out that if they started smashing quarterlights and boosting stereos the bar would close down and the junkies would return, and nobody wanted that.

"What have you got in your briefs, a pound of sausages?" Woody released a high laugh, then quickly lowered the timbre, looking guiltily around.

"This is all me," said Jack, looking down at his underpants. "Can I help it if God was bountiful? This is yours." He passed Woody a pint of strong lager, which she had ordered in the belief that it would provide her with additional gender camouflage. She took a sip in a way that showed she was unfamiliar with holding such a glass, like a nonsmoker drawing on a cigarette. As she did she took covert glances at Bax's sculptured torso.

"I'd drink that slowly, if I were you," said Jack. "There's no ladies' room in here. You may be able to pass for a man but I doubt even you can convincingly pee standing up."

The room was starting to fill. The temperature had begun to climb with the volume of the music. Woody clutched the glass to her flattened chest and took a deep breath, drawing in the smell of bitter hops that had soaked and impregnated the surrounding wooden bar for more than a century. All old pubs had this odor, but here there were other scents; traces of aftershave, cologne and the musky maleness of nearly a hundred stripped, sexed-up and overheated men. She felt herself becoming aroused, even though she was aware of the paradox; they would only be interested in her if she could successfully prove herself to be male, and that was the one thing she could not do. In the dark beyond the dance floor she sensed naked torsos touching, arms and legs shifting across each other. Maybe she had made a mistake coming along, and they were right when they'd asked her what she was trying to prove.

"You okay?" Bax laid a hand on her shoulder.

"I have a faint suspicion," she said, narrowing her eyes, "that there may be people fucking in here. It smells like fucking. Don't you think?"

"A fuck's just a way of celebrating life, princess, like a champagne toast. Look, you asked to come along with us."

"I know—I just didn't realize I was going to end up in the House of Testosterone. Who's Jack talking to?"

Bax looked over his shoulder. Behind him stood a vague, thin-limbed boy of about nineteen. He had carelessly cropped blond hair, watery blue eyes and the self-absorbed stance of a piece of minor Victorian statuary. He also had a dog chain tightened around his pale cigarette-burned neck. "His name's Simon. He knows us from evening classes. Gives me the creeps. He's into humiliation. Likes to take punishment. They say his dad sexually assaulted him for years and nobody found out about it until after the old guy was dead. I don't know why Jack talks to him. I never do."

"You mean he's a masochist?"

"Yeah, why? You wanna interview him for your thesis?" Bax drained his beer and set the glass down on the cigarette machine. "He won't be very interesting. People who are into role-playing never are."

"Why's that?"

"Because they're selfish, working out their childhood shit. They just take what they want from sex."

Woody peered around Bax's chest. The boy was flirting shamelessly with Jack.

"Perhaps he has no choice."

"You're right there. Kids like that are just whipping boys, put on earth to suck up all the bad vibes and take the blame."

"Don't you get jealous when guys flirt with Jack?"

Bax looked surprised. "Me? We've been together for six years. I hardly think he's about to run off with someone else, and if he did I'd like to think he'd choose someone attractive. Besides, we have a deal. It's simple; if he ever leaves me, I'll kill him. You want another beer?"

"I can keep pace with you, no problem," she said defensively.

"Come and give me a hand."

The two bartenders were ignoring customers in order to conduct some kind of odd argument with each other. Something was clearly wrong for them both to look so worried. "What's going on?" Bax shouted over the music as one of the boys distractedly took his order.

"They found some little kid on the wasteground this afternoon," explained the barman. "Dead. Raped. A little boy."

"Christ. That's terrible."

"Yeah. One of the customers just told me there's a crowd hanging around outside."

"What do you mean?"

"A bunch of people who live on the estate. At least, that's where he thinks they're from."

Bax was appalled. "They don't think the person who did it is in *here*?"

The barman looked at him as if he was stupid. "I wouldn't be surprised—would you?"

News of the boy's death had swept around the estate with electrifying speed, and as it passed along each street it gained gruesome new details. The boy was local and liked by all. Some other kids had seen him talking to a man, not someone from around here, a visitor, a stranger. The only people who came to this area did so to frequent *that place* across the road. The pub was just five hundred yards from the wasteground, the perfect sanctuary. They were shielding him inside, protecting one of their own. In the minds of the growing mob, deviants of that nature knew no difference between love and rape, between adults and children. At first there had only been a handful of people on the pavement outside, but over the last hour the numbers had swelled until now there were more than a hundred restless men and women. The police had been called to control the crowd, and at the moment were nervously discussing the problem in the next street while they awaited the arrival of the two Armed Response Vehicles they had requested. Their relationship with the estate residents had never been an easy one, and at this point one wrong move, one misunderstood command, would start a riot.

They lingered outside, the dark faces of the multitude, muttering to one another, cupping matches in their hands to light cigarettes, shifting back and forth from one group to the next trying to glean details, waiting for news, waiting for action, and not prepared to wait much longer.

—∿—

"When you think about it, this is really silly. A bunch of grown men standing around in their underclothes." Woody slid her arm around Jack as they watched the dance floor, but her eyes kept straying to the dark recesses beyond. Bax was still at the counter having an intense conversation with Simon and the barman. "Oh, I don't know," said Jack. "It's kind of like having X-ray vision. Didn't you ever see Ray Milland in *The Man with the X-Ray Eyes*? Anyway, nobody's hurting anyone else, so where's the harm?"

The noise of the brick cut through even the fuzzing bass sound of the track playing over the speakers. It clanged against the steel shutter next to the entrance and the bruit echoed through the club. A moment later the DJ cut the music. Muffled shouts could be heard outside. A chunk of concrete resounded against another of the shutters. Scuffles and angry yells broke out behind them as the rear door to the bar was hastily slammed shut. One of the barmen crashed a heavy iron rod across the door and locked it in place.

"What was that?" Woody looked back, shocked by the noise.

"They've broken in through the window of the corridor between the bar and the cloakroom," said Jack. "They can't get in here. But we can't get in there."

"What does that mean?"

"It means, my dear, that we can't get our clothes back."

"Let me get this straight," said Woody, raising her hands in rising panic. "We're locked in here, in just our underwear, with what sounds like a lynch mob outside howling for someone's blood."

"*Our* blood," said Jack. "You're one of us now. Congratulations. You always wanted to be one to the boys."

"Well, someone will have to go out there and tell them there's been a mistake."

"Good idea, Woodson. You wanna handle that?"

Bax reappeared beside them as another hail of rocks clanged against the shutters.

"The cops should be here in a minute."

"Well, *that's* reassuring. I feel better already. Let's have another drink, turn the music back on, and dance." Jack raised his glass just as—incredibly—

the techno-track really did resume, bleeding a thudding beat through the speakers. "Jeezus, I don't believe these queens!"

"It's like I said, they could tango their way through the stations of the fucking cross."

"Somehow I think it's gonna take more than a sense of rhythm and a pair of cha-cha heels to get us out of this situation." A few guys had returned to the dance floor, mainly the ones who were tripping. Everyone else was standing back by the bar, watching the sealed-up windows with increasing nervousness.

"How many of them do you think are out there?" asked Woody.

"A couple of hundred by now," replied Simon, who had appeared beside them.

"Oh yeah?" Bax wasn't prepared to allow the newcomer into their circle just because Jack sometimes spoke to him. "How do you know that?"

"I'm sensitive to shifts of mood. A bit psychic. My mother, my *real* mother, was a medium."

"Just great," moaned Bax, "we've gone from *Twilight Zone* to *The X-Files.* I'm gonna see what's happening." He headed off to the entrance, where the club's bouncer was watching the street from his peephole in the door.

"What's going on outside?"

"Some kids just climbed that pole over there and cut our phone lines. Now they're all just standing around like a bunch of . . . lemmings or something. Like they're waiting for a signal." The bouncer motioned him away. "I'd get back from the door if I were you."

Another hurled chunk of concrete hammered against the panels, shaking the air. The noise level on the street was rising as the crowd gained confidence and found its voice. "Can't someone call the police on a mobile?" asked Bax.

"You won't get reception in here. The cops are probably waiting for ARVs. They're equipped to deal with stuff like this. Nothing for us to do but wait." The sound of glass exploded on the other side of the door, and suddenly a pool of burning petrol was fanning through the gap beneath it, illuminating the room and turning the air acrid.

"Fire over here!" bellowed the bouncer. Bax jumped back, grabbed at the stack of listings magazines behind him and stamped a pile of them over the searing patch, spattering gobbets of flame over his boots and bare calves. The bouncer, the only fully clothed man in the building, found a small CO_2 extinguisher just as another burning cocktail tore through the plywood-covered window to the left of the entrance. The wood panel quickly heated and caught fire, then the inner window cracked with a bang and burning petrol began to drip down the interior wall. They could hear the mob outside cheering each direct hit.

This time the dance music stopped for good. Some clubbers were arguing with the staff, others were shouting at each other, but most were just standing around in shock, unable to go anywhere or do anything. Woody looked around to find herself left alone with Simon, whose face had drained of blood. He had the exotic look of an albino.

"Are you all right?"

"He wasn't frightened," he said in a clear loud voice, as if answering a distant inquiry. "Not until the very end."

"Who wasn't frightened?" she asked in alarm. The boy's skin was prickling, his eyes staring off at something, a view, a tableau she could not see. He was breathing too fast, starting to shake. "Here." She grabbed a plastic bottle of Evian from the bar, snapped off the cap and made him drink.

"It's too late," said Simon, water spilling from his mouth. "The man has gone now."

"Which man?"

"The one who hurt him, who made him bleed. The one in the big car." He was shaking uncontrollably now, edging into spasms. "He said he only wanted to look, to touch. He lied, he lied—"

"Can you help us?" she called to a man standing behind her. Simon was thrashing violently in her arms and then, before anyone could come to her aid, he was still once more and breathing normally. The attack had ended as quickly as it had begun.

"I'm fine now, really." He disentangled himself from her embrace and rose unsteadily to his feet, a look of mild surprise on his face.

"Are you quite sure?"

His colour was returning. He gave a wan smile to show that he was fine. Frustrated by his own inaction, Jack was asking one of the barmen what he could do to help. "Is there any other way out of this room?"

"No, only through the bar and upstairs onto the roof."

"We can't stay in here. We'll be burned alive. Do you have a sprinkler system we can turn on?"

"No," said the barman helplessly. "The place still qualifies as a pub, not a music venue. It's not big enough to require one. The only water supply is in the sinks and dishwasher behind the counter, and out with the clothes-bags."

"Then I guess we'll just have to hold out until the police take charge."

"There are enough of them outside to murder us all," said Simon softly. "They won't stop until they've performed a sacrifice."

"That's bloody cheerful," snapped Woody.

He threw her a sudden odd look. "Why are you pretending to be a man?"

"Just give me a hand with this." She and several of the others shifted one of the heavy drinks tables away from the wall and set it on end, blocking the broken window nearest the entrance. Bax and the bouncer were training extinguishers on the fiery fluid seeping through the windows from more burning Molotovs. People were motivating into groups, at work on separate sections of the room. It was as if a collective intelligence had kicked in to make them perform the necessary protective actions.

The explosion of wood and glass that erupted near Woody caught everyone by surprise. "Fuck me, what are they using?" Jack straightened up and looked out through the jagged hole that had been punched through the shutter by some kind of large-caliber ammunition. Following its flight path, he found one of the barmen clutching his shoulder as blood pumped between his fingers. The bullet had passed though the boy's T-shirt, grazing the soft flesh of his armpit, and had gone on to explode a bottle of Smirnoff above the bar. Within moments, two customers had torn tea towels into strips and were stanching his wound. Another gunshot blast ripped through the steel sheeting on the main window of the dance floor, but failed to find a target, smashing into the plaster ceiling rose in the center of the room. Surprisingly, nobody screamed.

"Everyone seems so calm," said Woody as Bax reappeared.

"Never underestimate the balls of a queen, honey. Half these guys grew up getting punched out by parents who won't speak to them until they're on their deathbeds." He didn't say whose deathbeds he meant, and Woody didn't ask. The rending noise that began at the farthest window alerted them to the fact that someone outside was levering the sheet steel away with a crowbar. "Oh shit."

Suddenly the sheeting was off and the inner window was being smashed out with boots and batons. Wood and glass splintered everywhere as dark figures struggled to climb in through the gap.

Jack swept the beer glasses from the other huge drinks table. He and Bax upended it, and with the help of four others ran it face-out at the breach. The heavy oak top crashed down over the limbs entering from outside. There were yelps of pain and rage as injured body parts were withdrawn. Everyone fell against the back of the table, determined to hold it in place by sheer weight of numbers.

"The cops aren't going to get here in time, are they?" said Woody, pushing with all her might.

Another gunshot exploded the piece of window that still showed above the table edge. The bullet plowed into the ceiling, and a shower of plaster cascaded over them. Bax wiped his hand across his neck to find flecks of blood from the fragments of glass. The guttural roar from outside sounded like football fans raging against a missed penalty. The table swayed and rocked but remained in place. More petrol bombs were being thrown at the windows beyond the bar. The bouncer left his post at the doors and ran toward the spreading flames with his extinguisher. The room was filling with dense smoke. There was an explosion of glass on the floor above them, but they had no way of knowing whether it had been caused by a rock or a petrol bomb.

"Simon?"

The boy drifted through the crowd and passed Woody like a wraith, staring hard ahead. He was moving quickly toward the club's temporarily unguarded entrance.

"SIMON!" Woody left the others rammed against the great table and ran toward the boy, who was reaching up on tiptoe to release the bolt at the top of the door. He had drawn it halfway down when she barreled into him, knocking him aside. *"What the hell do you think you're doing?"* she heard herself screaming.

When he turned his translucent eyes to hers, his serenity was the peace of inner madness. "Let me open the door."

"They'll come in and they'll kill us, don't you understand? You can't reason with them!"

"I don't need to reason with them. I have the boy within me." He ran bony fingers across his chest. "I reached out to him and took his pain. It's safe inside me now." There was another terrible eruption on the far side of the room. Somebody fell back with an agonized yell. "How can that be?" she shouted, shoving at him, *"How can that be?"*

"I know his suffering. I've lived with such pain all my life, I'm a fucking magnet for abuse and I'm dying from it, do you understand?" He tore himself free of her and stood alone.

Others had seen what was happening and were moving toward them. "They'll kill you, Simon," she said. "They'll tear you apart with their bare hands."

"Of course they will. They must have someone to blame. A whipping boy."

"But the real culprit—"

"*The real culprit* is far away. I can't catch him. I'm not clever, all I can do is take the pain. From my father, from the crowd outside, I can absorb their darkness. It's what I do, how I survive. Feeding on the violence of others." He held her with a look she would never forget to her dying day. "Someone once told me about the army."

"What army?"

"Everyone has an army in their heart, an army that rallies when its host is most in danger, an army that fights back with all its might until every last one of its soldiers is dead. But I don't. I have no army. There's nothing inside me fighting back, there's just a black hole." He smiled at her. "Don't look so worried. I know how to make the most of it." As he had been talking to her he had raised the entry door's floor-bolt with his boot, and now he shrugged himself away to release the top bolt in one swift, simple movement. The door suddenly opened inward and he slipped through it before anyone could realize what was happening.

Woody screamed after him but the others had crashed forward to slam the door shut once more. She begged them to open it, screamed and pleaded until her throat was raw, but they carried her away to the side of the room, where Bax gave her water and sat her down. She regained her breath, stopped crying and waited. They all waited.

—~—

Outside, Simon stood before the seething crowd with the placidity of a medieval child-saint, a sickly hermaphrodite that raised its arms in preparation for final absolution. His moon-blanched face was tense with sexual anticipation, his body illuminated by dozens of flashlights as the figures around him surged and erupted forward. In the distance the riot vehicles could be heard arriving. The mob took the sound of their sirens as a call to action and fell upon the boy, slashing and punching at him with everything they were holding, machetes and carpet-cutters, butchers' hooks, bread knives, daggers and carving forks. Obviously those inside the club were unwilling to take the rap for the murderer and had forced him to step out in the open. They had no loyalty to one another and probably all deserved to die, but this one, *this* one had to suffer properly for what he had done.

But then the swinging boots and arcing knives slowed their rhythm. Gradually the shouts died down and stopped. For a few moments total silence descended on the neighborhood. Then a few of the women started to scream. The crowd slunk back from the grotesque remains of their victim, slipping in crimson mire. A sense of shame and horror descended over them as they listened to those inside the building putting the remaining fires out. Weapons were released from bloody hands as men began to cover their faces and weep. Some fell to their knees. Others stumbled into the arms of their women like lost children. As the police disembarked from their grid-covered vehicles, one of the wives came forward and laid her coat across the shattered skull of the boy who had drained their rage away.

Inside the club, the sudden silence was eerier than anything they had heard so far. Woody put her eye to one of the bullet holes and watched as nearly three hundred men, women and children were herded back to the far side of the street. At the corner of her vision she could see the edge of the pavement, and a pale leg lying in a pool of blood, its foot severed at the ankle.

Bax had been standing up at the window. He had seen the boy hacked apart, and was crying uncontrollably. Jack and the bouncer were opening the club's main entrance doors, trying to clear away the suffocating smoke. Woody stepped numbly down and walked off through the guttering fires of the club, toward the chill clean air outside. She pulled her vest over her head and let it drop, then tore away the strips of tape and released her breasts from their confinement. She looked back at Jack, who returned her rueful smile. They both knew that she wasn't one of the boys anymore.

She didn't need to be.

She had her own army.

Whispers in Walled Tombs

O'Neil De Noux

Guy let the phone ring ten times before finally answering, "F.D.F.U.U."

The caller fumbled with the receiver and hung up.

Grinning at Chantal, Guy hung up and said, "Works every time."

With his feet up on his well-worn gray metal desk in the tiny office of the First District Follow-Up Unit, Guy congratulated himself again for coming up with the idea of using the unit's initials when answering the phone. It was the easiest way to get rid of pain-in-the-ass citizen callers.

Chantal, perched on a beat-up gray metal folding chair next to the only other desk in the small office, leafed through her collection of crime scene photos. She paused for a particularly gory scene—two victims of a knife attack lying in pools of blood on a barroom floor. Guy recognized the picture and remembered how she told him she liked the way the blood was bright red in places and orange where it was smeared and black where it was thickest.

Watching her, Guy wondered how she managed to contort her legs like a pretzel without getting a cramp. She looked almost frail, her petite body twisted like that. Her milky white skin looked paler than usual, especially with the deep crimson lipstick on her full lips.

She brushed her long, straight dark brown hair away from her eyes as she flipped through more photos. Then, as if she knew what Guy was thinking, she looked up and blinked her wide, dark brown eyes at him.

"You okay?" he asked.

"I'm hungry."

He nodded and felt that jittery feeling in his stomach again. He knew the feeling wasn't from hunger. It was nerves, plain and simple, and he had no idea why he felt nervous on a particularly dull Wednesday evening.

Thirty years old, Guy was thin, six feet tall, and had Chantal's dark brown hair and eyes. He could pass for her older brother. They'd tried that a couple times working undercover and, it had always worked.

Although she was twenty-four, Chantal could put on a pleated skirt and a white blouse, white socks and tennis shoes and pass for a high school girl. That had worked, too.

"How about Chinese?" he asked.

"We had that last night."

"Cajun?"

"The night before." She didn't look up.

"Then you tell me." Guy ran his hand through his longish hair, then patted his mustache down with his index fingers.

"I feel like a little Mexican."

"Fine." He looked at the electric clock on the wall, which read nine o'clock. "Let's roll."

She nodded, but didn't get up.

Guy reached his left foot over and kicked the small air conditioner sputtering in the lone window of the office at the rear of the First District station house. The semicool air smelled of mildew.

"All right," Chantal said. "Let's roll." She didn't sound too excited.

Twisted in her seat, with her full breasts pressed against the front of her tight-fitting dress, she looked sexy as hell. Royal blue, the dress had buttons down its front. Guy could make out the outline of both nipples. He reached down and adjusted his dick.

Chantal put her crime scene photos away and disentangled herself from her perch.

Rising, Guy stretched, then pulled up his belt with his gold star-and-crescent New Orleans Police badge clipped to the front just above the left pocket of his blue jeans. He reached around and adjusted the blue-steel 9mm Beretta tucked inside his belt on his left hip.

Chantal wore her 9mm Beretta in a canvass shoulder holster, the weapon neatly tucked under her right arm, butt facing out. She wore a light blue cotton jacket over her sleeveless dress to hide her shoulder rig.

Guy grabbed his short-sleeved dress white shirt on the way out and pulled the shirt over his black T-shirt but left it unbuttoned. It covered his badge and weapon, barely.

They took the back stairs down to their unmarked black Chevy Caprice. The night air was clammy and hot and smelled of exhaust fumes. Before climbing into the front passenger seat, Chantal reached down and unbuttoned the bottom four buttons of her dress, then pulled off her jacket and shoulder holster.

Guy caught a glimpse of her dark pubic hair when she climbed in and adjusted his dick again before starting up the car and juicing up the AC.

Chantal must have spotted his deft maneuver with the front of his jeans because she grinned at him as she shoved her shoulder rig under the front seat. Sitting up straight, she draped her jacket over the back of the seat and crossed her legs.

Not bothering with signals, Guy wheeled the Caprice out onto Basin Street, took a quick U-turn and headed uptown past St. Louis Cemetery Number One, the Iberville Housing Project, Canal Street, and through the dark concrete Central Business District.

Pausing momentarily at red lights, Guy punched it when he saw it was clear and in no time was on Magazine Street, cruising the Latino areas of the Sixth and Second Police Districts.

Chantal uncrossed her legs and pulled the sides of her dress open so any passerby peeking in would get a clear view of her bush.

Guy took a peek and struggled to watch the road.

They drove past El Zarapé Mexican Restaurant and the Latin Music Store all the way to El Lobo Bar at Napoleon Avenue. Guy spotted two couples outside the bar, but no lone wolves. He tooled the Caprice back around to Magazine and over past the Latin-American Apostolate on General Pershing Street, but the street was empty.

Chantal shook her head in disgust, leaned back, and closed her eyes.

Guy wheeled the Caprice up to St. Charles Avenue and punched it. Rounding Lee Circle, he thought he spotted a loner sitting on one of the benches, but a streetcar moved up on his left and made him turn right onto Howard Avenue. By the time he got back to Lee Circle, the bench was empty.

So Guy drove over to Camp Street to Lafayette Square and slowed as he approached the small dark square surrounded by tall concrete buildings.

"All right," Guy said aloud. "Where did the bums go?"

Chantal opened her eyes, pulled her long hair back with both hands, and said, "I guess it's gonna be one of those nights."

Guy nodded as he circumnavigated the circle.

"I don't believe it," Guy said. "I've never seen this place without at least one bum."

He motored over to Poydras Street and took a right toward the river, slowing as they passed the front entrance of Piazza D'Italia. It looked empty, too. Taking the next two rights, Guy pulled the Caprice around to the back of the well-lit piazza. He looked carefully through the columns and friezes and spotted a man sitting on one of the black wrought-iron benches near the rear wooden fence that divided the piazza from a private parking lot.

Guy parked the Caprice against the curb. Opening the trunk, he pulled off his white shirt and put his badge and Beretta inside. He dug out the Nikon they'd lifted from a Kansas tourist a couple months earlier.

He showed the camera to Chantal and asked, "What was his name?"

She smiled slyly and said, "Kenny Clark from Kansas. He sure was a limp dick, wasn't he?"

"When *you* finished with him."

Chantal unbuttoned the top four buttons of her dress.

Guy snapped the strobe unit to the top of the Nikon and followed Chantal into the piazza.

Chantal fluffed her hair with her hands, then led the way through the arched rear entrance into the slate-covered piazza. Her high heels clicking as she walked to the middle of the piazza, she moved like a cat, smooth and feline and sexy. She stopped next to the reflecting pool, which looked like glass under the lights.

Guy smiled when she turned and posed, her hands behind her head, her torso twisted slightly. He moved in front of her, between her and the man sitting on the bench, and focused the camera, framing her with a series of columns and friezes in the background. He snapped a shot, then took two steps to his right and looked around to see if anyone else was in the piazza.

He could hear the traffic moving along Poydras Street a good block away now, but they were alone with the stranger on the bench, who under closer inspection turned out to be black and younger than most street people, maybe thirty years old.

Chantal opened the top of her dress so that Guy could see her nipples. She smiled at the stranger and called out, "Would it bother you if I take my dress off?"

"What?"

Guy focused on her again as Chantal unbuttoned her dress, pulled it off her shoulders, and let it drop. Immediately, he reached down to adjust his swelling dick.

"Whoa," the stranger said behind Guy, who snapped a picture of Chantal standing naked in the middle of the piazza. The strobe's white light flickered across her sleek body, her full round breasts and dark pubic hair.

Guy refocused the Nikon when Chantal took a step toward him and spread her feet wide, putting her fists on her hips. He snapped another picture and caught Chantal's slight nod. Looking over his shoulder, he saw the stranger standing now. Big, the man looked to be at least six-two, a good couple inches taller than Guy. A typical street person, he wore too many clothes, including a long jacket.

The stranger took a hesitant step their way and Guy told him, "You can take a closer look. She's not shy." He snapped another picture.

Chantal moved to a series of marble and slate steps next to the water and leaned her back against a small square marble post. Guy felt the stranger move next to him as he squeezed off another shot. Then Chantal put her hands behind her, shoulders pressed against the post, and moved her feet apart, even wider than before, and arched her back, her thick bush sticking up and out at the men.

Guy's dick could have sliced a diamond.

"Man-oh-man," the stranger groaned as Guy took another picture.

Chantal turned and gave them a good ass shot before sitting on the top step. As Guy moved in front of her, the stranger in tow, Chantal leaned back on her hands, drew her knees up, and opened her legs, giving them a good look at her pink slit. Guy focused carefully and the strobe bathed her body again.

Chantal grinned at the stranger when he started rubbing his dick and said, "You want me to take care of that?"

The stranger froze.

"I wouldn't want to leave you with blue balls," she said.

The stranger looked at Guy, who shrugged and said, "We do this a lot."

Chantal climbed up off the steps and said, "He likes taking pictures of me giving head to strangers."

"Man-oh-man!"

Chantal stepped up to the big man, tapped him on the chest and said, "Follow me."

She gave that cat walk over to the bench where the stranger had been sitting, the stranger following her swaying hips. Guy scooped up her dress and hurried behind them. Chantal stopped before the bench, turned, and pulled her hair away from her face.

"Whew, it's hot," she said with a sigh.

Guy looked around and realized no one could see them unless they drove up Lafayette Street as he had.

Chantal told the stranger, "I've shown you mine. Let's see what you got." Her gaze moved down to his crotch.

The man pulled off his coat and unbuckled his pants. Guy moved around to get a good picture. Chantal stepped forward and helped the stranger with his zipper, reached in, and pulled out with a wide, thick black dick in her creamy hand.

"Oh, my. Did I cause this?"

"Oh—yeah." The man gasped as she moved her hand up and down the length of his dick. Guy took a picture. The stranger closed his eyes. Chantal turned to Guy and stuck out her tongue as he snapped another shot of her with the dick in her hand.

Chantal's face became serious when the stranger cupped her breasts in his hands and began to knead them. She reached up with her free hand and pulled the big man's head down. She kissed his lips softly and then kissed his cheek and chin before moving down to his neck.

She kissed his throat.

Guy took a picture.

Her hand still jerking the man's dick, Chantal continued kissing his throat, her head moving from side to side. The man moaned. Guy took another picture and watched as the man's dick went slowly limp in Chantal's hand.

Guy threw her dress over his shoulder, along with the camera strap. He backed away and took another look around before going out to the Caprice. His stomach felt jittery again, but he ignored it. He unlocked the trunk and put the camera inside and closed the trunk. He started the engine and moved the car next to the arch. The AC cooled his face immediately. Climbing out, he opened the rear passenger door.

When he got back to them the man was teetering. Guy stepped up behind the stranger.

Chantal's head continued moving from side to side until Guy touched her shoulder and said, "It's time."

He pressed a firm hand behind the stranger's shoulder blades.

Chantal pulled away from the throat and her eyes glistened, bright red blood staining the sides of her mouth. She took a wobbly step back and wiped the blood away from her mouth with her left hand, then licked the blood off her fingers.

The stranger staggered. Guy guided him backward and caught him as he fell, scooping the big man in his arms. He walked back to the Caprice quickly and slipped the stranger onto the backseat. Chantal followed slowly.

Guy pulled her dress off his shoulder and helped her into it. He guided her to the front passenger seat. No longer pale, she was flushed and rosy and looked . . . satiated.

Guy slipped the Caprice into gear and took a quick right on Tchoupitoulas back to Poydras and up to the Interstate for the fastest way to their Mid-City crib. He watched Chantal lean her head against the door, her eyes closed now. She looked so pretty. He reached over and touched her arm and it was hot and sweaty. He put the AC on "max."

It only took a few minutes to get to the City Park Avenue exit, where Guy had to wait behind two slow-assed city buses before taking two quick rights to head down Canal Street past Cypress Grove and Odd Fellow's Rest and St. Patrick Cemeteries. He took another right at South St. Patrick Street and slowed immediately.

Looking ahead, he saw blue and red lights on the right side of the street. He slowed even more as they approached Cleveland Street. Two police cars were parked in front of their crib, one with its tail still in the street, its lights flashing.

His stomach jumping now, Guy took a right on Cleveland and drove up a block to park beneath the gnarled branches of a huge magnolia tree. He turned off the ignition, reached over, and tapped Chantal's arm. She blinked groggily at him.

"Wait here," he said.

She nodded and closed her eyes, snuggling her face against the back of the car seat.

Guy looked at the stranger, who still lay facedown on the backseat. He climbed out of the Caprice, crossed the street, and walked back up the narrow one-way avenue toward South St. Patrick. Stopping beneath the overhanging branches of a huge southern oak, he closed his eyes and stood very still. He took in a long breath and slowly, ever so slowly, felt his feet rise from the sidewalk, felt the hot summer air flow through his body. He drifted up through the heavy oak branches and like a mist slid across the rooftops to the green shingle roof of the shotgun house he and Chantal had used as a crib for the last three years.

Oozing across the roof, Guy slithered around to the small front yard, where two patrolman stood talking. He slid into the camellia bushes next to their front porch.

". . . never," said a tall white officer. "Gotta be a real fuckin' sicko."

A stocky black officer took off his hat and wiped his brow with his wrist. "Man. They been bound up like that for God knows how long."

An ambulance pulled up in front of the house.

Guy spotted a lieutenant approaching from down the street and noticed two more patrol cars parking now. He recognized the man but couldn't remember his name. A crusty veteran with snowy hair, the lieutenant was in his forties and weighed more than both officers standing in the front yard.

"All right," the lieutenant snapped, "what the fuck we got here?"

The black officer stepped forward and explained how a woman neighbor had heard cries, how he'd knocked on the door but didn't get an answer, except even louder cries.

"Man, it was pitiful," he said. "Then I heard a crash and more screaming." The officer wiped sweat from his brow again.

"So I kicked in the front door and found two victims bound to chairs."

"Go see for yourself," the other officer told the lieutenant. "It's a fuckin' sight."

The lieutenant followed two emergency medical technicians from the ambulance into Guy and Chantal's crib. Guy slipped in behind them and watched an EMT work on the Chinese waitress from How Toy strapped to their sofa. The second EMT worked on Chantal's Cajun dockworker, tied to the recliner of their small front room.

The lieutenant asked the waitress her name. She blinked her milky eyes wildly at him and opened her mouth, but nothing came out. The dockworker started crying and shaking. The lieutenant moved over to lend a hand. A high-pitched howl came from the man as his chest heaved.

"He's throwing a fit," the lieutenant said.

The EMT reached for his medical bag.

The dockworker screamed and tried to bite the lieutenant, who fell away. Straining at his restraints, the dockworker howled again and then collapsed back against the recliner and didn't move.

As Guy started for the door, another cop came out of their bedroom carrying a police hat from one of their dress uniforms.

"Lou," he called out to the lieutenant. "I think a cop lives here."

"Jesus fuckin' Christ!"

Guy eased out of the house and back down South St. Patrick and up Cleveland to the Caprice. His stomach was so shaky and his feet so rubbery when he landed on the sidewalk that he had to lean against the Caprice a minute to catch his breath.

When he climbed in, Chantal's eyes blinked open. He started the engine. She sat up, pulled her hair away from her face again to let the AC bathe her neck, looked at the backseat, and told Guy, "I left enough for you."

"Our crib's blown."

She recoiled as if he'd slapped her.

He punched the steering wheel, then put the car into gear and took a right down South Bernadotte back to Canal Street.

It took a minute for Chantal to ask, "What happened?"

He told her about the cries and the nosy neighbor and the cops and the EMTs hurrying into their house. Accessing I-10 now, he hit the accelerator.

"It isn't fair!" Chantal sank back against the door, her chin down, her eyes suddenly wet. "It's just not fair."

He nodded slowly.

"We had a good three years," he said. "Better than most stops." He reached over to turn up the AC and noticed his hand shaking.

"Pull over," she said, her voice stronger now.

"I'm okay," he said, but knew better. He held on to the steering wheel with both hands and sucked in a deep breath and felt such a hollowness inside. He looked at her and shrugged. She grabbed the steering wheel and helped him pull over and stop along the shoulder of the Interstate.

Guy reached to open his door and found he hadn't the strength.

He felt the door open and Chantal reach in and gently pull him out. She guided him around to the back door and eased him in with the stranger.

"I left enough for you," she reminded him before closing the door. "But be careful."

Guy leaned over the stranger and knew what she meant. *Don't kill him.* He would be careful, he told himself as he opened his mouth and his tongue touched the side of the stranger's neck. Salty and sweet, the taste sent a shiver through Guy's body.

Opening his mouth wider, he sank his teeth into the flesh and felt the hot, coppery blood slide down his throat and burn with pleasure all the way to his stomach. He closed his eyes and fed and the jittery feeling slipped away, the weakness faded, and he fell into the deep and delicious rapture.

He felt her shake him. Guy pulled his head up and looked at her. Lying facedown on the backseat, he reached around for the stranger.

"He's gone," Chantal said. "I propped him outside a barroom." She began to rub his back softly.

He tried to rise.

She put a hand on his back and said, "We have time."

He couldn't hear anything outside so he asked, "Where are we?"

"Back on Cleveland."

Guy looked out the side window at dark magnolia branches. He pushed himself up and looked out the back window. Chantal had parked the Caprice beneath the same magnolia on Cleveland Avenue, a half block from their crib.

"There's a unit in front and crime scene tape sealing off the crib." Her voice was quieter now, sadder. "They're probably waiting for IAD."

Guy nodded. Internal Affairs were day-shift people. She was probably right. They'd come in the morning and discover the blacked-out windows and their photo collection and everything, even the brick dust between their mattresses. They might even figure it all out—maybe.

He sat up, reached over and hugged her, smelling the perfume in her hair. She squeezed him back. He looked at his Seiko. It was three-thirty already.

"Damn, I was out a while, wasn't I?"

She nodded, then said, "You get enough to eat?"

"Yeah. And you?"

She nodded, her hair brushing his cheek. She let out a long sigh and said, "I'm so tired of starting over."

He was, too.

"It was so nice living in a house. Sleeping together." Her voice cracked.

He kissed the side of her neck. She kissed his cheek and pulled away, then looked out the rear window and said they'd better do it now.

They both climbed out the door next to the sidewalk. Guy shut the door quietly and followed Chantal across the street and down to the corner. Stopping beneath the wide branches of the oak, they closed their eyes and rose softly through the tree and over to the back door of their crib.

They glided across the small wooden back porch, then Chantal slipped through the rear door keyhole while Guy slid under the door. Standing up in their kitchen, Guy stretched and twisted the kinks out of his back.

Chantal moved into their bedroom and went down on her knees to reach under their bed. Guy watched her pull up the floorboard beneath the bed and reach inside. Her ass looked nice, pointed up at him.

She stood up and dangled the three keys as she rose and walked back to him. Handing him the keys to their three safety deposit boxes, she brushed her lips across his and said, "Ready?"

When she turned to step away, she paused a second. "I'm going to miss this place."

"I know." He let out a long breath. "It could be worse."

When she didn't respond, he added, "It could be raining."

She elbowed him in the ribs and walked back into the bedroom to light a candle.

He put the keys in his pocket and moved to the stove. Lifting the top of the stove, he blew out the pilot lights, then put the lid back down and turned on all four burners. He went down on his knees, opened the oven, and blew out its pilot light. He left the oven door open and turned it on, too.

Chantal tapped him on the ass as she moved back to the door. He got up and joined her there. They took one more look at their crib as they faded.

Chantal parked the Caprice on Basin Street next to the fire hydrant behind Our Lady of Guadalupe Church. Guy climbed out with her Beretta and shoulder rig and tossed them into the trunk next to his Beretta and badge.

"Just leave it," she said.

"Hey, I'm still a cop. Some scumbag'll break in and steal them."

She laughed. "Still a cop, huh?"

He dug out the Nikon and exposed the film before tossing it all back in. Chantal threw the car keys inside and slammed the trunk shut.

He took her hand and they crossed Basin to the wide neutral ground, then continued on to the other side of the street to the white wall of St. Louis Cemetery Number One. They walked along the wall on the St. Louis Street side of the cemetery and up the narrow side street to a dark spot between the streetlights, where they stopped for a moment before floating over the wide wall.

They drifted over white masonry sepulchers and gray cement crypts of a cemetery built entirely above ground, like a little city of the dead. They floated to the front of the cemetery, to a small grassy area just inside the wall along the Basin Street side.

They sat together on a black wrought-iron bench—their bench. Guy lifted the cup at the top of the bench's right arm and placed the safety deposit box keys inside. He put the cup back and said, "At least we have something to start with next time."

Chantal nodded slowly. It was her idea, stashing cash in boxes in three separate banks, under different names, names from long ago, names no one remembered anymore, except them.

Guy took her hand and squeezed it as he inhaled the familiar, moldy scents of home. He tasted the sweet, thick air and ran his free hand across the warm metal of the bench. They hadn't been home for three years and he hadn't realized how much his senses had missed it. And, for the first time that evening, his stomach was no longer jittery.

Chantal leaned her head against his shoulder. He let go of her hand and wrapped his arm around her. And for a long time, they stared at the walled tombs. Outside, facing the street, the long brick wall was covered with masonry and looked white and pristine. Inside, the brick tombs were crumbled and decaying, the three rows of tiered tombs timeworn and brittle. Most of the marble and granite headstones had crumbled and fallen away, along with the names of the dead. Guy closed his eyes and remembered the feeling as his casket was slid into its oven tomb in the wall.

"I'm going to miss air-conditioning," Chantal said.

"And cable TV," he said.

"And all my clothes." She lifted her head away. "And my crime scene photos!"

"We'll get more clothes. New clothes," he said. She always liked to shop.

Chantal pulled her head away and looked over her shoulder and said, "Do you think they'll come for us this time?"

"No way." Guy said it with conviction. "And they never will."

"You'd think they would—finally figure." She put her head back against his shoulder.

He used to worry about them coming for him and Chantal, but not anymore, not after all the years.

"They'll just think we were two sickos," he said. "We'll need to be careful for a while."

She nodded, her hair brushing his cheek again.

"Work the streets," he said, "like we used to."

He didn't say it, but both of them knew it would be hit-and-run nights, sleeping back home—no AC, no cable TV, not for a while.

Chantal turned her wide eyes toward him and said, "Know what I'll miss the most?"

He knew she'd say it again.

She let out a long sigh. "I'll miss sleeping with you."

Guy cupped her face in his hands and kissed her softly on her full lips. She closed her eyes and a tear rolled from each. Guy moved his tongue against hers and felt her body press against him. He felt his heartbeat rise.

He unbuttoned her dress. She unbuttoned his shirt and then went to work on his belt. He cupped her breasts in his hands, his tongue still working against hers. He pushed her dress open. She pushed his jeans down.

They pulled away from the kiss to climb out of their clothes.

Standing naked next to her, Guy ran his hands down her back to squeeze her ass.

She hugged him and moved her body against his, her thick bush pressing against his swollen dick, the weight of her warm breasts against his chest. Then she took a step back and sat on the bench. Reaching for him, she grabbed his stiff dick and guided it toward her mouth. Her tongue flicked against the base of his swollen dick. She licked her way up, all the way to the tip. She let her sharp teeth brush across the tip and Guy winced in pain and pleasure. She sank her mouth on his dick and sucked, her head moving up and down.

Guy moaned and ran his hands through her hair. Pumping his hips, he fucked her mouth and felt so hot so quickly, he had to pull her from him before he came right away. It took a couple seconds to pull her off.

Chantal, his dick still in her hand, leaned back on the bench and opened her legs. She guided the tip of his dick to the opening of her pussy and rubbed her bush against it.

Guy felt how wet she was and felt his dick slide between the folds of her pussy. She shuddered at the initial penetration, then pumped back against him. Guy grabbed her hips and fucked her in a long, grinding ride, his balls slapping her ass.

Her pussy was so hot, he almost came again and had to fight it. Stopping momentarily, he caught his breath, then went back to a deep, grinding fuck, working his dick deep within her.

Chantal gasped and cried out. "Oh, babe. Oh, babe!" She grabbed the back of the bench.

Guy leaned forward and kissed her neck and felt her arms wrap around his, felt her head move forward, felt her kiss the side of his throat. The needle prick of her teeth burned his throat. The pain was deep and delicious.

He opened his trembling mouth, leaned down, and bit her neck, tasting her sweet blood.

His throat burned with her sharp kiss.

His dick throbbed inside her.

His mouth filled with her blood.

The pain was excruciating, the pleasure so complete, so deep, so hypnotic. Guy let it engulf him, let it smother him, let it pull him deeper and deeper with each scintillating sensation, each luscious moment of agony and pleasure.

Guy came in her and she gyrated back against him, but they didn't stop.

Later, much later, Guy felt her pull away from his throat. His mouth fell away from her neck. Chantal licked the wound on his throat until the pain went away. Guy licked her neck until the wound was neat and clean.

Tingling from the pain and the warmth of the pleasure, Guy fell next to her on the bench. He looked up at the sky and saw it beginning to lighten, blackness turning into charcoal gray.

Standing unsteadily, Guy reached down and picked up Chantal's dress. He handed it to her and then dressed himself. He was fastening his belt when Chantal moved to the wall and stood in front of an oven tomb along the second tier. Moving slightly to her right to allow the dim streetlights to illuminate the headstone, she read it aloud and then ran her fingers over the chiseled words—

> Guy Gaston LeRoux
> born 25 May 1819
> died 7 October 1849

Guy moved up behind her and touched her shoulder.

He ran his fingers over the words chiseled in the marble headstone of the walled tomb next to his. It read—

> Chantal-Marie Champollion
> Janvier 10, 1770
> Juillet 28, 1794

Looking at the dates, he felt his throat tighten as he remembered how she'd told him of the long years of loneliness before she'd found him.

As if she'd read his mind, she said, "We still have each other."

He looked down at her beautiful face, glowing orange now in the faint streetlight, and said, "I'm going to miss sleeping next to you."

She smiled weakly and said, "It's time."

"I know."

She sucked in a deep breath. He kissed her again, softly, and tasted the blood on her tongue—his blood. Then they stood next to one another until the ground slipped away.

The scent of brick dust filled Guy's nostrils as he breathed the rich deep smell of home. The scent was intoxicating and sent his heart racing. He blinked his eyes open to a blackness so complete it sent a shiver through him.

A second later he felt brick chips sharp against his back. He reached around and brushed the broken bits of brick from under him into the corners of his oven tomb, where the decayed linen and wood of his casket lay.

He ran his fingers along the roof of the tomb, then along its sides. He knew every bump and crease as well as he knew the curves of Chantal's body in the dark. He sucked in another breath and smelled old wood now—the scent of his casket.

He heard Chantal whisper, "Babe . . . Babe . . . "

"I hear you," he whispered back.

"It's so . . . cramped."

"I know." He stretched his legs and felt them brush against the end of the tomb.

"I can't sleep," she said, her voice so soft he could barely hear it.

"Just breathe deeply."

Guy closed his eyes and breathed evenly, trying his best to let his even breaths lull him to sleep. It didn't take long to feel himself drifting. And as he drifted, he saw her in his mind, saw her as he had on that fog-shrouded autumn night so long ago. Standing beneath a gas streetlight in the alley next to St. Louis Cathedral, she wore a long, black dress, her white shoulders bare, her eyes glimmering. He remembered how his breath slipped away when he'd first seen her. The most alluring, the most delicious creature he had ever seen, she reached her hand out to him and led him to the side of the alley.

She leaned back against the wall of the cathedral and pulled him to her, parting her legs to pull him close. She closed her eyes and tilted her head and kissed his lips so softly he barely felt her lips. He felt her hands work her dress up and then felt them on his belt and felt himself slip into her and they made love against the wall of St. Louis Cathedral, beneath the spire of the saints, and it was heavenly.

He remembered the absolute rapture of his death there in the alley—the absolute rapture. And he remembered his casket sliding into the wall and all the nights of their eternal blood dance along the dark streets of New Orleans. He remembered them all in rapid succession and as one, long tango.

His eyes opened and he realized it was Chantal, whispering in his ear.

"Yes?"

"I can't sleep," she said.

He smiled. "Me either."

The first night back in the tomb was always the longest.

"I was thinking," Chantal whispered, "that we should start right away."

"Okay."

"Go to the bank, get a crib immediately."

"Okay," he agreed.

"I think I'll be a blond, again. You liked me as a blonde."

A vision of Chantal the blonde cabdriver flashed in Guy's mind.

"You could be a blond, too. Maybe with no mustache this time." She was picking at him now. He always had a mustache—always.

"Yeah. Right," he said.

She was teasing him. That was a good sign.

"Just no more eating at home," he said.

She laughed, her soft voice echoing through the bricks.

"I was thinking," she said a minute later, "about the coroner's office. We'd be naturals working there. They have a graveyard shift, don't they?"

"Yes." Guy smiled. "And you can start your crime scene collection again."

Ceilings and Sky

Lucy Taylor

—∞—

Tonight the Master sucked the blood from a cut I'd opened up on the inside of my thigh. Afterward, he kissed me with his crimson lips. I felt Reborn.

I am sitting in the back row of a Greyhound bus hurtling through the desert toward Las Vegas, reading over and over the journal that my twenty-two-year-old son Nigel kept in the months before he hanged himself. The journal, along with a few of his effects, was sent to me by one of his ex-lovers, a bearded, raven-haired boy named David whom I know only from a photo of himself and Nigel that he included among the items forwarded to me.

"Nigel and me, in better days," he'd scribbled on the back. "Before he joined the Blood Cult."

The photo shows the two young men with their arms around each other, swaggering out of a Perry Street brownstone in New York's Greenwich Village. Nigel is wearing a white muscle shirt and scruffy shorts. His smile is shy, disarming, his eyes glittery and slitted—a boy either stoned or in love, perhaps both. I wouldn't know—it's been a long time since I had the pleasure of enjoying either state.

To look at him, you would never think this boy had ever hungered—for love or sex or anything else—a day in his charmed life.

Alas, if Nigel's life was "charmed," it was by an evil angel.

For one thing, at the time he was conceived, I was a nineteen-year-old drug-addled hooker. When I wasn't sucking a john's dick, I was pushing a needle into my arm. I'd already had two abortions and decided to keep this child, not because of any latent maternal instinct that surfaced between the bedroom and the abortion clinic, but because at the time, I thought a baby would help me hold on to the man I suspected was Nigel's father. The scheme was as old as my lover's sudden disappearance was predictable.

"But I love you," I remember crying out, as though merely saying the words would garner reciprocation. I was always in love with someone in those days—I needed to be in love as much as I needed to breathe. Being in love was the ultimate fix—it buffered me against reality and the self-hatred that I carried inside me like a ticking bomb while I used uppers and downers and heroin and the wrong kind of men to murder myself on the installment plan.

I thought if only I could meet the Right Man, he'd wave the magic wand between his legs and take away my pain.

Like the man that Nigel grew up to be, I hungered desperately for love and squandered myself in search of it.

And along the way, I found that answered prayers are often the first step toward damnation.

The summer that Nigel turned nine years old, I met The One, the man I'd waited for all my life—beautiful, wealthy, powerful. The man I knew I'd die for. I quit the streets, stopped shooting dope, quit being Nigel's mother. My life was different now. Soon after meeting my new lover, I sent Nigel to live with my widowed sister, a woman as austere and taciturn as I was wanton.

At first I tried to keep track of Nigel through sporadic correspondence with my sister. He was a shy child, I was told, very loving, attentive and eager to please. *He pines for you and keeps asking if he did something wrong to make you send him away,* she wrote. *He keeps asking why you never call or visit.*

But I had other things to keep me occupied by then, and Nigel wasn't one of them.

How I long for the Master to love me. . . , Nigel writes. *When I lie beneath the open dome of the Star Room, watching the swirling procession of the planets while the Master's mouth describes its own wondrous constellation of kisses down my belly, when I feel his hardness against my ass, between my thighs, I know the meaning of adoration, know that I would give myself to him entirely, commit any crime, endure any torture, if only he might feel for me one fraction of the love I feel for him.*

Oh yes, I understand, son. At your age, I felt the same way—that love was a tiny form of death, to be purchased with the heart's blood and paid for with the soul. Not a give-and-take between two equals, but the conquest of the vulnerable by the mighty, a lush and languid bloodletting, be it emotional or all too literal, of a submissive's life force.

When the Master opens up a cut on me and sucks the oozing wound, I feel a kind of ecstasy. I want to bleed to death for him, to be emptied out, drained dry by my beloved. His beauty makes my eyes ache. His skin has the pallor of paper and seems preternaturally sensitive to touch—I think he feels pleasure more intensely than others. When he kisses me, I know that I would die for him, if death indeed were the price of his affection.

I rest the journal on my lap as the bus plunges through the darkness of the desert. The head of the sleeping woman in the seat in front of me lolls back, frosted strands of hair matted into bird's-nest clumps. Across the aisle, a little boy sits wide awake, staring at me in a way that makes me want to scrunch up my face in a monster leer and hiss, "Boo!" Instead, I offer him a small go-back-to-sleep smile with a tiny tilt of my eyebrows. He turns away and grinds his spine into the seat back, as though hoping it will slide open like a secret passage into some other realm.

I try to sleep, but the bulky silhouettes of the Joshua trees slick with moonglow, the night textured with stars and what might be the leathery winging of bats, the sense of my own mission make me want to leave my seat and pace the aisle like a penned mustang.

Instead I try to remember everything that my research since Nigel's death has gleaned about "the Master" (née Edgar Lauren, forty-five years old, former real estate salesman, bit-part actor in some soap operas and a couple of MTV videos, Protestant by birth, sex-god and Creature of the Night by avocation). I've not found much—a few paragraphs on the subject of vampire cults in *The New York Times*, a page in *People*, and an analysis in *Psychology Today* on the phenomenon of people who either pretend to be or actually believe themselves to be vampires. A sidebar interview with an ex-follower described the Master as seductive, exploitative, an utterly narcissistic combination of vanity and charm. "He drinks human blood, exerts almost hypnotic power over his followers. Is he the *real* thing?" the magazine reporter asked coyly at the end of the interview.

When I read that question, I felt a frisson of horror and titillation. A vampire? My Nigel in thrall to such a creature?

I know that Nigel gave Edgar Lauren not just his body, but his material wealth as well—the trust fund I'd set up for him to receive when he turned twenty-one went entirely into Lauren's coffers.

But then the Master seems to have a talent for seducing those who have more wealth than wisdom, the decadent and trust-funded, the nouveau flush. It's known that the granddaughter of a famous deceased actor, a man who ironically enough had once played Count Dracula in a stage production, funded the Master's palatial digs outside Vegas a few years ago. Since he moved there, it's rumored the Master never goes outside, that the closest he gets to daylight are the facsimiles of skies painted on each of the ceilings in his desert residence.

At times the bloodletting is copious. The dozen or so of us who live here partner each other at random for sex and for the drinking of blood. Only those most fortunate are chosen by the Master. I understand the awful danger in the blood-drinking and yet, I find the sweet, thick taste of blood to be invigorating. It seems to act as an aphrodisiac, but more than that, it fills me with a sense of connectedness, as I take the very essence of the others into my own self.

I read that paragraph several times. If I could cry, then maybe I'd feel cleansed. But my eyes are as dry as the desert scrub sweeping past the edges of the Greyhound's headlights.

Around 3 A.M., just before the bus reaches Vegas, I open my dinner and eat quietly so as not to disturb the sleeping passengers. I put on fresh lipstick and rouge, run a brush through my blonde hair, and smooth out the collar of my blue silk blouse. Nigel writes that the Master's favorite color is blue. Sky blue. Like his eyes.

At the rental car company across the street from the bus station, a silver Volvo waits for me. When I tell the girl behind the counter where I'm going, no flicker of amusement or disgust crosses her varnished-looking features. "Skyland?" she says. No problem. This is Las Vegas, after all, and why shouldn't I be headed for the desert lair of a reclusive salesman turned MTV extra turned sex cult guru in the wee hours of an August morning?

She draws directions on a map. As I drive through the desert night, I can imagine the fierce heat of midday lancing down, white hot and blinding, but long before the sun breaks like a bloody egg on the horizon and drains into the desert sand, I have arrived at Skyland.

The Master says we acquire inner peace through the gift of our material possessions, the gift of our bodies. He accepts material wealth only to relieve his pupils of the desire for acquisition. Our bodies are a kind of tithe. Last night I worshiped him on my knees, suckling like a child, finally swallowing every drop of his gift to me, what he calls the Baptism of Holy Semen.

From the looks of Skyland, I can tell the Master has spared no effort to take onto himself the moral burden of his followers' unholy bank accounts and corrupting blue-chip-stock portfolios. The cult headquarters is an ornate domed castle of pink-orange sandstone, plunked incongruously in the center of the desert moonscape. It's like finding a Fabergé egg in the middle of the Kalahari—bizarre in the comic/scary way of a Salvador Dali painting.

To add to the off-kilter mystique, there's a Harley parked next to the door, a Jag and a couple of pickup trucks that must be used by the Devotees to bring supplies from Vegas. A lighted fountain by the door spews bile-colored water. Borders of stumpy teddy bear cacti that resemble malformed gnomes surround the palace like a profusion of warts.

No twinkle of light seeps from its windowless facade. As I approach the double doors inlaid with Spanish tile, I feel like I am entering the Byzantine necropolis of some corrupt and ancient pasha. It shames me that the feeling is not at all unpleasant. Perhaps it is my own adrenaline-fueled anticipation, but the place seems to reek of sex and blood, hormonal heat—essences that, even on this most serious of missions, make my cunt contract with longing while desire seethes along my spine. A corrupt, pheromonal perfume hangs languidly over the premises, like the promise of a rainstorm that will never come.

My arrival is expected. A lawyer I acquired in the days when I was amassing my quite considerable fortune has made sure the Master knows who I am, within certain discreet limits—a bored and wealthy eccentric, a one-time call girl, now in search of erotic thrills cloaked in pseudo-occult gibberish. Although I've been told the Master prefers young boys and girls, it seems greed's given him a hard-on for my more mature affections.

A scrawny, dark-skinned girl with gold rings through lips so plump and crimson they mimic vulval folds greets me at the entrance and ushers me into a waiting area. Simple benches, fringed throw rugs, a profusion of pillows flanked by teakwood griffins decorate the room. As the girl turns to leave, I see the ridged scar tissue along her upper arms and neck, more recent cuts across her back.

I shiver and gaze upward. As I expected, the ceiling is a replica of sky, robin's-egg blue, dotted with cream puff clouds and the gauzy, languid haze of heat rising. Track lighting gives the illusion of faint sunlight gilding the edges of the cumuli.

A young man with the pouty mouth of a errant schoolboy and an ugly sore marring the symmetry of his lower lip brings me a glass of tsai. Although I'm hungry, the curdled-milk look of its steamy contents turns my stomach.

While I wait, I continue reading Nigel's journal.

Tonight, lying in the Master's bed (while the other Devotees were fiercely envying me, no doubt), I dared to ask the question I'd been putting off for fear of appearing either ridiculously naive or unforgivably impudent. I asked if—should we both desire it—he could truly transform me into something more than human, powerful and immortal. In reply, he used his silver knife to open a gash at my neck and fondled my cock while he drank from me.

But he did not answer my question.

"Corrinne?"

I hear my name pronounced in syllables sweet and smooth as clotted cream. My head jerks around as though tugged by an invisible leash. *The Master.* Time slows and thickens as in a sluggish dream, as I take in every lithe, cobra-sleek inch of him. The man that Nigel loved.

He is as beautiful as I'd expected, yet somehow—for a man who wields such power over his Devotees—also more innocuous. No inkling of corruption here—unless one considers a too-pale and perfect body to imply some inner evil.

He looks much younger than his age, hair lustrous and black as enamel against meringue-white skin, limpid eyes that seek and penetrate while giving away nothing, forearms ropy with muscle and pelted with dark, lickable hair.

And hollow. The void in his soul vibrates against my flesh like a kind of psychic sonar. Perfectly, immaculately empty. Neither saintly nor corrupt, this Master, but an exquisite masculine vessel in a state of eternal spiritual, hormonal hunger.

He's dressed differently from what I had imagined. Perhaps I had expected a cape or flowing avatar robes, silk purring around bare toenails, some satin and velvet costume out of a B-grade vampire flick. Instead, he's wearing gray sweatpants with a drawstring waist, a plain blue, loose-fitting shirt. But for his extreme pallor, he might be an off-duty lifeguard or a lounging tennis pro.

When he takes my hand, his fingers are unusually dry and cool—as if they've been dipped in paraffin. He asks me a few questions to determine the extent of my interest in and knowledge of his so-called Blood Cult. Apparently my answers satisfy him—or maybe it's the dime-sized emerald on my left hand that convinces him I'm fit to be admitted to the sanctum. He grants me a tour. "You understand what you're getting into? You've read *The Work*?"

"Many times," I say—a pompous diatribe of sex and occult prattle and life-eternal rot that was included among Nigel's things. "It's what influenced me to seek you out." I decide to press my luck a bit. "That, and the fact that I had a son who recently died quite young. His death has given me a new perspective on life's brevity and the importance of sampling pleasure in all its forms."

He still has not released my hand. His sated-predator eyes assess me shamelessly. The way he looks at me, I feel he'd like to fuck me down to sweat and moans, lap the moisture from my cunt, then peel my skin and drape himself inside it, wear me like a cloak.

"The other Devotees are occupied with chores," he says with sudden brusqueness. "Let me see how well you serve me."

I smile up into his empty eyes and too-beautiful face, but it is Nigel's face I see—Nigel's kisses on his lips, Nigel's pain behind his eyes when I answer, "Fair enough. Let me see how well you fuck me."

The Master's palatial residence has no windows, but as we move from room to room, shyly spied upon by scarified and pale-cheeked Devotees, I know the sun has risen outside, the earth's commenced to bake, and shadows—red-hot wraiths that mime the phallic lengths of cacti—claw their way like those dying of thirst across the burning sand. Beyond the subtle burr of air conditioners, I'm also aware that heat assails the domed abode and sun-basking lizards flick forked tongues in our direction, as if anticipating a moment when the curved white roof cracks like an egg and sunlight dazzles in.

"Is it true you never see the daylight?"

He grimaces, as though the very thought induces goose bumps. "I see no need to leave my residence. I prefer to let my pleasure come to me."

We stroll along a dimly lit corridor where the scent of blood permeates the air like incense in a cathedral. Each time we pass Devotees, they bow in obeisance.

"There are those who say you stay inside because you have no choice—that sunlight would destroy you."

He allows himself the subtlest smile, but it's clear he's flattered. "Perhaps that's true . . . or maybe I suffer from some deficiency that makes my eyes acutely sensitive to sunlight. Maybe I crave blood as a way to compensate for some vitamin deficiency. Isn't that one of the explanations given for the universality of the vampire legend?"

"If it's a legend."

"If you're afraid, you're free to leave here if you like. Later on, I may not be able to make you the same offer."

I take his hand and guide his wrist to my lips, tongue the purple veins wending their way heartward.

"I want to learn all you can teach me."

"About pleasure?"

"And other things."

"Erotic pleasure is the path to higher wisdom." He sounds as if he's reading from a fortune cookie.

Then, perhaps because he realizes his observation sounds facile, he expostulates on his philosophy of salvation through the flesh until we arrive in what he calls the Morning Glory Room, a bedroom whose ceiling offers a pastel facsimile of a dawn sky so delicate it might have been painted on the inside of an eggshell.

His clothing slithers to the carpet like a discarded skin. Beneath it, his body is fetchingly muscular, his alabaster chest the white canvas against which spreads a tree of ebony hair. There's a sureness to the way he moves his muscles—more a swimmer's body than a weightlifter's, more dancer than quarterback.

He slides a hand behind my neck. Undoes my blouse. Cool dry hands, finger pads like insect husks. Lust plucks at me like hot, sadistic fingers—heat and hunger supersede all else. How can I so desire the creature I hold responsible for my son's death?

But I know: because he *was* Nigel's lover and now he will be mine. Because knowledge of his skin, his taste, of the musk wafting up from his pores will bring me as close as I will ever be again to Nigel, the child I betrayed.

The Master has a little game he plays with me. In private, when he snaps his fingers, I'm to drop to my knees, take his cock in my mouth. Humility and submission are the twin paths to enlightenment, he says. Freedom of the soul through bondage of the flesh and abdication of the will.

As he continues to disrobe me, he turns expostulatory. "You see, religions have had it all wrong through the centuries. What's denigrated as sexual debauchery is really the path to ecstasy and wisdom. The wisdom of the flesh. Mortify the flesh and bleed it dry. Devote ourselves to the arts of pleasure and pain. Through satiation of the body, we are able to transcend it and have peace."

And your own desert Xanadu and a different piece of ass every night, I think.

He cups my cheek and turns my face to meet his. Something in my eyes—perhaps the fact that they aren't closed, but open, seeing him, *really* seeing him and he *knows* I see him as he is . . . he hesitates a flicker. Then his ego muscles back to take command and he delivers a kiss hot and moist and penetrating enough to unravel the senses. These lips kissed Nigel, I think. This mouth took Nigel's cock into its hot dark and anointed it. These are my thoughts as I relax and melt into the kiss, let him mold my mouth to whatever shape he wants it.

"You're lucky," he says. "You're special. You have a need greater than most to be . . . filled in every sense . . . physically, spiritually . . . For a long time now your life has been as barren, as devoid of love as the dried-up, cracked arroyos splitting the desert."

I neither confirm nor deny this assessment, but lie back on the bed and allow his strumming tongue to play its song between my thighs. Time seems to be passing underwater. There's a slow-motion quality to each movement of his hands, his mouth. His caresses are stretched out like slick, moist taffy until we lie so close that the surface of his skin defines the boundaries of mine. I feel appalled at myself for enjoying this travesty of seduction, but the erotic has always had a self-renewing quality for me—it's always new, it always hits with a surprisingly strong jolt of YES, as if a small electrode has been fired in the pleasure center of my cortex.

Above me, the pale light illuminates a radiant, mother-of-pearl sky, dewy with captured moisture, streaked with soft curlicue clouds that range out like tassels toward what should be the horizon. The artist is to be congratulated. With my lids half lowered, it looks so real I nestle my head in the crook of the Master's shoulder to shield my eyes from the impending sunrise.

Tonight I took a razor blade and cut the Master's name into my chest. Soon I was white and red as a barber pole. The Master, when I showed him what I'd done, only looked at me with contempt. I felt appalled, ashamed, and filled with a self-loathing that I cannot seem to shake. I feel myself getting ever weaker, my sense of myself more ephemeral. My will feels as porous and crushable as vertebrae made cracker-thin by osteoporosis.

Adroitly as a Baryshnikov of the bedchamber, the Master maneuvers me through a ballet of sex, never breaking rhythm, never pulling out. It's like a dance, choreographed to perfect erotic rhythm, crescendos of force and near violence followed by long languid adagios of touch so tender as to verge on excruciating.

We move to yet another bedroom, accessible from the first one through a connecting door. The bed here is swathed in ivory-colored silk; above it shimmers a fog-shrouded sky where a veiled sun glimmers weakly. I slide down between his legs, bathe his length with my tongue. No blood courses through the blue vein that worms along the shaft, but he stiffens anyway. No surge of blood, but a fuck-you-senseless hard-on just the same.

I run my hand along the shaft, exploring, marveling at what I feel beneath the skin.

"A prosthesis." The irony astounds me. "The guru of a sex cult and you're impotent."

"Hardly impotent." He sounds offended. "Before I had my device implanted, I could get several erections a day—nothing to be ashamed of. Now I can have dozens and satisfy one partner after another. My lovers don't complain."

I decide to tease him a little. "Not to mention the fact that an implant adds to your mystique. A vampire would require such a device, wouldn't he, to get an erection?"

"If such a creature existed."

The tang of promised danger wafts off him like a drug. Lust rules me. "I want you to fuck me in every room," I whisper, "underneath each of your skies."

From a drawer that slides into the headboard of the bed, he takes out a slender silver knife, the handle elaborately carved to resemble male genitalia.

"You know what making love with me involves. May I make the first cut now?"

My gaze travels up the perfect silver shaft, the point glittering like the eviscerating tongue of some Aztec god. I think of spilled blood lapped in coppery tonguefuls. My head spins with wooziness.

"I need more time before I bleed."

"But bloodletting is part of making love here."

"Just a little more time . . . to get used to the idea."

He stares at me as if he's trying to decipher some secret inscribed behind my eyes. "I'll give you a few days," he says, "but then you'll have to let me cut you." And he puts the knife away.

As part of my initiation, I agree to stay in seclusion and be entirely at the Master's service for one week, with each of our sessions taking place in another of his many bedrooms. Our lovemaking familiarizes me with a multitude of skies—one broils with ocher-lined thunderheads while lightning lashes the clouds, another pays homage to dusk: thin tendrils of late sun, a delicate amber kudzu that creeps among clouds so gold-tinged and ethereal that they might harbor angels.

A variety of Devotees—haggard-looking, lily-skinned men and women with downcast eyes that never match the eerie, suffering little smiles that play upon their lips like incestuous caresses—bring me my meals. I have no appetite and, besides, there are other hungers to distract me. Some of the Devotees appeal to me—a blonde girl with breasts like pink-tipped figs and downy pubic curls; I feed her chunks of melon and oranges from my lips and make the many rings that pierce her labia chime like temple bells.

I ask her if she knew a young man named Nigel who hung himself in a domed bedroom that opens up to see the real sky. She listens with sweet solicitude, as though I'm reading her a fairy tale, then says she can't remember.

It seems my desirability has diminished as my personal resources have been depleted. The Master has grown bored with me. We have not made love alone in weeks, and when I try to catch his eye, he either ignores me or sends me off on some errand. I'm terrified he's going to ask that I leave, as I have seen him do with others but, in my egotism, never dreamed he would demand of me. The other day, he asked if I had family anywhere. Family? What a cruel joke! I thought I'd found my family within these walls.

More and more I anticipate my time spent with the Master, lust infected with that raptor hunger of rage mixed with arousal—for that flesh that so enraptured Nigel captivates me now, and I bury my face in the sweet curve of his groin, in the meat of his chest and the jut of his jawline, in the musky nest under his arm.

Almost a week after my arrival here, I am finally allowed inside the domed bedroom that I've been waiting to see, the one that Nigel described in his journal, the one in which he chose to die.

A four-poster bed with a satiny purple comforter occupies the center. There is a table with a pitcher of cold water on it and a variety of implements laid out: whips and clamps and various restraints. Metal rings festoon the walls at different levels—a plant in a wicker basket droops from the highest. I don't know if it's a deliberately mirthful touch or if the Master really likes his slavish Devotees to submit to his indignities amid a bit of foliage.

He has requested that I leave tomorrow—the Master, the Father, the man I adore. I've begged and pleaded and threatened to harm myself. He is unmoved. The old demons from my childhood bay at me like rabid hounds—once again, I am abandoned and betrayed by the person most important to me in the world. Once again, I am unworthy. Once again, I am alone.

"This is my favorite room, my special room. Soundproofed for greater privacy," he tells me as he fondles a leather riding crop that dangles from a hook near the single touch of greenery. "I think I've given you time enough. I want to see you bleed."

"Beneath the stars?"

He nods. "There are those who believe I never see the real sky, but they're wrong."

He presses a button by the bed. The ceiling, which bears a replica of desert day at its most scalding, when the sun is at its zenith, spirals back and the night opens up above our heads like a pinpoint pupil slowly dilating until it fills the entire eye.

As the ceiling opens, so do I. On my back, legs supported by his shoulders, I can see Venus and her entourage pulse and blaze. The star patterns seem to dance, dipping and wheeling like the constellations of pain that flash behind the eyelids after a blow.

"Are you willing to give up all that you possess for me?" the Master says.

"Are you willing to sacrifice all that you have and all that you are and could ever be?

"Are you willing to be one of the Devoted?"

The yeses come as easily, as unthinkingly as my climaxes. His tongue feasts on my neck. A bite above my collarbone, a nip beneath my hair. His teeth are gentle. The skin remains unbroken while above my head the stars twirl like drunken Sufis.

"You drink the blood of others," I tell him, "but when do you bleed? Or is it that you like your followers to think you don't bleed at all, because of what you are?"

But then before he answers, I pull him down to me and make fierce love to him, and this time it is really love we make, for I have always felt a strange, almost euphoria-inducing affection for those whose lives I am about to end.

It is decided—I know how and where I will die. Tomorrow in the room that is the Master's favorite I will tie a noose around the highest of the hooks and hang myself. I will make sure to do the deed at night, after I open up the dome, so that in my last moments I can see the night sky. The real sky, not another of the Master's painted ceilings.

I wonder where my mother is. I wonder who—if anyone—will tell her what I've done.

Afterward, when we have finished making love, the Master pushes the button by the bed again, replacing the night sky with a false and vivid noon. We lie entwined, him sated, me with nerves as keen as tiny wires, before I straddle him and let him feel my strength. I see the astonishment and then the terror in his eyes—terror not because he thinks I'm going to hurt him but because he's being overpowered by a woman, because his masculinity is being compromised as his wrists are forced above his head and fixed into the leather bonds that attach to metal clips around the bed-posts.

I pat his porcelain cheek and run my finger across the punctures that my kisses have left behind his ear.

"Do you understand that you've become what you pretend to be?"

He gives me his benevolent, mildly chastising smile. Christ looking down from the cross: Forgive them, Father, they know not what they do. "I don't believe in vampires."

"But you are a vampire—a human one who sucks the life force from your victims. I think that kind of vampire's more despicable. At least you have a choice."

His lower face cracks in a laugh, which ends abruptly when the heel of my hand smacks his jaw out of its socket.

"The son I lost? His name was Nigel and he killed himself in this room, because you used him and then cast him aside.

"I know how Nigel must have felt. I was obsessed with a beautiful man once, a man I was willing to die for. I *did* die for him, to become like him, just like you're going to die to become like me."

I bite him hard.

Smile redly.

This time I let him see my fangs.

I lean down to give his wrist a lacerating kiss that penetrates the bones. The sensation of my fangs popping his flesh and sinking down through fat and skeletal system is like an orgasm that explodes in my mouth and travels to the far reaches of my body. Eternal Death flows with my spittle. His sweet blood stains my teeth.

He screams for help, and I remind him that the Star Room's walls are soundproofed.

"It's hard not to finish you off right now. I haven't eaten since a sleeping woman with ratty hair on the bus that brought me to Vegas. I could have had my chauffeur drive me out, but it's nice to snack along the way."

A final, deep drink from his screaming throat: for Nigel.

When I turn the switch to make the painted ceiling spiral open, unveiling the night sky, he begins to struggle, but I've drained too much of his blood by now. Not having fed, he has no strength to break his bonds, so he makes empty promises.

He'll partner me, he'll be my lover, we'll hunt and kill together. A perfect, if unholy, pair.

Perhaps those words are what make me realize more than ever why I can't let his existence continue as one of my Kind. We are so much alike, except he feels no shame, no guilt. His hunger and his evil exceed mine.

I stand on the other side of the door, relishing the agony of his anticipation. Once I peek in and see that the inkiness of desert night has faded to the gentler, blue-tinged black preceding dawn. Then I shut the door again, but leave it cracked a hair.

When the desert sun begins to rise and his dead flesh starts to scorch, I hear the savage music of his screams.

The Fly Room

Th. Metzger

The key groaned in the lock.

"Welcome to the fly room." Jason entered and immediately an acrid pall enveloped him, an odor both sourish and sweet that went perfectly with the sunset swelter and the faint buzz of ten thousand tiny wings.

Tommy held the door for her new lab assistant. "It's mostly bottle washing," she said, "and preparing the mash, the food, for the flies. We use a mix of cornmeal, agar, molasses, and yeast."

"Sounds delicious."

Jason's feeble joke went unremarked. Like a jailor, Tommy stood dangling her overloaded ring of keys. She was a graduate student, and though only a few years older than Jason, something about her made him feel like a child. An abyss—not just a few years—separated them. Already he was contemplating the leap.

She was tall, and had her red-black hair pulled back in a ponytail that evening. She wore jeans, a threadbare T-shirt, and running shoes repaired with electrician's tape. In a crowd—in the dining commons or on Cornell's Libe Slope—she would have been invisible. Except for the eye patch. Jason had realized, meeting her yesterday for his five-minute interview, that he'd never known a girl with a patch. One-eyed women—he'd assumed—always wore a prosthesis. She wasn't pretty, not exactly. Her figure was unremarkable. Yet that night when Jason lay in his dorm room, it was Tommy—her long pallid fingers, her unblinking eye, and sad, wan smile—who slid with him into dreams. He hadn't touched a girl since saying good-bye to Wendy three weeks before.

"You'll get the hang of it pretty fast," Tommy said.

There were only two windows in the room, high on the west wall. They were filthy and probably had been painted shut long before Jason was born. The sun was just setting, making the air a beautiful red-ochre haze. Along one wall were hundreds of old-style milk bottles in wire racks. Lightbulbs dangled overhead like glowing fruit. In the center of the room was a long trestle table scarred with a hundred names. A few filing cabinets, a battered steel desk, and a pair of institutional sinks crowded the remaining space.

A small office used mostly for storage was connected to the fly room by a door of pebbled glass. Tommy gave Jason his keys the first night. "This one's for the outer door, this one's for the inner." She had him try the keys and when he found them hard to turn in the corroded brass lock, she guided his hands. That close, her scent was strong. Not a feminine perfume, but something slightly off, gamy and glandular. Not bothering with any subterfuge, he breathed deeply, and felt himself getting drunk.

Jason started that night with a routine task: cleaning dozens of milk bottles where the fruit flies lived their entire lives—a week; a whole life in a week. Then he moved on to mixing up the fetid mash and replacing lightbulbs in the makeshift incubators. Tommy had explained the night before that she was working on her doctorate in the history of genetics, recreating the experiments of Thomas Hunt Morgan, who'd done his work at Columbia almost a hundred years before.

"He was the one who discovered the XX and XY chromosomes that determine sex," she said, holding up one of the fruit flies with tweezers, staring at the tiny dot of life through a jeweler's loupe. A half dozen adolescent sex jokes came to mind, but Jason knew she wouldn't laugh. "*Drosophila melanogaster* normally has red eyes. But a mutant white-eyed strain was found and Morgan discovered the link between the mutation and the Y chromosome."

Jason stood at the sink with his bottle brush and long rubber gloves, soap suds oozing to the floor. Tommy kept flicking back her head, trying to get a lock of hair out of her face. She caught Jason staring and gave him a half-smile. Challenge, encouragement, or mere reflex?

Unsure how to respond, he turned back to the sink and went through a few dozen bottles before speaking again. He thought of Wendy in her stylish high-tone clothes and perfectly coiffed hair. She could have been a model, but comparing her with Tommy was like holding a guttering match next to an acetylene torch.

To break the groaning silence, Jason asked Tommy again about her work. The short explanation was that she was trying to re-create Morgan's experiments not to study genetics per se—this fly business, she pointed out, was all very primitive—but to analyze his methods, expectations and conclusions, and how they influenced each other.

A charge was building in Jason's body, quaking and buzzing like a lightbulb about to blow. As the red dusk faded, the feeling grew worse. The air became crystalline, as if the fruit flies had all escaped and were swarming hungrily around their mistress.

XX, XY, sex-linked chromosomes—it was all meaningless to Jason, just an excuse to be near Tommy. The light faded from the high lancet windows. He faded with it. Only his eyes remained, soaking in the artificial light. She felt his stare and turned. No smile this time, her face so fierce and flagrant he wanted to look away to keep from dissolving there like the sweet goo they fed to the flies. But he clung on, refusing to avert his eyes. He was weak and woozy. It might have been the smell of the flies, the muggy overheated September air. More likely it was the power of her naked cyclops gaze.

Three weeks away from home and he felt that he was mutating. Twenty days and he'd evolved so far from what he'd been that he barely remembered his former life. At home, expectations kept him locked in place; the eyes of his family, of friends, of Wendy, trapped him like pins holding a wriggling bug to a corkboard. That was all gone now.

Stripping off his rubber gloves, he let them fall like fish skins to the floor.

As though the whole room was charged with X rays, it took no effort to see through Tommy's clothes. Tiny, girlish nipples. Sculpted plain of her belly. Sleek smooth thighs.

The flies' buzzing grew louder, more insistent. Tommy stared back at Jason, unblinking, as though he were naked.

A bulb rattled and went black. The sudden pop broke them both out of their trance.

"I'm married," she said. She wore no ring.

Jason nodded. "I have a girlfriend back home." Wendy seemed infinitely far away, packed away with all the other junk now moldering in the back bedroom.

"What's her name?"

He hesitated. "Wendy."

"That's nice. What's she like?"

Jason shrugged. It didn't make any difference what she was like.

Turning back to the sink, he rushed through his work and left without filling out a time card. He didn't get to sleep until three and missed his morning classes the next day.

After buying a six-pack, he spent most of the afternoon at the bottom of Fall Creek Gorge, listening to the water pound the crumbling rock shelves. Steep ravines sliced the campus, lush with swollen, groping vines and hypertrophied creepers, like glimpses of some primeval world. Above him were the Victorian redbrick palaces, the ugly glass boxes put up in the sixties, the ranks of frat houses. Here below, Jason could look up and see only a glimpse of this civilization. A suspension bridge spanned the abyss, silvery gray, looking very fragile as the late afternoon sun congealed around it.

He waited for the sun to go down, watched the ruby-russet throb spread across the crack of sky he could see from his hiding place, then climbed the slick rock steps and headed across campus toward Beckwith Hall.

He counted twice, three times, to make sure. Yes, she was there; shadows moved in the high arched windows.

He waited a while, pacing the crisscrossing sidewalks like a ball caroming around the quad, telling himself he was acting like a little kid, telling himself he had nothing to fear from her.

When the last of the light had drained from the sky, he went up the scalloped stone steps. The corridor was dark by then, only a few meager bulbs in the frail metal cages. His steps echoed on the tile floor. His breathing seemed amplified by the hard surfaces of the hall.

But coming to the fly room, he realized that the labored breathing wasn't his own. In and out like exhaust whistling through the vents of some machine made of meat.

He stood paralyzed. The organic rhythm came from the fly room, the slap of wet skin on wet skin, a steadily rising cry-and-moan. He turned to flee, but the sound held him, trammeled him like the straps of a strait-jacket.

He fit his key into the door of the adjoining room, wiggled it weakly. He slid inside, eased the door shut, and stared through the pebbled glass.

Two silhouettes were framed there. One was definitely Tommy. The image was like an old fluoroscope: shadowy bones and misty flesh. It appeared she was on a table, facedown, but the banks of lights all at conflicting angles, the irregular surface of the glass door, made a prism image. They could have been anywhere in the room: the floor, straddling a chair, hanging upside down from the ceiling.

The rhythm got louder, harder. Her noises might have been weeping. His sub-bass grunt shook the floor.

Jason crouched shamed and secret, his breathing synched to theirs, terrified that they'd look through the glass and discover him, as drunk on his fear as he was on the splintered image.

They finished at last, in a shuddering growl. Before they could unlock the door and find him there, Jason snuck out and scurried down the hall, a freshly hatched larva fleeing its ruptured shell.

He had no choice now; he had to return. At seven o'clock the next evening he was at the fly room again. Tommy was at her desk, holding an invisible insect up to the quaking lamplight. Jason nodded a greeting and before she could speak, apologized. "It won't happen again, ever. It's just that I had a major test in calc today and I kind of panicked. I would have flunked for sure if I didn't study all last night. I'll get myself better organized from now on. I promise."

"Fine." She barely looked at him.

The room appeared to be undisturbed by whatever had gone on the previous night. Jason tried to visualize Tommy there on the table. But he couldn't keep the fractured, prismatic image in his head.

There was twice as much work to do that night: bottles, hundreds of bottles with black slime and dead flies inside. Big pots of foul-smelling mash to be mixed up. He stayed late to get it all done, and she stayed too, as though waiting for him. They locked up together and by unspoken agreement decided to walk home—at least part of the way—with each other. Down the pitted marble steps, into the hazy night air. It had rained while they'd worked and the ground was now breathing the moisture back into the air.

As they walked, she said almost nothing, but seemed to want him there with her.

What he'd seen the night before was real: he was sure of that. Not just his fevered adolescent imagination, not overheated fantasies projected on the pebbled glass like a cheap porn loop.

They went down a flight of wet wooden steps and started across the suspension bridge that spanned Fall Creek. In the misty dark, it seemed an even huger emptiness loomed below them, as if the night sky and the ravine had switched places. He heard water running through the rocky sluice, the wind moving tiredly in the trees that clung to the gorge rim.

A man stood at the midpoint of the bridge, waiting for them. As they approached, he remained as dim and unfocused as seen from the far side of the bridge. Tommy took Jason's hand; her breathing came sharp and shallow. He felt something—not quite fear, not exactly excitement—transmitted across the skin-to-skin connection.

"Right on time." The man's voice was a hoarse blur.

Closer now, Tommy squeezed Jason's hand.

"You like her so far?" the man said, a little smile forming on his lips, which seemed to shine an iridescent purple-red. He wore sunglasses. His skin was dark, but shiny, as though coated with spent motor oil. His hair looked like charred grass. Suddenly he jabbed a finger at Jason. "Well, do you like her?" Anger flared, and just as quickly dissipated to a smarmy smile.

"I got every right to rip your lungs out, sneaking around with my wife." He smiled more broadly now, showing ranks of tiny opalescent teeth. "But that wouldn't be too friendly, now would it? And I think Tommy'd be kind of disappointed to lose another fly helper."

He reached out abruptly and grasped Jason's face. Jason tried to pull back, but Tommy held him there. The man's touch was cold and wet as meat. His breath was rank acid.

Suspended like a spider's thread above the gorge, the narrow bridge swayed as they struggled. Below, far below, the water hissed and muttered, cutting like a fine silver edge into the bedrock.

As quickly as he'd lunged at Jason, the man backed away. "Pretty boy. Very pretty boy. Tommy's got such good taste."

"All right, Vin, that's enough."

"Kind of young though. But I guess I shouldn't complain about Tommy robbing the cradle. I can see you'll work out better than the last one."

"I said, *enough!*"

"Okay, okay." Vin backed off, hands in the air, a mock surrender. "Fine. Two's company, three's a crowd."

Squeezing Jason's hand, Tommy hurried him across the bridge. On stable ground again, Jason looked back. Vin was still standing in the middle of the bridge, a night watchman guarding his post.

They went up Fall Creek Drive as fast as they could. With the bridge gone, the gorge hidden in the trees, the roar of the creek muffled to a distant whisper, Tommy relaxed a little. The adrenaline, however, still burned in Jason's veins.

"Are you really married?" he said.

She nodded. "Sort of. It was over, but then he . . . No, I'm not really married."

"I don't have a girlfriend either." Jason was surprised to hear these words come out of his mouth. "I just said that last night because I thought—"

"I left Vin over a year ago. He followed me. He always follows me."

"What does he want?"

"What does anyone want?" At the top of the hill, she stopped and said, "Where do you live?"

"Hasbrouck. The north campus."

"I'm going the other way from here."

"You'll be all right?" He was the one still shaking.

"Yeah. Sure. Don't worry about us."

"Okay then . . . I guess I'll see you tomorrow."

She let go of his hand, sticky and hot, and it felt as though a power plug had been yanked out. He went back toward his dorm and she disappeared down an unlit path.

When he got home, he found his hands were smeared with brown-red stain. Streaks of it on his neck and arms too. He looked in the mirror and on his cheeks were finger marks, as though Vin's hands had rubbed eight lines clean, exposing darker skin below.

It came off with some scrubbing, but still he could smell Vin's oily scent on himself. He stood in the shower far too long, thinking of Tommy and Vin, trying to picture exactly what they'd been doing in the fly room the night before—if in fact it was Vin who'd been there.

The gamy smell was still on his hands when he returned to work the next evening.

It had been a sweltering day, the last blaze of a blast-furnace summer. Tommy was wearing a thin sundress, the first time Jason had seen her legs and shoulders. She had her hair pinned up on top of her head, making her neck look long and frail.

Jason said hello, asked how she was.

"Okay."

He squeezed her hand but she slid away. He asked if everything was all right and she shrugged.

"Did you see him again?"

"No."

They worked a while in silence, or near-silence, the buzz of the fly colonies making a cottony undercurrent in the air.

Jason wanted to ask a hundred questions but didn't know where to start, and wasn't sure he really wanted to hear the answers.

He stood at the sink, dumb, numb, cleaning bottle after bottle like a machine. Endless in and out with the brush.

"Here, take a look," Tommy said after a while. She passed him a tiny silver forceps and her jeweler's glass. Jason looked. Two fruit flies mating, like ten thousand others there, except the male's eyes were white instead of the usual pink-red. "Peep show. Mutant love." She shook her head, as though suddenly disgusted with her work.

Embarrassed by her embarrassment, he handed the forceps back.

Tommy's exhalation might have been a tired laugh. "Jackpot. You see what you expect to see."

She laid the specimen on a slide. "Mr. White Eye. Big deal."

Suddenly she grabbed one of the milk bottles and heaved it at the wall. These bottles, made decades ago, were quite strong. It bounced off the wall and rolled, unbroken, beneath the table.

She went for another but Jason grabbed her hand. She struggled, though not very hard.

"Tommy, what's going on between you and Vin?"

"Nothing."

"Tell me the truth. You're married, right?"

"I said, *nothing*."

"What does he want?"

"What do you think he wants?" She stared at Jason, fury burning on her cheeks. "He's my husband and he wants me."

"Then what was all that last night? Jesus, Tommy, I was covered with goo when I got home. What is the story with—"

"This is your first semester at Cornell, right? You didn't hear about Jon then. I started here last year. I got my funding and I hired a lab assistant to do the things you're doing now. He killed himself, jumped off the Fall Creek Bridge. Every year there are suicides here. Nobody is surprised. Too much pressure, family expectations . . . Jon wasn't very stable. I guess on top of everything else, I pushed him too hard. Vin hadn't found me yet. I got involved with Jon. He killed himself right after Vin showed up." She stood, took his hand. "Vin says that I made Jon do it. And now he likes to stand on the bridge where Jon jumped."

As though suddenly afraid Vin might burst in on them, Tommy went to the door and made sure it was locked. Jason felt the dull metallic click like a blow to his chest.

The air in the fly room was stained red, harsh, and heavy as wool. "When I came here, Cornell I mean, last year I thought I was finally free. But he tracked me down. I should have known I couldn't get away from him." She kissed Jason, and the fevered air seethed around them. The kiss went on a long time. They fumbled at each other's clothes, but when

Jason's hand ran up the inside of her thigh, she pulled back. He stood there, dazed, taking shallow breaths as though he'd just woken from a midsummer's nightmare of sweat and tangled sheets.

He undid his belt, and she said, "No, let me." She unzipped his pants, worked them to the floor. He reached for her again but she backed away. "No." She unbuttoned his shirt and ran her hands over his neck, chest, belly. "Sit down," she murmured, "over there," pointing to the floor, in the shadow of the incubator banks. He did as he was told, hating and at the same time excited by his helplessness.

She pulled her dress off over her head and skinned off her panties. The only covering left, the tiny circle of cloth over her eye, made her nakedness seem even more extreme. Jason could see his breath, jets of smoke in the stifling air. She sat down next to him, close enough for Jason to feel her body heat but not quite touching. "Go ahead," she said. Jason reached for her uncertainly and she shook her head again. Finally he understood as she slid her own hands up between her thighs.

Her mouth was half open; her eyelid drooped. Jason stared, hypnotized, as her hand moved in tight circles. "Go ahead," she whispered. "I want to watch."

It didn't take any more encouragement. They sat there in the motionless air, eating each other with their eyes. Once or twice more Jason moved toward Tommy, unthinking, and she shook her head. "It's better this way. Pure."

Wendy had never let him see her totally naked; always there was a wall of propriety, even in the skimpiest bathing suit. He'd gone a few times with friends to a strip joint, but the atmosphere there was so fake, money coloring everything. He'd seen his share of porn, gawked at the beach, but nothing came near to this. Real, his and his only, close enough to smell but untouchable.

The incubator bulbs throbbed, they flickered, they caught the humming undertone of the myriad fly wings and amplified it.

Friction, frantic rhythm, the steadily rising arc of pleasure. He'd close his eyes for a moment or two, overwhelmed, then open them and be struck again by the strangeness and power in such a simple act.

She reached up at one point, stroking gently at the patch, as though the hidden eye served the same function as the glistening molten crux between her thighs.

How long it went on he couldn't have said. Every time he'd get near the end, she'd sense it and say, "No, wait for me." He'd do as he was told and fall back a short distance on the slippery curve.

It was the sound, finally, that told him they were at the top. The lights crackled, the flies batted themselves against their glass prisons, the air itself seemed to vibrate like countless tiny beads. "All right, all right, all right," she hissed. And with a last judder and moan, it was over.

She crawled over to him, kissed him once, lightly on the lips, and reached for her dress. Before he could get his clothes on, she'd unlocked the door and was gone.

Though he went home, slept, showed up for a few classes, and ate three meals in the interim, it was as though he'd merely blinked and a day had passed.

A message for him was tacked on the door. He opened the envelope and found inside a scrap of paper with an address written in green ink and below it the word "Tonight."

The street was on the other side of Fall Creek, in the tangle of narrow blind drives and culs-de-sac he'd yet to navigate successfully. He hiked through the twilit campus, crossed the bridge, pausing only a moment to look down at the spot where Tommy's last assistant had jumped. Fog and shadows roiled beneath him. Treetops appeared and disappeared. He knew there was a building below in the misty murk, a turn-of-the-century generating station, but it had vanished.

He sped up as he approached the house, doubling back twice in dead ends overgrown with vines and overladen willows. But he did find the place eventually, a tumbledown little bungalow between two frat houses. The weeds in front made it lush as a riverbank. A car—up on cement blocks—filled the entire driveway.

He went to the front door and knocked. Voices inside, shuffling. The door wheezed open and there was Vin, again wearing his sunglasses. A slight pause, as though he didn't recognize Jason.

"I got a message . . . ," Jason said. "Tommy left a message for me."

"Come in, come on in." Vin smiled his iridescent smile and stepped awkwardly to one side. "We've been waiting for you. Tommy said you'd come. She said you wouldn't let us down."

Vin took him by the arm and ushered him through a dank alcove. In the living room the light was somewhat stronger, but still the place had a blue-green out-of-focus quality to it, like a badly maintained aquarium. Tommy was nowhere to be seen. On shelves above the brocade-crusted sofa were rows of crocheted dolls with plastic cupid faces. A paint-on-velvet version of *American Gothic* hung on the nearer wall, though the eyes of the couple were far too large for their heads. On a glass table covered with Coke bottles and cassette tapes was a large knockoff of Dürer's *Praying Hands.* "Come in, come in," Vin said, tightening his grasp on Jason's arm.

"Is Tommy—"

"Don't worry about her." Vin leaned in close to Jason, as if sniffing for some rare scent.

The TV was on, but the picture was rolling, a steady wave after wave that augmented the seasick atmosphere.

"Jesus, Vin, why didn't you tell me?" Tommy rushed over from the kitchen entry and snagged Jason away. "How long has he been here?"

"I just—"

"What's wrong with you, Vin?" She steered Jason to the sofa and had him sit down. "You want something to drink?" He had the feeling he'd been transported back a few decades, a guest at some ratty Eisenhower-era cocktail party. However, he suspected there wouldn't be anyone else coming. "No, no thanks."

"Tommy's been telling me all about you," Vin said. He plopped down in a chair and kept speaking, but seemed to be looking a few feet to the left of where Jason sat. "She can't say enough about you."

It finally hit Jason: he's blind; Vin is blind. And as though Jason had spoken the words out loud, Vin pulled off his sunglasses and stared with pinkish filmy eyes in Jason's direction. "Yes, indeed. A real looker. Just like my Tommy. Everybody staring at her. I can tell. But I never once seen it. Never, not once." He leaned forward, gazing at Jason with his boiled-egg eyes. But these eggs had been fertilized, with the tiny fetuses and webby veins all exploded in the cooking heat. "Goddamn, what I wouldn't give to have what you got, Jay. Just one look. One little look at her."

"Okay, Vin, enough. He didn't come over to listen to your hearts-and-flowers routine." Tommy put her arm around Jason's shoulders, pulled him close as if in defiance of Vin's empty stare.

"Don't try whispering," Vin said. "I can't see a goddamned thing but there's no way in hell I won't hear it."

Silently, she slid her hand onto Jason's thigh, edged it upward.

Vin lunged up from the chair, but instead of grabbing Tommy's hand away, he felt for the *Praying Hands.* "Look here," he said pressing the switch on the underside. The hands opened and closed like a clam. "Ashtray. You smoke? Didn't think so. Put your ashes in here." He pressed the button a few more times, as though making the hands clap for some unseen performance.

"We just rent this place," Tommy said. "It came with all this junk. I needed a place quick after I got accepted into the program. Only thing here that's ours is the TV and some of the books."

"That's right," Vin said. "A house is not a home without the TV and VCR." He smiled, and his eyelids puckered like tiny mouths on sour candy. "You want to watch some TV?"

"Vin," Tommy said, "just shut up for a minute, would you?" Her lips were close enough to Jason's ear that he felt her warm breath. Vin stared, smiling, and for a moment Jason thought that the blindness was a ruse, that perhaps Vin really could see. But Tommy's hand moved higher on his thigh, fingers splayed. Her mouth brushed his ear.

"No whispering!"

"I think maybe I'd better be—"

"Stay right where you are," Vin growled. "You're our guest. Tommy said she wanted you over for a little party." Vin's voice descended, hoarse, almost too low to hear. "You know what kind of party she means."

"Vin, leave him—"

"Tommy spends all day in the lab, picking flies to put together. Matching them up, watching them go at it. Watching."

The three of them sat silently. A few drunken hoots drifted in from the frat house next door. On the TV an exercise queen was thrusting her pelvis at the camera. Her distant murmur: *"Make it hurt, make it burn."*

"It's okay, Jay. Go ahead. I want you to. Nobody will see a thing. Go ahead and do it. I'll just sit here and I won't say a thing. Ask Tommy. Go ahead, I'll behave myself. Ask her! I really can't see a goddamned thing. You might as well be a hundred miles away."

"I've got to get going," Jason said, trying to stand. But Tommy pulled him back to the sofa.

"What's the rush? The party's hardly gotten started yet," Vin said, then got up and felt his way to the kitchen. He came back with a plastic platter heaped with pumpernickel and sliced olive loaf. "Go ahead, Jay. Take as much as you want." He waved the plate under Jason's nose, but Tommy told him to take it away.

"Okay, okay. Maybe you'd rather watch a little TV. Maybe that would put you in the mood." Vin rattled through the pile of videos and jammed one into the VCR. He hit a few buttons, squatting inches from the screen, then backed away. "How's that? The picture okay?"

On the screen a pair of naked women were writhing together. The picture was still skewed. The bodies flickered in and out of focus, making it appear that one of the women had crawled out of the other, a snake sloughing her skin. "That all right?"

"Fine," Tommy said.

"So what is it?" Vin said. "Which one did I get?"

"Two girls."

"You like to watch, Jay? Watching's better than doing sometimes."

"I really have to go," Jason said, struggling out of Tommy's embrace, but Vin, sensing the movement, shoved him back down. "We're trying to be good hosts here, Jay. So it's your job to be a good guest. Now sit down and tell me what's on the screen."

"Like Tommy said, two girls."

"What are they doing?"

"What the hell do you think they're doing?" That morning, in Jason's Intro to Lit survey course, they'd been working on *Paradise Lost.* The professor, a leering old goat with a reputation for hitting on students, had made the best-looking girl in the class read from Milton's description of angels mating. "Easier than air with air, if spirits embrace, total they mix." The atmosphere in the dank little room was like the class that morning: a grinning lecher pushing his perversions on others. Nonetheless, the two girls on the screen—scrambled and fractured—did look like angels to Jason.

"Go ahead, tell me, what are they doing?"

"Tommy, listen, I really have to get going."

Her hand slid up between his legs, circling languidly. She snagged his ear between her teeth and tugged gently. "He can't see a thing," she said. "He's stone-cold blind."

"I can't—"

"What are they doing?" Vin shouted. "Tommy, what are they—"

"One's got her face in the other's cooze and they're both—"

Jason threw himself out of the sofa and bolted past Vin for the door. Suddenly the sound on the video exploded, two fake orgasms erupting from the tiny TV speaker.

"Get back here, you son of a bitch!" Vin shrieked. But Jason had made it to the door and out into the night air. As he ran from the bungalow the sound of the two women followed him, ghostly moans and sighs. He ran the entire way to his dorm and collapsed in one of the lounges. A dozen different sound tracks pounded from the rooms above. Shouts, drunken laughter, a girl screaming punctuated the din.

Classes the next day were a meaningless blur. He ate but tasted nothing. Wandering the campus, he saw nothing but Tommy naked, Vin's bleary pink eyes, and the two angelic girls on the TV.

The sun was already down when he unlocked the fly room. Tables were overturned, a hundred lightbulbs were smashed, files had been pulled out and scattered. Containers of fly mash had been smeared on the walls in crusty brown swaths. The floor was a carpet of tiny insect corpses and broken glass. Jason stood there staring, unsure as to whether he should call security or just close the door, slide his key under it, and never return.

He went in, the air around him dense with swarming insects. He sat down in the wreckage with the lights off, listening to the flies eat and breed and die. A new generation every week. Liberated, they gorged on the spilled mash and flew off to lay their eggs. Out into the world, red eye, white eye, thousands of them carrying mutant genes.

"I knew you'd come." Tommy's voice came from the shadows.

"Why'd he do it?" No answer. "Shouldn't we call somebody?"

"What difference would it make? I'm not going to start all over. There's no point in fighting him. It's over."

They sat there in the darkness, like ghosts trapped in a shipwreck. Broken glass and twisted metal, overturned furniture, snarls of paper moving as though stirred by undersea currents. And the flies: clouds of them swarming in slow whirlpools. She'd been their god, and this room their entire universe. With Tommy no longer there to rule their lives from birth to death, to pair them off and watch them mate, their reason for being had vanished.

Jason put his hand on Tommy's shoulder to draw her close. But she shrugged away and swept her hand across the floor. Another few bottles crashed. She liked the sound and picked up another bottle. Jason stopped her before she threw it.

"Don't touch me," she hissed.

He let go and she brought her foot down on a lightbulb, squashing it like a great glass beetle. "It's over. All over." She kicked at a drift of papers. "You and me. Everything. Over."

"We could call the police, have him . . . what do they call it? Get a restraining order."

"No. You don't understand. That's why I came back, to tell you in person. Fill out the time card; put a few extra hours on if you want. You'll get paid. But don't come back tomorrow."

"What about—"

"It's over. I give up." She turned and hurried down the corridor. Jason stumbled to his feet and followed, calling to her, and though the echoes were long in dying, she didn't seem to hear. He stopped at the main door, deciding there was no point in trekking across campus, wailing her name like a little lost kid.

Then it came to him: it had been Tommy, not Vin, who'd smashed the fly room. After all that had happened in the past few days, there was no way for the work to go on. The research had been an escape for her, a place to hide from Vin. Clearly it had failed. She'd come back and wrecked the place to get rid of Jason, to put an absolute end to it.

He stood a long while on Beckwith's steps, dismal and directionless. Then it seemed he heard Vin's voice, but speaking the words of his lit professor. Sniggering about angelic sex: "Union of pure with pure desiring."

He set off and soon was on their street again. The front of the bungalow was dark. Not caring who saw him—drunken frat boys certainly wouldn't pay him any notice—he cut through the side yard and peeked in the back window. A pair of silhouettes moved behind the tattered screen. Standing in the pine-heavy gloom, Jason pressed closer to the window. There was just enough light to see two figures on the bed. And voices: Vin and Tommy together again. Springs creaked; something tore away. Silence and shadowy heat for a while, then the same hard, ugly rhythm he'd heard at the fly room. Her breathing and his animal grunts. It got louder, faster. Jason felt his blood turning to steam, leaching out through his pores to make a vaporous halo.

They shifted position and Jason got a glimpse of a long white leg, a glowing orb about the size of a plum.

He went around to the front and pushed on the luminous button. No answer. He pressed his ear against the door and used the bell again. It didn't work. He tried the door and it swung open.

He hesitated only a moment, listening to the steadily mounting grind of flesh against flesh. Down a dark hallway smelling of stale clothes, trash, wallpaper that had absorbed fifty years of cigar smoke. He stopped at the bedroom door. Tommy was whimpering. Pain and pleasure, control and helplessness, they were all the same in that room. The noise rose suddenly, a rapid in-and-out cry as though he were running a hot wire back and forth through her chest. Jason went through the door, reached out and found the light switch.

Vin was on top. He reared back like a predator disturbed at the kill. They were both naked, but what struck Jason hardest was the color of Vin's skin. From the neck down he was white as a grub, his skin almost luminous. Without sunglasses, his pink-red eyes glowed sickly and feverish.

To see him this way was sickening, but the sight of Tommy was worse—caught, exposed. They looked like cannibals, starved, eating the worst of each other, an act of mutual desolation.

Vin's greasy fingerprints were all over her: streaks, blurs, blotches of red-brown stain. Her face was daubed like a two-year-old who's forced at her birthday party to gorge on chocolate cake and make as big a mess as possible. Spotlights for the cameras. Everybody looking, laughing, clapping.

"You came to watch?" Vin said, his voice seething with contempt. "A little private show?"

There was no move to cover themselves. The scene was appalling and at the same time—now Jason had to admit to himself—beautiful. Then Tommy turned her head and Jason saw she'd taken off the patch. Her eye was swollen, milky, with a faint marbling of veins: red, blue, purple. She looked directly at Jason and his viscera went molten.

Vin touched Tommy's forehead like a priest bestowing a blessing. "You can watch," he said, sneering, "if you want." His thumb left a faint brown print.

The sensation woke her from her trance. "Get out," she moaned. Jason didn't move. "Please, get out." The eye throbbed as she spoke, ragged spots moving like figures in a seer's crystal ball. Jason was disgusted by what he saw, but the small tooth of excitement continued to gnaw at him. And this made his disgust even stronger. The eye swelled, her pulse showing on the glossy surface. "Please," she begged. "Leave."

"I think your little boyfriend likes what he sees." Vin rubbed the back of his hand between her breasts, as if wiping dirt on a rag. "This is the way he really likes you." The dye was on the sheets too; the pillow bore the faint outline of five outstretched fingers.

"Get out of here, Jason." Still she didn't cover herself. With her voice she was telling him to leave, but the eye—gibbous and unblinking—insisted on the opposite.

"Let him watch. That's what he came here for, right, Jay? You came to see how it's done. The big time. The real thing."

Vin planted a big sloppy kiss on her side, leaving his stain. Then he bit her, and when he let go there were teeth marks on her skin. "Go away, please go away," she murmured, but he knew she wanted him to stay.

The fluids in her eye boiled, churned. Jason approached, but before he reached the bed, Vin slid upward and fit his greasy purpled lips around the weeping orb. Tommy mewled as his mouth surrounded her eye, but she didn't push him away. Like a baby at the nipple, Vin lay sucking, and immediately waves of bliss cascaded through his body.

Tommy writhed weakly as Vin drew from her, the two of them tangled like half-knotted ropes. Vin pressed both hands around her head to steady her as he gulped and guttled. The sound was horrible, like wet fingers stroking a balloon. Squeaks; wet slobbery suction. "Please, please, please," she begged.

Finally Vin fell away, sated. Tommy rolled over to face Jason. The eye was darker now, as though drained, but some of the luminous mottling remained, flecks floating in the turbid matter.

"No," she whispered. "No." But here no meant yes, just as black was white and blindness was vision. Vin shook, helpless now, a baby who'd sucked his fill and was descending quickly into gorged dreams.

Jason stood beside the bed, mesmerized by the eye. On the surface, tiny shapes flitted, rose, and dove down again.

"Jason, don't—"

He bent and reached his tongue out. The eye was hot, a slick fevered membrane. Shivers passed through her and a spark of light exploded in Jason's mouth. He climbed onto the bed, easing Vin to one side and kneeling over Tommy. His tongue went out again, but he didn't back away this time as the jolt hit him. His lips closed around her eye and a liquid fire oozed into his mouth. He sucked at the smooth blissom ball and the light—poured into a clotted lambent flow, brilliant ooze with tiny shapes swimming in it—

Vin had sucked most of the vision from her eye, but there remained the dregs, secondhand memories coalescing now inside Jason like contaminated photos. Half-formed figures, images that bled into each other. There was Vin, not as he really was, but as Tommy saw him: taller, almost regal, not a tainted freak but a dark prince. The image dissolved as Jason sucked harder at the eye. There was Tommy, seen as she saw herself. No less attractive but in some odd way motherly. A magnetic maternal air about her. Not a temptress but a caretaker, a healer of wounds, a comforter. Jason tried to pull away from her eye but a vacuum drew his lips back to the swollen sphere. His tongue plunged forward, probing the cornea's febrile surface. Another pulse of glowing fluid and he saw himself as Tommy saw him. A teenager, a mere kid. Handsome, almost pretty. But barely out of adolescence. The image came and went quickly: Jason a beautiful naked boy. Sleek muscles, hairless chest, clear eyes. More a child than a man.

He wrenched himself backward and felt shreds of his lips peel off, then aftershocks of fiery pain, tiny flames glimmering in his mouth. He fell away from the bed, but lay there only a moment. Tommy was moaning like a sick animal; Vin lay hunched and fetal, quaking as the tremors coursed through him.

Jason bolted from the room, ran down the hall and out the front door. He ran blind in the spongy midnight air. He ran and the images blistered and bubbled up. At times he could see nothing but her face, or Vin's. Then the real world would swim out from the phantoms. Trees, a car, a streetlight. Then his own face—pure, guileless—would take shape again.

He stumbled against a metal pole, reached out to steady himself. Groping in the fire-shot shadows, he found a cold stone wall, waist high. He heard the rush of water far below and knew he was on the Fall Creek Bridge. Vin stood at the midpoint as he had the night before, a lone, leering sentry. Jason rushed at him and plunged through the specter. Tommy called and Jason spun around. He reached for her and she too evaporated. The bridge shook as he staggered from side to side. The pain in his lips was awful, as though he were still drinking from the fiery fountain. He thought of the water in the creek hundreds of feet below. Cool water to heal his scorched mouth.

He climbed onto the bridge's parapet and pawed at the shadow-choked void. Swaying, seeing Tommy out there in the empty air, he reached for her. She beckoned, coaxing him as though he were a two-year-old just learning to walk. But then her voice came from behind. He turned, losing his balance, and fell.

Tommy's face flickered like a flame and went out. Vin's ugly grin, too, disappeared. And Jason was left with himself: a handsome boy, a mirror image made of fire.

He lay on the bridge deck a long time. The water far below hissed, swirled, plummeted downward. He touched at his lips and felt the weeping blisters.

Eventually, though, he knew his mouth would heal and he'd be able to go back to Tommy. She'd welcome him, give him some of Vin's cream to protect his lips. She'd make sure he was safe as he went back to the source, again and again.

The Subtle Ties That Bind

David Niall Wilson

Smoke swirled in wisping clouds about her feet, capturing the colored floor lights like projected images on a movie screen. She did not look down from the stage at the eyes beneath her, did not acknowledge the sweat-coated faces that held them or the murky darkness that was their backdrop. They were not real, not to her, not when the music played. The eyes worshiped her, but she did not love them. They were the denizens of fantasyland, her people, and she was their goddess.

She concentrated on the lights, waited for the sound. As the drums began their sinuous backbeat, timing themselves with the beating of her heart, she felt as though strings were rising up through her, felt the tug of each note, each syncopated beat on her passive body. Performance itself was a rhythm, a thread she could follow by touch, closing herself off from the outside world and moving on instinct.

Her head jerked back as the first chorus of the song gripped her, and she hesitated—nearly stopped. The eyes held her. Not those beneath her, or surrounding her, but a single set, glowing slightly in the gloom at the back of the club. They were surrounded by darkness, that of the poor lighting and a different, more subtle shadow. A shiver rippled through her, then was gone, lost in the music.

The strings were pulled, and she danced. The music ruled her, pounding through her in comforting waves, leading her through sound into motion. There were dancers, and then there was her. The former created motion, reveling in individuality. She performed with a grace that was not wholly her own.

When she danced, she was detached. She *was* the music, manifesting its own creativity back into the world that had spawned it. She was a reflected, off-world vision, secondhand from the musician to the netherworld and back. Fingers danced over keyboards, caressed the necks of guitars, and the strings—silken ties that bound her to the notes, drew the art from her gyrating form, painting the music across the stage. She was the medium, not the artist.

As the sound died, slipping away as subtly as it had begun, the curtains drew back and the world seeped in. Lewd voices, stale smoke surrounded her, and the memory of a single set of eyes drew her gaze into the shadows. She watched the shadowed booth for a flicker of light from those eyes, the flash of a smile.

There was nothing. He was a silhouette, devoid of light. She was intrigued. The final notes of the music drained from her world, and the strings slipped loose from her limbs, releasing her into a limp bow that draped her long, white-blonde hair over her like a silken curtain to sweep the dusty surface of the stage.

She slipped off the back of the stage, another dancer taking her place in fantasyland, and moved through the room slowly. The scented air parted for her reluctantly—stale smoke, cheap perfume, equally cheap cologne, all groping for one another in an olfactory war of loneliness and dreams.

She felt focused. The music played, but not for her. She could still feel the subtle, tickling touch of the strings as they teased at her body, but she ignored them. There were other strings at work—different strings. She felt compelled to move into the shadows, toward those eyes. She shivered.

Sliding into the booth across from him, she reached without comment for his cigarettes and helped herself. Her eyes remained averted, an illusion of freedom that her presence in the booth negated. She had come to him.

She turned to him quickly, drinking in his face in a glance: long, aquiline features, handsome, but nondescript—shadowed.

"Who are you?" she asked. No greeting. No pleasantries. No bullshit. "Who are you?"

He did not answer, not right away. She could feel the steps of his eyes across her skin, the subtle imprint of his fantasies worming their way into her psyche. She felt the strings tugging at more intimate, private places and blew a cloud of smoke through her nose to try and calm her nerves. Then he spoke.

"You feel the strings, the ties that bind you to the world. You dance beautifully, but you are not *one* with the dance. Not yet. I can set you free." Just that. Nothing but a simple phrase, softly spoken, but with authority.

She fidgeted nervously, crossing her legs under the table and drumming her fingers. "Who are you?" It did not matter. For the moment, he held the strings. She slid free of the booth and moved into the night, feeling the threads being played out between unseen fingers, knowing his eyes traced patterns on her back as she moved.

Her apartment was a cold, lifeless shell. She lay across her bed, naked, waiting for dreams to slip in and wipe away the shadowed walls and ache of loneliness. She had always been lonely; he had pulled it to the surface. She waited in vain.

His outline—the etched crevasses that marked his profile as it was embedded in her mind—was bereft of emotion. He held her prone, awake, with his image alone. She stared intently at the spider's web of cracks that mapped the plaster of her ceiling, reaching finally for a cigarette and lighting it quickly. Her memory of his image did not waver. She closed her eyes; nothing changed.

"You are not *one* with the music. Not yet. I can set you free."

The next night, when the lights of the club flickered on and those who remained scuttled to the exits to escape the reality that was threatening fantasyland, she followed him into the night without a word. He slipped into the darkness like a wraith. She floated in his wake, unseen lines of force binding her movements to his. She had not slept. She had not eaten.

"Who are you?" she asked again. "Where are you going?"

Her answer was the sound of his feet slapping the pavement, one in front of the other, carrying them off into—what? Still, she followed, smoking furiously, one after another.

There was no color in the room. She lay on his bed—she assumed it was his—and he paced slowly about the room, gazing at her from all angles. She was nervous, but he'd moved the cigarettes out of reach. His gaze lingered on every curve of her body, slid between her thighs and up the sides of her stomach, sliding over sensitive skin like liquid, molding itself to the contours of her form.

"What do you want?" she asked, feeling her legs slide farther apart, subtly, invitingly. She could feel the arousal coursing through her. Not a single touch. Not a single word. She was his.

"I want to see you dance. I want to set you free."

She tried to form a protest as strong hands grabbed her left wrist suddenly, as a silken scarf circled soft skin and was fixed to the bedpost. Then the right wrist. Then her legs. There was no pain. The silk caressed her skin and she felt herself moving against its electric touch. She wanted more, wanted to feel his hands, his skin, but he still circled her slowly, watching her.

He turned away, walking to the dresser against the far wall, then returned. There was a box in his hand, finished in black lacquer and gleaming in the meager light. He propped the lid open slightly and turned it so that she could see what lay inside.

Pins. Each had its own ceramic head, like the one on an old-fashioned hatpin, though somehow more elegant. They were like nothing she'd ever seen. The glitter of their shafts gripped her mind hypnotically, each sheathed in a block of black velvet.

Her eyes rolled back in momentary fear, but as her body trembled, the silk brushed once more across her wrists, worked its way up her ankles—but not far enough—and the fear melted to desire.

He plucked free one of the pins, setting the box aside, and gripped her right thigh with one strong, cool hand.

"Do not move."

She watched as he ran his fingers softly over her skin, felt the tremor of nerves as they searched for just the right spot, felt the sudden prick of sharp metal biting into her skin, felt nothing. He had already moved to her other side, her other leg. She stared at the black head of the pin as his fingers went to work again. The caress, the bite, nothing.

She could almost hear the snap of the strings as he clipped them, one by one. Arms next, then earlobes, the soles of her feet. She could see the black heads of the pins protruding from her limbs, but she felt nothing, nothing but the heat that was growing, emanating from the very center of her being and flowing outward.

The silk held her, but no longer caressed. His hand lay gently across her breast, twisting her nipple back and forth distractedly. She felt nothing. She could see it, could imagine the feel of his skin on hers, but she felt only the heat, and it was centered lower.

"It is a focus. Do not think of what you cannot feel—concentrate on what you can. There are levels of release from that which binds you. At this moment, you may only find release through the core of your heat."

His hand drifted between her thighs, one soft brush of fingertips. She lost control. Her vision swam, and she could not steady her mind. Every distraction had been removed, the pins acting just as her personal curtain of darkness did when she moved across the stage of fantasyland. Her body remained stationary, relaxed, except for her vagina, except for the orgasm that rippled through her soul. Gasping, groping for reality, she tried to speak.

"Wh . . . who are you?

He did not answer. Moving a few feet away, he watched. She could feel his eyes, the soft, undulating impact they made on the center of her being.

There was a movement, a shadow, blurring against the darkness. He did not move. He watched. A sleek, ebony cat leaped from the pools of shadow that surrounded them and onto her torso, staring at her with huge, green, glowing eyes. She felt nothing. The cat moved toward her face, settled between her breasts—stretched. Claws extended, kneaded, digging short, white furrows that ran with sudden crimson. She felt nothing.

Her eyes shifted away—he was moving forward, ignoring her, ignoring the cat. He reached down, touching her again, more fully than before, sliding his fingers inside her, and she lost consciousness. Waves of pleasure and release pounded away at her insides like a relentless surf, eroding thought, dragging her into a vortex. The center of the vortex was an eye, a cat's eye, green and glowing.

When she awakened, it was still dark—or was it dark *again?* The pins were gone, her limbs her own. She flexed her legs, trying each muscle separately, testing, probing. Stretching, she looked about herself, trying to pierce the gloom, trying to find the answers he would not provide. Instead of the freedom the return of her body should have brought, she felt confined—bound. She could sense the strings.

She heard nothing, yet suddenly, he was there. He stood at her side, gazing down at her, holding out one of the pins for her inspection. She felt herself trembling again, felt questions bubbling to the surface that she knew would be futile wastes of breath.

Without waiting for approval, or even for her reaction, he seated himself beside her, his hands moving directly to her thighs and sliding up slowly to tangle in the curls of her pubic hair. She watched him, her nerves wild—on edge. She wished for a cigarette, wished for the sensations she'd felt, what, hours ago? Days?

He massaged her slowly, and she felt herself growing warm, moist. Her lips parted, and she moaned. It was an animal sound. He ignored her. There was the soft caress, the lingering touch on that most tender of spots, the bite of steel—nothing.

She gasped. The sensations of pleasure were cut off so sharply that her eyes immediately filled with tears. The loss was incredible—overpowering. She whimpered, moving a hand down toward his, toward the invading steel. She did not feel the pin, but a ring, cold and metallic, numb.

"You cannot remove it." The words were without passion, without hope or compromise. Empty. She knew without doubt that he did not lie—there was no deception in him. He was cold, like the ring, like her heart.

Tears flowed in a sudden, steady stream from the corners of her eyes, running down to wet the skin of her breasts and the trailing ends of her hair. She felt the salty liquid as it dribbled across the edges of her lips. It was intense, biting.

She could feel the texture of the sheets beneath her, the cold touch of the sweat that coated her skin. His slow, even breath brushed across her and she could feel it molding itself to the curves of her, could feel the bond of air to flesh in ways she'd never imagined. There was no heat.

"There is more than one focus," he said. "Each sensation is important. Your desire, the focus of your heat, interferes with your art. It bars you from the music. It is late now, and soon you must dance."

The music coursed through her. Her arms and legs were tied in bonds of gossamer, threads of spider silk that twisted about her gracefully as the melody played its 3-D symphony with her soul. The chords rippled down her skin, skittering through the nerves that controlled her muscles, picking intricate pizzicato notes from her tendons. She flowed with the sound, within it—cold and beautiful.

She watched it all from the distance of the artist, watched also the dark silhouette against the back booth. She dreamed of a different sensation, a different focus. She begged for it, sending mental waves of supplication to blend with her movements. She watched him through bitter tears that would not pass her eyes, swimming within the harmonies.

The music slowed, releasing the strings, and she drooped toward the floor, less a bow than an act of supplication. Her corn-silk tresses caressed the wood of the floor, and she could feel the grain of the wood through nerves previously unheeded—undreamed of.

Below, tucked into a fold of skin that imprisoned her thoughts, she knew that the ring still violated her. She reached to it with her mind, groping desperately with mental fingers for the heat that was her passion. She felt nothing.

The floor lights receded, cutting off the eyes, erasing the world, and there was only darkness. Against it he moved, his shadow approaching over the plains of fantasyland. Sweeping her into powerful, icy arms, he carried her into the night.

In her ear the softest of whispers teased at her desire. "There is more than one focus. You have been one with the music. You have been one with the heat. Now I will set you free."

They stopped, and she slid down his form. They were bathed in moonlight; she could feel it against her skin. His fingers moved unerringly down, sliding over skin that rippled and tingled at his touch, slipping free the pin. The flood of heat was intense. His fingers continued to caress, black slivers of shadow, moving over her, through her.

She felt him pluck gingerly at her mind, her thoughts, her dreams. She felt him linger, searching; felt him focus unerringly on the center of her being. Felt the bite as ivory punctured flesh—as sensation enveloped thought.

She felt the snap as the strings burst free, untangling, whirling, a kaleidoscopic vision. More than a vision: a release—an end—a birth.

She looked at him in wonder, with new eyes. She turned her face upward, bathed herself in the light of the brilliant moon. She saw everything. She felt nothing.

"I have set you free."

When Memory Fails

Roberta Lannes

Some evenings Anton awoke suddenly, as if roused by a voice or the careless kick of a still slumbering bed partner, and found himself terrified, alone, and completely unaware of where or who he was. He'd sit up, his thin arms going around himself even if it was warm, his eyes wide, heart thudding arrhythmically, mouth open like a fisherman's catch on the boat's deck, gulping for air. His mind would feel tethered in a void, the need for thought, a design by which to navigate back to himself, vital as survival. In time, the darkness around him and within him would dissipate, and he'd know everything. That was when he'd wonder most what his life was about, what he was.

This evening had been like that. The sun had barely set. A red-brown shadow from the tree outside his window burned on the wall in effigy to the day and there was still birdsong in the dusk. He couldn't recall ever waking so close to twilight before. Worrying his sheets with his bony fingers, he watched the wall until the shadow grew faint, then disappeared.

The sound of footsteps in the hallway of the old boardinghouse he owned caused his heart to lurch. It was the girl, coming home from work. He'd managed to dodge her since she'd moved in three weeks ago. That he was painfully shy and averse to conversation had to be clear to her by now, he thought. At first she, too, appeared timid, but with Anton's avoidance came her growing mettle.

One evening after she moved in, she came down into the parlor to read just as Anton was about to leave.

"Excuse me, Mr. Valjean, I have a question."

Anton stopped at the end of the hall, his hand on his coat.

"Yes?"

"Could you come into the parlor?"

Anton sighed, he hoped loudly enough to signal his resentment, then stepped slowly into the room. She sat down, her book in her lap. Her hair, which had been twisted into a knot on her head whenever he'd seen her previously, was hanging in waves over her shoulders, nearly reaching her waist. He couldn't remember if she'd been wearing makeup when he'd last seen her, but her face was now washed, scrubbed clean, the pink in her cheeks making him shiver. She was more attractive than he'd thought at first.

She averted his eyes, but smiled primly. "I'm sorry to bother you, but you said linens and towels were in the cabinet in my room. I've only found one set of each."

Anton knew there had been more. The last tenant had been difficult when he'd asked her to move. She'd taken her revenge on him with his sheets and hand cloths.

"Well, then buy what you need and I'll reimburse you." He turned to retrieve his coat, but she wasn't through with him.

"Mr. Valjean, I just started work, remember? I gave you the last of my money for rent."

"Of course." He reached into his pocket for his wallet. As he took out a hundred-dollar bill, he noticed that his hands were shaking. "I'll leave you money here on the hall table. Now I have to go." He shoved the bill under the base of a lamp, grabbed his coat, and hurried out.

The next night, she insisted he see what she bought. She corraled him in her room for an eternity—the agony of it! God, she'd gone on about fabrics, cotton, percales, thread counts and nap. He'd wanted to scream. In the aftermath, he found himself paralyzed in isolation, waiting for her to go to sleep.

Now, as he sat in bed, he knew she would be up using the house, spreading herself out and taking up all the space. Because he'd awakened early, he was now going to be trapped far longer in his rooms than he found acceptable. He couldn't go out to his studio in the back to work even if he'd wanted to—he'd run out of wood for the carvings and sculptures he did.

Standing, he felt woozy. He'd gone without feeding for far too long, and he was growing dangerously undernourished. He glanced down at his stomach. His hipbones and ribs were exposed like bleached dunes on a vast desert plain. His penis hung limp between his thighs, long and hungry and wasted. Why had he been cursed so? To need something that was so common, so accessible to any man able to seduce a woman, yet to be so damnably, pathologically, socially inept. And after centuries of existence, he'd only grown more reticent.

Once, it had only been awkward for him. His looks were not exceptional. He was androgynous, almost a sexual cipher; his hair long, his body slim, his features almost handsome, yet soft and full in a feminine way—an appearance found only oddly attractive in the 90s. His personality had always been melancholy, introspective, intelligence and creativity being his strong suits. Women didn't flutter about him, as they did big, dull-witted, but blustery men. So he'd created personae; gentlemen and cads, clowns and intellectuals, sportsmen and healers, each drawing a certain type of woman close enough to share his bed. To provide him the liquors of their climaxes. But they'd fallen in love with whomever he'd become to lure them in. And that kept them about. The only lesson Anton recalled from this period of his youth was that to his kind, love was lust's depletion and possession's fomentation. So he moved on, quickly, furtively, often.

Anton spent a half-century living in brothels as a laundryman, or in asylums as an aide, using willing women to satisfy his hunger. But even then these attachments leeched him and the inorgasmic women made him anorexic. He longed for the company of his kind, but over the centuries, the others were killed off; murdered by jealous husbands, by angry fathers, by gluttony and, a few, by love, or so legend had it. He had no friends, no one to tell his woes to. Yet even if someone did come along he could confide in, he'd grown so bashful, he couldn't get the words out. The simple truth was that Anton Valjean was terrified. And it had become easy to be alone.

He stood naked before his mirror, brushed his auburn hair and secured it in an elastic band. His pallor was accentuated by the rosiness of his lips and cheeks, the rouge of his nipples and his rubicund cock. His body was hairless, and where testicles should have descended, there was a rise of skin that folded over an orifice which took in libation gleaned when his prey peaked under his sexual attentions.

When he was bored, he often masturbated, an act he found only slightly gratifying and that stimulated his hunger many times over. Still, tonight, he had a longer wait than usual until the girl went to bed. He took his penis in his slender fingers and held it toward his reflection. He licked his other hand wet, then began stroking himself. He dared not close his eyes as he worked the flesh or he might see a face or remember another time, and the moment would be ruined. Instead he let the intoxication of his own image bring him to a familiar fever. His twin, his other, supplicating himself to his hand, the pleasure on that identical face bringing him closer to his zenith.

Anton groaned; his breath caught in his throat, then left him in a long hiss as he ejaculated, the jism hitting the mirror, dripping in pearlescent rivulets to the wooden frame. Then he closed his eyes. Light flashed there, brilliant, safe.

"Are you all right, Mr. Valjean?"

Her! The girl was at his door! Anton crumbled to his knees, his hands going over his face. My God, he thought, she heard it all. I can never show my face again.

She tapped lightly on his door.

"Mr. Valjean?" She went quiet a moment, then in a much more sheepish tone said, "Oh, I'm sorry, sir. I didn't think . . . " Then he heard her padding off down the hall.

Weakened, he crawled back to his bed and pulled himself onto it. Every cell in his body ached to be out, away, coupling with a woman, drinking of her, yet his mind was a whorl of shame and panic.

Slowly, his hands gathered into fists. He thought of her standing outside his room, listening, holding him hostage in his own house, depriving him of sustenance, and he was enraged. He hurried to his bathroom and managed his ablutions in a blind fury. Dressing in his most provocative clothing, he remained full of wrath. He stood before the mirror, the cum dried in the center of his reflection, and he frowned. What would he say should he meet her in the hall?

At his door, the fear returned, freezing his hand on the knob. He fought the feeling and yanked open the door. He smelled, wafting up from below, the faint, familiar cooking scents she left behind each dinner hour, and her feminine odors—her skin, the musk he craved—and his heart began to slam in his chest. The enchantment had begun.

No, not her. No.

Anton put one foot before the other, struggling against this ancient dearth of his strength until he reached the top of the stairs. He paused in relief. His eyes traveled down to the hallway and the front door, knowing he only had to make it that far and he was out. Then he heard her.

It was as if hearing had become his only sense. Her breath sounded in his ear as if her lips were there. The rustle of her sheets beneath her hips was coarse and loud. Wet sounds of her fingers gliding into the soft passage and glands working their juices were powerful song, as potent as a siren's call. His feet betrayed him as he turned and walked stealthily to her room.

The floorboards creaked under him, and her sounds ceased. He stood still, the aperture behind his cock opening to the promise of an elixir of the musk he smelled so distinctly. A tongue of his flesh unfurled from inside, caressing the base of his penis, making him swoon.

She resumed her movements in the silence and Anton hurried to her door. It was ajar and he could see her lying on her bed, her legs spread, her dress pushed up around her waist, her panties puddled around one ankle. The mass of her hair against her pillow was a dusky aura. Something saintly. His heart tugged a moment and his erection flagged.

He gently pushed the door open. Her eyes were closed, but he could tell by her movements that she was aware he was watching. Going to her bedside, he removed his shirt and pants, slipped out of his shoes and stockings. The smell of her sex was heady, inebriating. His eyes took in her hand as it stroked the glistening nub of flesh that, prodded to an apex of pleasure, would bring him his sustenance.

Her name. He couldn't engage his mind to recall it. He knew prey needed endearments, that they always responded most to the use of their names.

"I . . . I . . ." He was no less timid when victuals were waiting, and words escaped him.

She didn't open her eyes, but she moved her hands away from her mons and unbuttoned the top of her dress to expose her breasts. She put her hands over her face, then opened an eye behind her fingers.

"Your name," he whispered, his throat closing.

"Ursula."

"Ursula." He repeated it. Again. And again. His voice sounded distant to him. "It's all right?"

"Just . . . yes. Please." She sounded frightened, and something else.

Anton slid onto the bed. The sheets were smooth, as smooth as she'd claimed. He lay beside her, looking. Her breasts were small and high, her nipples hard. His fingertips danced lightly over his own, drawing the crowns of flesh up until an amber milk oozed onto them.

His words were plaintive. "Please . . . suckle me."

"You . . . ?"

He took her hand from her face and leaned over her so that her lips could find his nipple. "Here. It's sweet." His hunger was growing, making him bold.

Her eyes still shut, she reached up with her tongue until it made contact. His liquid dribbled onto her lips and she drank it in.

"Suck on them." It was an order now.

She obeyed, and the aphrodisia sent her into passion's hold. As she suckled wantonly, his mind turned on an axis of ecstasy, the thrall cremating the body of his despair.

Until he was sure she'd imbibed enough of him, he let her moan beneath him. When she began to slip away, drunk, he lifted himself and slid down, putting his lips to her labia.

"Lick me, please." Her voice was husky with passion.

He breathed in slowly, the fruity, musky odor intriguing him. Her pheromones had a peculiar note. Rather than disgust him, as some women's did, he found hers exhilarating. He nudged her clitoris, tickling it.

"Please." She began to wriggle.

He moved her legs farther apart and held them still. Tongue to flesh, he found her taste exquisite, and he licked her thirstily. Only the flow that came from her orgasm could nourish him, so he worked her carefully, gauging the tone of her moans.

"I . . . I never . . . I've never . . . " She slipped closer to the edge, a place she'd never been before. Anton gently put a finger into her, stroking the velvety cat's tongue of skin at the crown of her vagina.

"Oh!" she shouted, and a cascade of shrieks began, her body writhing under his lips, his finger still planing her nether reaches.

While she was bucking, he swam up her body, his cock entering her. His thrusting began as usual, the mouth below consuming, its tongue guiding fluids home, as he continued to please her. Pressing deeply to the spot where he'd kneaded her to orgasm, he felt a subtle jolt, an electrical *and* chemical charge each time his glans glided over it. The feeling was unlike anything he'd ever felt, and was clearly fouling his concentration.

Pleasure was overtaking him. Suddenly his body went still, her vagina holding him firmly, massaging him, debilitating him. The mouth that fed on her elixir lapped hungrily, but he felt himself losing consciousness.

He then did something he knew was dangerous while feeding—he closed his eyes. Ursula's face blossomed brightly behind his eyelids, luminescent from within, her eyes no longer a dark jade color, but yellow-gold, her hair woven with stars. She spoke, her lips moving, but there was no sound. His deafness infuriating him, his eyes fluttered open. Ursula was looking at him, her eyes dark, lips closed but in a wry smile that confounded him.

She whispered, "Are you all right?"

Were they finished? Had he climaxed? He moved his hips slightly, enough to feel he was still hard, the heat of her radiating around his cock.

"Yes."

Ursula closed her eyes and seemed to become shy again. But her next words belied that. "Please. Come for me."

He bent his head, focusing on the intense burning, pulling sensation that began to work its way to the root of his prick and pulse upward. Ursula began moving her hips in that primitive rhythm and the pain turned into pure liquid bliss. One flurry of thrusts and Anton was ejaculating. Ursula responded as if she'd been shot full of molten steel, her scream feral and anguished, yet Anton could not stop. He forgot her sounds and closed his eyes again, this time seeing a place of white and gold, where peace was everywhere.

When he was empty, he slept.

Anton felt the fear before he was fully awake. What had happened? He'd never slept into the night with his prey before. Sated, he usually walked, allowing the fluids he'd taken to travel through his body and nourish him. Now he was bloated with a glutton's bounty, feeling only inertia. He managed to open his eyes, expecting to see Ursula beneath him. The lamp on the night table cast a rosy light over the wasteland of sheet she'd abandoned. He was alone. The fear didn't pass.

He listened for her, sniffed the room. Somewhere in the old house she made the floorboards creak, but it was not here, upstairs. Her scent was intense—it was on him, on the soft cotton he lay upon. Would she love him now, killing any chance he had to feed freely? Panic, traveling its well-worn path, crept into his heart.

Scrambling up, Anton gathered his clothes and hurried into his suite. He shut the door just as he heard her footfalls at the bottom of the stairs. How was he going to explain this to her? If he was fortunate, she would find his mutiny cause to leave his house and never return. Yes. He hoped that. His mind took to picturing her packing. He'd find another boarder.

She passed his door without stopping, went to her room, and shut the door. There was no hesitation, as there might have been had she looked in to find Anton gone and wondered what had become of him. Anton leaned against his door waiting for her to come back out, to search for him.

Nearly an hour passed, and Anton grew weary of listening to nothing. His panic had gone, but anxious thoughts played in his mind, a favored playground. Why had she not come after him? Had he not pleased her? Was she dismissing him now that she'd had her way with him? Was she so much more bashful than he that she was actually thankful he'd run off? Yes, of course. That was it. Her timidity would be his saving grace.

As he sat at his dressing table, he looked down to his nipples. They were still distended, suckled to bruise. Milk had dried on the tips, turned pink with blood that Ursula seemed to have drawn as well. He reached down to his penis, limp and raw on the tapestry-covered seat. The prepuce was covered with flakes of dried elixir—hers mixed with his. In the yellowed light of his lamps, the scales he brushed off appeared an opaque, pearlescent gold, like the leaf he sometimes applied to his carved pieces.

He stretched, his body already less gaunt. When he was well-fed, he occasionally thought himself beautiful. He held his hands out, flexing his fingers, then smelled them, captivated with their fragrance. His hands were his favorite part of himself. It was because of them that he wrought true beauty.

His thoughts turned to his carving, and to the fact that he needed wood. He'd shower, dress for scavenging, go out into the early morning before it was light. Yes, his other need required his attention and indulgence. His fingers ached to hold his tools, find the life inside a block of basswood.

Just as the sun was rising, Anton slipped the last cord of wood into the barrel in his studio. He'd found a stash of wormy rosewood burl in someone's trash, and a box of scrap behind the lumberyard.

As he crossed the lawn to the house, he glanced up to the window of her room. She'd be watching him now: eyes hungry, heart longing, loins aching. She'd be wherever he was, her desire viscous, pumping like blood in her veins. The notion made him shiver as he stepped inside and quietly went up the back stairway to his room.

That wouldn't do. Not at all.

Anton shrugged off his clothes and crawled into bed, certain that he'd know just what to do when he awoke that evening. He had to.

He waited for that terrible feeling of mindless dread upon waking, but instead he felt entirely calm and right. That was it: *right.* As if he'd felt wrong all his centuries on earth, and suddenly every cell in his body knew things were different now. He grinned. Was he happy? Not quite.

He noted the time. Well past eight. She'd be in the parlor or bed, reading. No matter—he would move about his home as if he were alone. Why not? Wasn't this his place?

He bathed, considering going out to feed. Ursula would be asleep by ten. First, he powdered his nipples and cock, still ruddy from the previous evening's abuse. He pinched his lips and cheeks to rouge them, though they didn't require it. Then he dressed nicely in tight black jeans, a blue shirt, and his boots, and tied the hair at the end of his braid with blue string.

As he descended the staircase, he smelled her through the sweet scent of home-baked cookies. He rarely indulged in foods, but when he did, it was usually in cakes, cookies, and breads. Almost to the door, he stopped. Perhaps he would taste just one of her cookies before he went out.

Ursula sat at the kitchen table, a photography book spread out, her glasses on the end of her nose, hair piled haphazardly atop her head. Two sheets of freshly baked cookies sat on cooling racks on the stove. She looked up at him, caught his eye, then went back to her book.

"May I try one?" He stood at the counter.

She nodded, turning a page.

"Would you like one?" He reached out and peeled up an oatmeal raisin cookie.

"No. Thank you." She turned another page. Speaking seemed to pain her.

Anton bit into the cookie. It was warm and tasty. "Mmmm, it's good. I don't eat them much myself."

He stared at her. She refused to hold his eyes. In the glaring light of the brightly lit kitchen, her skin appeared luminous—and her scent oddly pungent. He felt his penis stiffen. The hunger was arriving unexpectedly. He moved toward her. She failed to notice he was beside her until he was leaning over to see what she was looking at. When she realized his proximity, she gasped, her hand going over her face.

He ignored her reaction, fascinated. The book was an album, a scrapbook. The pictures were of couples and children, or families, cut from magazines, books, and newspapers. Some of the photos of children were in ornately drawn frames. He found it curious, but his interest began to pale against passion's flourish.

He swallowed, afraid any words that came would be commitments from which he could never extricate himself; yet he was compelled.

"I want . . . to be inside you." He didn't know why this was happening. She would have to stop him. His hand went to her cheek.

Ursula shut the album. "Don't." She held her breath. "Oh." She appeared to grow suddenly weak. "I . . . please." She reached out for him, her hand landing on his chest, her fingers going to an erect nipple.

Anton fell to his knees and turned her in her chair to face him. He tore the front of her dress open, exposing her breasts, and began suckling hungrily. Her hands were suddenly on his head, her fingers running through his hair, loosening it until it fell around his face in waves.

He tasted something then. Milk. Not the sort he'd known when he'd suckled lactating women. This was thick, rich, nutty stuff that made him dizzy. The sounds of her moans, her words of encouragement charmed him, erasing the thoughts in his head.

Her legs parted and she prodded his head downward. She pulled up her dress and slid to the edge of the chair. Anton pulled her panties aside, attacking her sex, lapping at her, tasting the odd flavor, breathing in the strange pheromonal note. His tongue wriggled into her vagina, bent on examining the curves of it, the crenulated terrain. The top of her vagina twisted down, and a velvety cat's tongue met his. He recoiled, suddenly sober.

"What was that?" He looked up—her head was back, her eyes rolled up, mouth gaping. Her hand went to her mons, and her fingers worked her clitoris in his absence.

"Ursula!"

Her name spoken aloud stopped her dead. Her head dropped and unfocused eyes took Anton in. "What . . . "

As she realized she was sitting completely open to him, she yanked her skirt over her knees and pulled closed her blouse, then turned away.

Anton began apologizing. "I'm sorry. I don't know what possessed me. I just—"

She held up a hand, avoiding his stare. "Please, don't say anything. Just leave. Go."

His cock went flaccid, his lust for her slowly ebbing, an ache in his heart replacing it. *"Ursula."*

She ventured a glance, and tears filled her eyes. "I thought . . . nothing. Go." She covered her face.

Anton was torn. He put his hand on her head and her hair came loose, cascading down. It just made the moment worse for him and he rushed out, cursing under his breath.

He didn't pay attention to where he walked, just kept moving away from his house, from the anguish and confusion. Breathing in the night air and feeling his appetite return, even in its vague and rootless fashion, reassured him. Anything to keep from asking himself questions.

Anton ventured into the part of town known as The Sticks. Wooden shanties and dilapidated old clapboard houses lined weed-infested streets where lawn ornaments consisted of discarded wheel rims, crankcases, and broken furniture. He'd gone there once before, intentionally seeking game, and found a love-hungry teenager who'd just been beaten and thrown out by her father. He'd thought then that there'd be more of that if he ever came back.

Sure enough, new prey was sitting on a sagging porch. A pale woman with thin hair and thick legs, she fixed him with a hard, angry glare, daring him to respond. He held her eyes as he continued past her, breaking contact only when he reached the corner and went around it. When next he passed her, she followed. They walked along in silence, their eyes and bodies speaking for them, until they came to a deserted house.

She led him inside, where a filthy mattress lay beneath a canopy of torn sheets. By the way she took him, he knew she'd been there often. He had to work her for hours before she finally climaxed. He saw that her anger was holding back her release, so he baited her, let her fight him until she was weak. She never uttered a word, only growled fiercely when she came. Finally, he drank copiously of her liquors.

When he stood there, she still basking in the pleasure she'd been robbed of for so long, he told her he was grateful. Tears welled in his eyes. He felt so old and tired looking down at her, and something came unwound in him. He told her of his life, his hunger, his sorrow, unburdening himself of his secrets. He didn't care if she thought him insane. Wiping his face dry, he saw her hands flutter in the air in front of her, speaking for her, and he realized she was deaf. He recalled a vague memory of some sign language, the movements for "Sorry, I don't understand." She shrugged up at him, then rolled onto her stomach to sleep. He hurried out.

All the way home, he tried not to think of Ursula. He'd never thought again of a woman once he'd fed. Rarely, a woman had some unique quality that stayed in his mind, the same way a spectacularly prepared dish might linger in a diner's memory. A woman's coloring or her voice, a magical trick of movement. But no one woman had ever occupied his thoughts as this woman did.

He went back in his mind to what had occurred in the kitchen, his tongue reaching deep within her. Had he imagined what had slithered down to parry with him?

He stood on the porch. His house dark save for the parlor light, which burned all night. She would be in bed—her job started at an ungodly hour in the morning. He wouldn't be well-received if he went to her room, not this late. But he wanted to talk to her. Learn for himself what was happening to him, with her.

The fear grew on itself in minute quantum fragments until he stood paralyzed in the foyer, staring up the stairs. Whatever she was, whatever lay up there, terrified him in a way, was at once exhilarating and petrifying.

He breathed deeply, fear having closed his lungs to all but shallow breaths. Her scent made his cock taut, his hunger fevered. Without conscious willing, his feet took him to her door. He pushed it slowly open. It took a few moments for his eyes to adjust to the darkness. Expecting to see her there, he saw shadows on her bed and approached.

"Ursula?" he whispered.

There was no response, and suddenly his panic returned. Had she packed up and left him while he was rutting in The Sticks? He reached out to the bedcovers and felt them. Flat. She was gone, though her smell was still strong.

Anton flew to his bathroom, enraged. Under the warm water's spray, he washed off the common odors of the deaf woman, ruminating on Ursula. Why had he wished her gone? Now he'd never understand.

He rubbed the towel over himself, tossed it aside, pulled on his robe, and stalked to his bedroom. He threw open the door and slapped the light switch.

"Damn!"

Ursula was on his bed, awakened by the light and his shout. She curled instantly into a pill bug of a girl, her eyes wide.

Anton grabbed his chest, his heart threatening to beat through. "I . . . I . . . I thought you were gone."

She shook her head, pushing hair away from her face. Then she sat up, her arms around her knees, looking at him timidly.

He went to his bed and sat beside her. "Why are you . . . *here?*"

"I felt bad about . . . for what happened. Before." Her hand covered her face.

Anton's prick ached; his heart blushed with tenderness for her.

"I'm sorry. Look, I'm just confused."

She nodded. "Yes. I am, too. I've waited to know this, what it is. It's too much, and yet . . . I can't say no to it."

Anton kissed her softly, slowly, letting the almost floral taste of her mouth fill his. When he leaned away, he held her face. Her eyes were yellow-gold.

"Nor can I. I wouldn't believe it possible. And . . . " He looked away, then back at her. "It's dangerous, it's so . . . "

"Dangerous . . . " She seemed absorbed, her eyes unfocused. He waited, glancing at her hands, clasped like pale shells over her knees. When she spoke, she did so with an assurance.

"I need you, Mr. Valjean, in a way I don't understand." Her fingers went to his lips, her desire for him flaring, now obvious in her bearing.

As she peeled the sheets from her naked body, he could barely find the breath to speak. "I need you . . . too."

He let her take him. Whatever she wanted, he would be that, tonight. Even just a man.

His bed was empty when he rolled over in the middle of the day, he recalled his body calling out for her as he fell back into sleep. Later, that evening, it was Ursula's footsteps in the hall that woke him and sent him rushing naked from his room to hers.

She stood by her bed, glowing, a package in her arms. She smiled at Anton without the usual anxious averting of her eyes.

"Hello, Mr. Valjean."

"Please." He put his hand out to take one of hers. "Anton."

She blushed as she shook his hand. "Anton. Well, that will take getting used to." Then she looked at her feet. "I've brought you a gift."

"A gift? But why?" Women who had loved him had brought him things. Meaningless things, with meaningless emotions attached to them. Here, he found himself enthralled.

"I don't know. It felt right." She held out the package.

He took it, set it on her bed, then looked at her. "May I?" He made a tearing motion. She nodded.

Brown paper fell to the floor as he took the scrapbook from its wrapper. He ran his hand over the etched leather cover. It said his name in large scrolled letters. "Valjean." He opened it to find that it wasn't an ordinary album full of cardboardy paper jammed into a string binding. The pages were of heavy stock with fine vellum sheets between, and they were bound with gold wire.

"This must have been expensive." He marveled at it, then thinking of her meager savings, began to worry.

"Actually, I've had it a very long time, but I took it to be inscribed today, for you. It's an heirloom." She swelled with pride.

"How old is it?" He examined it. The work was undoubtedly that of an expert craftsman, and had to have been preserved archivally to be in such fine condition.

She went to the chair at her dressing table and sat down.

"Anton, please. Sit down. I have to talk to you about this. But, first . . . I think perhaps you should put something on."

His brow furrowed in curiosity. He clasped the scrapbook to his chest, aware of his nakedness, but suddenly a little afraid. "All right."

In his room, he pulled on a shirt and pants, wondering into foreign territory. He hadn't sat for a talk with anyone in years. And he couldn't recall having one with a woman that didn't require a firm good-bye afterward. When he returned to her, she was still at the dressing table.

"I'm scared." She knit her fingers in her lap. Anton thought he'd never seen a lovelier woman.

"Ah, yes, well, all this talking terrifies me, too . . . as you know." He hoped this would assuage her fears.

"So it seems." She licked her lips. "I want to tell you things, secrets I've carried all my life, and for reasons I can't grasp, I want more than anything to tell *you*."

"Well, I want to know," he reassured her, yet unsure himself.

"Yes." She held herself. "You'll find it unbelievable, but even I can't explain what there is between us, or within me. Who I am. What I am." She waited for his reaction.

"Go on." He managed a smile.

Ursula took a deep breath and exhaled slowly. "I am not just a girl . . . a woman. I am a thing. A thing that is so ancient, so primordial in instinct, I've forgotten everything else. What I am. I've lived hundreds of years, all over this world. During that time, I've coupled innumerable times, but always . . . always with regret. And sorrow. A kind of heart-weariness that's turned me cold to men for ages. But I've always found myself searching again, never knowing for what, or who. Men have always followed me, fought for me, died for me, for what I did with them. But I felt nothing. It's been as if I was cursed. They could feel pleasure, joy, love, yet I only felt a kind of physical well-being from our unions." She stopped, eyes squinting. "Am I scaring you yet?"

Anton was delighted, but he didn't trust what he'd heard. He spoke carefully. "Actually, you're not. I'm fascinated."

"Good." She relaxed a bit. "I've always kept a scrapbook, for as long as my memory allows. Like the one you saw before. Early on, before I can recall, I kept drawings, pressed flowers, etchings in them. When photographs became available, I pasted those in. Always of places, buildings, the sky, the forest, the city. Never people. At the turn of the century, when I came to this country, I began to cut out pictures of people. Men, women, alone. I filled many books." She sighed. "Are you with me?"

Anton nodded. "Oh, *yes.*"

She grinned, pleased. "Twenty years ago, I began collecting pictures of couples, kids. The jobs I took involved caring for children. And I got my teaching degree. Now I know part of my purpose is to care for the young. I'd contemplated for an eternity on why I'd been alive so long, knowing only that I was not like . . . like other women."

He whispered, too softly for her to hear. "As I am not like men."

"Anton, I was drawn to your house, to you. I don't understand it, nor can I walk away from it. I don't want to frighten you, yet I know telling you the truth may very well do that."

He shook his head to clear it, then steeled himself to reveal the truth to her.

"Ursula, it isn't you I'm frightened of—it's what I feel. If this will make any sense to you, it's because I, too, am centuries old. Somehow I was born to live in ways that aren't . . . human, unsure of what *my* purpose is. I've been with many women, and I am not speaking as a man who is full of ego. It hasn't been to find love, or to amass quantities of conquests, or to compare myself to men. I am not their kind. I haven't felt love or compassion or need for women beyond what I must have to keep myself alive." He looked away. "This sounds so cold as I hear it leave my lips. Until last night, I'd never told a soul anything of my real nature."

Ursula stood. "Anton, could it be . . . ?" Her eyes implored him to agree.

Of course. That was the pull toward her. Legend had it that the female of his species were few. Centuries ago he'd come to believe they were extinct, as he'd come to believe he was now one of the last. He'd certainly never met a female of his kind, as memory served.

"Ursula, it can't be anything else." He went to her and embraced her. "We've found each other."

She leaned away slightly and fixed him with her eyes. "I want to be glad, yet . . . "

"Yet what?" The old panic crawled into his heart.

"What's it all mean? What are we to do about it?"

Anton went limp. He had no idea. Were they to marry? Cohabit like humans? Travel, seek their prey, no longer solitary in their venture? He'd been alone his entire existence. So had she. And what of the emphatic feelings, the bond to her he felt powerless to undo?

"You want answers to questions that only bring more questions. I don't know."

She hugged him. "Me either, but whatever it is we'll be doing, it must have something to do with *this.*" She began slowly rubbing her hand against the swell of his cock. Her mouth went to his, and their tongues sought contact.

Anton, almost lost in the coming swirl of oblivion, felt a twinge of grief for his eons of loneliness, then allowed the lethe to swallow him.

For weeks, Anton's creativity surged. His usually highly modern, abstract sculptures began to change. The shapes became more lifelike, natural. He carved delicate lacy climbing vines flowing over earthy women growing up from garden beds. He found in hunks of wood angels and cherubs with wings as fine and feathered-looking as a butterfly's.

Until the morning light, he worked in his studio, his eyes always turning from his handiwork to Ursula's window, watching for the light to go on, signaling her rising. Only then would he quit, hurry up to her, the smell of wood and coal oil on him, and kiss her deeply before he went to bed.

They made love, as he now knew it, when she came home from work and the sky had gone dark. At first they needed only each other, but it became clear after the first month that their bodies needed the panacea of others. She'd noticed it first.

"I'm hungry lately, Anton. I don't want to be. I feel I must apologize for it. It's . . . it's not you, I know that."

Anton rolled over to look at her. She was growing almost plump. How could she be hungry? But he was experiencing it, too.

"Oh, why? I've gotten used to it being just you and I." He stroked her face. "Yet . . . I feel it as well."

"Then, maybe we must. It's been our way. . . ." She didn't sound convinced.

Anton felt her breasts. They were firmer, larger lately. "I don't imagine we'll enjoy it."

She frowned at him. "I never have. Not really."

"God, we sound so melancholy."

Ursula nodded. "It's just food."

"Yes. Simply sustenance. This . . ."—he kissed her nipples—"this is succor."

She giggled, purring.

He rose up on his haunches and looked at her. "Where will you hunt?"

"When I get hungry enough, prey flocks to me. It's the nature of the beast that females have it easier than men. After all, we bear the young."

That was it. "Ursula, are you . . . could you be pregnant?"

She lay back against the pillows her hands on her belly, no swell there.

"I might be. I wouldn't know how to tell. I haven't been pregnant before."

"Damn. I know we can't go to a doctor and ask for a test—our chemistry isn't human."

"So where does that leave us?" She pulled him to her.

"Enjoying what we know." And he made certain they did.

Ursula began to show three months later. She was going out every night after work to feed. Anton learned that along with the emotions of joy and sadness and anger came jealousy. Though he fed a few times a week, it didn't take any time away from Ursula; he just waited until she was asleep. She complained that as she grew plumper and more pregnant, she'd have more difficulty securing quarry, so that she had to get everything she could now. As her mate, he accepted this, but having lived among humans all his life, he also found it contrary to a loyal pair bonding. He was torn.

One evening, Ursula came in late. She had the sated look he'd come to expect, and as usual, it inspired hurt in him.

"Anton, what is it?" She crawled onto his lap as he sat in the parlor.

"You're getting heavy."

She frowned. "I am. But that's not it. There's something on your mind."

"The standard petulant thoughts of a deserted mate, is all."

Her arms went around his neck and she kissed his forehead. "I'm sorry, love. But, listen. I've bought us a wonderful thing. Don't you want to know what?"

Anton pouted. "What?"

She leapt off him and ran upstairs, returning with a small box. "Open it."

He saw by the label that it was a camera. "Why do we need this?"

"Oh, Anton, for the children. Neither of us can remember our childhoods. Our parents. Now I know my scrapbooks have been for them. If we take photos, they won't have to remember."

He smiled. "You think of everything. I . . . I . . . "

"You love me?" She nuzzled him.

He became sullen. "I'm not sure what love is."

"Why can't you give me that one little thing? Those three words?"

He screwed his mouth and said derisively, "You're so human sometimes."

She ran off crying. For Anton it was a relief. Something inside him was causing him to backpedal, to seek comfort in what he knew he was, how he was different from humans. Their feelings. It was the beginning of a detachment that confused him, made him bitter.

But when the children came soon after, it was she who pulled away.

There were five of them. Anton instinctually knew what to do as they were born, one by one. He ate their placentas and licked them clean. Ursula and he nursed the babies until their nipples were too painful to touch, then they nursed them some more.

He hardly spoke to her, nor she to him. They became shy again, their focus completely on their young. They spoke just enough to give names to the three girls and two boys, names she told him came from the Bible; Samuel, Adam, Rachel, Sarah, and Mary. And they talked to the children of everything they could remember.

Neither knew what to expect in the way of growth, and Anton was alarmed when the children developed at an accelerated rate. Ursula took many photographs, chronicling each inch and pound, each foray into the world, gluing the pictures into the leather-bound book she'd given Anton. There were even photos of him and Ursula. The children would know their parents someday.

Ursula and Anton went out to feed nightly, then fed their babies. In six months the youngsters were adolescents in emotion, physique, intellect, and sexual precociousness. If any of this astonished Ursula, Anton saw no sign. He felt very alone in his bewilderment.

Anton had one of his rare exchanges with Ursula after he'd found Adam and Samuel slipping into bed with her. "That was wrong, Ursula."

She'd grown sullen, stubborn, and nasty. He couldn't recall the passion he'd once known with her.

"How are they to learn, Anton? You'd have them starving before they're a year old?"

"It's time we move on. We'll start over in another state, let them learn like humans. No one would know they're not as old as they appear." Anton knew the children were huddled outside the parlor listening. He could hear them breathing, shushing each other.

Ursula folded her arms. "I'll tell you what we'll do: I'll stay here in the house with the boys and you can take the girls with you anywhere you want. That way I can keep my job."

"You want to sever our relationship?" He felt an icy fist grab his heart. It surprised him, because he hadn't felt anything for Ursula since the children were born.

When Ursula spoke, she did so as a stranger. "You've served your purpose. Move on. Do what you do. We'll be fine here."

"What about the children? You'd separate them?"

She chortled. "Don't be stupid, Anton. They'll be flying off like dust motes in a breeze soon enough, each their own way. It won't make any difference if we part them."

"It's wrong, Ursula. I can't tell you why. I don't know. It's just not *right.*"

Anton turned and walked out, passing his beautiful spawn, to his studio. He sat at his workbench, staring at his unfinished sculptures, and began to weep. He had no idea why he was so full of sorrow. The sadness, all the emotion, had begun when he'd first lain with Ursula. How would he ever be as he once was? Now that he was losing his children. His home. Her.

His hands went to a chunk of ash half-carved on his workbench. It was his five babies as they'd emerged from Ursula, each seeming part of the other, their mouths open, hungry; their eyes closed; their arms out, reaching. He took a chisel and began working on the mouth from whence they came, making it universal, not Ursula's. Wood chips flew around him, disappearing in his peripheral vision like snowflakes in a blizzard.

The light rapping at the door startled him from his reverie. He had no idea how long he'd been sitting there thinking, working.

"Yes?"

One of his daughters peeked in. "It's me, Father, Rachel."

He wiped his tears, though his throat was still constricted with anguish, and motioned her to enter.

The lithe auburn-haired beauty stepped in, her sensual grace an inbred characteristic. "You're all wet." She knelt beside him.

He chuckled. "Yes, I seem to be leaking."

"Can we talk, Father?"

Anton was somber again. "Is there anything to talk about?"

"Mother said something to me that I want to tell you."

He frowned. "What could she say that I need to know?"

Rachel grew strident. "Don't pretend you're so smart." She looked away, then to him. "Sorry, I don't want to hurt you."

He put his hand on her cheek. "Talk."

"You're sure?" She paused, waiting for his nod. "She said that you and she were so old that you'd both forgotten what your ways were as children. That perhaps both of you should trust us to find that way ourselves. Let our instincts lead us."

Anton thought about this. Ursula was correct—he had forgotten. "That very well may be the way. I'm just feeling so . . . so useless." He teared up again.

"Oh, Father." Rachel embraced him.

Her scent was not like Ursula's, but was intensely sweet, fragrant, and exciting. He nestled his face in his daughter's neck, under her hair, and breathed deeply. He froze, his mind in opposition to his body's reaction.

Rachel drew her arms from around him and pulled her dress over her head. Her bone-pale body, with its ruby nipples and rusty-haired mons, stood before him. Anton was paralyzed—his eyes averted, his head hung in resistance. Her hand went under his chin and made him look at her.

"This is what my instincts tell me to do, Father."

She then removed Anton's shirt and opened his pants. His cock stood straight out at her, the ache in his groin as powerful as it had been when he'd first been with Ursula. She curled herself around him, letting her scent waft up.

"Teach me how to feed so that I may live."

Anton, inebriated, kissed his daughter full on the mouth, taking her breasts in his hands. He kneaded them until he felt his own nipples begin to weep.

"Suck on them," he instructed her, and she did as he asked.

His head went back and he felt her slip her cunt over his cock. Pleasure rocked him as his ears filled with her moans. He didn't hear Rachel's sisters enter, each peeling off her dress, each anxious to learn. But he felt them as they took him to the floor of his studio, spending him deep into the night.

Anton awoke in his bed, his back burned from the rug in his workroom, his body aching from having pleased three females. Rachel and Sarah and Mary were sprawled on the floor around his bed, covered in blankets and coats. It was dark and for a moment, he didn't know where he was, or what he was. It had been ages since he'd last known that amnesia of the soul. He worried over it until he remembered.

"Rachel?"

She roused slowly, languorously. "Father."

"Where's your mother?"

She shrugged.

He mirrored the shrug and lay back. Sarah, the fair-haired daughter, woke and slithered into her father's bed. She went immediately to his penis, her mouth going around it, soothing and arousing him.

The door to his bedroom opened and he saw handsome Adam and Samuel. They were naked but for the blankets cloaking their broad shoulders.

"Father, it's time for *us.*" Samuel went to the bedside and firmly moved Sarah's head away from Anton.

Anton frowned. Trust his newborns to teach themselves? What had he been thinking?

Startled, he found Samuel's mouth replacing Sarah's on his prick. Adam sat on the edge of the bed, stroking his father's distended nipples, then licking the trickle of milk that oozed forth.

Anton had never been with a male before. Or had he been like his own sons as a child? Had he suckled his father's nipples? His cock? Entered his sisters and tasted their fruits? He was too old, his memory rusted. Regardless, his body responded instinctually, taking his son's cocks into his mouth, teasing the tongues in the orifices hidden behind their pricks, pleasuring the boys into manhood, holding them close, kissing them deeply. Their nipples gave forth the same intoxicating milk as did their parents', and he became drunk with it. He lay in the mass of his boys and girls, breathing in the sweet young scent of them, listening to their erotic purrings, giving in to the piquant pleasure of it.

Samuel suckled Anton's nipples as Adam's tongue explored the mouth at Samuel's crotch, making him wet, ready. As Adam pressed his cock into Samuel, Anton closed his eyes, feeling the movement of his sons at his chest. For an instant, he saw an image: a pale blond male, sucking his cock, his eyes staring up, old and wise. His father? Suddenly, he felt Samuel's mouth on his penis, pale blond Samuel. So like his grandfather? Anton's heart swelled as he came full force into his son.

Exhausted finally, he left his children to play together and went to seek refuge in Ursula's old bed. He wondered idly where she might have been all this time. Wasn't it she who had first intimated that taking the children into her bed was the natural way? She was missing it all.

As he pushed into the room, he knew immediately that something horrible had happened there. Ursula's scent was no longer about. Instead, an odor of rot filled the air. He reached for the lamp. As the light came on, he saw her there on the floor. What was left of her.

Anton had read about what vultures left of carrion, and there was not much more than that left of Ursula. She'd been scalped, her head cracked open and her brains eaten. Her bones were picked clean in spots, muscle left to trail on the hardwood. Her eyes were gone; her face as well. He stared, feeling no revulsion, no guilt, no loss—nothing of what he'd have expected after all the emotion he'd known with her.

He just felt tired. He climbed into bed and pulled the sheet over him.

The sounds of his children in the room down the hall gave him what little emotional resonance he was aware of having. Pride. Yes, that was it. And a sense of purpose.

Later, he'd show them the albums, let them see their history and heritage as kept by their mother. Give them what he'd never had—a sense of who they are, the knowledge that they have roots, that one day they'd be able to teach their own children of these things. So that if they took him, as they had Ursula, and there was no one left to remind them, they would never forget.

The I of the Eye of the Worm

Janet Berliner and
George Guthridge

“Loa loa is an uncommon disease outside Africa.”

—DAVID GENDELMAN

Infectious Diseases

In the light of a single candle I see the soft fluttering of eyelids. My lover has begun to dream. I feel the pulse of the loa loa worm as it begins its midnight journey across my eye. Soon it will make its nightly demand.

I know what the worm wants. As gently as the whisper of a summer breeze, I weave its web around the face of my naked lover. Then I lie down and accept the dream that passes through me into the eye of the worm, the eye of the dream stealer. I cannot truly understand the dream, for it does not belong to me, but it is all I have to induce sleep. I have long since been denuded of my own dreams. I can sleep only for the brief moment when another’s dream passes through me.

I wake at dawn and watch light seep under the shanty door.

“Mandela’s release,” I want to tell my people as I look between the boards at the dawn sweeping over Soweto, “will puncture all of your dreams. I know, for in my blood beats the souls of the races of men.”

“Why are you not sleeping, Nssessebe?” my lover asks, using my African name as he reaches for me. I am named for the swiftest antelope in our land—slim, dainty, slender ankles, and fleet as the wind. In the white world, my name breaks their tongues and they call me Ness. I do not mind. "Your name is as beautiful as you are," he says. In the dawn light he cannot see the swelling of my eye where the worm's passage has inflamed the tissue.

I try to avoid his hand but it is too quick. He plays with my nipple and I hear his breathing grow heavier. I enjoyed making love once, when I did it for pleasure. Now, though I do it, it revolts me. By tomorrow he will begin to hate me. Tonight and every night for the rest of his life his sleep will be dreamless. Eventually he will know that I caused this.

Ti e, n !ka ssho au !ko-ssho-!kui, sse !uonniva, kke, n see !kuiten n-ka !oe, n sse ttumm-a !ke-ta-ku ka kko-kkommi, I say, using the old tongue. *I sit waiting for the moon to turn back, that I may listen to all the people's stories.*

He knows that I have spent my life as a storyteller in the white man's world, that I travel the land, telling them the tales of my people. He is content with my answer. I would like to tell him the true story of my life, but I clench my teeth so that the truth remains in my throat. He would not believe it anyway. Instead, I spend the time remembering, as I do each dawn while I lie in a stranger's bed waiting for the moon to turn back.

The remembering has become a ritual . . .

. . . I heard the buzzing of the horsefly as I sat in the narrow outhouse adjacent to my home, buttocks on a board stained black with the urine of a generation, knees and forehead against the door, peering out at light breaking across the tin and cardboard roofs of my shantytown home. When it landed on me, I slapped it away, trusting that the speed of my reaction had stopped it from depositing its eggs. I though nothing more of it until the worm came to me, crawling beneath the fragile subcutaneous membrane of my eye, and even then I did not know what it was, not until I went to the clinic. My eye was troubling me. Itching and inflamed. Worst of all, I had lost my dreams and woke out of the night's blankness more fatigued than when I'd lain down. My powers of concentration were gone and I had trouble writing.

"The disease is unique, Ness. May I call you Ness? Let me put it in medical terms first, and then I'll translate. The loa loa is a necrotic, subconjunctival worm which sometimes takes up residence in the superotemporal quadrant of the eye. It comes from the eggs of the horsefly."

I was educated in the white man's world; my master's degree attests to that. My father's magic bought me that—a European education, graduate school at Copenhagen's Polytechnick Institute, fieldwork in Zaire, beneath whose jungle canopy there still are wild men crazy enough to paint their faces with radium. I am clever, all right, just not smart. If I were smart, I would not be living in Soweto.

"The worm, how do I get rid of it?" I asked, indicating that I understood.

"There are those who say that you cannot. It feeds on the tissue of the eye and then produces its own eggs. . . ." The clinic doctor looked uncomfortable. "You could try to drive the worm from the eye by using cold compresses or onion compresses. You could have it removed surgically—"

"I fear the knife," I said. "If I do nothing, what will happen?"

"At best, fever, itching, a general malaise—"

"And at worst?"

"Corneal conjunctivitis, meningoencephalitis, for starters. Who knows what else. It can grow to the size of a hen's egg and will not be pretty to look at. Damn thing takes a year to mature and can live as long as fifteen years. It is unnerving having a foreign body in your eye."

I could see by his body language that there was more. "Will it be painful?" I asked.

"Not *physically,*" he said. "Ness, listen to me. Loa loa will cross your cornea at precisely the same moment once every twenty-four hours. The waiting, the watching for it, can make you insane. You will imagine it feeding on you, and waste away. Our Africa and its diseases can be enigmatic and exasperating."

The disease is unique, Ness. May I call you Ness?

"This new mixing of the races can be so enigmatic and exasperating" is what the white doctor meant.

"Doctor Ras—may I call you Doctor Ras?" I asked. I felt strangely relieved. "Society, too, has a worm crawling across its vision. I will find out what the worm wants of me and bow to its demands. When you figure out how to excise society's worms with your knife, I shall return to see you. Meanwhile, you must give me something to help me sleep. To help me dream."

"I can help you sleep," he said. "That's easy. But medical science has no idea how to create REM sleep. We know that deprivation wreaks havoc with your nervous system." He paused thoughtfully. "I have a theory, Ness. I think perhaps the worm has stolen your dreams. I have heard before that it can do such things. If that is true, it will demand to be fed regularly."

"Fed?"

"Here's the thing. If I'm right, loa loa feeds on dreams. If it isn't provided with dreams, it feeds on its host. The kicker is that once you give it your dreams, you cannot get them back. Not as long as loa loa is with you."

I came away feeling joyful that I was being punished at last, though I did not understand the form that the punishment was taking. I had longed for punishment since Nelson Mandela's arrest. I had known him well. As a child, I sat on his knee and called him uncle. When he was taken away, I cried because I wished to go with him; he was the only family I knew. I saw him move from incarceration to house arrest, saw him living in lice-ridden cells and in a white man's house. Now he has the power, and he cannot remember what color he is. He, too, must be a victim of loa loa, for he has forgotten his dreams . . .

. . . The man in whose bed I lie awakens again. This time I cannot refuse him. He is strangely gentle, and despite myself, I enjoy the quality of his embraces. When he enters me I arch toward him and, for a few minutes, I forget that he is a stranger who will soon hate me, forget that tonight or tomorrow—when I can stand the sleeplessness no longer—I will grace some other man's bed.

When he is done with me and I with him, I leave his bed. In the full light of day, I anticipate the worm's march with a balance of fear and joy. I count my victims as I walk through the township and men who were once my friends turn away as I approach them, their eyes filled with fury. Strangers whom I assume to belong to my one-night-stand club spit in my path. I try to remember something about each one—the size of a cock, a hand grasping my breast, a tongue thrust too deeply into my throat. They fear me, these men, but they do not know why. They have not heard of loa loa. Each morning when I return to my house, my shack, I look in the mirror, wondering when the egg will begin to swell. When it does, they will speak among themselves. They will visit the witch doctor and he will tell them where their dreams have gone.

When that happens, they will send the Tsotsis to destroy me and take the worm. I do not fear much, but I fear them, these young gangster-boys who roam in groups, predators who feed on their own kind. They are children to whom the intrinsic value of human life means nothing. Their youth and tenacity mirror the depths to which we have descended. They are the offspring of men without dreams, the progeny of fathers who nightly stain women's thighs and daily board buses to spineless work in Johannesburg or Pretoria or mindless toil in the oil or coal or diamond fields.

These are the children of the worm.

When they come for me, my heart will cease to beat with the souls of the races of men, because it will no longer beat at all. Until then, I glory in the punishment I have both dreaded and longed for ever since they took everyone I loved and left me behind.

I return to my shack, cleanse my body, and examine my eye. A node has begun to show itself. I hear the echo of Dr. Ras's voice: *It can grow to the size of a hen's egg.* I lie down to rest and prepare myself for the night. As I close my eyes, I wonder anew why it is that, somewhere in the arrest that was never made and the beating and sodomizing I never received, I became a victim; as I fall asleep, into that black dreamless void, I wonder how many more of me there are, women who spread their legs and feed the worm in atonement for never having been raped by white men in starched khakis, sweat popping from their straining chests. We are all victims of the worm.

In my blood beats the souls of the races of men.

I awaken feeling as if I have not slept at all. I twist the ring on my finger, a pitifully small diamond I found in my mother's belongings after the Tsotsis killed her for the few rand she had in her pocket. The ring was a gift, I assumed, from my father, who could neither confirm nor deny the supposition from the cell where he died. I packed up his amulets, his phallic sticks, and the jars of juju magic he had brought with him when he moved the family here forty years ago, saying, "Your uncle Nelson wishes us to come to the city."

I was born in Soweto.

I will die in Soweto, of the worm, of Tsotsis, of sleep deprivation. I will fuck myself to death.

"I have paid my dues, Loa Loa," I say, crying because I have paid nightly for the crime of survival and now I want to be free of the guilt; free of the worm. I want to sleep, but what is sleep without dreams? *My* dreams, not stolen ones which slide through me into the maw of my oppressor, a worm half the size of a heartbeat?

In the seven months that have passed since my visit to the clinic, Mandela has taken over the reins of power. I am more concerned with the nodule in my eye, which has already grown to the size of a pigeon's egg. The sight of my face in the mirror disgusts me and I turn away from my own ugliness. Desperate to have the worm excised, I return to see Dr. Ras.

"If it is about your eye," the receptionist says, "I'd advise you to go into the city and see an ophthalmologist. Things have changed since Mandela took over. All of our good doctors have moved away. They are practicing at the white man's hospitals. Looks like you need to have it cut, but surgery will cost you a lot of money. You should have let him cut it before. . . ."

I leave. "Should have" doesn't even count in horseshoes. I have used up all of my money buying sleep. The itching and the redness have become unbearable, the worm has grown to the size of an egg.

That night and for the next four nights, I seek out no man. I do not sleep much, and when I do the black of my dreamless state is replaced by a single image. I see a worm, headless, entwined in a spiderweb. Always the same image.

I am otherwise dry of dreams.

On the fifth night, precisely at midnight, I sit in readiness in the outhouse, a hammer in my hand. In the streets, I hear the sounds of anger. I imagine that it comes from the men I have robbed, that they are gathering to seek retribution. Forever sleep-deprived, they have become as crazed as I. This time, surely, I will summon the nerve to smash the worm. If I do not, I will become a victim of the victims of the worm. Somehow, I must show them that I could not help myself. That I was forced to do what I did. I must show them because I have paid my dues and I want to survive.

"Kill me and you will be without dreams forever," a voice in my head says. A voice in my eye. "I allow you to dream the dreams of the men you sleep with before I claim them as my own. Only I can make that possible. Only I, the I in your eye."

I raise the hammer, imagining my blood staining the dungarees pushed down around my knees.

In that blood beats the souls of the races of men.

I grip the hammer, wondering how long it has been since I last slept. The haft of the hammer, like the head, is iron, rust-brown from years of use, the shape of the eye of a giant needle. I peer through the cracks in the boards, aware that Soweto is out there but able only to focus on my right eye—my *wrong* eye—the culprit.

Beyond the outhouse the dawn continues to spread. A carpet of sunlight rolls under the door and into the outhouse. With all-consuming envy, I imagine people awakening, and I lust after their ability to dream.

It is envy, I admit, and not the worm that has been my undoing. The horsefly must have smelled it in my sweat.

I tighten my grip on the hammer and my resolve, but I cannot do it. I cannot kill the worm. I guess I have always known that. As on so many other mornings, I ask myself what I would do should the worm leave its eggs behind in the bloodied socket. What might come crawling then across my flesh?

Someone pounds on the outhouse door. Is it my enemy, or someone simply obeying the demands of nature?

"I'll be right out," I say, without moving. I must have a plan. Now that everyone knows my catalytic responsibility in their loss of dreams and sanity, they will soon kill me. They will, or their families, or their messengers. Perhaps, I think, there is still time for me to escape to my parents' old Homeland, where there are herds and rivers and the fresh smell of dew on the morning grasses. He used to tell me, my father, how the poor hung a hunk of meat or a single fish above the heads of their families as they ate their mealie pap. She would tell me, my mother, that she could taste the flesh even as her tongue pushed the maize into her hungry belly.

I sigh, put down the hammer, pull up my clothing, and emplace the eye patch I have taken to wearing. As has been so often true since the coming of the worm, I have delivered no stool. I release the wooden latch and ease into the morning. Smoke pours from a fire lit in the upholstery of two car seats ransacked from God knows where. It chokes the sky, tinging the sun rust-brown. Liquor bottles, most of them broken, litter the narrow streets.

I look for the men whose angry murmurings invaded the outhouse and see only two turbaned women, children clutching at their skirts.

I have made it into one more morning, but I have nothing left to trade. The worm demands to be fed, but those men who have kept their dreams intact have heard the warning cries of the others. If they do not join their friends in battering me to death, they will kill me with their refusals to allow me into their beds.

Walking back to my shanty, I listen to the talk of the women in the streets. Slowly, I begin to understand that, this time, I am not at the root of the fury that I hear.

The fury comes from a very different place; it comes from a new hatred—a growing hatred for the man who was once their hero and who is now, they say, the white man's concessionary tool. He wants to give us *their* dreams, they say, and we do not want them. We want our own.

That is when I realize that I do indeed have something to trade, something only I can give to the people of the township.

I know Nelson Mandela. I can take their message to him. I can tell him that it is not refrigerators or manicured lawns for which they yearn, but lives of value by their own standards. I will take their night dreams in trade, and give them back their daydreams of a dignified, black African life.

—~—

Almost midnight. Alone and walking the dark streets of Soweto I inhale the smell of paraffin—the drink of the hopeless—the reek of sex, and the sound of tin drums and pennywhistles.

It has happened as I predicted.

Almost.

In the year that has passed, the men of Soweto gave me their night dreams and I fed the worm; I carried their daydreams to Mandela. He listened . . . and did nothing. He gives fine speeches and has good intentions which serve to pacify the world and gain him honors, but nothing has really changed.

Nothing except my eye, which bulges beneath its patch and the hatred of the people of Soweto that is now my only companion. I have not looked at my eye for weeks because I am afraid of what I will see. No one halfway decent will talk to me, let alone bed me. I have no money to leave the township, no courage to remove the scourge from my eye. I no longer hate myself, envy the survivors, or pity my . . . the worm's . . . victims. They avoid me like a leper when I walk the night streets of Soweto, begging to gain entrance to any stranger's bed. I am suffering so severely from sleep deprivation that I often do not know who I am, frequently cannot find my way back to my own home. I refuse to entertain the possibility of there being any sense or order to the maze that is Soweto, and blame this randomness for my confusion.

Though I do not know where I am going, I move quickly, silently, feeling an odd sense that, despite the jagged chaos of the streets, I am about to come full circle. I have stopped looking over my shoulder for attackers out to take revenge upon me, and I even sleep without aids, mostly in the heat and clatter and chatter of the afternoons. My sleep remains without dreams. As all the sleep of Soweto is, one way or another, without dreams. Except for the dreams Mandela spins, hallucinations of false security. I no longer envy or deny him his punishment, power, or position, but if I could I would tell him that I understand that one man cannot satisfy all the longings of mankind.

No more than any number of men can satisfy the worm who has swallowed my dreams and those of the males of Soweto.

I stop at a door—the door of this night's hope. The owner of the home is a man who may not yet know of my affliction, for he only today returned from a year in Johannesburg, where he went in search of the better life he was promised during the choreographies surrounding Mandela's release. Before he left, he painted his door a bright red, with a single white chalk mark down the middle. The decor, he claimed, signified the role of the African in the white man's world, though how or why he wouldn't say. Frankly, I doubt he knew. None of us here know anything really, despite our protestations. I'm not sure we ever did. Know. Anything.

Only loa loa claims to know what is worthy, and what it knows it won't reveal.

I knock lightly on the door and enter without invitation. It opens easily to my touch, as if in a dream, almost as though someone else were opening it and ushering me inside. The ceiling is so low that I must stoop; the tools of a leather worker's trade are cluttered on the floor. From the back of the room, I hear raspy breathing, broken intermittently by sleep-mutterings. I have forgotten his name, though I have known him since childhood. The names have disappeared along with my dreams since the worm invaded my eye.

I draw back the dirty curtain separating his sleeping area from the rest of the room, wondering what silly modesty spurred the man to hang up the thing in the first place. I stand with my back to the moonlight that is filtering in through the small window, so that he will not be able to see me clearly.

"It is Nssessebe, come to welcome you home," I say.

He opens his eyes and smiles.

I picture his face crisscrossed with the silky threads of the worm's web and crawl into his bed.

We make love greedily, he avoiding the eye after I explain that I have a bad case of conjunctivitis. When he falls asleep, I do the work of the worm. Then I sleep, too, sucking in his dreams before the worm devours them. I wake refreshed, for the first time in months, and roll away slightly, making no effort to cover my naked belly or my breasts, and stare at the wall. His hand falls from my shoulder, his mouth sputters, and I turn to watch as he scratches his face, the web mildly irritant, as if slapping at a fly. I lean over, his breath hot against my neck, and peel away the web. Again he stirs, the intoxicant lifted.

In the space behind my eye, like the darkness behind the moon, the worm writhes, and in my blood beats the souls of the races of men. *"Leather worker, woman-worker, Soweto swine,"* the worm whispers, *"this man's dreaming is done. Forever."*

For a moment I am filled with sorrow at what I have done, for I know that the anger this man brought with him when he returned to the township is as nothing compared with the chaos this new loss will bring in its wake.

Chaos, and more anger.

Men without sleep die in agony, but without dreams they die a more terrible death.

The old-friend stranger who will soon be my enemy touches the back of my hand as I rise to depart, web splayed between my fingers like the threaded make-believe of a clever child. I have never taken one with me before and I do not know why I do so now. Perhaps I know somewhere in the depths of my being that this is the last time.

There are no more strangers to bring me temporary peace.

I am glad he cannot see me clearly as I leave in the semidarkness. If he could he might see that the mockery is gone from my good eye and that in its place there is pleading. I look down hard at him and think of my belly that never cocooned a child, my thighs stained with his sperm. There have been so many. Men. Webs. Whispered words.

When, with what man, did I cross the chasm into madness, my sanity siphoned by the inexhaustible need of loa loa?

"It was the worm who cajoled me," I whisper. "The worm in my eye."

I back out of the room. The web seems to sing with dreams between my fingers. I determine that, after I wear it for a night on my face in the hope that some vestige of a dream will return, I will lay it amid layers of damp dirty chamois acrawl with grubs, and watch it die as the cloth dries. Or perhaps I will place it in a container, like the silkworms my father raised in boxed darkness, his phallic sticks thrust up like flagpoles at each corner. Were they kin to the worm that inhabits me? They were as white as the loa loa is made of shadows.

Is Mandela kin to de Klerk?

Are dreams related to nightmares?

Is Mankind father to man?

There is much that I fear to know.

I step into the street, dust puffing with each footfall, and can hear the din as I hurry away. It seems to come from all sides, like termites eating away at Soweto's edges.

For the first time since this all began, I pose the old question: Why, when I fought apartheid as vigorously as the rest, was I spared from punishment?

I suspect that the worm knows.

I suspect that, could I but dream again, I would learn an answer I would fear to share, even with myself.

The din grows louder, and I see dark men scurry between shacks like cockroaches trying to stay out of the light.

I move faster, but it is difficult to run, lest I break the web and dispel what may be left of its dreams. Fear ruffles like feathers along my spine. I glance back to see my last lover staring at me from his doorway, and I wonder how many men's balls I have held since the dream-feeding frenzy began.

Running now, hand over the eye patch like a naked woman trying to cover too much with only two hands, I know that this is not the first lynching the worm has inspired—that men have made love to loa loa throughout history.

To their dismay.

To the demise of their dreams.

Children spill from between shacks, from around corners, gripping pieces of rusted metal and sharpened sticks roughly fashioned into assegais, their shirts hanging open, buttonless, their tattered trousers and jeans chevroned with paint stripes vaguely reminiscent of those worn by warriors in the stories their grandparents have told them. Their eyes are hungry. Hungry.

For blood, not food.

Four of my former lovers, linked as much by their madness as by the chain they are holding, outflank me before I can reach the alley to my house, where a Karbiner 95 awaits from the years when Mandela strode in defiance rather than compromise and accommodation. I find myself walking backward, glancing from face to face as the circle tightens.

"Have you forgotten what I can do for you?" I call out. "I can bring you hope."

Hope, fragile and lethal, I think.

The men's faces remain impassive.

"Don't you know who I am?"

They come on, lifting their weapons.

They know who I am. I am the servant of the dream stealer.

I raise the web as if to emphasize its significance, wondering if these men who no longer dream know what a dream catcher is. Or care.

I turn and sprint between shanties, sending hens squawking, tearing past clothes hanging to dry, knocking over a pail of soapy water. Looming as if in a dream, the open door of the outhouse beckons.

There is nowhere else to go.

I enter, slam shut the door, and latch it as my lovers converge.

"Go away, I tell you!"

They do not go. They beat on the walls—first with fists, then with sticks and with metal. The building rocks. I let go of the web and brace my hands against the walls as the outhouse tips and yaws. My eyes are so wide that even in the dimness I can see something dark crawl across my pupil, making an untimely passage as if in protest against my murderous thoughts. While the building pitches my fingers search for the hammer I left leaning against the wall.

It is still there. As I seize the thing, the shaking stops and the building settles.

There is a clanking and rattling. Then, silence. In some faraway recess, the words I hear each morning when I awake from a night of single-image dreaming returns: *In my blood beats the souls of the races of men.* I summon a strength I have not known since those days long ago, the times of confrontation: "What now, you little bastards!"

There is no answer.

Clutching the hammer, I release the latch. I push at the door. It opens just enough for sunlight to slip through.

The door has been chained shut.

I hear the roar of raised voices. At first I think it is the men outside, but then I realize the sound is further away. Cheering follows, and applause, and then the cacophony of drums and untuned trumpets. I hear the raised voices of my lovers, the men of Soweto.

"Mandela," they shout.

"Uhuru." Freedom.

I hear them and I raise the hammer and release the blood in which beats the souls of the races of men.

Stigmata

Jean-Daniel Brèque

Richard turned to her and said, "This must be the safest place in the city. Who would be crazy enough to plant a bomb in a cemetery?"

Kelly didn't feel safe at all. They had just arrived in Paris, and the whole trip was already looking like a bust. First there was that long and exhausting flight. She'd felt pretty smart at O'Hare asking for a seat near the emergency exit, but the door was right behind her, and she couldn't lower her seat. Richard had slept fine, thank you, but she'd only managed a nap, and the nightmare had awakened her.

It was an old friend, this nightmare. She wakes up alone in her bed. Richard's shirts and pants are gone from the closet, his toothbrush from the sink, his favorite records from the shelves. She walks from room to room, touches his favorite chair, picks up drinking glasses in search of his fingerprints. And all the things he has ever put his mark on slowly disappear, even the wallpaper (he'd selected it as soon as they moved in together) and the garage-sale furniture (there wasn't a piece he hadn't fixed). Until the whole apartment is empty, bare walls and bare ground. Even her clothes are gone, for she always asked for his opinion before buying a dress, a blouse, a skirt.

Alone in the emptiness, she wants to cry, but her eyes remain desperately dry. She lifts her hand to wipe off her absent tears, but it never touches her cheek. For it is disappearing, too. She sees the wall through her skin and bones, but the wall is almost gone—or rather, her eyes are. Then she realizes that, without Richard, she is nothing.

She'd managed to put the dream out of her mind, but they had no sooner landed than the real problems started. Their suitcases did eventually appear on the luggage claim belt, but it seemed that the backpack with her maps and guidebooks had been flown to Madrid.

On the way to the city, the taxi driver upped the volume of his radio. It was not a song he wanted to hear, however, but a news bulletin. When Richard asked him what the fuss was about, he went into a long-winded rant that Kelly's high school French allowed her to translate only in part. Richard was glad to oblige. "There's been an explosion in the Quartier Latin," he said. "Not far from our hotel, actually. Some fundamentalist Muslims planted a bomb in the subway." She was almost tempted to ask the driver to go back to the airport, but said nothing.

"Tell me when we'll see the Eiffel Tower," she asked Richard.

He burst into laughter. "C'mon, Kellog. You should have studied your damn maps better. We're entering Paris by the east side; the tower is way out west."

How she hated it when he called her Kellog! "My cornflake girl," he sometimes added. Could she help it if she was tall, blonde, and healthy-looking?

He snapped her out of her reverie. "C'mon, let's see if we can find Jim Morrison's tomb."

She followed him reluctantly. The Père Lachaise cemetery, it seemed, also doubled as a park and was full of pram-pushing young mothers, elderly Parisians out for a stroll, and students out for a lark. They had been walking there for half an hour, but she had yet to see genuine mourners. The trees and the sunshine would have made them out of place, she thought.

Kelly couldn't remember the cemetery's precise location inside Paris. Her sense of direction was dreadful, and she hadn't had time to get her bearings in the city. And besides, she had learned at least one thing that made fun of all her efforts: Paris was full of various signs supposed to point the way to museums, monuments, and the like, but only the Parisians were able to decipher them—which they never bothered to do, nonetheless flowing from one place to the other with unfailing accuracy.

Richard used to say she was addicted to maps, and she'd thought the ones she'd got in Chicago would help her. "Forget it," he'd said this morning when she wanted to buy some in a bookstore near their hotel. "I've spent two years in the City of Light, and I know my way around it." Which was true, she had to admit. If only he'd consented to plan the day's outing, she would have been willing to trust him. But only chance, it seemed, guided him in his expeditions.

They had walked around the old Opéra; then he wanted to show her the new one built on *Place de la Bastille*—"I'm told it's a real eyesore," he said—but the subway line was closed when they went down into the station. The bombing that took place the day before had claimed five lives, plus caused an untold number of flesh wounds. Policemen were on the lookout, and the Métro was subject to various dysfunctions: as soon as somebody reported a suitcase—or even a paper bag—lying on the ground, the alert was given and traffic came to a standstill. "I've got an idea," Richard had said. "Let's take the number three line and have a look at Père Lachaise."

She looked around her. She had to admit it was a nice place, and maybe a safe one. The cemetery was built on a hillside, and most—if not all—of the lanes wound their ways downward. From time to time, the trees parted to reveal a vista of roofs and chimneys. She heard the sinister wail of a police siren, but the sky was perfectly blue, the leaves perfectly green, and she allowed herself to relax.

Richard was a bit disappointed, however. "The place has changed a lot since I was here," he said. "Looks like they're trying to prettify it." He pointed to a row of tombs. "These are new. I remember that this part of the grounds was grown over with weeds."

"Hush," she said to him. "There's a party of mourners over there."

He smiled. "Those people are not mourners. They're celebrants."

The tomb she had just noticed was quite weird. It looked like a set of standing stones, full to bursting with flowers, with a bust nestled among them. A small group of people were walking around it, mumbling verse and stroking the stones.

"This is the grave of Allan Kardec," Richard said, "the founding father of spiritualism. Still a cult figure today. Speaking of which . . . "

He turned to her and gave her a dazzling smile. How she loved that smile! Richard had a homely face, nondescript hair, and a five o'clock shadow that only his antique razor seemed able to smooth off, but the first time she'd seen that smile, she'd nearly melted. They'd been living together for two years now, they'd had their ups and downs, but she couldn't imagine life without him—"cornflake girl" or not.

He took her hand and led her among the graves. "There's another spot you have to see. We'll get to Jim Morrison later."

She saw several tombstones with American names as they walked. Could any of her countrymen actually have wished to be buried here? She shuddered at the thought of her grave being looked over by tourists. Still, some of the tombs were worth the sight. Richard explained that, given the number of celebrities buried here, a lot of nouveaux riches had bought plots in Père Lachaise during the nineteenth century, building for their last sleep huge mausoleums which were paeans to bad taste.

After meandering through the tombs, they stopped in a tree-shaded alley and Richard said, "Here he is. Victor Noir."

She looked down at the grave. It was decorated with a bronze statue of a man lying prone with a hat at his feet, who looked as if he had died just after saying hello to someone. "Who was he?" she asked.

"Essentially a nobody. A young reporter who was sent by his editor to interview the emperor's brother. That worthy was so outraged that he shot young Victor in the head. He died instantly, and there was a great uproar in the country. Victor Hugo himself attended his funeral—Napoleon the Third and his immediate family weren't among his favorite people—and a sculptor was asked to make a statue of his corpse."

"So he became famous by dying?"

"Not quite. His *statue* became famous." Richard smirked. "Look at it closely and you'll understand why."

She did so. At first she saw nothing out of the ordinary, but then she noticed that a part of the statue looked considerably more worn down than the others. Richard laughed when he saw her blush.

"I don't know if poor Victor Noir was as well-endowed as this in real life," he said, "but the artist made a stallion out of him. Soon, women started coming here to touch him in the hope that they would get pregnant." He put an arm around her waist. "According to some rumors, Victor's feet are also honored, though in a different way." He looked in all directions. "Nobody around. Want to try?"

It took her a few seconds to understand his meaning. "Are you crazy?" she said—but she couldn't help looking at the statue's upturned feet. They looked worn down, too, but nevertheless quite solid. She was surprised to find herself a bit excited. Richard had asked her to put on a skirt this morning, instead of her usual jeans. Had he intended right from the beginning that. . . ?

He took her in his arms and kissed her. She tensed a bit, then allowed herself to relax. When he broke the kiss, he smiled and took her hand. She sighed inwardly when he walked away from the statue.

"All right, let's try and find the Lizard King," he said. "It's easy: look for the graffiti."

"What?"

"All the people who come here to have a look at his tomb scrawl directions everywhere. As soon as you see 'Jim,' follow the arrows."

But they never got to Jim Morrison's last home. As they came to a crossroads, Richard decided to take a shortcut among the tombs, and they soon had to ascend a small wooded hill. Richard was enjoying the scenery now. "This is the Père Lachaise I remember," he said, pointing to a big tree whose gnarled roots were springing from an open grave. "Look, you see this kind of thing everywhere."

Kelly saw two tombs stuck together; from each of them grew a stone arm, and the two hands were joined. "Husband and wife," Richard said. "Even death couldn't part them."

Kelly was about to say something—what, she couldn't remember afterward—when she stumbled on the uneven ground and fell on one of the twin graves.

Richard came to her rescue, and if he had put his hand on her waist instead of her ass, maybe nothing would have happened. She gasped, and he must have mistaken her surprise for excitation, for his hand started to wander under her skirt.

It took her a few moments to realize what he was doing. The thought of him making love to her in a cemetery was so preposterous that her mind didn't register it at once. When it did, it was too late, for Richard's fingers were slipping into her, and she *was* excited.

"No," she tried to say. "Not here—"

But he closed her mouth with his.

All things considered, it was not the best of experiences. Although they were in a secluded spot, she kept looking around fearfully, and she hardly felt Richard tearing off her panties and slipping his penis into her. Maybe she would have given in to the moment if she hadn't glimpsed some potential witnesses. She almost cried out, but then she saw that the five people she had noticed were totally oblivious to their coupling.

The most startling of them was the sole woman of the lot, a fat fifty-something hag who was standing on a tomb. She seemed to be in a trance, and the four men who surrounded her watched her with hungry eyes. She unbuttoned her blouse, then threw it on the ground. Her breasts were enormous. She exposed them to the admiration of the four men, then took her breasts in her hands and lifted them. The men tensed.

"What the fuck is this?" Richard said. He had noticed the group, too. "Hey, we're not the only ones who like to fool around among the dead." He fondled Kelly's breasts, somewhat more roughly than he was usually wont to. She wanted to tell him to stop, but couldn't say a word.

A mouth had appeared under the woman's right breast. First it was a pale scar, but then it got steadily redder and redder, until its lips parted and a trickle of blood started to seep from it. The woman seemed to be satisfied by her audience's reaction, for she let go of her breasts, hiding the bloody mouth from view.

But the ceremony—for such it was, Kelly felt certain—was not ended. The woman opened her arms and turned her hands toward her congregation. Kelly was not at all surprised to see a mouth in each palm.

"Stigmata," Richard whispered.

He seemed to be in a trance, too, and Kelly noticed that the rhythm of his thrusts was following the pulsations of the woman's wounds. The mouths' lips were slowly moving, like an obscene parody of a vulva, and she saw the men starting to sway on their feet, following the same rhythm.

The woman pointed toward one of them, and he walked to her, knelt at her feet, and kissed her right hand.

Kelly almost threw up, but Richard continued to fuck her, and his frenzy grew as the kneeling man hungrily sucked the blood that was oozing from the woman's hand. She could see his tongue darting out from his mouth like a fat leech. He must be the woman's favorite, Kelly thought, for when he was done, she let him suck at her other hand. Soon he was shuddering from head to foot, and at the same instant he took his bloodied face from the pulsating wound, Richard came in her.

His hand fell from Kelly's breast, and she turned around to give him a dressing-down he would remember for a long time. But she saw with dismay that he had fainted.

She turned toward the celebrants, who were already starting to walk away. The woman was buttoning her blouse, and her favorite was cleaning her hands with a handkerchief, which he put to his face afterward, then dropped on the ground.

Kelly decided to wait until they had gone before looking at Richard. When nobody was in view, she got up from the tomb, but felt a trickle of sperm run onto her thigh. Maybe Richard needed to get to a hospital, she thought, but she had to clean herself before she started looking for an ambulance. She rummaged in her handbag: there were a few tampons, a hotel brochure, but no Kleenex. And Richard's pockets were empty.

She turned toward the handkerchief left by the celebrant. She had no choice. If a tourist had come upon her as she walked the few yards from one tomb to the other, he or she would have been intrigued by her steps, which were very similar to those of a clumsy hopscotch player. But none appeared, and she managed to get to the handkerchief, pick it up, and clean herself—more or less. It was by sheer reflex that she folded it into the brochure and put it in her bag: never in her life would she have left litter in a cemetery.

When she came back to Richard, she saw her torn panties on the ground, and she put them in her bag, too. She zippered up Richard's fly, then slapped him a few times, but he didn't wake up.

"Is he dead?" said somebody behind her.

She noticed two things simultaneously: that piping voice belonged to a child, and he or she spoke English. She turned around and saw a boy with a Disneyland Paris T-shirt. His eyes were huge.

"No," she said, "he had a sunstroke. Are your parents nearby?"

The boy nodded.

"Could you please tell them to come here?"

Another nod, then the boy fled.

Thank God for take-charge American tourists, Kelly thought fifteen minutes later in the taxi. Mr. and Mrs. Avila of St. Teresa, Florida, had fussed over her for only two minutes. Then, after making sure that Richard was definitely not dead—their son had somewhat distorted the truth—they had led her to the cemetery's main entrance, Mr. Avila helping a still-dazzled Richard to walk, and hailed her a taxi rather than calling for an ambulance. Mrs. Avila, who was a registered nurse, told Kelly that her husband—Kelly made no effort to correct her on that point—was most likely suffering from jet lag.

The taxi reeked of cigar smoke, but the driver knew their hotel. They arrived there before dark, she told the clerk that everything was okay, thank you, and then she dumped Richard on the bed and allowed herself a huge sigh.

Today's lunch was only a memory, and she was hungry—sex always had the same effect on her, cemetery or not. But seeing Richard sleeping so soundly made her realize how tired she was.

She took off her shoes, pushed him aside, lay down, and fell asleep at once.

When she woke up, he was gone.

The nightmare had become reality. Richard was gone, and everything around her—the wallpaper, the furniture, her clothes—would soon start to disappear, until it was her turn to slowly fade away. She tensed, stared at her surroundings.

But nothing happened.

She wasn't at home. She was in a strange room, in a strange city. This wallpaper hadn't been selected by Richard; he had never fixed this chest of drawers. As for her clothes, she was still wearing them, and she clutched at them desperately. They felt solid.

When the tears came, it was as if scales were falling from her eyes. Even though a liquid veil was blurring things around her, she *knew* the world was here and would stay here.

Even though Richard was gone.

She filed this thought in her mind. It needed to be examined more closely, but she had to act fast. She reviewed her options while she took a shower, then selected a blouse and a pair of jeans from the closet.

The nightmare came back to her as soon as she stepped out of the hotel—or more precisely, a part of it she had never remembered until now: there were some things of hers that Richard never touched. He claimed he didn't need them, and it was true.

Kelly looked around her. Richard had chosen to stay in this hotel because it was right in the middle of the Quartier Latin. This was, he said, one of the friendliest parts of the city, home of the university he had attended eight years ago; thanks to the student population, the streets were full of cheap restaurants, art-movie houses, and bookstores. The one on the other side of the street had a full display of maps and guidebooks.

Fifteen minutes later, she was sitting in a café, sipping a cup of dreadfully strong coffee and perusing a map of the City of Light. She located the cemetery, quickly selected the Métro lines that would take her there, then walked to the nearest station.

While she waited on the platform, she noticed a map of the subway network and began to study it. Colored lines were uncoiling among the white-on-gray streets, and every time she followed one from end to end, she felt her heartbeat grow stronger, more steady. It was as if she had in front of her a diagram of her body, with all her veins and arteries duly laid out. Still, the diagram was not complete, for graffiti hid some parts of it, as if the city were bleeding many-colored inks.

She noticed that her fellow passengers were tense, and that the Arabs who boarded the trains got some mean stares. If Richard had been with her, his dark hair and five o'clock shadow would have marked him as a potential suspect. She changed lines twice, and saw black-clad cops in the hallways. The city was under siege.

When she walked into the Père Lachaise cemetery, the first thing she saw was a board announcing: *Carte du cimetière: 10 francs.* She thought at first that *carte* meant postcard, or playing card, but she remembered that the word also meant map. Well, that was a map she would play for all its worth.

She quickly located Victor Noir's grave; from there, she would have no trouble finding the twin tombs upon which they had made love.

There was nobody around the grave upon which the fat woman had stood. Kelly sighed. What had she expected? To burst among the celebrants, grab Richard's hand, and run like hell? Richard had probably joined the bleeding woman's flock, but it was unlikely she lived in the cemetery, and maybe the ceremony didn't take place daily.

As she walked back to the gates, a man rose from behind a tree and stood before her. "Give it to me," he said.

She froze, then took a step backward. The man jumped at her.

And fell to the ground.

"Please," he said. "Give it to me."

She recognized him: it was the fat woman's favorite, the one who had sucked at her hands. What could he possibly want? Then she knew. She opened her bag, took out the handkerchief. His eyes lit up and he raised his hand toward it.

"Not so fast," she said. "First, I need some answers."

"Please—"

"Where is Richard?"

"Richard?" The man coughed; a trickle of pale blood ran onto his chin. "So his name is Richard? No matter now."

"Where is he?"

"You'll never see him again. Give me what's mine."

"Come and get it."

The man tried to stand up. Failed. "I beg you—"

"What do you want this thing for?" Kelly said. She unfolded the handkerchief. "It's too dirty to be of any use. But it's quite nice." Was she really saying these words? Was she really able to taunt this poor excuse for a human being who drooled at her feet? "I think I'll keep it. But I'll need to clean it, of course."

"Please, give me a drop, just a drop."

She looked at the handkerchief, and she almost let it go when she saw that the woman's blood—which had been dry when she unfolded the thing—was now wet and spreading over the linen. She took pity on the man and dabbed his lips with it.

He sighed. "Thank you, thank you." A beat. "More, please."

"Where is Richard?"

He looked up. His eyes seemed more alive now. "He came to her place tonight. She had called him, of course. I never imagined her new lover would be a stranger."

Kelly flinched. "What do you mean?"

"You don't understand, do you?" The man started to laugh, then spat out a gob of blood. "Forget your boyfriend and go back to America. I wish I could take the first plane out, but I will die shortly. I can't live without her blood—and she doesn't want me anymore. She wants your *Richard.*" A brief pause, then: "Please, give me this handkerchief."

"Where does this woman live?"

The man laughed. "Look, she betrayed me, all right. But I won't betray her." He frowned. "I can't help it."

"I'll keep it, then." She put the handkerchief into her bag, then waited. The man stared at her.

"What are you waiting for?" he said after a few moments. "Go away!"

His voice was barely a whisper, and Kelly noticed with dismay that his skin was starting to dry up. His hair was falling from his skull; a yellowish tooth rolled down his chin, then another, then another still. The end of his nose detached itself, and suddenly there was a hideous gap under his eyes. "This is what love does to you," he gasped. "It bleeds you dry."

Kelly closed her eyes. When she opened them, there was only a bunch of clothes on the ground. And the handkerchief in her bag was dry again.

The days that followed saw her falling into a routine. Her alarm clock awoke her at seven o'clock, she ate breakfast at the nearest café, then she took the Métro and spent the whole day in the cemetery, leaving it only at noon to buy a sandwich in a bakery. She saw nothing of Paris except the subway and the streets around Père Lachaise, but it was enough to realize that the City of Light had fallen under a cloud of darkness. People were eyeing each other with suspicion, and it seemed that the darker your skin was, the more dangerous you were. Policemen were everywhere, like antibodies whose mission was to expel foreigners from the bloodstream. Kelly was often ashamed of her "cornflake girl" looks.

She soon knew the Père Lachaise as if she'd been born there. The numerous cats that prowled the grounds came to beg scraps of food from her. She did her best to go unnoticed, and rather than staying near the place where she had seen the woman, she spent her time walking among the graves.

One day, her wanderings brought her to Jim Morrison's tomb. Richard had been right: she had seen the word "Jim" scrawled on a tombstone, and arrows had pointed the way to him. But she didn't need them; neither did she need the map she had bought at the cemetery's entrance. She knew it by heart now.

Her heart missed a beat when she arrived at the singer's resting place. A group of people were milling around the tomb, and she thought at first that it was the fat woman and her congregation. But these celebrants were much younger, and it was a substance other than blood that they were absorbing. A needle went from arm to arm, a teenage girl fell on the ground and moaned, an unshaven man shuddered ecstatically. Not far away a young boy was eyeing the proceedings with a hungry look; Kelly recognized Mr. and Mrs. Avila's son. She felt her throat tighten: his turn would come. Maybe his body would be found among the graffiti-strewn tombs that surrounded Morrison's bust, whose nose was conspicuously absent. She thought of the fat woman's favorite and shivered.

Whenever her feet brought her to the top of a hill, she turned toward the cemetery sprawled before her and mentally connected the alleys she glimpsed here and there with the ones on the map. The Père Lachaise was a city within the city, with its squares and avenues, its crossroads and gardens. And just as the map of Paris she had studied in the subway had made her think of her body, the map of the cemetery conjured the image of another body inside her own, a dormant mind that was slowly awakening.

It was alive, this mind, although she associated it with a dead place. It was pestering her, asking questions for which she had no answers. Was it this mind which had taken control of her when she had met the fat woman's favorite? She couldn't say. Every time she took the subway to go from the hotel to the cemetery, her fellow passengers seemed dead to her eyes, as if terror had struck their very souls, as if the city of the dead was growing tendrils that were slowly invading the city of the living.

Richard did look dead when she saw him again.

His clothes were dirty, his cheeks grubby, his eyes without light. The fat woman had taken refuge in a mausoleum whose walls were crawling with obscene graffiti; Richard had joined her in the cramped space, and the other disciples were watching the ceremony from outside. They parted before Kelly as if she had been expected.

She felt the gaze of the fat woman upon her, but she only had eyes for Richard. He was oblivious to her presence; his lips were glued to the woman's hand, and he stopped sucking her blood only to utter little moans of pleasure. Kelly saw that the more blood he swallowed, the paler his skin became.

"Richard," she said. "Come back to me."

"He will never go back to you," the woman said. "He'll never go back to Belmont Avenue."

Kelly started. How could that woman know their address? What could Richard have told her?

The fat woman smiled. "He belongs to me now. Body and soul. I know everything about him, everything about you." A beat. "He loves me, more than he has ever loved you."

Kelly said nothing. One glance at Richard was enough to realize that the woman had told the truth. If she wanted him back, there was only one way.

She opened her handbag, unfolded the handkerchief, grabbed Richard's razor, and put the blade on the palm of her left hand.

Then she froze. She had darted a glance at the fat woman and read terror in her eyes. Kelly had been right. Maybe she didn't have natural stigmata, maybe she would have to cut herself with steel, but the end result would be the same: Richard would come to her, like a junkie to a needle.

But did she really want their love to become an addiction?

She came forward, the razor blade on her hand. "Richard," she said.

He turned to her, withdrew his lips from the pulsating wound, let the woman's hand drop, and started to get up.

She waited until he stood before her, then raised her hand and slashed his throat.

He was not as far gone as the favorite had been, and he took a long time to crumble away. Kelly didn't watch him die, for she had left almost at once. She had forgotten the other disciples, but she needn't have worried about them. As soon as she'd gone, they'd pounced on the fat woman, rushed into the mausoleum, and started to drink from her wounds. Her screams had soon been cut short.

On the way out of the cemetery, Kelly glimpsed a tomb similar to the one where Richard and she had made love a few days before. The two stone hands would be linked for eternity, or at least until the grave fell into neglect and was replaced by another. She now had the answers to the questions her new mind had asked her. It would always be with her, this mind, or at least until the day she died.

She had to find a name for it, and she did when she missed her next period.

The Dripping of Sundered Wineskins

Brian Hodge

I. *Media Vita in Morte Sumus*

It's said that William Blake spent nearly all of his life experiencing visitations by angels, or what he took to be angels, but my first time came when I was only seven, and I'd never heard of William Blake and was unaware that anything miraculous was happening. It may have been that my young age kept me from seeing her as anything other than entirely natural, much as I took for granted the checkpoints and the ever-present British soldiers who tried in vain to enforce peace in the Belfast of my childhood.

Or, more likely, I was in shock from the bomb blast.

It was years before I understood what was known as, with wry understatement, the Troubles: the politics and the hatreds between Protestants and Catholics, amongst Catholics ourselves, loyalists and republicans. As I later came to understand that day, the pub that had been targeted was regarded by the Provo IRA as a nest of opposition, lovers of queen and crown. To those who planted the bomb that should have killed me, a few more dead fellow Irish were but part of the cumulative price of independence. Funny, that.

Belfast is working-class to its core, and made mostly of bricks. They rained out of the blast erupting within the pub across the street from where two friends and I were walking home from school, late and chastised for some forgotten mischief we'd gotten up to. I knew the gray calm of an early autumn day, then fire and a roar, and suddenly I stood alone. One moment my friends had been walking one on either side of me, and in the next had disappeared.

"Don't look at them," she said, in a gentle voice not of the Emerald Isle, the first of two things I fully recall her telling me, even if I didn't know where she'd come from. It was only later, from the odd translucence of her otherwise light brown skin, that I realized she was unlike any woman I'd ever seen. "Don't look."

But look I did, and I remember the feel of her hand atop my head, although not to turn me from the sight; lighter, it was, as if even she were rendered powerless by my schoolboy's curiosity. *Well, now you've done it,* her touch seemed to be telling me. *Now you've sprung the lid on the last of that innocence.*

They both lay where they'd been flung, behind me, cut down by bricks propelled with the velocity of cannonballs. Nothing have I seen since that's looked any deader, with more tragic suddenness; and there I stood between them, untouched but for a scratch across my bare knee that trickled blood down my hairless shin.

I felt so cold my teeth chattered, and thought she then told me I must've been spared for a reason. It's always made sense that she would have. It's what angels say. And whatever reason she had, in the midst of an afternoon's chaos, for stooping to kiss away that blood from my knee, I felt sure it must've been a good one.

"Oh yes," I think she said, her lips soft at my knee, as if something there had confirmed her suspicions that in my survival there lay design.

Even today I can't say that the mysterious touch of her mouth didn't inspire my first true erection, if stubby and immature.

She looked up, smiling at me with my young blood bright upon her mouth. She nodded once toward the smoking rubble of the pub, once at the pitiful bodies of my lads, then said the other thing I clearly recall: "Never forget—this is the kind of work you can expect from people who have God on their side."

When I told my mother about her that night, how the smiling woman had come to me, I left out the part about her kissing away my blood. It had been one of those moments that children know instinctively to separate from the rest, and keep secret, for to share it would change the whole world. I saw no harm in sharing what she'd said to me, though; but when I did, my mother shook me by the shoulders as if I'd done something wrong.

"You mustn't ever speak of it again, Patrick Kieran Malone," she told me. Hearing my full name used meant there was no room for argument.

"Talk like that sounds like something from your uncle Brendan, and a wonder it is *he's* not been struck by lightning."

The comparison shocked me. The way she normally spoke of her brother Brendan made him out to be, if not the devil himself, then at least one of his most trusted servants. I protested; I was only repeating what the angel-lady said.

"Hush! Word of such a thing gets round, they'll be showing up one day to sink us to the bottom of a bog, don't you know."

Of course I wondered who she meant, and why they would feel so strongly about the matter, but as I think about it now I don't believe she even fully knew herself. She only knew that she had one more reason to be afraid of something at which she couldn't hit back.

There are all kinds of tyranny employed around us. Bombs are but the loudest.

To those things that shape us and decide the paths we take, there is no true beginning, not even with our birth, for many are in motion long before we draw our first breath. Ireland's monastic tradition predates even the Dark Ages, when the saint I was named for returned to the island where he'd once been a slave, to win it for Christianity. While that tradition is now but a sliver of what it used to be, when thriving monasteries housed hundreds of monks and friars, on the day I joined the Franciscan order my whole life felt directed toward the vows of poverty, chastity, and obedience.

For as long as I could recall, the mysteries of our Catholic faith had sparked my imagination, from the solemn liturgy of the priests, to the surviving architecture of our misty past, to the relics that had drawn veneration from centuries of believers. Ever thankful for my survival, my parents exposed me to as much of our faith as they could. They took me to visit the Purgatory of Saint Patrick, and to his retreat on Cruachan Aigli in County Mayo. Down in County Kerry we undertook pilgrimages to Mount Brandon and to the shrine of the Blessed Virgin in Kilmalkedar. I touched Celtic crosses that had been standing for a millennium, the weathered stone hard and sacred beneath my fingers.

Most mysterious of all to me was the three-hundred-year-old head of the newly canonized Saint Oliver Plunkett, staring from the splendor of his reliquary in Saint Peter's Church in Drogheda. Blackened skin stretched over his bald skull like leather; his upper lip had shriveled back from his teeth to give him the start of a smile, and I could stare at him in full expectation that those dry lips would continue to move, to whisper some message for me alone.

It held no terrors for me, that severed head of his. I'd seen the dead before, and a damn sight fresher than old Oliver was.

Of the ethereal woman who came and went unnoticed on that day death had come so close, for years I hoped she might show herself again so I could put to her the questions I was old enough now to ask, and felt a deep ache that she did not. The mind reevaluates what's never validated, giving it the fuzzy edges of a dream, and as I grew taller, older, there were days I almost convinced myself that that was all she'd been; that I'd hallucinated a beautiful, compassionate adult because she was what I needed at the moment, since so many others around me were busy killing each other.

But on those nights I dreamt of her, I knew better. I could never have invented anything so radiant out of thin air. Every few months, a dream so crystalline would unfold inside me it felt as if she were in the same room, watching. Angel, phantom, whatever she was, she was as responsible as anything for my joining the Franciscans of Greyfriars Abbey in Kilkenny, for she had done so much to open my eyes to the things of the spirit, and to inspire my hunger to let them fill me.

"Does it hurt to become a saint?" I asked the first time I set eyes on those sunken leathery sockets of Oliver's.

"Some of them were hurt staying well true to the will of the Lord," my mother answered. "But on that day they were made saints they felt only joy, because they'd already been in Heaven a long, long time, in the company of their angels."

"Then that's what I want to be," I declared.

She smiled at such impudence, waiting until later to tell me that no saint had ever aspired to such, as the first thing they'd given up was ambition for themselves. Sainthood was something that happened later, usually decided by people who'd never known them in the flesh.

While I didn't claim to understand why it had to be that way, I tried to put vanity behind me like the childish thing it was . . . and remember I was still alive for a reason that would be revealed in God's own time.

II. *Corpus Antichristi*

The greatest irony about what drove me from the Order of Saint Francis is that it was nothing that hadn't been experienced by the very founder himself, nearly eight hundred years before.

The first time it happened to me was a Sunday morning in the abbey chapel, near the close of Mass. The Host had been venerated and the brothers and I knelt along the railing before the altar as Abbot O'Riordan worked his way down the row of us.

"The body of Christ," he would say, then rest a wafer upon a waiting tongue, while in our mouths the miracle would happen again and again—the bread become the actual flesh of our Lord, and the wine His Saviour's blood. "The body of Christ."

Awaiting my turn, I often contemplated the crucifix hanging on the wall before us: life-size, a plaster Christ painted in the vivid colours of His suffering and passion. His dark eyes gazed heavenward, while from His brow and nail wounds blood streamed in the other direction. Every rib stood out clearly as He seemed to labor in agony for each breath.

"The body of Christ," said the abbot, before me now.

Only when I drew my hands from the railing to cup them beneath my chin, to catch the Host should it fall by accident, did I notice my own blood flowing from each wrist, where a nail might have been driven by a Roman executioner. Beneath my grey robe, my feet felt suddenly warm and wet.

And when the Host slipped from Abbot O'Riordan's fingers, it fell all the way to the hard floor, with no hands there to catch it and spare it from defilement. There it chipped into crumbling fragments of proxy flesh, to mingle with drops of blood that were entirely real.

—⁓—

There was no pattern to the stigmata's recurrence after the first time, just a gradual worsening of physical signs. Initially, blood only seeped like sweat through unbroken skin, but later the wounds themselves manifested in my flesh, deeper on each occasion, layer by layer—for scarcely a minute to begin with, until at last they lingered for as long as two hours before sealing up again.

I was examined over several months by a hierarchy of church representatives, all of them seeking a simple explanation, and I soon realized this was what they were hoping to find. The length and sharpness of my fingernails were checked repeatedly, and my routines became of intense fascination as they sought to discover some habit that might inflict deep blisters which would on occasion burst and bleed.

But Greyfriars was no reclusive monastery far from the modern world, where medieval-minded monks were turned out each sunrise to till the fields. In the quiet neighbourhoods of Kilkenny I taught Latin in the parochial school adjacent to the friary. The closest I came to fieldwork was teaching the declensions of *agricola.*

At least until the day I bled in class, and was removed from active staff.

For a faith founded on the resurrection of the dead, and sustained by centuries of miracles accepted as historically real as wars and plagues, the Church of my era I found to be reluctant to admit to the possibility of modern miracles. Worse, I began to feel I'd become more of an embarrassment than anything, a smudge of unfortunate dust that may have been *only* dust, but that they weren't yet willing to say was not divine, and therefore dust that they above all wished they might sweep aside so they wouldn't have to debate what more to do with it.

I believe what unsettled them most was that the wounds opened on my *wrists,* an anatomical verisimilitude shared by no stigmatic I'd ever heard of. Centuries of art and sculpture have depicted a crucifixion that never would've taken place, not with any self-respecting Roman soldier on the scene with a hammer and a fistful of nails. Say what you will of the Romans, they were no incompetents when it came to killing. They knew better than to nail some poor bugger up by his palms; the bones are too small. Nailing through the wrists was the only way to support the weight of the body and keep it on the cross without its tearing loose. But old images, fixed in the head and worn round the neck, are hard to kill, although I should think they'd give anyone a handy means for weeding the miraculous from the merely hysterical: If Jesus were to go to all the trouble of manifesting through the flesh of another, you'd think He'd at least want to get the facts straight.

This, more than anything, was what seemed to keep my priestly examiners from comfortably dismissing the whole matter. It'd been going on for nearly half a year before I was told, finally, that I was to be examined the next day by a tribunal arriving from Rome.

"I would ask you to spend the hours between now and then in prayer and fasting," Abbot O'Riordan told me. We were alone in his office and the door that he almost never closed was shut tight.

"All due respect, Father," I said, "I've been praying for a bit more insight ever since this started."

"Not for insight, that's not what I'm asking of you, but for how you'll answer their questions tomorrow. What you send back to Rome with them . . . *that's* what you need concern yourself with now."

"I thought all I'd send them back with was the simple truth about what's been happening."

"Do you even *know* what's happening to you, Patrick? Can you tell me the cause of it? There's been no getting to the bottom of it for six months, and you don't know how I prayed for an end to it before it got *this* far."

He lowered his head to his hands for a moment, as if he'd said too much; then, with those hands folded loosely together on his desk, he avoided my eyes and looked about the austere room.

"The Church," he said in a slow hush, "is built on a solid foundation of miracles from the past. But it's my belief—and I'm not alone in this—that the past is where they should stay. What's in the past remains fixed and constant. There's no reason to doubt it, no need to demand from it any greater explanation. There's no need to question it . . . only to believe in it. There it is and there it remains for all time, and it need never, ever change . . . because it's safely protected by time."

I stepped closer to him, aghast. "What threat could I pose to any of that?"

"Have you not yet understood why we've tried to keep this as quiet as we can? Spontaneous healings at shrines and apparitions of Mary are one thing. But give the laity another human being they see miracles in, and it opens up an entirely new channel for their faith. You don't want it any more than I do . . . because *they'll* want more from you. They *will.* No pun intended, Brother Patrick, but they'll bleed you dry, and in the end you can only disappoint them because you can't possibly give them as much as they'll want from you. And then they'll doubt, because disappointment can lead to cracks in the foundation of their faith. Cracks that might never appear if we but leave well enough alone."

He looked as sad as any man I had ever seen. "I'd never tell you how to conduct yourself tomorrow, or how to answer their questions. But God gave us a mind, Patrick . . . and the ability to anticipate the consequences of our actions. All I ask is that you go do that for me, and for the sake of the Church."

After the abbot sent me from his office, I paused in the cool, empty hall and stood before a painting that hung on the wall. I'd admired, even envied, it ever since first coming to the abbey.

It showed the martyrdom of Saint Ignatius, having been brought from Antioch to Rome to be tossed to the beasts in the Coliseum. With his left hand on his heart and the right outstretched in glory, as if he were making a grand speech of his suffering, his transcendent old eyes looked wide to the heavens. Supposedly he'd been eaten by two lions, but the beasts set upon him in the painting more resembled savage dogs, although no dogs I'd ever seen, with piglike snouts and eyes human in their cunning. The paws of the one tearing into his shoulder were spread wide like clawed hands. Often I wondered if the beasts weren't subtly intended to portray demons instead. But whatever they were, Ignatius had looked forward to meeting them. They were his transport to a Heaven he couldn't wait to get to.

"You were lucky," I whispered. "When you knew what tomorrow was bringing, they hadn't given you any choice in the matter."

—~—

I ate nothing for the rest of the day, nor that night, hoping that a fast would clear my mind. Long after Compline, the rest of the brothers asleep in their cells, I remained on my knees before the altar rail in the chapel. The only eyes on me were those of the cruciform Christ hanging on the wall. The only light was cast from the rack of votive candles to my left, filling the sanctuary with a soft glow and warm, peaceful shadows.

For hours I prayed for a resolution between my conflicting loyalties—to the mission of the Church, and to the purpose of whatever had chosen to work through me. I couldn't see why these two aims had to exclude one another.

In the chapel's hush, I heard the soft plink of drops as they began falling to the floor nearby. Distracted, I checked both wrists but found them dry. Probably some leak in the roof, I told myself. I pushed it from my ears, and from my heart tried to push the pique I felt over that reflex to check for my own blood in the first place, that this ordeal had done such a thing to me.

I prayed for the ugliness rising in me to recede like muddied waters. There should be no place within me for anger, I believed, but felt it more and more as the hours passed. Part of me raged against Abbot O'Riordan and the others like him, so concerned with the status quo that they preferred to turn a blind eye on anything in their midst that threatened to disrupt their lives of routine.

The dripping sound seemed to become more insistent, as if the flow had increased—or perhaps my growing annoyance with it, I reasoned, was only making it appear louder.

There was more at work here than blood and transitory wounds, yet they all behaved as if what was happening through me was happening mindlessly, devoid of purpose. Yet there had to be a logic behind it, and therefore a reason . . . else why should it occur at all?

The dripping grew heavier still, like the thick spatter of rainwater on the ground beneath the clogged gutters of a house. It killed the last of the prayer on my lips. When the chapel's broken hush was ripped by a scream that resounded from the chilly stone, at first I wasn't sure it hadn't come from me.

But no—I hadn't the lungs for any cry as terrible as this.

I stood at the railing, facing the back of the chapel to see who might've walked in on me, but no one was there; the door hung motionless. From the shadows I heard the wet sound of something tearing, and a rustle, then a moist heavy thud, like that of an animal carcass collapsing to the killing floor, except that with it came a grunt that sounded unmistakably human.

When I turned round to the front again, to see if someone might have come through unnoticed from the sacristy, it took several moments for what I noticed to penetrate the layers of disbelief.

The cross on the wall hung empty, no Christ nailed to it now. Blood ran darkly gleaming down the stones from the foot of the cross and from both sides, and from each of these points jutted a crooked spike shellacked with coagulating gore.

From the deep shadows behind the altar there issued a rasp of breath, and a groan of agony. In none of it did I hear any hint of meekness—these were not the sounds of a man who'd gone willingly to his cross. And when from his concealment he began to rise, I started to back my trembling way down the aisle.

By the time I reached the rear of the chapel, he was standing in shadow, little of him to see in the flickering votives but for wet reflections of flame. He doubled halfway over, quaking in pain beyond imagining, as he began to move out from behind the altar.

My first impulse was to retreat all the way to my room—yet what if this truly was meant for me to see? I chose to seclude myself in the flimsy shelter of the confessional—remaining, but giving this apparition every chance to vanish. I drew the curtain behind me as I sat pressed against the far wall and hoped to be spared this sight, hoped that it was no more than a waking dream brought on by one night's hunger and six months of stress.

But closer it came, and even when I could not see it, I heard it. Down the aisle it moved, harsh breath growing more ragged as it neared me, each shuffling footstep louder than the one before, a meaty wet slap of torn flesh on stone.

The Christ seemed to linger outside the confessional, then I heard the rattling of the door to the priest's booth. On the other side of that thin wall the Christ settled heavily upon the seat, bringing with him a stifling reek of blood and sweat.

I pushed the curtain back again and in the dim light thrown by the votives looked down at my wrists, unbloodied, then at the partition separating me from this Christ who'd ripped free of his cross. The panel between us scraped open; through the screen I saw the outline of his head, misshapen with its wrapping of the crown of thorns. Fingers next—they clawed at the screen, then battered away until it buckled and fell out. The hand looked mangled beyond repair, and he held it up so I could see the damage it would never have sustained had that life-size crucifix been accurately rendered.

"Do you understand now?" he asked, in Latin.

"I'm . . . not sure," I whispered, but I suspected that I did. If sculptors couldn't get anatomical details right, how much easier might it have been for scribes to propagate other fallacies?

The Christ's head tilted forward to fill the tiny window. I was spared the worst of his burning and pain-mad gaze, his eyes veiled by the hair straggling blood-caked from beneath the thorns.

"Save me," he begged, again in Latin. "Save me from that impotent, slaughtered lamb they have made of me."

"You mean . . . you never died?"

"Everyone dies. Everyone and everything," he said. "But there is no salvation in anyone's death but your own . . . and sometimes not even then."

"What . . . what of your being the Son of God, then?"

"There are many gods. There are many sons conceived by rape." For a moment he was still, almost contemplative; then he reached through the opening with a filthy arm, torn hand clamping upon my wrist. "The things I've seen, the secrets he keeps . . . if babies were born remembering these things, they would tear apart their mothers trying to return to the womb."

His hand felt hot and wet, the splintered bones as sharp as nails, gouging deep scratches where before my flesh had opened of its own accord. He held fast as our blood mingled.

"*Demon est Deus inversus,*" he said, a phrase born of ancient heresy, yet coming now from the one I'd thought to be my Saviour.

He released me then, his arm withdrawing like a serpent back to its lair. A moment later I heard him abandon the confessional, and hurriedly I drew my curtain again, so I wouldn't have to see him passing before me, lacerated and limping.

The footsteps receded into the chapel silence. For a moment I thought it might be safe to leave, but what I heard next persuaded me to remain until morning light had driven away every shadow:

The pounding of hammers.

When I came awake a few hours later and left the booth, the dawn showed no blood upon the walls, nor sticky footprints along the aisle. But I don't think I was expecting any, really.

Later on in the day, I told the tribunal from Rome that I'd been causing the stigmata myself, and showed them the fresh wounds on my wrist as evidence. The matter was officially closed. Abbot O'Riordan seemed greatly relieved, and only mildly distressed when I informed him that I planned to leave Greyfriars.

The prior night could have been a dream, and I might've found it easy to convince myself of that, as I'd nearly done with the spectral comforter who'd at least been substantial enough to kiss the blood from my knee. What evidence to the contrary did I have, except for some deep scratches on my wrist that I could've made myself?

None, but for unshakable conviction . . . and the other thing.

It went unnoticed until my last day with the order, as alone I stood in the chapel gazing silently up at the lurid crucifix and its Christ frozen in suffering like an ancient fly trapped in the amber of another epoch. The change in it was so subtle I doubted anyone else would even notice, and if they did, they'd merely dismiss their memories of how it had looked as being mistaken.

Surely, they'd tell themselves, their Saviour had been nailed up there through the wrists all along.

III. *Excommunio Sanctorum*

After the pinched faces and ectomorphic frames of most of my Franciscan brothers, the robust lumpiness of my Uncle Brendan came as a welcome change. He drove me away from Greyfriars with a ruddy scowl for the abbey, and only when we were rolling west through that green and treeless countryside did he break into a relieved grin and slap his big hard hand upon my leg.

"So. Which vow should we have you breaking first?" he asked.

Penniless, I'd turned to Uncle Brendan for help in making my new life. By renouncing the order in disillusion, I had become a shame to my devout family in Belfast. As they'd regarded Brendan the same for as long as I could recall, it was inevitable that two such black sheep as ourselves throw in together. I'd long realized he was hardly the devil my mother—his older sister—had painted him to be, for refusing to set foot in a church since before I was born and scoffing at nothing less than the Holy See itself.

"Some choose to face the world with a rosary in their hands, and some get more out of holding a well-pulled pint of stout," he said. "Not that one excludes the other, but at some point you *do* need to decide which is more fundamentally truthful."

I lived with him in Killaloe, northeast of Limerick, where at the southern tip of Lough Derg he rented out boats to tourists and wandering lovers. I helped him most days at the docks, on others motoring down to Limerick to earn a little extra money tutoring Latin. In this way I slowly opened up to a wider world.

Early evenings, we'd often find ourselves in one of Brendan's favourite pubs. Great pub country, Ireland, and Brendan had a great many favourites. Poor man's universities, he called them, and we'd further our educations at tables near fires that crackled as warm and welcoming as any hearth in any home.

Guinness for Brendan, always, and in the beginning, shandies for me;

I was little accustomed to drinking and inclined to start slow. But they relaxed me, and this I needed, often feeling that I still didn't belong outside cloistered walls. I would look at all these people who knew how to live their days without each hour predetermined as to how they'd pass it, and I'd wonder how they managed, if they knew how courageous they were. I'd listen to them laugh and would feel they had no more than to look at me to see that I was only pretending to be one of them.

More to the heart, I began to regret all the years I'd never truly known my uncle, letting others form my opinion of him for me. When I told him this one night, I was glad to learn he didn't hold it against me, as he waved my guilt aside like a pesky fly.

"You've a great many relatives, but I daresay not a one of them could understand how you'd be feeling now any better than I can," he said. "After all . . . *I'm* the one who once left seminary."

Astounding news, this. I'd never been told; had assumed Uncle Brendan to have been an incorrigible heathen from the very start. "*Father* Brendan, it almost was?" I exclaimed, laughing.

"Oh, aye," he said, mischief in his eyes. "I was going to win souls back from the devil himself, until I began to really listen to those claiming to be out of his clutches already, and started wondering what he could ever want with them in the first place. Not a very bright or ambitious devil, you ask me."

"You left seminary because of . . . who, the priests?"

"Oh, the whole buggery lot of them. Them, and that I woke up one day to realize that all I'd been studying for years? I didn't believe a word of it. Now, love and compassion, aye, they've their virtues . . . but a message that basic doesn't need any act of divine intervention." He winked. "Not as dramatic as your experiences with those collared old pisspots, but you're not the only one to give in to a crisis of faith."

He knew of the stigmata; I'd freely told him of that. Of the rest, that awful Christ come down off the wall, I'd been silent.

"But we're in good company, we are." He toasted his stout to companions unseen. "Hardly the Church's finest hour, not a thing they're any too proud of, you understand, but last century, I think it was, the pope decides he's a bit fagged of hearing the Bible attacked on educated terms. Science, history. If the Church fathers didn't have the wee-est clue what they lived on was round, and orbited the sun, then why in hell assume they knew what they were talking about when it comes to eternity? Or, fifteen hundred years after he's dead, you still had minds like Saint Augustine's setting down doctrine. Augustine had said it was impossible that anyone could be living on the other side of the world, because the Bible didn't list any such descendants of Adam. So the pope, under that big posthole digging hat, the pope decides he's heard quite enough of this shite from these smart-arse intellectuals, so he decides to establish his own elite corps of priests who can argue their faith on the same terms . . . scientific, historical, like that.

"Except the more they studied, tried to arm themselves, the more these buggers quit the priesthood altogether." Brendan gulped a hearty swallow of stout and wiped the foam from his mouth with the back of his hand. "Game called on account of brains."

"You're a hostile man, Uncle Brendan," I joked, setting no accusation by it. In truth, I admired the courage it took to make no secret of such opinions in a mostly Catholic country.

"Aye. Ignorance brings out the worst in me, it's true, and the Church has never been much bothered by facts getting in the way of the dazzle. Like a magic show, it is . . . the grandest magic show anyone's ever put on, and the fools who pay their money or their souls are plenty keen on letting themselves *be* fooled." He shook his head. "Like with the relics. Never mind all the saints' bones that actually came from animals—the Vatican won't even keep its own records sensible. What are they up to now—more than a hundred and fifty nails from the crucifixion? Used that many, why, they'd still be taking him down off the cross to this day. What else . . . ? Ah—nine breasts of Saint Eulalia. Twenty-eight fingers and thumbs of Saint Dominic. Ten heads of John the Baptist. Ten! You show me where in the gospels it says anything about John the Baptist being a fucking Hydra, and I'll still not believe it, but at least I'll admire their bloody audacity in trying to pull that one off too."

Quite in my cups by now, I lamented how sad it was that faith and reason were so often at odds with one another. What a joke it would be on the whole planetary lot of us, I added, if it turned out that whatever made us in its own image had then filled the books with the most improbable bollocks imaginable, and put incompetents in charge of keeping them, just to make it that much harder on us and weed out everyone but the truest of true believers.

"Who's to say it hasn't happened that very way?" my uncle said. The seriousness with which he was taking this surprised me, even unsettled me. "But what've you got then? It's no god of love and mercy. What you've got then . . . is a master who wants slaves."

"Uncle Brendan," I said, "I was only joking."

"I know you were. But even jesters can speak the truth. They just do it by accident."

"Forget all the dogma, then," I said. "You don't even believe in something so basic as a god of love?"

"I believe in love itself, oh, aye. But, now, love could just as easily be our own invention, couldn't it? Took a few billion years of bloody harsh survival of the fittest before we'd dragged ourselves out of the mud far enough where we could even *think* of love. So why should we take for granted that something out there loves us any more than we love ourselves? I'll tell you why: Any other alternative is too horrible for most people to contemplate."

I remembered the way my mother reacted when I told her what the blood-kissing angel had said on that day of the bomb. *This is the kind of work you can expect from people who have God on their side*. I'd not made it up, only repeated it, but my mother hadn't wanted to hear another word. Hadn't wanted to know any more about that woman who'd comforted me as my friends lay dead. It hurt me now much more than it had then. How rigid our fears can make us; how tightly they can close our minds. I wondered aloud why the uncomplicated faith that ran like a virus through the generations of our family hadn't been enough for Brendan and me.

"Wondered that myself, I have," he admitted. "Who knows? But I like to think it might be our Celtic blood. That it's purer in us, somehow, than it is in the rest of the family . . . and the blood remembers. Greatest mystics that ever were, the Celts. So you and I . . . could be we're like those stones they left behind."

"How's that—the standing stones?"

"Aye, those're the ones," Brendan said, and I thought of them settled into green meadows like giant gray eggs, inscribed with the primitive ogham alphabet. "Already been around for centuries, they had, by the time the bloody Christians overrun the island and go carving their crosses into the stones to convert them . . . like they're trying to suck all the power out of the stones and turn them into something they were never intended to be. But the stones remember, still, and so do we, I think, you and I . . . because our blood remembers, too."

The blood remembers. I liked the sound of that.

And if blood could only talk, what stories might it tell?

The stigmata still came, the flow of blood awe-inspiring to me, still, but there was something shameful about it now, as if leaving the Franciscans had made me unworthy. Worse, it terrified me now more than ever, for I exhibited the wounds of a Christ who had denied himself. They came like violent summons from something beyond me, indifferent to what I did or didn't believe in.

They knew no propriety, no decorum. One night, soon after I'd confessed to my uncle that I'd never been with a woman, he paid for me to enjoy the company of one who certainly didn't live in the area, and then stepped discreetly from the house to share a drink with a neighbour. They'd scarcely tipped their glasses before she ran from the house and demanded he take her back to Limerick. Brendan first came in to see what had upset her so, and found me sitting on the bed with my wounds freshly opened.

"Oh suffering Christ," he said, weary and beaten. "Ordinarily it's the woman who bleeds the first time."

For days I felt stung by the humiliation, and the loneliness of what I was, and tried to pull the world as tight around me as it had been at the friary. Once a cloister, now a boat. I'd leave the docks early in the morning, rowing out onto Lough Derg until I could see nothing of what I'd left behind, and there I'd drift for hours. Chilled by misty rains or cold Atlantic winds, I didn't care how cruelly the elements conspired against my comfort. The dark, peaty waters lapped inches away like a liquid grave.

I often dwelt upon Saint Francis, whose life I'd once vowed to emulate. He too had suffered stigmata, had beheld visions of Jesus. *Francesco, repair my falling house,* his Jesus had commanded him, or so he'd believed, and so he'd stolen many of his father's belongings to sell for the money it would take to get him started. *Repair my falling house.* Whose Jesus was more true? Mine appeared to want from me nothing less than that I tear it down.

But always, my reflections would turn to that which to me was most real: she who had come on the day of the bomb. Who had smiled reassuringly at me with my blood on her lips, then never seen fit to visit again. A poor guardian she'd made, abandoning me. Since I'd been a child kneeling beside my bed at night, I had prayed to every evolving concept of God I'd held. I'd prayed to Saviour and Virgin and more saints than I could recall, and now, adrift on the dark rippling lake, I added *her* to those canonical ranks, praying that she come to my aid once more, to show me what was wanted of me.

"You loved me once," I called to her, into the wind. "Did I lose that, too, along with all the blood?"

But the wind said nothing, nor the waters, nor the hills, nor the skies whence I imagined that she'd come. They were as silent as dead gods who'd never risen again.

In the nights that followed these restless days, I learned to drink at the elbow of a master. No more shandies for me—the foamy black stout now became the water of life. Women, too, lost much of their mystery, thanks to a couple of encounters, the greater part of which I managed to remember.

And when I couldn't stand it any longer, I broke down and told my uncle the secrets that had been eating away at me—the one for only a few weeks, the other since I was seven. It surprised me to see it was the earlier incident that seemed to affect him most. Brendan grew deathly quiet as he listened to the story of that day, his fleshy, ruddy cheeks going pale. He was very keen on my recounting exactly how she'd looked—black hair shimmering nearly to her waist, her skin a translucent brown, not like that of any native I'd ever seen, not even those called the Black Irish.

"It's true, they really do exist," Brendan murmured after I'd finished, then turned away, face strained between envy and dread, with no clear victor. "Goddamn you, boy," he finally said. "You've no idea what's been dogging your life, have you?"

Apparently I did not.

He sought out the clock, then in sullen silence appeared to think things over a while. When at last he moved again, it was to snatch up his automobile keys and nod toward the door. Of the envy and dread upon his face, the latter had clearly won out.

IV. *De Contemptu Mundi*

"Somebody once said—I've forgot who—said you can take away a man's gods . . . but only to give him others in return."

He told me this on our late-night drive, southwest through the countryside, past hedgerows and farms, along desolate lanes that may well have been better traveled after midnight. A corner rounded by day could have put us square in the middle of a flock of sheep nagged along by nipping dogs.

Or maybe we traveled by the meager luster of a slivered moon because, of those things that Uncle Brendan wished to tell me, he didn't wish to do so by the light of day, or bulb, or fire.

"Wasn't until after I'd left seminary that I understood what that really meant. You don't walk away from a thing you'd thought you believed your whole life through without the loss of it leaving a hole in you, hungering to be filled. You've still a need to believe in something . . . it's just a question of what."

Sometimes he talked, sometimes he fell silent, collecting his remembrances of days long gone.

"I *tried* some things, Patrick. Things I'd rather not discuss in detail. Tried some things, and saw others . . . heard still other things beyond those. You can't always trust your own senses, much less the things that get whispered about by people you can't be sure haven't themselves gone daft before you've ever met them. But some things . . .

"That woman you saw? One of three, she is, if she's who I think she was. There's some say they've always been here, long as there's been an Ireland, and long before that. All the legends that got born on this island, they're not *all* about little people. There's some say that from the earliest times, the Celts knew of them, and worshiped them because the Celts knew that the most powerful goddesses were three-in-one."

We'd driven as far down as the Dingle Peninsula, one of the desolate and beautiful spits of coastal land that reached out like fingers to test the cold Atlantic waters. The land rolled with low peaks, and waves pounded sea cliffs to churn up mists that trapped the dawn's light in spectral iridescence, and the countryside was littered with ancient rock—standing stones and the beehive-shaped huts that had housed early Christian monks. Here hermits found the desolation they'd craved, thinking they would come to know God better.

"There's some say," Uncle Brendan went on, "they were still around after Saint Patrick came. That sometimes, in the night, when the winds were blowing and the waves were wearing down the cliffs, a pious hermit might hear them outside his hut. Come to tempt him, they had. Calling in to him. All night, it might go on, and that horny bugger inside, all alone in the world, sunk to his knees in prayer, trying not to imagine how they'd look, how they'd feel. No reason they couldn't 've come on in as they pleased—it was just their sport to break him down."

"Why?" I asked. "To prove they were . . . more powerful than his god was?"

"Aye, now that could be. More powerful . . . or at least *there*. Then again, some say that by the time Sisters of the Trinity finally got to their business on those who gave in, all the hours of fear had . . . flavoured the monks better."

"Flavoured . . . ? Their blood, you mean?"

"*All* of them. It's said each consumes a different part of a man. One, the blood. One, the flesh. And one, the sperm. It's said that when they've not fed for a good long time? There's nothing of a man left but his bones, cracked open and sucked dry."

I couldn't reconcile such savagery with the tenderness I'd been shown—the sweetness of her face, the gentle sadness in her eyes as she looked upon us, two dead boys and the other changed for life. Only when she'd tasted my blood had anything like terrible wisdom surfaced in her eyes.

The sun had breached the horizon behind us when Uncle Brendan stopped the car. There was nothing human or animal to be seen in any direction, and we ourselves were insignificant in this rugged and lovely desolation. We crossed meadows on foot, until the road was lost to sight. Ahead, in the distance, a solitary standing stone listed at a slight tilt; it drew my uncle on with quickened steps. When we reached it, he touched it with a reverence I'd never thought resided in him, for anything, fingers skimming the shallow cuts of the ogham writing that rimmed it, archlike.

"It's theirs. The Sisters'. Engraved to honour them." Then he grinned. "See anything missing?"

I looked for chunks eroded or hammered away, but the stone appeared complete. I shook my head, mystified.

"No crosses cut in later by the Christians. It wouldn't take the chisel. Tried to smash the rock, they did, but it wore down their sledges instead. Tried to drag it to the sea, and the ropes snapped. So the legend goes, anyway. Like trying to pull God's own tooth. Or the devil's. If there's a difference." He shut his eyes, and the wind from the west swirled his graying hair. When he spoke again his voice was shaking. "Killed a boy here once. When I was young. Trying to call them up. I'd heard sometimes they'd answer the call of blood. Maybe I should've used my own instead. Maybe they'd've paid some mind to that."

On the wind I could hear the pounding of the ocean, and as I tried to imagine my generous and profane uncle a murderer, it felt as if those distant waves had all along been eroding everything I thought I knew. I asked Brendan what he'd wanted with the Sisters.

"They didn't take the name of the Trinity just because there happens to be three of them. Couldn't tell you what it is, but it's said there's some tie to that *other* trinity you and I thought we were born to serve. Patrick, I . . . I wanted to know what they know. And there's some say when they put their teeth to a man, the pleasure's worth it. So what's a few years sacrificed, next to learning what's been covered up by centuries of lies?"

"But what if," I asked, "all they'd have to tell you is just another set of lies?"

"Then might be the pleasure makes up for that, too." He took a step toward me and I flinched, as if he had a knife or garrote, as he would've had for that boy whose blood hadn't been enough. Brendan raised his empty hands, then looked at mine.

At my wrists.

"Maybe you've the chance I never had. Maybe they've a use for you they never had for me."

And in the new morning, he left me there alone. I sat against the old pagan stone after I heard the faraway sound of his car.

The blood remembers, he'd once told me, *and so do we.*

Demon est Deus inversus, I'd been told by another. *Save me from that impotent, slaughtered lamb they have made of me.*

On this rock will I build my church, some scribe had written, putting words in the latter's mouth.

The blood remembers.

Three days later my flesh remembered how to bleed.

And the stone how to drink.

Regardless of their orbits, planets are born, then mature and die, upon a single axis, and so the stone and those it honoured had always been to me, even before I knew it. Now that I was here, I circled the stone but wouldn't leave it, couldn't, because, as in space, there was nothing beyond but cold dark emptiness.

They came while I slept—the fourth morning, maybe the fifth. They were there with the dawn, and who knows how many hours before that, slender and solid against the morning mists, watching as I rolled upright in my dew-soaked blanket. When I rubbed my eyes and blinked, they didn't vanish. Part of me feared they would. Part of me feared they wouldn't.

As I leaned back against the stone, she came forward and went to her knees beside me, looking not a day older than she had more than twenty years before. Her light brown skin was still smoothly translucent. Her gaze was tender at first, and though it didn't change of itself, it grew more unnerving when she did not blink—like being regarded by the consummate patience of a serpent.

She leaned in, the tip of her nose cool at my throat as she sniffed deeply. Her lips were warm against mine; their soft press set mine to trembling. Her breath was sweet, and the edge of one sharp tooth bit down to open a tiny cut on my lip. She sucked at it as if it were a split berry, and I thought without fear that next I would die. But she only raised my hands to nuzzle the pale inner wrists, their blue tracery of veins, then pushed them gently back to my lap, and I understood that she must've known all along what I was, what I was to become.

"It's nice to look into your eyes again," she said, as if but a week had passed since she'd done so, "and not closed in sleep."

Since coming to the stone I'd imagined and rehearsed this moment countless times, and she'd never said this. Never dressed in black and grays, pants and a thick sweater, clothes I might've seen on any city street and not thought twice about. She'd never glanced back at the other two, who stood eyeing each other with impatience, while the taller of them idly scraped something from the bottom of her shoe. She'd never simply stood up, taken me by the hand, and pulled me to my feet, to leave me surprised at how much smaller she looked now that I'd grown to adulthood.

"He stinks," said the taller Sister. From the feral arrogance in her face, I took her to be the flesh-eater. "I can smell him from here."

"You've smelt worse," said the third. "Eaten it, too."

As I'd rehearsed this they'd never bickered, and my erstwhile angel—Maia, the others called her—had never led me away from the stone like a bewildered child.

"Where are we going?" I asked.

"Back down to the road. Then back home to Dublin," Maia said.

"You . . . you drove?"

The flesh-eater, her leather jacket disconcertingly modern, burst into mocking laughter. "Oh Jesus, another goddess hunter," she sighed. "What was he expecting? We'd take him by the hand and fly into the woods?"

The third one, the sperm-eater by default, slid closer to me in a colorful gypsy swirl of skirts. "Try not to be so baroque," she said. "It really sets Lilah off, anymore."

V. *Sanguis Sanctus*

They were not goddesses, but if they'd been around as long as they were supposed to have been, inspiring legends that had driven men like my uncle to murder, then as goddesses they at least must've posed. They were beautiful and they were three, and undoubtedly could be both generous and terrible. They could've been anything to anyone—goddesses, succubi, temptresses, avengers—and at one time or another probably had been. They might've gone through lands and ages, exploiting extant myths of triune women, leaving others in their wake: Egyptian Hathors, Greek Gorgons, Roman Fates, Norse Norns.

And today they lived in Dublin in a gabled stone house that had been standing for centuries, secluded now behind security fences and a vast lawn patrolled by mastiffs—not what I'd expected. But I accepted the fact of them the same way I accepted visions of a blaspheming Christ, and ancient stones that drank stigmatic blood, then sang a summons that only immortal women could hear. All these I accepted as proof that Shakespeare had been right—there was more in Heaven and Earth than I'd ever dreamt of. What I found hardest to believe was that I could have any part to play in it.

They took me in without explaining themselves. I was fed and allowed to bathe, given fresh clothes. Otherwise, the Sisters of the Trinity lived as privileged aristocrats, doing whatever they pleased, whenever it pleased them.

Lilah, the flesh-eater, aloof and most often found in dark leathers, had the least to do with me, and seemed to tolerate me as she might a stray dog taken in that she didn't care to pet.

The sperm-eater was Salíce, and while she was much less apt to pretend I didn't exist, most of her attentions took the form of taunts, teasing me with innuendo and glimpses of her body, as if it were something I might see but never experience. After I'd been there a few days, though, she thrust a crystal goblet in my hand. "Fill it," she demanded, then pursed her lips as my eyes widened. "Well—do what you can."

I managed in private, to fantasies of Maia.

I'd loved her all my life, I realized—a love for every age and need. I'd first loved her with childish adoration, and then for her divine wisdom. I later loved her extraordinary beauty as I matured into its spell. Loved her as an ideal that no mortal woman could live up to. I'd begun loving her as proof that the merciful God I'd been raised to worship existed, and now, finally, as further evidence that he didn't.

My devotion was reciprocated, and the time we spent together lovers' time. But while I shared her bed and body, I tried not to delude myself that it meant the same thing to Maia as it did me. Millions of people may love their dogs, but none regard them as equals. I kept alive the cut on the side of my lip, where she'd bitten me that first morning, the pain tiny and exquisite. But her teeth never returned to the spot, or sought any other.

"Why not?" I asked one bright afternoon. Now I understood why Aztecs had allowed their hearts to be cut out, and islanders went willingly into live volcanoes. "Is there something wrong with my blood?"

"Is that all you think you are to me?" Maia looked at me with such intuitive depth it felt as if she could take in my whole life between eyeblinks. "I can get blood anywhere."

"I didn't say you had to take it all."

"Yours is special. It shouldn't be wasted."

When I suggested they must be reserving me for something, she only smiled with mystery and allure. We were out walking, had gotten far from home by this time of day, Maia showing me some of the mundane, everyday sights of Dublin. Her arm looped in mine, she steered me down a side street, more purpose in her stride now than before. When we were across the street from a brick building that looked like a school, we sat atop a low wall. Before long the doors opened to release a flood of young boys in their uniforms—dark blue short pants and pullover sweaters, with pale blue shirts and red ties. We watched them swarm away, and one in particular she seemed to track, until he was lost from sight.

"I had children once . . . but they were killed by soldiers," she said, as if the grief still came unexpectedly sometimes. "Life is cheap enough now but it was even cheaper then. Before I could have any more, things *happened* to me, and then . . . I couldn't. So I just watch strangers, children whose names I never know. I'll pick one out, pretend he or she is mine, and it goes on like that for a year, maybe two. And then I go to another school and pick out a new one because I've noticed the other's looking older and I don't want to know what becomes of him. Or her. It's easier to imagine a good future than to deal with the truth, watch all that bright potential start to dim."

"Then obviously I'm an exception."

"Exception. Oh, you're that, all right." When she touched my leg I could feel the thrilling heat of her. "I was following you that day. Like I always did. I'd first noticed you six, seven months before. Such a pious little thing—it was the most adorable trait. Like little American boys growing up wanting to be cowboys, before they find out the world doesn't have cattle drives anymore. I wanted to save you from yourself, if I could. And then the bomb almost took care of it for me."

I'd never once imagined our history predating that day.

"You were standing there between your friends' bodies. Too shocked to cry. I wish I could tell you I steered the bricks away from you in midair, but something like that's a bit beyond me. I think I was as surprised as you that you were okay. But I couldn't walk away without touching you. And then . . . then I saw your knee."

Across the street, the flood of schoolboys had been reduced to a trickle: the laggards, the stragglers, the delinquents.

"Sometimes—and it *is* rare," Maia went on, "I can taste more than life in someone's blood. I can taste all the truth of that person. Lilah's the same way. The blood and the flesh of a special or gifted person are full of images. Take them in and we can learn things they might not even know about themselves." Her eyes locked on mine, clear and hard. "If you think the rite of Holy Communion is only two thousand years old, you're a few thousand short.

"When I licked the blood from your knee that day, I knew you were either going to be a saint, or a butcher."

I thought at first she meant working in a meat shop. Then I realized what sort of butcher she meant.

"From one to the other—that's quite a jump," I said.

Maia shook her head. "They're closer than you think. There's always been a certain type of man, if he can't save a soul, he's willing to settle for exterminating it. Your Church has attracted more than its share. And I tasted that potential in you."

She'd kept track of me ever since, she admitted, always knew where to find me when she felt like watching me sleep. And while it disturbed her to see me hand my life over to the Church, she was patient enough to let it run its course without interfering, knowing all along that it wouldn't last.

"What made you so sure?"

"You were too raw and open for it to last forever. There's no faith in anything so strong it can't be shattered by one moment's glimpse of something it doesn't allow for. And I knew someday you were bound to see one of them . . . and it'd leave its mark on you."

I looked at my wrists. Maia was right. *There, in the flesh, over the veins* . . . Weeks had passed, yet there was still a mark where that tormented Christ had grabbed me with his handful of shattered bones. From the day he'd pierced the skin and his blood had mingled with my own, a transfused message I was to carry inside until, perhaps, I found someone able to read it.

His commission: *Save me from that impotent, slaughtered lamb they have made of me.*

With one fingertip, Maia touched the healing split on my lip. "I've tasted you before," she said, "and I've tasted you after. So I know the difference, Patrick. He's in there. You still carry him. We can use that."

VI. *Haereticae Pravitatis*

I didn't know what she was waiting for, one day being as good as another to bleed. I was used to it. I wondered how much Maia would require; if it made a difference to her where it came from, wrists or throat. Wondered if she alone would be involved, or Lilah, too, or maybe all three of them, opening me like a heretical gospel written in flesh and blood and semen. It was Lilah I feared most, because if she were involved, I could only be read once.

Still, I never considered running.

They indulged their appetites, neither flaunting them nor hiding them from me. Only Lilah's necessitated fatality, and as I came to understand their habits, they didn't always feed together, but when they did it was usually at her instigation. Most often, Lilah or Salíce would disappear for a few hours, some nights both of them, then come home after they'd coaxed some man into joining them. As huntresses, they had an easy time of it.

"After more than two and a half millennia," Lilah told me one morning, when she was in especially good humour, "I can personally vouch that one thing about men has stayed exactly the same, and always will." She grinned, relishing the predictability of my gender. "Every one of you thinks you're virile enough to handle more than one woman at a time . . . and you're *soooo* embarrassingly eager for your chance to prove it."

I'd never seen the room where the Sisters took them. It was always locked, like the room where Bluebeard kept dead wives. Nor did I see the men themselves; didn't want to. But on those nights when I knew one would be coming, I'd sit nearby in the dark and listen to their laughter, their ignorance-fueled anticipation. I'd hear the latching of the door. Then it would go on for some time. Often the men grew vocal in their passion, bellowing like love-struck bulls. The Sisters would laugh and squeal. Eventually I'd hear a sudden snap, or worse, a thick ripping. The overwhelmed voice would screech louder still, but I never could discern any clear division between ecstasy and agony, even after their cries degenerated into whimpers and moans that never lasted very long.

The final cracking open of the bones was the worst.

One morning after they'd fed, Salíce found me huddled before the hearth and a blazing fire. I was disheveled from having been up all night, and clutched a blanket around my shoulders because I couldn't seem to get warm.

"Awww, look, he's . . . he's *shivering*," Salíce announced to an otherwise empty room. "He misses home, I'll bet."

I wouldn't answer, wouldn't turn around to look at her. Maia and Lilah would still be upstairs sleeping it off. Maia wouldn't let me see her for the next several hours after she'd gorged, but I found that easy to live with.

"Well, he *was* a noisy one, even by the usual standards, I'll admit that much." Behind me, she was coming closer. "'Tendons and ligaments like steel bands,' Lilah said. What a snap those made."

I could feel her directly behind me, warmer than the fire, and I jumped when she bent down to snake her arms around me in an unexpected hug. Patronizing, I first thought, but when she kissed me atop the head I wondered if instead she wasn't trying, in her way, to tell me that she wouldn't bite.

"Nobody forces you to listen, you know," she said. "There're plenty of places in this house where you wouldn't hear a thing."

I nodded. Salíce didn't need to tell me this, though, just as I shouldn't have had to tell her that listening to them feed was the best way of putting my future in perspective.

"You're worried about the divination? That's all?" She almost sounded amused. "Forget about Lilah, why don't you. So she looks at you like a kidney pie. The thing to remember about Lilah is, if it wasn't for scaring people, she wouldn't have any fun at all."

Salíce told me to wait right there, that she really shouldn't show this to me, but so what. She disappeared into an adjacent room that overlooked the back lawn; it was full of tall windows and sunlight, locked file cabinets and computers. When she came back she handed me a small news clipping.

"It was a bigger story in Italy," she said, "but I'm assuming you don't read Italian."

It was dated the previous week, about a theft from the church of a small village seventy-some kilometers north of Rome. During the night, someone had smashed a spherical crystal reliquary and stolen the relic inside, which wasn't identified but was only described as dating from the earliest years of Church history.

"Our friend Julius had this done. He lives in Capua, with a beautiful castrato boy named Giovanni. He used to throw the best parties, until Vanni deafened him with a pair of nails, so they're pretty sure he's dying now . . . but I think he wanted it that way, because he still loves Vanni even after what that little eunuch did." She rolled her eyes. "They want to grow *old* together."

Since I didn't know who or what she was talking about, I read the article again. It still struck me as an incomplete puzzle. "I don't understand what this has to do with me, or Maia, or—"

"Don't you get it? The relic—it's for the divination. Lilah can't bother you with those lovely white teeth of hers if she's got them busy on something else, now, can she?"

Ghouls already; now body thieves? Asked what the relic was, Salíce just laughed and told me to be patient, adding only that if it was genuine it could prove to be quite illuminating. Pour my tainted stigmatic's blood into the mix, and it might be their best opportunity yet for stealing the secrets of Heaven and Hell.

"I'd've thought you already knew them," I said.

"You think because we've lived a long time we hold privileged information?" She shook her head. "There's some older than we are, and they're no better off. We've all got our ideas, but there's too much we can never agree on.

"At Julius's last party, two years ago, we managed to summon down and imprison an Ophanim. We thought we might get some answers out of it. But it was already insane. And wasn't flesh and blood like Maia and Lilah are used to. So we raped it and sent it back, out of spite, and that was the end of it. We didn't learn anything that most of us hadn't already suspected.

"But you," she said, with a faint smile. "We're thinking we might learn more from you than even one of Heaven's inmates. We don't even have to summon you down—*you're* already here. And all you have to do . . . is bleed."

When she learned how much Salíce had told me, Maia wouldn't speak to her for two days; after it got to be too much to contain, they shouted at each other for half an hour.

"You didn't have any right!" Maia cried. "*I* should've been the one to tell him those things."

"Then what you were waiting for?" Salíce asked. "Until he got too old and decrepit to run away from you?"

I listened to them argue as I listened to them feed: out of sight, and out of reach.

"The problem with you, Maia, is that there's still a part of you that refuses to admit you're not like the rest of them, and never can be again. Aren't you ever going to accept that? *Ever?*"

"Because I'm not strictly human anymore, that means I can't still be humane?" Maia's voice then turned bitter, accusing. "Of course, you do have to possess that quality before you can slough it off."

"Inhumane—me? They always *thank* me when I feed on them. What *I* take they're already swimming in to begin with; they can't wait to give it away. You can't make any such claim, so don't you even try." Salíce groaned with exasperation. "My god, you still think you can fall in love, don't you? You pick them out when they're children and you dream about what might've been, and on the rare occasion you meet up with one again when he's grown, you think if you put on enough of a front you'll both forget what you are."

"Keep your voice down," Maia warned.

"You're afraid he'll hear something he doesn't already know? Oh, wake up, he's got excellent hearing. The only thing he doesn't know is how you look after a meal. That's the one thing you can't pretend away, isn't it? Not even you're *that* naive. And damn right you are that most of them would have a problem loving you back if they saw how bloated your belly gets with all the blood."

Whatever Maia said next I didn't hear; I was too busy facing Lilah when I realized she'd been behind me, watching me eavesdrop.

"It'll blow over. It always does," she told me, and nodded in the direction of the argument. "Salíce always has had an attitude of superiority because she never has to get any messier than some little cocksucker bobbing her head beneath a table at Mr. Pussy's Café."

"Do you ever resent that?" I asked.

"Do *I?* God, no. But then, I know what really makes Salíce so cocky over it in the first place." She laughed, her long hair uncombed and tangled in her face as she leaned into mine. "Nobody's afraid of her. She hates that. Maia and me—they fear us. But nobody fears Salíce."

"I'm not afraid of Maia, either."

Lilah loudly clicked her teeth. "But you are of me." She stared triumphantly through the crumbling of my self-assurance. "Then maybe you're only half-stupid."

As she'd predicted, the argument soon blustered away, ending when Maia stormed from the house and cooled down out on the back lawn. Through the windows I watched her, a slight, distant figure in somber grays, walking slowly amidst grass and gardens, finally sitting beneath an oak, where she distractedly petted one of the slobbering mastiffs that had the run of the grounds. When I braved the dog and joined her, we sat a while in that silence that follows the clumsy dropping of another guard from around the heart.

"After that first day, and the bomb," I said, "why didn't you come to me again? I've always wondered that. I'd've followed you anywhere. I'd've been anything you wanted."

"There's your answer, right there. It's too easy for someone like us to take whatever we want. Where's the joy in that? After so long, it's only gratifying one more appetite." She watched her hand scruffing the black fur across the dog's huge head. "It's important to me that if someone like you comes back . . . it's because you do it on your own."

"Because it's more real to you then?"

Maia shrugged, stared off into the gray sky. "What *is* real, anyway?" she asked, and while once I thought I had those answers, now I wasn't even sure of the questions.

In the black-and-white faith I was raised in, there'd been no room outside of Hell for the likes of the Sisters of the Trinity. And while I realized that they weren't goddesses, neither were they demons. I no longer believed in demons, at least not the sort the Church had spent centuries exorcising. Where was the need for them, other than keeping the Church in business? One pontiff with a private army could wreak more havoc than any infernal legion.

Because of Salíce, I now understood that the Sisters weren't the only ones of their kind. When I asked how many of them there were, Maia didn't know, or wouldn't say, and I realized with an unexpected poignancy that whatever monstrous acts it was in their nature to commit, those acts were no worse than what went on between wolves and deer, and that those who committed them were still as lost in their world as the most ignorant of us mortal fools in ours, working and loving and praying and dying over our threescore and ten.

Black-haired and black-eyed, hair tousled in the breeze, Maia turned her unblinking serpent's gaze on me, so unexpected it was almost alien.

"How much would it take to repulse you?" she said.

At first I didn't know how to respond; then I asked why she'd even want to.

"Because it obviously takes more than eating men alive to do it. You don't find that interesting about yourself?" She wouldn't look at me, instead smiled down at the dog. "I've made lovers of grown-up children before, and sometimes they've run and sometimes they've stayed, but do you know who I've noticed is most likely to stay? It's you refugees from Christianity. Now why do you suppose that is?"

I had no idea.

"My guess is it's because, most of you, you were *weaned* on the idea of serving up your god on a plate and in a little cup and eating him in a communal meal. Then when you can't believe in him anymore, and you find us, and see how willing we are to eat others just like you, how we *need* that . . . then isn't a little part of you, deep inside, relieved? Because that means *you're* the god. Your ego is still too fragile to see yourself as just food. So you *must* be God, right . . . ?

"So let me ask you again: How much would it take to repulse you? To sicken those romantic ideals out of you?"

"I don't want to talk about this anymore, Maia. If you want me to leave,

I'll leave, but have the good grace to ask me rather than talking your way around it."

"Hear that, Brutus? Doesn't want to talk about it," she said to the mastiff. "You know, Patrick, where we get these dogs, they claim the lineage runs directly back to war dogs used by the Roman army. Like barrels, they were . . . with legs and teeth and fury and spiked leather armor. And you know something, Patrick? That's no empty claim on the breeders' part—it's absolutely true. Do you know how I know this?"

I shook my head.

"They're extraordinary dogs. With extraordinary bloodlines."

She hugged the dog, then slammed it over onto its back, and I could only watch appalled as Maia buried her beautiful face in the coarse fur at the mastiff's bull neck. It yelped once, and those powerful legs kicked and clawed at the air, its body all squirming steel muscle, and yet she held it down with a minimum of struggle. When after several moments Maia tore her face away and let the dog go, it rolled unsteadily to its feet and lurched to a safer spot. Dazed, it looked back at her and whined, then ran off as if in a drunken lope.

She was on me by then, had flipped me back and down before I knew it was happening. She straddled me, her hands gripping my shoulders, then pressed her smeared face to mine and opened her mouth in a violent kiss, let gravity take the blood straight into me. We spit and we spewed, but I couldn't fight her.

It would've been like wrestling an angel.

So I pretended the blood was her own.

When she sat back against the oak, Maia was breathing hard. I was still lying flat and trying not to retch. She wiped her mouth with the back of one hand, and trembled.

"Julius has always hated the dogs," she murmured. "He hated the Romans, so he hates the dogs. He still blames the Romans for what he became. And he hates the dogs."

"Became," I echoed. "None of you were born this way, then?"

"Nobody's ever born this way," she said. When I asked what made them all, she told me it was different on the surface in each case, and that sometimes that surface was all they knew. When I asked what made *her*, Maia did not speak for a long time, nor look at me. At last, after we heard the mournful howling of an unseen dog, she said, "If you're still around late tonight, I'll tell you."

VII. *Ignominy Patris*

"We were Assyrian," she began, in our room filled with silks and dried orchids, "and we were just women. Devalued, and with no formal power. But we still had our ways. You know the Bible; so you know the sorts of men who made Assyria, don't you?"

I told her I did. A nation of warrior kings ruling warrior subjects, Assyria had been so feared for its savagery that an Old Testament scribe had called it "a land bathed in blood."

"In Assyria, as in Babylonia," Maia went on, "each woman was expected, once in her life before she married, to go to the temple of Ishtar and sit on the steps until a man came and dropped a coin in her lap as the price of her favours. So off they'd go and their bodies became divine vessels for a while, and that was how a woman performed her duty to the goddess of love.

"My sisters and I decided to go to the temple all on the same day, and the men who came then, they showered us with coins and started to fight each other over who'd end up having us. Lilah loved it, thought it was hilarious. At night, in secret, she led us and other women in worshiping the demoness Lilitu . . . the one the Israelites took and turned into Adam's first wife, Lilith, and thought she was so horrible just because she fucked Adam from the top instead of lying on her back like a proper woman was supposed to. I'm sure you can see the appeal she had to those of us who didn't feel particularly subservient to men.

"After that first day at the temple, when we saw what kind of power we had over them, we kept going back. Our fame grew, and so did our fortunes, and the rumours of the pleasure we could bring . . . until we were finally summoned by King Sennacherib. He wanted to restore a rite that was ancient even then, from Sumerian times: the Sacred Marriage. The king embodied a god and a priestess stood in for the goddess—by then, we were held in much higher esteem than mere temple prostitutes—and out of that physical union the gods and goddesses received their pleasures of the flesh."

Maia uttered a small laugh. "Lilah never believed Sennacherib really meant any of it, said he only wanted some grandiose excuse for an orgy with us. Probably she was right. After that, we became his most favoured concubines, and whatever in Nineveh we wanted, we had. And I . . . gave birth to twins, a daughter and a son. Of course, the king didn't publicly acknowledge them as his own. That was only for children born of his queen. But *I* knew whose they were.

"In 701 B.C. Sennacherib invaded the Israelites. He captured forty-six cities before getting to Jerusalem, but by then, the Jewish king Hezekiah had had an underground aqueduct dug to ensure the water supply. Sennacherib besieged the city, as he'd already done at Lachish, but by now they were in a position to outwait us almost indefinitely. I know, because we were *there.* He might leave his queen at home, but Sennacherib wouldn't dare leave us behind. Not with the addiction he had to our bodies. So we were there for it all. Waiting for weeks under that merciless desert sun, a few arrows flying back and forth, an attempt at building a siege ramp . . . but mostly each side just waiting for the other to give up."

Maia seemed to lose herself in the flickering flame of a pillar candle. "Do you remember what supposedly happened to part of our army there?"

I nodded. It was said that an angel from the one true God of Israel came down and in one night slaughtered 185,000 Assyrians.

"Not true, I'm guessing?"

"Oh, do you even have to ask?" she said. "It was more like four thousand, and it was Sennacherib's own fault. He was starting to fear he might lose the siege, so he went to the priests, the ones he knew practiced sorcery . . . and he had them conjure a demon from out of the desert wastes. He'd meant to send it over the city walls and turn it loose on Jerusalem. But the priests lost control of it and it began slaughtering our own soldiers.

When they wrote about it later, the Isrealites just exaggerated the casualties and credited them all to the Archangel Michael." Maia shook her head. "They did a lot of that sort of thing. Anything to boost the stock of their god Yahweh.

"What our priests had created, they finally got some control over, but they couldn't get rid of it. I call it a demon, but it's not like *you* think of demon. There've always been spirits, like unshaped clay, waiting to take whatever form someone with enough knowledge or devotion gives it, and that's what the priests had done. But with the appetite they'd given it, and fed on the blood of four thousand warriors, it'd reached a degree of independence. Finally it consented to banishment, but only on condition of a sacrifice. It . . . it wanted flesh and blood from Sennacherib's own lineage. Even then he got the priests to bargain with it: The thing didn't care if what it received was a legitimate heir to the Assyrian throne; it was the flesh and blood alone that mattered.

"*They took my children, Patrick.* He sent soldiers into our tent and they took my beautiful babies and they *fed* them to that thing. It opened up their bellies and spread their insides out on the desert floor, and ate them piece . . . by . . . piece."

Maia was silent for a long time, and I didn't go to her as I might've. I wasn't made to ease a grief some twenty-seven hundred years strong.

"Hezekiah was horrified by what he'd heard happened, and he eventually paid tribute—he ransomed the city, really—so our army went back home again. But Sennacherib left us behind, Lilah and Salíce and me. Now that he'd killed my children he couldn't trust us, so he made a gift of us to Hezekiah, to be his concubines. Seems even *he* had heard of us, from spies he'd sent to Assyria.

"Even though we were betrayed by Sennacherib, we still didn't have any love for the Israelites, or their god. So it was mostly a very antagonistic relationship we had with Hezekiah. But then one night, before he took us, he became very drunk, and we were amazed at what a state of *terror* he was in over their god. He talked to us, I think, because we were the only ones he *could* talk to, the only ones who didn't share his religion.

"He was still haunted by the butchery of my babies. It wasn't their deaths so much as the . . . the consumption of them that was so abhorrent to him. And this one night, drunk, with his guard down, he confessed that he couldn't see any difference between that and certain things the Israelites' god Yahweh had demanded.

"Then he mentioned some text he'd acquired from a Chaldean trader. He wouldn't tell us what it said, specifically—he was too horrified to do that—but he hinted that it was written in angelic script, and that it couldn't be burned, and that it had something to do with Yahweh and the blood sacrifice of a child."

As Maia told me these things, they plucked at old misgivings I'd once chosen to ignore . . . like all those scriptures that plainly had God demanding that his chosen people lay waste to enemies, down to the last innocent baby and ignorant animal.

Might these, too, have fed him, along with faith?

"When Hezekiah finally had us that night, something became very different about him. In spite of how drunk he was, he was inexhaustible. His erection had swollen to twice its usual size, and he kept after us long after it was raw. Hours, it must've been, and he still hadn't released once. I don't know if it was something in his eyes, or the way his throat ballooned out, as if his flesh couldn't contain whatever was inside him, but we knew it wasn't Hezekiah any longer. It was the Sacred Marriage, all over again . . . except this time, it was *their* god inside *him.*

"And when we realized this, Lilah and Salíce and I, that was when he orgasmed. His screaming was like a slaughtered pig's. You can't have any idea what that sounded like echoing down the palace corridors and back again. And his semen . . . was like venom. He held us down and filled us with it, and there wasn't any end to it, and it burned us from the inside out. . . ."

When Maia went to the window, pressing her hands to the panes of leaded glass, we both gazed on the risen moon that watched over a land once filled with people who'd had no need of anything from the scorching deserts of Palestine. And I thought how right it was that she and her sisters had come to live amongst the Celts, and wait for that day when some magic in our blood might be turned to their advantage, if only to know the enemy a little better.

"And that was the seed of what we became," she finished. "The punishment from their god for who we were; what we'd heard. He turned us into their idea of what we'd worshiped at home. Turned us into Liliths. And then he turned us away. Forever."

—∞—

VIII. *O Magnum Mysterium*

Even before they came to Dublin for the divination, I'd begun collectively thinking of them as the Misbegotten.

They came from as near as across the Irish Sea, from as far away as the other side of the world. They came, and they were not all the same. Some drank blood while others ate flesh; and then there was Salíce. The one called Julius? Before his castrato deafened him, Maia told me, it was the resonances of extraordinary sounds that kept him young. I'd been told of an aborigine who'd been eating eyes since the British used Australia as a penal colony, claiming it kept his view into the Dreamtime clear. I'd been told of a Paris artist who could be nourished only with spinal fluid. They walked and talked like men and women, but only if you looked none too close. For one who knew better, it was as though the gates of some fabulous and terrible menagerie had been thrown wide, and its inhabitants allowed to overrun creation.

Nobody's ever born this way, Maia had said, but I saw them as misbegotten all the same, of monstrous second births that had, by chance or perverse design, left them equipped to demand accounting for what they'd all become. And even if in the end they might only shake futile fists at Heaven, I felt sure their voices would carry much farther than the rest of ours.

In a way I envied them.

In a way I regretted they hadn't the power to turn me into one of them.

But to aid their cause, all I had to do was spread wide my arms, fixate my soul upon the Christ, then do what came naturally.

"We're of two minds on God, Patrick," she'd explained to me. "But if he

really had a son, and there's even a little bit of him in that son, and if there's even a little bit of that son now in your blood, and in that single tiny scrap of flesh he left behind, then maybe that's enough for us to do what men and women have always wanted to do: understand the true nature of God."

"What tiny scrap of flesh he left behind?" I'd asked.

Having heard stories of their revels and debauches, I'd half-expected them to behave like barbarians as they filled the cellars beneath the house. But they took their places amongst the stones and great oaken beams with grim and solemn faces, and waited with the kind of hungry patience that could only accrue over lifetimes.

When the Sisters came for me I was preparing myself in silent contemplation. The Order of Saint Francis had taught me well in this much, at least. I turned around to find they'd quietly filled the doorway, and when Maia laid her cheek to my bare back, the other two turned theirs, to give us our moment alone.

"We're of two minds on God," she'd explained. "Some fear he might really be the creator of everything. In which case, we have no hope at all. Even if there is *some lost paradise that was once promised, we'll never regain it."*

They led me into the chamber, in the center of eyes and teeth and throats, and naked, I lay down upon the waiting cross.

"But there's another way it might be," she'd said, reminding me then of how the Assyrians had made their demon by taking that malleable form and imprinting it with all the traits they desired in it, until they'd fed it to the point of independence, so that it broke away on its own.

They lashed my arms to those of the cross; secured my feet as well. The crown of thorns came last. And when they raised the cross upright, and dropped its foot into the waiting hole, all the old devotions came back to me again, and once more I became as one with Father, with Son, and with Holy Ghost.

Whatever those were.

"Some of us wonder if religion hasn't gotten it backwards," she'd said. "If what the world now calls God wasn't born in the desert out of the needs of people who had to have something bigger than themselves to worship. So it heard them, and asked for more, and they fed it burnt offerings, and the

blood of their enemies, and their devotion, and later on they exported it to the rest of the world. But even before then, it was getting stronger, until after enough centuries had passed, they'd all forgotten where that god of theirs came from and thought it'd always been there, and had created them instead . . . and by then, it was ready to feed on them."

The Sisters of the Trinity took their places while my weight tugged at the lashes that held me aloft. My every rib stood etched against flesh as I laboured for breath. At long last, the empathy I'd always sought with Christ had come. I was no longer in a Dublin cellar; rather, atop a skull-shaped hill called Golgotha, dying in the hot winds and stinging desert dust.

"Who better to feed on than those who considered themselves his children?" she'd explained. "They've always called themselves his chosen people . . . but chosen for what? You have to wonder. From the time of the Babylonian exile, to the destruction of Jerusalem by the Romans, right up to the Holocaust . . . he's been eating and drinking them all along, like no other people on earth."

Salíce stood before me, below, and slowly, reverently, took me into her mouth. Minutes passed as I writhed upon the cross between the agony of breaths, until it happened anew—the flesh of my wrists splitting layer by layer, the blood freed at last in a gush of transcendence and ecstasy. It trickled first along my arms toward my rib cage, then began to flow more heavily, drizzling down into Maia's wide and waiting mouth. So that none would be wasted, bowls were set beneath my other wrist and my feet.

I turned my eyes toward the heavens, wide and seeing so very clearly now, like those of the martyr I'd once dreamt of being: Saint Ignatius, in that painting hanging in Greyfriars Abbey. I'd so admired it, always wondering if I could show his sort of courage when the teeth of the carnivores began to close. Perhaps, now, I'd equaled him, even bettered him; or maybe I'd fallen short by the depth and breadth of the darkest abyss.

There was no truth but this: I was not the father's son I'd once been.

"What tiny scrap of flesh he left behind?" I'd asked.

"Don't forget, he was *circumcised. In the temple, when he was eight weeks old. The Holy Foreskin—that's what you papists call it," she'd said, with a teasing shake of her head. "You people and your morbid relics."*

When I looked down the bloody length of my body, I could see that tiny dark scrap in Lilah's fingers, stolen from its crystal reliquary north of Rome. Still soft and pliable, it was, neither rotted nor gone leathery; incorruptible.

But flesh is flesh, and beliefs something else altogether.

"*Save me from that impotent, slaughtered lamb they have made of me,*" he'd asked, and while I'd never known for sure what impact I might have, perhaps the truth alone would be enough.

The truth, they'd insisted he said, will set you free.

Then again, doubt works miracles, too.

Lilah lifted her hand and touched the foreskin to my flesh, to wet it with my blood; then it disappeared between her teeth.

And in the convulsive rapture of fluids and tissue, in that moment that makes us one with gods, I gave them all they'd asked for, all they needed, all I had to give.

It was explosive.

The greatest revelations usually are.

IX. *Descendo Ad Patrem Meum*

"You can take away a man's gods, but only to give him others in return."

It was Carl Jung said that. My uncle had only borrowed it.

I nearly bled to death on that night of the divination, the stigmata persistent and reaching for the very core of me. In the weeks that followed, as the Sisters nursed me back to health like a faithful dog they couldn't bear to have put to sleep, I often fondled an old pewter crucifix while my thoughts turned to the subject of fear.

Fear the Lord thy God, we were taught since childhood in my family, and how we quaked. How we trembled. How we fell daily to our knees and supplicated for continued mercy.

I'd long ceased to fear; fear is for children, no matter what their age. But when fear is no more, that's still not the end of it, because beyond fear lies despair, and so far, I don't know if there's any end to despair at all.

Once I was well enough to get about again, to stand without dizziness, to walk and run without weakness pitching me toward the nearest chair, I decided I could no longer spend my life with the Sisters of the Trinity. They, and the rest of the Misbegotten, were so much more than I could ever be. Their eyes saw more, their ears heard more, and with their tongues they tasted it, and their feet had walked it, and their minds comprehended it, and they had lived the histories that others only analyzed, and wrongly. . . .

And still they were not gods. They'd have been the first to admit it.

To see them day by day was too hideous a reminder that I was nowhere near their equal . . . and worse, that I'd never really gotten past that deeply instilled need to *believe,* but had now been left with only the Void.

"So what did you learn from it?" I'd asked the Sisters, soon as I could, from my bed; asked more than once. They'd look at one another and smile, with something like sadness and pity and even embarrassment for my sake; but for their own, with maybe just the tiniest ray of hope. Or maybe I saw that only because I wanted to. And then they'd tell me to rest, just rest, their twenty-seven hundred years to my thirty-one like quantum mechanics to a dog.

On my own for the first time in my life, I hiked my homeland like a student tourist, my old possessions sharing backpack space with something I thought of as belonging to a newer Patrick Kieran Malone. The knife was large, with a contoured Kraton haft, a huge killing blade of carbon steel, and a sawtoothed upper edge.

I walked an Ireland different from that of the times of the Troubles, when a bomb had left me standing on a new road. Up north there were no more bombs going off, nor bullets flying, the IRA having decided to lay down its arms—for the time being, at least—and I saw that most everyone was caught up in a cautious optimism that people with differing ideas of the same god really could live together after all.

I wondered if, somewhere, in his jealousness, he missed the smoke and blood of those earlier days. But time was on his side. The old blood lusts never die, they just lie dormant.

Saw a bumper sticker while on my way back up to Belfast. *Nuke Gay Whales for Christ,* it said.

Had to come from America.

"So what did you learn?" I'd asked the Sisters, refusing to give up, and finally Maia sat down on the bed where the marrow in my bones frantically churned out new red blood cells.

"How can I tell you this so you understand it?" she said, and thought a while. "What's God really like . . . ? Imagine an arrogant and greedy and demented child on a beach, building castles in the sand . . . only to kick them over out of boredom, leaving what's left for the waves. Which of course begs one more question:

"Where did the sand come from?"

In Belfast I returned to the church I'd grown up in, and as I entered the sanctuary that quiet afternoon, it smelt the same as it always had, old and sweet with wax and incense. It took me back twenty years, more, the shock of it overwhelming and unexpected; smells can do that to you. It was here where my family gave thanks for my life being spared on that day of the bomb, where they lit candles for the souls of my friends who'd been killed.

I genuflected before the altar, out of old reflex.

Or maybe it was disguise.

The priest didn't recognize me at first, but then it *had* been a while, a decade of monasticism and nearly another year of heresy in between. Such things leave their mark on a man, and even his blood knows the difference. The priest had already heard that I'd left the order; clasped my hands warmly just the same; would be at least sixty now. He told me how deeply my leaving the Franciscans had hurt my mother, dashing so many of her expectations for me.

"Can't help that, Father," I said. "Wasn't my idea, but . . . I've learnt a brand-new doctrine. I just count myself lucky that I learnt it while I'm still a relatively young man."

I could see that he was puzzled. And I remembered a childhood friend who'd told me, when we were altar boys, how the Father had put his hands on him, and where. I'd not believed him. Nobody had. Everybody knew that God loves little children.

"Gospel of Matthew," I said. "Remember what Jesus had to say about new doctrines? Comparing them to wine?" The priest nodded, back on familiar ground. "Said you can't go pouring new wine into old wineskins. It'll just burst them, and what've you got then? Spilt wine and a wineskin that won't hold anything else."

From my backpack I took the sleek, dark knife, and when I unsheathed it, the blade seemed to keep on coming.

"Some days," I confessed, "I do wish that fucking bomb had done me in, too."

I don't know why I killed the priest. Don't know why I did such a thorough bloody job of it. Or why I killed twelve more in the coming weeks, or how I managed to get away with it for as long as I did. Blessed, I suppose, in my own way.

With that sacrificial blade I opened them, throats and chests and bellies, opened them lengthwise or crossways, and out of each poured their stale old wine. And then I'd have to sit a while and gaze upon their burst skins, and reflect upon the way they weren't good for anything else now; this was my main comfort. But I could never get them all.

That, too, was my despair.

So I imagined those beyond my blade, Catholic and Protestant alike, shepherding those even more desperate than I to believe, telling them about an impotent, slaughtered lamb whose history and words had been agreed on by committees. And in his captive name, the eager converts would rise from their watery baptismal graves to go forth and seek to propagate the species.

Over those weeks, I was not a particularly beloved figure in Ireland. Knew it couldn't be much longer before I was caught. And when at last I grew too tired, too sick at heart to continue, only then did I return to the one place, the one people, that would have me, and they took me in as one of their own.

I knew better, though.

No matter how much blood I'd drunk, it hadn't made me one of them.

"Hide me," I asked those voracious and beautiful Sisters of the Trinity. "Hide me where they'll never find me. Hide me where they never can."

Of course, they said. Of course we will.

But Maia wept.

X. *Consummatum Est*

And thus finishes this testament of a boy who wanted only to grow up and be a saint.

There are many who'd say he couldn't have fallen any farther short of such a lofty goal. After all, there are saints, and there are butchers, and they believe they know the difference.

But a few—a growing few, perhaps—would say that he achieved his dream all the same. But this depends on your idea of paradise.

"Think of it this way," Lilah tells me. "You struck some of the first blows in a coming war. Oh, you'll be venerated, I don't have any doubt about that. I've . . . seen it before."

And now, at the end of all ambition, where too ends the flesh and the blood and the seed of life, I can't help but think of my old hero, obsolete though he may be: Saint Ignatius, on his way to the lions in Rome. Would that he'd had such beautiful mouths to welcome him as I'll soon have.

Take me into you, Maia. Take me in, my angel, my deliverer, and I will be with you always . . . until the end of your world.

Caress then these beasts, that they may be my tomb, Ignatius wrote in a final letter, *and let nothing be left of my body; thus my funeral will be a burden to none.*

As for me, I'll not mind leaving bones, and I hope they keep them around, gnawed and clean, true relics for the inspiration of disciples yet to come.

I’m Not Well, But I’m Better

Pat Califia

A dolpha, dressed in her customary black leather and red silk, was the last to arrive. The room was too small for the six (now seven) women it held. There were some perfectly nice leather-covered sofas and chairs, but everyone had propped themselves up on large pillows on the floor. It was not Adolpha's way to lounge about. So she walked through the middle of the circle, picked a spot exactly opposite the therapist, and folded herself neatly to a cross-legged position on the carpeted floor. She did not look to the left or to the right to acknowledge the women who moved sideways, sliding awkwardly on their butts, to make space for her. Nor did she give the therapist a deferential smile or an explanation for her five minutes' worth of tardiness.

It would have been easy to spot who the therapist was, even if Adolpha had not been studying Amy Ross for the last two weeks. For one thing, she sat inside a slightly larger zone of empty space than anyone else in the circle. This gave her room to make expressive gestures with her hands, without the risk of bumping elbows with one of her clients. She looked prosperous—feminine, yet professional. She wore a strand of carnelian and onyx beads, a lacy Victorian blouse, and a broomstick skirt of organic cotton whose rich brown color was imbued with vegetable dyes. She had taken off her Italian sandals and placed them neatly, toes to the wall, behind herself.

Now Amy cleared her throat and began to talk. The women in the group looked at the floor and played with their hair. They seemed to wish desperately to be anywhere except trapped within this small room with its taupe carpet, the huge framed print of a fulsome Georgia O'Keefe flower, the handblown glass vases on the mantelpiece of the empty fireplace, the earth-and-sky hues of the dreamcatcher that hung on the back of the door.

Adolpha had buzzed her hair that morning, and by now it had grown out to half an inch of stubble the color of corn silk. She did not touch it, feeling no need to rearrange herself for scrutiny. She noticed then that all the other women in the group had taken off their shoes, in imitation of the therapist. So she stretched her legs out in front of herself, which gave Amy an excellent view of her riding boots. Adolpha had tucked her full-cut leather pants into the top of them. She looked like a Cossack on her way to Nordstrom's.

Adolpha felt someone else's eyes upon her, and tracked the stranger's gaze to the knife hilt that protruded slightly from the top of the right boot. Not that she needed it; her teeth were growing sharper by the minute, honed by boredom if nothing else. But Adolpha loved the drama of knives—their flashing beauty, the way they instantly reflected light and terror. It was Rhys who had seen it, of course. She was good at figuring out how other people could damage her. Adolpha idly made her forget about the knife.

The droning introduction to the group was finally over. The therapist had presented her credentials as an experienced healer of those who'd suffered the trauma of childhood sexual abuse. This was a group for survivors, she had emphasized, a group for those who had the courage to heal. She promised that the work would be successful, if they had the faith and strength to persevere. It was vitally important to conjure up the past and its misery, so that it could be reexperienced in a safe context, all the anger and fear vented, the old business finished. Then normal life could begin. A better body image, self-esteem, healthy relationships, healthy sexuality were some of the fruits that could spill from Amy's cornucopia, if they were worthy. Were there any questions?

Adolpha, who needed to worry very little about her health, thought that was probably a fine quality for a prey animal to possess, and yawned, taking a good long time to properly stretch her jaws. But wait—someone was daring to ask a question. It was the woman on Adolpha's right, a voluptuous femme dyke in her early forties who worked as a travel agent. Her curls shook as she stammered, "How much longer, I mean, in the groups that you've led in the past, I know you can't really be specific but to just give us a general idea, how long have other groups lasted before you felt like people were, um, well, I guess you shouldn't say *cured,* but . . . ?"

Amy gave her a smile full of pity that made the hair on the back of Adolpha's neck stand up in a silent shout of rage. "Well, we are doing depth work here," she temporized. "Incest is a serious trauma. It has long-term, wide-ranging consequences. We must be prepared to put in as much time as is necessary to address it."

The woman on Adolpha's left, a young musician with a mostly shaved scalp and an off-center, sapphire-colored mandarin braid, spoke out then. "That means we're never going to get well, doesn't it?" she said flatly. This was Rhys, not quite twenty-one. She wore her alien skeleton fresh and raw on the outside of her skin, having spent almost as much time getting tattooed as she would have spent in prison for manslaughter. Adolpha liked girls with tattoos, although she had to admit that choosing someone on that basis was as risky as picking a bottle of wine just because it had a pretty label.

Amy acted as if she had not heard that comment. "I think we should go around the circle. Each woman should tell us what name she'd like used in the group and a little bit of the history that brought you here." And there was another one of those smiles that Adolpha hated, a coy smile, like that of a cat who knows her sister is waiting by the mouse's escape hatch. Amy turned her head and sprayed the entire circle with that smile, except that when her gaze crossed Adolpha, two tiny creases sprang up between her eyebrows, two little lines of concern. Adolpha was amused. Dissent had sprung from either side of her. Without saying a word, she had been identified as a troublemaker.

She exerted her will slightly, and the woman on her right began to talk. Adolpha did not listen to the details. She was more interested in the flavor of being that emanated from each woman. Mortals had that strange effect upon her senses, as if each was a dish that her mind had to sample before she could sink her teeth into it. It made walking through a crowd a real challenge; sometimes there was just too much data, and it made her feel crazy. Automatically, to keep herself awake, she paged through the past of each woman as she spoke, separating truth from fiction, belief from actual event.

The travel agent had an alcoholic father and a mother who insisted on staying married to him. She believed that her father had molested her, but in fact, it was her mother who had crept into her room late at night and put her hand where it did not belong.

The next woman was a graduate student who was having trouble finishing her thesis. She had short, naturally red hair and a lean, athletic body. After two years of therapy, she had come to believe that the only explanation for her fractured relationships, uneven sex life, and confusion about her future was a history of incest. In fact, Adolpha found, nothing of the sort had happened. But that would not be a problem in Amy's group. Amy was a certified hypnotherapist. She could give you the past that your misery demanded.

And so it went around the circle, until it came time for Rhys to speak. Adolpha did her the rare courtesy of turning to look at her. She had so much enjoyed listening to her band play in a warehouse that weekend. It was thrilling to take blood in a thrash pit, right in front of the victim's friends. She had not even bothered to cast a see-me-not over herself that night. Of course, Rhys did not remember her. Adolpha frequently found it convenient to be overlooked by her conquests until the appropriate moment for confrontation came.

Rhys spoke in a rush, incomplete sentences piled on top of one another, uneven and jagged as broken glass. She was a victim—a junkie (although she did not mention that part of her life in the group), a habitual fuckup who could not hold down a job or a home, always on the verge of not surviving because she managed to alienate even the friends who offered her temporary places to stay, fed her, loaned her money that she never repaid. Rhys had a lot of friends for a girl who never put out. But it was no surprise to Adolpha that givers outnumbered takers in this world, and she did not think ill of Rhys for her unthinking consumption of other people's love, money, peanut butter, and smack.

Rhys had been raped by virtually every male relative she had, and by some of their friends. Pictures had been taken. Movies had been made.

Some of the violation had been scripted as satanic ritual. She did not need hypnotherapy or truth serum to remember this. She remembered it all. In fact, what she really wanted from the group was a way to forget.

When Rhys was done speaking, Adolpha, who knew what such a thing would look like, visualized each woman trying to sit quietly with her abdomen slit open and her intestines steaming in her lap. She got quite preoccupied with embellishing this vision, until she realized that the silence in the group had gone on too long for even a therapist's patience.

"Adolpha," Amy said pleasantly, "do you have anything you'd like to share with us?"

Adolpha gave her back a smile, exactly a copy of that I-feel-so-much-compassion-for-you-because-I-know-something-you-don't-know look. "Once," she said, deliberately spacing out her words to get their attention, "a long time ago, my brother did something to me that I did not wish him to do. And I have never forgiven him for it. One day, he will do penance."

Everyone kept looking at her, hanging on her words. When it became clear that there would be no more to the story, they shook themselves as if they were waking up or flicking water off their faces. Even Amy Ross had to shudder to cast off the spell of Adolpha's honeyed, foreign-sounding tenor.

The meeting went on for another hour. Amy managed to persuade the woman who had not been abused to pretend she was talking to her father, to confront him with accusations that Adolpha could hardly refrain from laughing at. Eventually she beat up a pillow that represented him. Then Amy dismissed them all with a short, upbeat speech about liberating themselves from the tyranny of the past, which would happen only if they kept coming back!

The therapist asked Rhys to stay behind. She wanted to tell her that there were more resources available for healing herself—in other words, she wanted Rhys to start seeing her for individual therapy, in addition to the group. Adolpha heard all of this from her place on the landing, where she was waiting so she could watch Rhys walk down the stairs. She heard Rhys complain that she could not afford so much therapy, and Amy offered to run a tab. Adolpha bit her own tongue to keep herself from laughing out loud. Rhys was going to go into debt to satisfy Amy Ross's appetite for suffering. That was like asking people to pay for the privilege of being bled. Although, come to think of it, there was Daytona Bitch, who worked Times Square and did exactly that.

Rhys said she would think about it, and left. It took only the lightest touch against her mind to stop her from wondering why Adolpha was lurking on the landing. The vampire descended two steps behind her quarry, aching to cup her hands around the cheeks of her ass. Rhys smelled like water lilies and snow. The aura she gave off was violet-tinged, and its texture reminded Adolpha of a Victorian quilt she had once seen, made out of one-inch squares of jewel-toned velvet. Inside her chest was the claw of an eagle, which tore and tore at Rhys's heart. She was in so much psychic pain, all the time, it was as if her own blood was scalding her to death.

It would be so sweet to take her now. Adolpha knew it could be done with ease. All she had to do was prevent Rhys's Shadow from starting, say she knew something about bikes, pretend to fix it, invite her out for a beer to celebrate. Of course, even these preliminaries were not necessary. Adolpha could simply take Rhys in her arms, rip her head off, and empty her right here on the street. People would part around them and keep on walking, as if they had seen nothing at all. Adolpha had the power to make even a grandiloquent kill invisible to innocent bystanders. But she loved the dance of seduction. She would never do what her foolish brother Ulrich had done and take a mortal consort. Still, there were pleasures other than blood lust.

And she did not intend to kill Rhys. At least, not yet, not now. So Adolpha satisfied herself with breathing into Rhys's body, a warm and subversive gust of air that started around her ankles, ran up her legs into her cunt, and from there spread into her chest and face, opening her up to a lightning flash of pure pleasure. Rhys made a small sound and stumbled. Adolpha caught her by the elbow, steadied her, and gave her a conspiratorial wink. It came to her, despite everything she did to shield herself from the information, that this was the first time Rhys had ever felt a delicious sensation of her own in any of her orifices, rather than being held hostage as a witness to other people's taking their pleasure there.

Adolpha shrugged. Human beings were cruel to each other. It was one of the things that justified her hunting among them. This was the latest episode in the predatory game of her life, and that was all. The musician's soul had been mangled, but countless others had been treated with even more brutality.

The darkness would last for another six hours. She squeezed herself as small as a fist—wrinkled face with a monkey-snout, soft brown fur, thin-skinned wings stretched taut between cartilage struts, and agile, grasping paws. In this guise, she flew to a much more interesting part of town, where the clubs were located. After spending so much time in the company of women, she had a fancy for boy meat, some brash young thing who would be appalled to find himself alone with a woman he could not force or intimidate. Frat boys were especially yummy, full of testosterone, their faces prickly with nubile beards. The scrape of male fur against her lips and tongue gave Adolpha goose bumps. She loved the flavor of brandy mingled with a human being's blood. It was her little way to sit next to her intended and manipulate the bartender into pouring and her beloved into drinking whatever flavor she thought would make her feeding most piquant.

It took two more weekly sessions for Amy to persuade Rhys to make an appointment for individual therapy. In that short amount of time, the lives of the women in the group had deteriorated quickly. Two of them had lost their jobs. The graduate student had severed all ties with her family, who were paying for school, which solved the problem of the unwritten dissertation. Some of them had broken up with their lovers. All of them were depressed. It amazed Adolpha to see them draw closer together, caught in the net of their despair. Why was it that adversity made human beings so stupid and stubborn? Any other animal would try to escape from a situation that was causing them such unhappiness, but these women simply dug their heels in and became even more loyal to their therapist and the process that was drowning them.

Amy Ross, with her turquoise jewelry and cloisonnée bracelets and silver earrings from Thailand, her cashmere cardigans and her batik skirts and linen jackets, and her promises of nurturance and healing, had them spellbound. She loved to dabble her clean white fingers in someone else's emotional wounds. If she saw any signs of healing, she did not flinch from yanking hard on the sides of it and ripping it open again. Women in her groups who were not sure they had been molested became convinced that it was so. Those who had been able to name one perpetrator were now able to name two, or half a dozen. Those who had remembered only fondling, which had been obnoxious but not painful, were now sobbing through hysterical narratives about being torn by penetration. They saw signs of abuse in every relationship they had, with employers, friends, lovers, family members. They stopped making love, stopped masturbating, and saw every sexual fantasy as just one more symptom of damage.

Adolpha had to admit it was a perfect scam. Find a group of people whose early life experience has convinced them that they are unworthy, that bad things will always happen to them, a group of people who expect to be hurt, who don't know what a healthy relationship is, and then put yourself in the position of their caretaker and promise to help them. After most of the group therapy sessions, Adolpha was convinced that if Amy Ross had tried to do real therapy with them and promote resolution or healing, she would have lost every client she had. They were that embedded in old patterns, the repetition of injury and insult and violation.

Rhys never spoke to her or even looked at her. But she always sat next to Adolpha, on her left, like a dog that automatically assumes its place at the feet of its master. Adolpha could not, of course, go a whole week without seeing Rhys. She had taken to feeding herself quickly and then hovering outside Rhys's bedroom window, every night, in the witching hours before dawn. There were so many games she could play with Rhys once sleep had dismantled some of her defenses. One of Adolpha's favorite ploys was to make Rhys's tattoos come alive. First she would warm them until Rhys threw off her covers and lay naked before Adolpha's hungry eyes. Then she would make them move slightly, quickly. It was like being caressed with the barest tips of butterfly wings. She would make the rings in Rhys's nipples and clitoral hood vibrate subtly, until the parts they pierced were swollen and erect. Slowly, gradually, Adolpha would pour sensuality into the ink, suffusing Rhys's body with delight until she groaned and came in her sleep.

The best moment of all was when Rhys would wake up, heart pounding and cunt wet, unable to remember exactly what had happened, rubbing herself all over, trying to figure out how the flat ink on her skin had become inflamed. Adolpha wanted her so much then, wanted to flick her tongue against Rhys's clit and sink her hand into Rhys's cunt. But she knew that Rhys took no pleasure in sex and would barely feel the most savage rapine. So she continued to devise new ways to make Rhys tremble in her sleep.

Of course, she could have simply walked into Rhys's mind and taken away the horrors that had made sex a ruined palace for her, but she did not. That would have spoiled the game, and Adolpha was relishing this hunt.

She was there the first evening that Amy Ross met with Rhys one-on-one to begin a new phase of treatment. Ironically enough, it was the weird evenings of onanistic pleasure that had made Rhys think the therapy was effective, and more of it would probably be a good idea. Adolpha slipped in the door behind her, accidentally catching the fact that Rhys had no idea where she was going to sleep tonight; probably the bus station.

Amy indicated the couch and told Rhys to lie down. She obeyed the order, as she had obeyed many others like it. Adolpha could barely contain herself when Amy began to hypnotize Rhys. She had to dig her fingernails (cut at sundown, now an inch long and sharp as razors) into the palms of her hands to make herself stay silent and hidden. It was a surprise to feel so much jealousy. The clumsy trance state that Amy Ross induced could not compare with the deep glamour that Adolpha could cast, but it was enough to peel back Rhys's inhibitions and make her suggestible.

Amy Ross began with the usual reassurances that Rhys was safe. They were going to watch a movie together, and maybe there would be some upsetting things in it, but it wasn't really happening, and Rhys could stop the tape at any time. The movie was about Rhys when she was little, and some bad people had done bad things to her. Did Rhys remember when that had begun? Who was there? What did he say? What had been done to her?

Adolpha hissed as she listened to the narrative. So far it was standard desensitization, giving Rhys power over the narrative of her life, allowing her to stop and thus control the replay of her memories. But Adolpha did not think it was standard practice for Amy Ross to keep demanding additional details (which Rhys gave her in the voice of a frightened child), or ethical for her to be putting her right hand inside her own panties and rubbing her bikini-waxed pussy. Adolpha was not surprised to find herself becoming aroused by the pathos of Rhys's tale of rape and voyeurism, but she didn't approve of mortals with gourmet appetites.

Then Amy suggested that it was hot in the room, very hot, and that it was hard to breathe, so Rhys should pull up her T-shirt and unbutton her jeans. Adolpha's eyebrows shot up at the sheer temerity of it. When Amy succeeded in directing Rhys to stroke her own nipples and finger her clit, Adolpha cracked. She would not tolerate someone else coming this close to the gift she had picked out for her own enjoyment.

The look on Amy Ross's face as Adolpha came out of the shadows was priceless, a mixture of fury and abject guilt. Still, she managed to cling to the mantle of her profession. "Adolpha, I am afraid I will have to ask you to leave. You are jeopardizing the confidentiality of one of my clients!"

Adolpha advanced on her, plucked Amy Ross's wanton hand from between her thighs, and thrust the fingers of that hand into the therapist's painted-pink mouth. "Is this what you mean by in-depth work?" she sneered.

She took Amy Ross's hand out of her mouth, so she could hear what she had to say. But she kept a tight grip on her wrist. The therapist did not try to escape. She seemed to believe that if she did not acknowledge her captivity, it would have no meaning. She gave the intruder that pitying trademark smile. "I'm afraid you don't have the background to understand the intricacies of psychotherapy, dear. Sometimes it takes unorthodox methods to clean up the garbage that's left behind by incest. But I stand by my results."

"Oh, really?" Adolpha asked, with one eyebrow raised. "What about Sue Harkness? Do you stand by the results you got with her? Because you might as well have been standing by her side when she blew her brains out with a .45."

"I must acknowledge that it's a great tragedy when a long-term client commits suicide," Amy Ross whispered. "But I can't take responsibility for her decision to end her own life. Each one of us is the only person who can really shoulder that burden."

"I don't know about that—you seem to have more burdens than most shrinks. Do you recall the name of Ellen Bauer? What about Linda Treat? Jocelyn Dewars? Or little Eddy Silverstein? Come on, Amy, I know you can't reveal the identities of your clients, but these people all happen to be very very dead. And I think it's your fault."

Amy Ross finally realized that she was in deep trouble, and began to struggle. But Adolpha was not ready to take her yet. "Wake Rhys up," she ordered, turning Amy to face the reclining woman. Rhys still lay there with her clothing askew and her mouth slightly open. She looked as if she was in REM sleep. One of her hands twitched a little as she dreamed.

"Tell her the movie is over, she doesn't need to watch it anymore, and wake her up!" Adolpha said, getting impatient. She shook Amy to let her know she meant business. The out-of-breath therapist snapped her fingers. Rhys sat up slowly, realized her breasts were exposed, and yanked her shirt down. Then she realized her fly was open and she glared up at both of them, humiliated and furious. "What the hell is going on here?" she yelled.

"Why, it's time for Amy Ross to realize that she's not the only vampire in this town," Adolpha said, feeling quite cheerful now. Amy Ross's eyes went wide as Adolpha took her by the shoulders. She was facing Rhys as Adolpha sank three-inch ivory fangs into her neck and sucked out her life as fast as it could come. She beat on Adolpha's back and tried to free herself, but it was no use. Adolpha was too strong, and too quick. Rhys made a muffled sound and tried to back away, but the couch was too heavy to move, and she was too frightened to think of a way out of its sticky cream-colored embrace.

Adolpha dropped Amy Ross's body. It fell akimbo, with as much dignity as she had allowed her patients. Rhys threw her hands out, an ineffectual gesture of warding as Adolpha came toward her with her fangs fully extended, a snake woman, a wolf spirit. Her face was bloody, and her eyes were full of glee.

"Don't hurt me," Rhys pleaded. "Please, leave me alone, don't hurt me!"

Adolpha shook her head, spraying Rhys with a little of Amy Ross's jugular vintage. "Don't hurt me," she mocked. "Please, leave me alone! What a wimp you are, Rhys, a weak member of a weak species. You have no idea how short your life is, do you? In fact, you imagine that your life has already gone on for far too long. You whimper and whine and live like a fool, and hope that fate will take a hand and deal you out of the game. I have lived for many long centuries. My victims number in the millions. Sometimes I take the best, the strongest, the most beautiful, the most talented. And sometimes I am in a mood to take the evil, the wicked, or the sick whose time is almost up. But I tell you this—every person I have ever embraced has fought to live. And now, it is your turn to learn how precious your life is, and find the will to keep it."

Rhys's sleeveless white T-shirt was speckled red, and a few fine drops of blood had been sprayed across her forehead. Her blue pigtail hung over one shoulder, and her guitar-callused hands dug into the leather upholstery, ripping it. She smelled like absolute terror. There was no hot, coppery smell of anger in her. She was a little brown rabbit who knew it had been spotted moving through the autumn leaves. The sight of her small breasts, rising and falling with her frail mortal breath, enraged Adolpha, and she hurled herself at her, lifting her until they were chest to chest, eye to eye. There was still no resistance. Rhys stared straight at her, but her eyes were blind. And so Adolpha gathered her up like a lover, nuzzled the crook of her neck, and went deep into the muscle.

The pain must have been intense. But Rhys didn't even scream. Adolpha thought she might be crying. So she worried the wounds that she had made, and at that, Rhys responded by pulling away slightly. "I can't do this," she cried, and Adolpha knew she was weeping. "I can't do this, I can't fight you. Take me, let me die, I don't want to live. I don't want to live. I'm a fucked-up mess, I'm a junkie and a loser. You're strong and beautiful, and it's right for me to feed you. So take what you want, just do it quick, and if you don't have to hurt me, please don't, I can't stand the pain."

Adolpha shrugged and resumed feeding. It usually took her no more than a few minutes to take a life, but she prolonged this kill. Amy Ross had sated most of her hunger and rage, and now she felt almost playful. She refused to take quite enough blood to make Rhys lose consciousness. Instead, she bit deeper and deeper, making multiple wounds, deliberately inflicting the pain that Rhys was begging to avoid.

Finally she lifted Rhys up and sank her fangs into the musician's left breast. Rhys was dangling from her arms, and she screamed when the sharp incisors penetrated her delicate tissues. Still she did not really resist. This was maddening. When her own brother had come for her, Adolpha had not been like the other girls in the cage, had not shrieked or tried to escape. She was too proud. But this was not pride, it was weakness, and Rhys had no right to stir the ancient pool of her memories!

Physical pain was not having the effect she wanted, Adolpha, forever flexible, changed tactics, and unleashed a series of fierce orgasms in her victim, keeping it up until Rhys's thighs were as wet as her neck. Rhys had never come in someone else's arms before. "You're going to get at least one good fuck before you die," Adolpha vowed. She threw Rhys back onto the sofa and herself on top of her, then ripped off the musician's jeans. Now she was struggling, calling Adolpha filthy names, trying to fend her off and protect her cunt. At last her will to live had emerged. But Adolpha brushed aside her hands and went in deep, saying, "You are under my power, Rhys, and you will come every time I say your name."

Then she proved that it was so. The only break that Rhys got were the few seconds Adolpha needed to lick the young woman's nipples in between the soft, caressing repetitions of her name. Adolpha put her hands everywhere that Rhys's abusers had: in her cunt, her mouth, her ass. And everywhere she touched, she left behind a legacy of inhuman pleasure, the total response that can only be wrung from human flesh when it is on the brink of death, or under supernatural sway.

"So there you are," Adolpha said, withdrawing from her victim. Her belly was full of blood, and she felt warm and replete. Ready for sleep.

"You're not going to kill me, are you?" Rhys asked, legs splayed against a couch that would never be pure white again. Her arms and legs trembled with fatigue from the combat with Adolpha.

"I don't think so," the vampire said.

"Where are you going? What will I do now?" Rhys sobbed with dry eyes, looking wildly about, smeared with blood.

"If I were you, I'd call an attorney," Adolpha said, stepping down. "Then I'd call the police. You might want to ask them to take a look at Amy Ross's private video collection, over there on the bookshelf, between Malamud and Goldsmith. She taped all of the private sessions." Adolpha took the Georgia O'Keefe off the wall. A tiny hole had been cut in it, and it concealed a niche in the wall that held a small video camera. "Just like she was videotaping you, sweet thing."

"But I didn't kill her. You—"

"Please be my guest, Rhys. Tell the district attorney that you were raped by a vampire who had just murdered your therapist. They'll still put you away, but I imagine mental hospitals are a lot more fun than prison. Or I guess you could tell the cops that the cult that was abusing you took revenge upon the kindly shrink who was trying to give you psychic first aid. In which case, you should probably destroy Amy Ross's library of dual-relationship pornography before you call anybody."

"I can't believe you're just going to walk away and leave me to deal with all this!"

Adolpha gave her a withering look. "Believe it or not, as you like. I'm out of here. You'll clean up this mess just fine, Rhys. You'll do it because you have to if you want to live. Like Amy Ross said, we're all survivors. You're not well, but you're better."

Adolpha opened a window and thought, *Fist-size, warm night sky, bouncing ping of radar, insect scooping crunchy-squishy midnight snack, soothing moonlight bath,* and vanished, eager to feel the narrow sides and lid of her coffin pressing against her well-fed flesh.

Kingyo no fun

Nicholas Royle

Everybody knows one. You've either met one or you know one by reputation. Not everybody suffers, however, to the extent that James has suffered. And while that's partly circumstance, it's also partly James's own fault, through his innocence—which has a lot to do with why I love him.

This one's name was Simon but it could have been anything. It could have been William or Terry, or Carolyn or Suzi. They're all the same. They're all *kingyo no fun.* I've known them, you've known them. And James has known them. Only James doesn't know how to shake them off like most people do.

We were in Amsterdam for the weekend. A long weekend. It was late spring sometime in the mid-1990s. I think it was late May. That summer would break all records for mean temperatures and hours of sunshine and already by the end of April it was beginning to get seriously hot. James was doing publicity for his new book and I was hanging around with him. He likes me being around when he's doing this stuff. It's not that we make a big show of it, but I'm always there, if anybody wants to know. If anybody's wondering. About James, you know. There's a light. Okay? And it's a red kind of a light.

He's not a gay writer, he's fond of saying. He's just a writer who happens to be gay. You come on as a gay writer and you get asked to do all the representative stuff. ACT UP and Outrage and fundraising for AIDS charities.

James says he's got nothing against doing some of that stuff—and he works hard for a good cause—but he doesn't want to get labeled. And I think that's cool. He doesn't want to cut his sales by half in order to please a minority. So I hang around and meet people but I don't, you know, stick my tongue down his throat and my hand down his pants while he's schmoozing some new agent or flirting with pretty-boy publishers. I do have a sense of restraint. I can be diplomatic. It's not half as much fun but I can do it.

The gig was some weird conjunction of writing and visual art in a small gallery off the Herengracht—*gracht* being the Dutch word for canal. The place was crawling with conceptual artists being studiedly unkempt and unshaven—boys *and* girls, this being the year Della Grace famously "stopped plucking"—and, frankly, a little bit dirty. I longed to take one of them aside and ask why they thought it necessary to go around looking like extras out of some Eastern Bloc movie of the 1970s. In whose eyes could it possibly make them look like better artists?

But I didn't, because I had to think of James.

The artists were all meant to be exhibiting new stuff and the writers reading from recently published work. One video artist showed his new "piece," which consisted of him wearing a gorilla suit and jumping up and down—quite strenuously for a self-proclaimed slacker. Over the course of twelve minutes—the overgenerous running time of this video—the gorilla suit gradually falls apart, leaving the artist naked and generally looking a bit of an asshole. Wouldn't have been half as bad if he'd had a decent body, I said later to James. Another artist showed a glass case full of miniature houses pinned down like dead butterflies. The work was entitled, *Househunting 1995.*

There was worse, believe me, but hey, you know, life's too short.

James was doing his thing. There was a microphone but James never uses them because he's blessed with a mellifluous, sonorous voice—he can project to the end of next week. And if he's reading from a book or script he prefers to keep one hand free. He ranges to and fro in order to include the entire audience, trying to give good value. He's a real pro. There was a photographer guy climbing all over the seats and crates that were stacked up at the side of the gallery, taking shot after shot after shot, and sometimes getting right in close, but James just carried on, totally unfazed. When he cracked jokes people laughed. His timing was good and I noticed he'd give them a look as he delivered a new gag. He knew that even given the language barrier he could make them laugh if (a) they liked him and (b) they realized *when* they were supposed to laugh.

When he'd done I noticed this guy go up to talk to him. Nothing unusual in that. People are always going up to get books signed or just to say hi, so they can say to their friends they met a famous author. This guy looked about thirty-six or thirty-seven, unruly hair and a thrift-store jacket, but perfectly normal compared to some of the freaks James occasionally attracts. I watched James politely listen to the guy and respond with some larger-than-life gesture—not to impress, that's just the way he is—and then, because someone else was waiting to say something, the guy stepped back and kind of melted into the crowd.

"Because that was the extent of it," James was to tell me much later, "I thought he was okay. But when he came up to me again at the end of the evening, when we'd all hung around with whoever we were hanging around with for just about long enough, and were all about ready to go and move on, he came up to me again and I don't know what he said but he started talking and straightaway I knew—I knew this guy was bad news. I don't know how I missed it earlier. I guess because he wasn't talking to me for long enough and didn't have a chance to show what a complete asshole he was. But as soon as he started, when he came up to me again later, as soon as he started I knew I was in big trouble."

"That look?"

"That look."

Kingyo no fun always have the look. Always. But you can't always tell on the look alone because other people can have the same look and be okay. It's a kind of a crazed look in the eyes. Hell, who am I telling this shit! You know this. You've seen the look. You do sometimes get normal people who have the look, or who appear to have it—the lights are on and there *is* somebody at home. With *kingyo no fun,* the lights are burning for sure, every goddamn fucking window, but there ain't *nobody* sitting in that house. And that's the whole problem in, like, a real small pecan shell. Never occurred to me before. You got the whole problem right there.

So when I ambled over to join James because it looked like people might be about to make a move, this guy—Simon—was hanging around like a bad smell. He appeared quite impervious to hints. No amount of subtle body language seemed able to shift him.

"So we going, James, or what?" I said with a trace of impatience.

James was turned the other way. "I think a couple of the guys are joining us for a drink." He turned to face me. Simon was side on to the two of us; he didn't turn away, just watched, this little smile like a worm making its way slowly across the lower half of his face. "You wanna go for a drink?" James said, sort of to both of us. Jeez, that stung. "Coupla English guys. Writers. They seem pretty cool. Tall guy suggested we go get a beer."

"A drink's a good idea," said Simon, the *kingyo no fun.*

"Why don't you go fuck yourself? You're not invited, pal," I wanted to say, but I heard James falling over himself to be nice to the guy.

"Wanna go get a beer, Simon? Whaddya say, huh?"

Jesus, James. Didn't God give you eyes? Don't you ever fucking use them? You wanna fucking use them, man.

"Yeah, that'd be cool," said the *kingyo no fun.*

Cool. Yeah, it'd be *fucking* cool. Mr. Kingyo No Fucking Asshole.

Calm, calm, some shrink was going inside my head. *Yeah, calm, you don't know what it's like, guy.*

So we headed out of the art gallery, James shaking hands with the gallery owner on the way, in pursuit of the two English writers, and with Simon, naturally, bringing up the rear.

"Where would you like to go?" I heard the shorter of the two English guys ask James.

"Wherever," James replied, looking around to include me.

The *kingyo no fun* said: "There's a nice place just up here. Shouldn't be too busy."

The tall English guy, whose name turned out to be Ben, acquiesced quite happily; his shorter companion, Matthew, fell uncomplainingly into line; and James, easygoing as ever, nodded brightly. I looked across the canal at a crowd spilling out of a bar, wondered what was wrong with that place, but Ben and Matthew had already struck off in the direction indicated by

Simon, who had fallen in next to James and was animatedly talking *art* with him. Because of some major construction work that ran alongside the canal, I couldn't squeeze alongside them and had to follow on behind. This, you will appreciate, pissed me off.

Kingyo no fun operate differently in different countries when it comes to bar etiquette. The goal is always the same: to avoid paying. Okay, okay, I know some of you will have come across people you *think* are *kingyo no fun* who *do* buy drinks in order to ingratiate themselves with the people they're leeching off of. But hey, get this, they're not real *kingyo no fun* because the *kingyo no fun* conforms to a rigid set of regs.

James and I, although we were both born and raised in New York City, live in London, England, and have done for about ten years. James likes the scene—by which I mean the literary scene, not the gay scene. He likes that too. A little too well. But that's another story. We met in Heaven about three years ago. We had both been in London seven years already, having come from pretty much the same neighbourhood in New York originally, and not having met previously in London. "Kinda weird, huh?" James would say to me later.

"What's weird?" I asked him.

"Well, you know. It's kind of a coincidence you turning up like that and, you know, we're both from New York, both in Heaven that night, both been on the scene some time and never met up before."

"Coincidence? There's no such thing," I said.

When we met, James was with a group of leathermen. I'd been following them with my eyes for about ten minutes when one of them approached me and asked if I wanted a drink. Sure, I said. Why not? And rather than let this guy take me off to some dark corner, which was what he appeared to have on his mind, I used him to help me enter the group. It was the tallest guy I had my eye on. The one with long sculpted sideburns and a Nick Cave T-shirt. The one with big eyes. The one called James.

So that was the night we met and from then on we stuck together—James slightly less convincingly than me from time to time, but he always came back, always apologized and I always forgave him.

Living in England you have to get used to pubs. A pub is like a bar without the sense of being in a bar. You can get a beer and all, but it's like getting a beer in a mall—it's kind of like Bar-Lite, you know, or Diet-Bar. I'm talking about the pubs in London. I can't tell you about the quaint little old country pubs because we haven't gone out to the country. We did go to High Wycombe once to score some powder, but I don't think that counts. Jesus, I sure hope it don't count. And one of the thing about pubs is that groups go there together, or they meet up there, and they kind of take it in turns to go get the drinks. Only there's no bar tab, so by the end of the evening everybody has bought everybody else a drink. Or that's how it's supposed to work. The *kingyo no fun* in any group sits right back in his or her seat whenever the glasses start to look empty. He is not going to buy anybody else a drink if he can help it. Because he's a fuckin' freeloader, man. That's his entire philosophy. He's gonna sit right back and let everybody else get on with it. Of course, he'll still accept his beer every time some other poor sucker goes up to the bar to get it. And somehow, don't ask me how, he gets away with it.

If you're in a group—jeez, even if that group is only two people and one of them is *kingyo no fun*—and you're walking toward the pub, the *kingyo no fun* starts to hang back, real subtle-like so nobody knows what's going on, but he hangs back and puts an arm around the last person to enter the pub ahead of him, just to make sure. This way he'll be the last person to reach the bar and there's no way he'll have to buy a drink if they're only staying for one or two.

In Amsterdam, Simon, *kingyo no fun,* led us into the crowded bar. *Jesus, what's this guy doing?* I thought. Could I have been mistaken? But once I, and the others, had fought our way through the throng and caught up with Simon, I realized he knew exactly what he was doing. He'd found the only free table in the place. And he'd sat down already. He was guarding our seats. We could hardly expect him to get up and go to the bar now because he was keeping our table for us. That was his job and boy didn't he do it well. So, Ben and Matthew went off to the bar and James and I sat down with Simon. I had this sneaking suspicion that the two English guys would take the opportunity to slip away, unable to take any more of Simon's company, but when I craned my neck I could just make out Ben standing at the bar talking to one of the bartenders—nice looking guy, about twenty, twenty-one, very tall, blond, healthy tan. Yeah, right—look but don't touch.

James had gone and sat right next to Simon. There was no need for that, I thought. We could have both sat right over the other side of the table—it was quite a wide table—in order to make sure we kept all the seats necessary. But James is like that. He doesn't think. Sometimes I have to think for him. Ben and Matthew reappeared, Ben carrying a tray with five opened bottles of Beck's on it. Matthew helped by distributing the beers and then we were all clinking bottles and saying stuff. Simon was grinning all over his face. Yeah, of course he was. He was doing okay.

No one was saying anything so I thought I'd start the ball rolling. "So what about all that art shit?"

"Oh, I know some of those guys," Simon said.

Yeah, he would.

"I think some of their stuff's fascinating, don't you?" He directed his question at James, who raised his bottle to his lips and nodded.

Simon was English and, unlike his two compatriots, talked like he had a ten-pound salmon up his ass. Like someone out of a 1960s movie. Someone who lives in a little mews flat off the King's Road in Chelsea. I looked at him looking at James. His skin was a little too white, like thin dough, and his eyes were punched into it like raisins. The left eye bore a slight imperfection on the iris. A little yellow fleck, like a tendril of broken egg yolk.

"Do you live in Amsterdam?" Ben asked him.

"Yes. I have a rather sweet little place not far from here," he said, looking around for a glass. "On Laurierstraat."

"What do you do?" Matthew this time.

"Oh, you know, I write. Not like you guys." The word "guys" sounded forced in his mouth. "I write about shows and films and art. I suppose I'm a critic."

"Who do you write for?"

"Oh, there's an English-language magazine, *Time Out Amsterdam.* I do some stuff for them. I speak Dutch so I can write for the local press as well. It's really rather a good setup."

Although it was Matthew who'd asked the question, Simon looked at

James most of the time while he was answering. And then he went too far. The guy crossed the line. James wore a ring on the second finger of his left hand. It was an impressive ring, a beautiful ring with a serpent design and a polished piece of jet set into it. I'd chosen it and I'd bought it and James wore it always. It occasionally won admiring glances, but people didn't normally go so far as to do what Simon did.

He reached across and touched the ring with his own second finger and his other fingers touched James's. I saw them alight on James's hand, as carefully and gently as Apollo 11 touching down on the moon, while he made pathetic little noises, practically cooing over the ring.

I exploded. I stood up abruptly, jarring the table across the floor and upsetting two bottles of Beck's, and I roared: "Get your fucking hands off of him! Right now!" I sprawled across the table in an attempt to grab at him. I saw my fingers curl like talons, my nails itching to sink into him. His face went completely pale as he staggered back, murmuring something unintelligible. James looked shocked. Ben was hunched over his Beck's snuffling and spluttering, lost somewhere between hysteria and bafflement. And Matthew had thrust an arm across my chest to restrain me. Still I struggled to reach him. People all over the bar had turned to watch. Wide eyes and open mouths were everywhere like a bar-load of Munch screamers.

I backed off and glowered at Simon for the last time before turning and stalking out of the bar, knocking the elbow of some guy near the door as I left. He sent me out into the night with a volley of abuse—in Dutch, fortunately, so that I didn't have a clue what he was saying. I was churning up inside, had to get out. It was either that or start a fight. With Simon; with the guy near the door; Jesus, even with James. Or with Ben for finding the whole humiliating episode so goddamn funny. Or Matthew for egging Simon on, asking his questions, instead of icing him out right from the start.

I barely slowed down for a couple of blocks, then I became aware how my heart was racing and I stopped. I leaned against a handrail on a bridge over one of the city's eighteen million canals. I felt some of the anger pass out of me and float away on the oily wake of a pleasure boat. Only some of it, though. I was still cursing Simon when I noticed a tall figure loping down the street from the direction of the bar. At first I thought it was Ben, come to snuffle at me, but then I recognized James's slight stoop, the rounded shoulders, the victim look. His long legs covered acres of cobbled street with each stride. He came alongside me and leaned on the parapet, looking out at the lights on the water.

"Don't," I said, expecting a lecture. "Just . . . don't."

I could hear his breathing, slightly faster than normal.

"Let's go back," he said softly. "To the apartment."

Back on Utrechtsedwarsstraat, where we were staying in a cute little apartment loaned by a former girlfriend of James's, we chilled out. ("Girlfriend," I'd said, my eyes popping out on stalks. Jesus, you just never knew. "Oh Christ, just a friend. I couldn't fuck a girl," he said, grabbing my hand. "I love them too much. I've got too much respect for them to do *that*." He pronounced "that" with genuine distaste.) We drank a couple of beers in the backyard, where we sat naked, because it was warm enough. And because we wanted to. There was a party going on two or three houses farther down and the frantic, hectic techno beats started to open me up a little. I apologized to James for the outburst in the bar and James asked me if I wanted to take an E. I didn't know if I did, so I said no, and I knew James wouldn't take one without me. We do everything together.

"Fuck it, why not?" I said after all.

So James broke out the little wooden pillbox I bought for him in Paris and produced a couple of white doves. I checked we had plenty water in the refrigerator and we took one each and sat around in the yard listening to the whooping and screaming taking place a couple of doors down. A Marc Almond single that I liked at the time came on and I started singing along. "I wanna be adored," I fluted. "And explored." I was dancing around the yard. James was watching me, still drinking steadily. Then I came on, with a real big whoosh. I just took off like a goddamn rocket. I'd come on so quickly because I'd had nothing to eat and because, in any case, they were real good doves. James was a little slower to get it, but pretty soon we were lying on the floor of the yard, the sounds of the party washing over us, staring up at the sky. James liked to watch the stars fade in and out. I looked for faces and stuff in the clouds. I ran my hands over his chest. James has a chest covered with thick, dark hair and on E it felt completely different—very, very soft. It seemed as if I could feel every single strand of hair as it passed beneath my hand and each one was indescribably soft. His skin became sort of rubbery. I leaned over him. His pupils were enormous. I told him. "Your pupils are totally immense," I said, and he put his hand around the back of my neck, pulling me down onto him, his tongue sinking into my mouth and his lips closing around mine. His free hand sought out my dick and played with it. It was pretty soft but James is an expert. There's never been anybody better. As we kissed he worked at my dick until it had become curiously big and long but still not very hard. This was pretty typical in our experience of E. I broke off the kiss and looked at his dick. It was like mine, lying flopped over his thigh, so I took it in my right hand and moved his foreskin up and down, over the glans. My jaw was clenching because of the E and I didn't have any spit to spare. I stood up. "Hang on," I said, my head spinning because I got up too fast. I went into the apartment and fetched a bottle of water from the kitchen. Standing over James I tipped the bottle back and chugged almost half a pint. I felt it trickle down my chin and knew James would be watching it run down my white body. "Wow," I said, my head back, staring at the sky. It was so big. The things you think! The things you say! I lay back down next to James, only the other way this time, and held his dick for a moment, feeling the soft downy hairs at its base before slipping it into my mouth and pulling back his foreskin. It felt and tasted beautiful, rolling around inside my mouth, but my jaw kept clenching. James was moaning softly. I knew what he'd be doing: staring at the stars, thinking weird thoughts. He was still stroking my dick as I sucked his and it was real nice but at some point you gotta face up to the facts: we weren't going to get hard enough to do it. Maybe we didn't even wanna fuck. I didn't wanna do it to James. The thought of him doing it to me was kinda nice but I could live without it and after a while we found we were both just lying there again, staring up at the sky, our blood ebbing.

Later, I don't know when, much later, we got cold and made it in to the bedroom, where we crashed out. If I dreamt, I didn't remember anything.

Kingyo no fun

When I woke, James was not around.

Ten minutes later, having checked the backyard, the bathroom, under the bed, and inside one or two cupboards, I established that he had gone. This was strange. James isn't that kind of a person. He never just goes out. He needs a reason. He needs a good reason.

It was twenty before eleven. We'd slept late because of the E. Or I had, at least. I had no way of knowing how long James had been asleep. I felt pretty rough, my jaw still clenching and my limbs aching, although we'd neither of us been very energetic while we'd been up. Outside it was another hot day. When I stepped out the front door there was a hooting of klaxons from the Prinsengracht and a clatter of bicycles heading down Amstel. From a pay phone I called the hotel where Ben and Matthew were staying. They hadn't seen James but Ben was able to give me Simon's address. Apparently he'd been handing out his business card after I'd stormed out of the bar the night before. I thanked Ben, who merely sniggered in reply, and I left the kiosk. Simon's street was close by the gallery and the bar, as he had said. I rang his bell, then stepped back to look up at the front of the building. The windows were all closed and there was no clear sign of life. A cloud shaped like a snowman drifted over the top of the building. My neck began to ache from leaning back and looking up. I cursed Simon. And James—he'd fallen for a routine.

Just across the street from the apartment house was a coffeeshop. The sweet, sickly miasma of dope overpowered even the smell of freshly ground beans. I got a large cappuccino and sat by the window, where I could watch the street door to Simon's building. I ordered a second cappuccino. A couple of tables away a woman wearing Oakley wraps sat reading a Dutch newspaper. There was a little direct light in the coffeeshop but not too much. I guess she could have gotten along okay without the shades. I looked back across the street. *Kingyo no fun* is a Japanese expression meaning goldfish shit. The first time I heard it, the significance was not entirely clear to me. Matter of fact, it didn't mean a damn thing.

The Oakley woman's partner came back from the bathroom. He was wearing a slithery, artificial snakeskin shirt in some shiny yellow and green fabric, tight black jeans, and beat-up Nike Airs a couple of years out of date. On anybody else the combination would have looked awful, but this guy wore it well. Real well. He had a kind of glamour. He almost shone. I figured he was a rock star on vacation or someone off of the TV. He was casually toking on a spliff the size of a California redwood, which again would have looked like an affection if he'd been anybody else. But this guy was genuine. Just like James is genuine.

Something somewhere clicked. Not just somewhere. In my head somewhere.

I dropped a couple of crumpled colorful bills on the counter and left the coffeeshop. So urgent was it that I reach Simon's door—I'd seen a guy go to enter it while I was reaching for my stash of guilders—I didn't look, but just dashed across the street.

It was real close. I heard a jangling bell, a woman's voice, and I escaped with a knock on the back of my left heel. *Uh-huh, pretty fortunate,* I thought in a daze as faces stared down at me from the windows of the tram which groaned slowly by. Cyclists weaved lenticular patterns around me as I gawped openmouthed in the middle of the street, bells ringing, horns hooting, whistles blowing. The guy who'd been about to enter Simon's building was poised on the threshold, the door held open by his hand. Maybe, if I hadn't nearly been knocked down by the tram, he wouldn't have still been there and I would have been unable to enter. Everything happens for a reason.

I snapped back, dodging more bicycles as I hurried to catch the big blond-wood door. A blur of bell pushes told me Simon's apartment number. The guy stood and watched as I mounted the stairs three at a time. I guess I didn't much care what he thought.

I stood outside the door to Simon's apartment. A big brass number seven on the door. I got my breath back. If I was right, though, there was no need to compose myself. I pushed the door with a finger and it swung open, creaking just a little for good measure. I went in.

I knew instantly that the place was not empty. At least not quite. Sure there was no sign of James, but then I hadn't expected there to be. Simon was good, real good. He was good *kingyo no fun.* There's good and bad, by which I mean how successful he got to be rather than what a good guy he was. Clearly, he was not a good guy. But then who is? Simon was a master of his craft. I knew that within moments of entering his place, because I could sense that part of him was still there. I scouted round to look for it. I have experience. I knew what I was looking for. The traces take different forms. Sometimes you see stuff lying right there in the middle of the floor, like fresh slough, picking up the light and handing it straight back to you—like the shirt the rock-star guy in the coffeeshop was wearing. It's like an old snakeskin or wings that an insect has no more use for.

There was nothing like that in Simon's apartment. He was more highly evolved.

I didn't want to waste valuable time looking for traces of Simon when I knew I should be out there hunting down . . . "James." But you can't help it. And I guess I still had a little bit of my mind that needed convincing. I stared hard at the surfaces in the apartment, the things he had lying around like props. The magazines and newspapers, the novels in English and Dutch with realistically broken spines, a word processor with the cursor blinking. An ashtray full of dead cigarettes—not Simon's—a stack of bland CDs: Prince, George Michael, Jesus Christ even the Gypsy Kings. Hal Hartley videos, some French shit: Eric Rohmer, Robert Bresson, Maurice Pialat. I wasn't getting anything except further evidence that he was good at what he did. This cultural vacuum—it was no coincidence, no coincidence at all.

I stared harder and tried first to shorten my focus, then to extend it, to focus beyond the walls. It's like goofing around with a stereogram: it can take time, but if you get a glimpse, the rest comes easy. And there on the wall, or through the wall, between the poster for the Van Gogh Museum and the Arnolfini print, I got it. I managed to lose the basic building blocks of the poster, the frame, the bare wall, the print, and in the interstices I saw him, a trace of him. The sneer, the twisted lip, even the fleck in the eye. His signature on the wall. Like the shadow of the Hiroshima victim or the casts at Pompeii. I looked away, then looked back and it was still there. He was still inhabiting this place, even in his absence. And *by* his absence I now knew that he was inhabiting James.

Trashing the place would do no good. Some things are eternal. And I had to find "James." It was an outside chance but worth a few minutes of my time to continue searching the apartment for any detail that might, in spite of his efforts, give me a real clue to the nature of him. Something that might tell me where to start looking. I swept the set dressings aside now—the CDs, the videos and the books, the cheap point-and-shoot camera, the bottles of liquor, and the unwrapped packs of Camel Lites. Most of the cigarette butts in the ashtray were rouged with lipstick, but in a city like Amsterdam you couldn't take that as proof they had been smoked by women. Or by transvestites, or transsexuals—you could take nothing for granted here. It was one reason why James and I liked coming here and why we'd leapt eagerly on the gallery invitation when it arrived at the end of a dull month-long trail of book launches in private Soho drinking clubs, the Museum of the Moving Image, and subterranean fetish joints in Spitalfields. Amsterdam was special, it was different. But I knew it could make finding "James" even harder.

The quotes. You want me to explain the quotes? Like I said, Simon is good *kingyo no fun.* He gets right inside, like all *kingyo no fun,* but then he stays there. He doesn't get shut out in a couple of days like the amateurs. He's there for keeps, or for as long as he wants to be.

Kingyo no fun try to get up their host's ass. They're shit trying to get back up the asses of bright shiny charismatic people—the goldfish of the world. Not the perch, the gudgeon, or the minnows. The goldfish. They hang around, the *kingyo no fun,* just like goldfish shit—you ever sat and watched a fish tank, seen a goldfish take a crap, and noticed the long string of crap that trails after it for as long as it takes to work loose? It can take minutes, hours, days. Some goldfish are never seen without *kingyo no fun.*

The world is divided into two groups of people: those who are not *kingyo no fun* and those who are. Not all goldfish shine as brightly, however. James shone brightly. The guy in the coffeeshop shone brightly, and the woman with him kept her shades on pretty much the whole time, you can be sure of that; he shone so brightly, she'd have had to.

At first they're just easing in, laying the groundwork. Later they'll strip naked, lose their clothes, their skin, their patina of ordinariness—leave it lying on the floor or fused into the fabric of the walls—and slowly, messily work their way in. Once inside, the less successful *kingyo no fun* stay there an hour or two. To the rest of the world they've just disappeared. But that's all the goldfish can bear, and the goldfish outgrows them, rejects them, and the *kingyo no fun* are back to being themselves again, but strengthened, nourished.

Those are the amateurs, the part-timers.

The business—and Simon was the business, that was clear—stays up there.

It's not a gay thing, wanting to get up somebody's ass in this way. It's a people thing. A weak-people thing. I know, I've seen it.

Further proof of that was to be found in Simon's bedroom. After his thoroughness in other respects I was astonished to find, nestling within the pages of a Jeffrey Archer novel—so far so good—a photograph. Just a little six-by-four glossy print, not very well taken, of a black hooker standing in a doorway in the Red Light District. It was the one thing in the whole apartment—with the exception of the stereogrammatical trace of the *kingyo no fun* himself, and the clothes I'd seen him wearing the night before dumped in the otherwise empty laundry basket—that was not entirely *faux*.

Apart from the girl herself, there was a clue in the picture. The rows and rows of doors in Amsterdam's Red Light District are pretty much homogeneous. Narrow doors that are almost entirely glass, with a brown or a red curtain on the inside that can be drawn across. Beyond the door a foreshortened passageway and another doorway, into the hooker's room. The girl stands in the street doorway, or sits on an elevated stool either in the doorway or in the room's picture window, which can also be curtained off. It all looks so artificial—a hurried though professional-looking construction of glass and alloy—and tacked on to whatever real buildings lie at the rear, that you wonder if behind the shallow little rooms with their air freshener and single washbasin lurk a league of unscrupulous gentlemen who sneak in from the back when the curtains are drawn to help themselves to your billfold and plastic.

Bounded by Zeedijk to the north, Kloveniersburgwal to the east, Oude Hoogstraat, Oude Doelenstraat and Damstraat to the south, and Warmoesstraat to the west, the Red Light District is roughly heart-shaped—a real, messy, asymmetrical human heart rather than its cartoon symbol. It rests, snug and reliable, in the oldest part of Amsterdam, functioning twenty-four hours a day on some streets. Men—and a steady stream of sightseers of both sexes—are drawn through its venous streets and capillary alleyways, past yards and yards of flesh that is stretched and pressed, twisted and uplifted.

James and I had spent an hour on our first day wandering round the district. We might not have wanted to buy, but that didn't mean we weren't interested in taking a look—it's something different, something you don't see in London, or New York for that matter.

Of course, most of the doorways face onto canals and the majority of those that don't are squeezed into narrow alleyways. The doorway in Simon's picture fell into neither of these two groups. His black hooker worked a street broader than the alleyways that connected Oudezijds Voorburgwal to Oudezijds Achterburgwal and the angle of his shot revealed that a stone building rather than a canal was on the other side of it. When I applied my recollection of the area to close study of the map I found I was able to narrow down the possible locations. The girls worked in six-hour shifts, so I wouldn't necessarily see the black girl even if I found her street, but it was all I had to go on.

I needed James back, if only for confirmation. And he needed me. Now more than ever.

If I knew Simon half as well as I thought I did, I was on the right track.

There were fewer streets that fitted the bill than I had thought. In fact, I only had to tour the area once more before I was able to pin down the location. The strongest clue was the fraction of stonework visible on the far right of the picture, which formed part of whatever building faced the hooker's doorway. I soon realized, as I walked around the outside of the massive structure for the second time, that this was the Oude Kerk—the Old Church.

The street was in back of the Oude Kerk, little more than an alleyway connecting one of the canals, the Oudezijdsachterburgwal, to Warmoesstraat, and along it, opposite the church, a row of hookers' windows and doorways. I walked by once, then twice, trying to identify the doorway, but they all looked pretty much the same. The hookers themselves were more varied. There were a few Africans, a handful of Thai or Filipino girls, and one or two Europeans. Several talked directly to me as I walked by; one black girl caught my hand and tried to drag me into her doorway. "Fuckee, suckee," she said, her painted lips and pneumatic breasts trembling. I held my ground and withdrew the photograph from the back pocket of my Levi's.

"Do you know this girl?" I asked her. She took hold of the picture with long-nailed glittery fingers and called out to a colleague two doors down. They spoke in French, which I did not understand, the second hooker looking at me appraisingly as I switched my gaze from one to the other. The first girl answered me. "She is not there," she said in halting but charming English.

"Where is she?"

"She is . . . later. *Plus tard. Plus tard elle sera là.*"

I understood that much.

"Where? Here?" I pointed to the doorway behind the girl who was talking to me.

"She is there," the other girl said, pointing at a closed door twenty-five yards farther along toward the canal. "Not now. Later."

"Yeah, later," I said. "Like, when later?"

The girls both shrugged.

There was a beat. The three of us stood there in a triangle of silence broken only by the clicking of the first girl's nails on a long string of beads she wore around her neck.

"Fuckee, suckee?" she said hopefully.

I went back later and recognized her instantly. The slightly haughty angle she held her head at. The red earrings. And, frankly, the enormous breasts, thrust upward and outward in apparent defiance of the laws of nature. I hesitated a moment before approaching her. In that moment, I knew, everything could still change. I could leave undone what I was about to do. I could walk away and never see "James" or Simon ever again.

But then neither would I ever be able to look myself in the eye again.

I took a different photograph from the pocket of my shirt and walked across the street to where she stood. As I accelerated so did everything else. A train of events had been set in motion, even before I spoke to her, simply by my deciding to speak to her.

She told me her name was Stephanie and that she was from the Cameroon. I said that was cool but had she seen this guy. She told me she saw many, many guys. This one was special, I told her. Had she seen him? I slipped a twenty from my pocket. Yeah, she'd seen him. Did she expect to see him again?

Yeah, she nodded.

"What about you?" she suggested. "You are a nice man."

I warned her not to get her hopes up, then took out my billfold and said we had business to discuss. As I watched her eyes greedily counting the notes, I knew she'd go for the deal. She sold her own body for hard cash, why not others' as well?

Crouching in a space no bigger than a closet, my breathing becoming wheezy, my knee joints seizing up, I plugged my eye to the tear in the curtain and watched and waited. Stephanie stood outside and touted for business. I had said that for the money I was giving her she should simply wait for "James" to show up, but she wouldn't buy that.

I said, "What if he comes and you're busy and he goes with someone else?"

She told me he'd wait. He didn't just want to fuck. He wanted to fuck her. I winced. He'd paid already, she explained. Paid up front.

I wondered whose money it was. I wouldn't put it past the little bastard.

When she led her first john into the little room and drew the curtains at the front, I asked myself again if I couldn't have waited in the street for "James" to show up and tackled him there. But I knew I couldn't. I had to be 100 percent sure before I did anything, and for that I needed a close-up view. I fastened my eyes shut as Stephanie unclipped her sturdy brassiere and the john—a nervous-looking Scandinavian type—put a hand to his belt buckle. It seemed to go on forever but could only have lasted five or ten miserable minutes.

Stephanie saw two more clients. I merely checked them out quickly, then tried to switch off while she got on with it. I began to experience the absolute vertiginous depression that naturally accompanies the destruction—or imminent destruction—of everything you live for. At the same time I was tortured by flashes of hope. Even when fully convinced that you face total disaster, your mind is a wellspring of mad optimism. You never know . . . even when you do.

I didn't even know what I would do when the time came. By not properly arming myself did I somehow think I was molding the future, fixing the right conditions for a better outcome? I was a fool, had always been a fool. I should never have trusted James. With him it wasn't a matter of choice—he trusted everyone. And got fucked as a result.

Maybe I was a fool to think it had been a matter of choice in my case. I was, after all, no more a free agent than Simon was. Only he was better at it than me.

I heard conversation, half-recognized voices out on the street. I stuck my eye to the hole. There it was, he was, they were—James's tall, stooping figure was twisted into a gangling, distressing compromise. Standing by the doorway leering at Stephanie as if she were a glossy six-by-four in a skin mag rather than a human being. I hunched up a fraction, tried to flex my muscles, oil my joints. I heard a sound behind me but guessed it was an acoustical trick and dismissed it.

"James" was inside the air-freshened chamber now, his spine bent unnecessarily beneath the artificial ceiling, his body contorted, limbs abruptly snaking this way and that like power cables brought down in a storm. His face writhed with tics and spasms as two souls fought for its control. Stephanie rounded him neatly, interposing herself between him and me so that I was spared the worst as he unbuckled his black Levi's, but I could still see his face—that once proud countenance become this battered canvas for a wrestling bout of light and shade. His eyes flashed once like a horse's—suffering but devoid of ordered intelligence. That look strengthened my resolve, but I found myself rooted to the spot, watching in horrified fascination as he started to thrust in and out of the still-standing Stephanie. His movements were ungainly but full of physical power, truly a case of mind over matter as Simon turned James's flesh into his servant. James's comments about fucking women came back to me and I don't think

I imagined that lost, hurt look in his creased brow. If I squinted I could just make out in his left eye a small but distinct fleck of yellow.

This time behind me I did hear a noise, but I was too late to do much about it. There was a rush of air and a scuffling noise, then a sudden cold sensation in the small of my back. I twisted round and felt something scrape against my vertebrae. Something inside my body. The wiry African who had stabbed me then tried to bundle me over, but I thumped him hard and low, dug the knife out of my back with one twist, and, when the man started to uncurl his winded body, opened him with it swiftly from groin to throat. I stepped right back to avoid the hot, slippery tumble of his intestines, and with a crash I brought down the curtain, rail and all.

"James" stumbled back, total confusion writ large across his crumpled face, and Stephanie spun round to face me. I quickly considered dispatching her for the double cross but in a split-second decision—I am at least conversant with humanity—chose not to. She couldn't be blamed for not trusting me.

I looked at "James," who tottered backward unsteadily, and had a brief true vision of his liver and lights slipping quietly from a sewage outfall into the Herengracht and the soupy green water closing implacably over the still, small muscle of his heart. I knew that Simon's viscera were packed into the much-loved body of the man in front of me, just as his sick thoughts and wicked desires coiled in the scoured cranium I had for ten years stroked and kissed each night in our bed. In my hand was clutched the means to guarantee James's release into oblivion from this squalid and barbaric tenancy.

Proficient, cunning, and ultimately successful, Simon would have believed himself eternal, but I was holding the gutting knife and he was in poor shape to resist. Some *kingyo no fun,* after all, are more eternal than others.

First Date

Richard Laymon

Shannon latched her seat belt, then turned to Jeff as he started the car. "Can we go someplace?" she asked. "I don't really want to go home yet. Okay? It's still early, and . . . I mean, I'd like to spend more time with you."

"Hey, fine," Jeff said, suddenly feeling shaky. "Great. I was thinking the same thing." He gave her a smile, then looked over his shoulder and started to back out of the parking space.

Oh God, he thought. Is it really possible that she *likes* me?

She must. She came to the movie with me. Now she wants to *go someplace.*

Unbelievable.

Swinging forward onto the road, he asked, "What time do you have to be home?"

"Not till midnight."

"So we've got a couple of hours."

"Looks that way," she said. "Is it all right if I roll down my window?"

"Sure, go ahead."

As Shannon lowered her window, Jeff shut off the air conditioner and opened his own window.

"It's such a lovely, warm night," she said.

"A night made for roving," Jeff said.

He glanced at Shannon and saw her smile in the dim glow cast by the streetlights.

God, she's so beautiful, he thought. And she's with *me.* She's sitting right there, Shannon Ashley, *smiling* at me. And she wants to *go* someplace.

He suddenly wished he'd had the guts to hold her hand during the movie.

Maybe she would've liked it, after all.

But he'd been too afraid to try.

I should've just done it!

Why not now? he asked himself.

NO!

"Are you hungry?" he asked. "We could go someplace . . . Pizza Hut or Jack in the—"

"I'm stuffed. Really." She suddenly frowned. "But if *you're* hungry . . . "

"No, no, I just thought *you* might be."

"I'm fine."

"So, where would you *like* to go?" he asked.

"Someplace . . . *different.*"

"Ah," Jeff said.

"Ah," Shannon echoed.

They looked at each other. Shannon was all blurs and shadows, dim angles and patches of darkness. She seemed to be smiling. Her teeth were as white as her blouse. Jeff found his gaze sliding down the front of her blouse, lingering on the rises formed by her breasts.

"Maybe you should keep your eyes on the road," she said.

Jeff looked forward fast, blushing. "Sorry," he muttered.

"I just don't want to end up in the hospital."

"It'd be *different.*"

"I hate hospitals," Shannon said. "The *morgue,* on the other hand . . . "

"Morgues are cool."

"Ever been to one?" Shannon asked.

"No."

"Me neither."

"No time like the present."

"No way!" Shannon gave his upper arm a gentle punch.

It felt *wonderful.*

He was tempted to give her a nice, soft punch in return—a way to touch her—but he didn't dare.

"What was that for?" he asked.

"Being an idiot."

"Ah."

"I mean, it'd be crazy. Even if we could *find* a morgue and get in, we'd probably end up being arrested."

"Jail would be different."

"I've got it!"

"What?"

"That old graveyard! The one out there by the church!"

"What church?"

"You know. Out on County Line Road."

"Oh!"

"You know?"

"Jesus. You don't want to go *there.*"

"Sure. Why not? I mean, wouldn't that be just *perfect?*"

The idea of it made Jeff feel shivery inside. "I don't know," he muttered.

"Scared?" Shannon asked.

"Who, me?"

"How about it?"

It seemed like a bad idea. An old cemetery behind a long-abandoned church in the middle of nowhere seemed like a *very* bad place to go, especially late at night.

But Jeff didn't want to look like a coward.

And, somehow, the idea of being in such a horrible place with Shannon made him tremble with excitement as much as dread.

"I'm game," he said. "If you're sure that's where you want to go . . . "

"I'm sure."

"Okay. We'll go. It's this way, isn't it?"

"Yeah, just keep heading out of town. I'll tell you where to turn."

"Have you been there before?" Jeff asked.

"Just driving by. I've never even gotten close enough to take a good look. But I've always thought it'd be a neat place to stop. I mean, it looks so *creepy.* I just *love* creepy stuff."

"Me, too."

"I know. That's how come it's so perfect, you and me going there tonight." She reached over and put a hand on his thigh.

Jeff struggled not to moan.

Her hand felt warm through his jeans.

"We're so much alike," she said. "I kept waiting and waiting for you to ask me out. I *knew* we'd be perfect together. We're two of a kind."

"What kind is that?" he asked, blushing so fiercely that he thought he might melt.

"Dark."

"Yeah?"

"Lured by the mysteries of the night, the gallows, and the grave. I knew it from the moment I first saw you."

"That's why you asked me out tonight?" he asked.

"We just *had* to see *Eyes of the Vampire* together. I didn't want to go alone, and everyone else I know . . . they would've *mocked* it. I *had* to see it with you. *Share* it with you."

"*Near Dark* was better."

"Ten times better." Her hand moved slightly higher, and her curled fingers rubbed the side of his thigh. "I wish we'd known each other then."

"You and me both," Jeff managed to say, squirming a little. Her hand remained where it was, barely moving, but caressing him.

Doesn't she know what she's doing? Jeff wondered.

She's so *close.*

"Here comes County Line Road," Shannon said. "You'll want to hang a left at the stop sign."

After he made the turn, she said, "This is going to be so exciting. I've never been to *any* graveyard at night. Have you?"

"No."

"So it'll be the first time for both of us."

"Guess so."

"And a full moon."

"Maybe we'll run into a werewolf," Jeff said.

"I'm not real big on werewolves."

He turned his head and smiled at her. "You're a vampire person."

"You bet," she said, and squeezed his thigh. "Wouldn't you just love to run into a vampire?" she asked.

"I think there's a pretty slim chance of that."

"But if you *could* . . . you know?"

"I guess it'd be pretty cool."

"What would you do?"

"Run like hell."

She laughed and slapped his thigh and took her hand away. Where her hand had been, the leg of his jeans felt warm and slightly moist.

"What would *you* do?" he asked. "Interview him?"

"You think he'd let me?"

"If you asked nicely."

"I think he'd probably be a lot more interested in biting my neck."

"More than likely," Jeff said.

"Or she."

"Good point. I'd *much* prefer a female, myself."

"Not me. If a vampire's going to chomp on my neck, I want it to be a *guy*."

"So then, I guess *ideally* we'll need to get attacked by *two* vampires—a guy for you and a gal for me."

"And they've got to be *heterosexual* vampires," Shannon added.

"Do they come both ways?"

"Do they come at all?"

Blushing, Jeff shook his head. "I guess it all depends on who you read," he said.

"What about *real* vampires?" she asked.

"What do you mean by real?"

"The kind that are really *out* there."

Jeff smiled at her. "I hate to break it to you, Shannon, but there ain't no such animal."

"Think not?"

He chuckled softly. "Hope not," he said. "Oh, I know there are nut-cakes who like to *think* they're vampires . . . but I have some serious reservations about the existence of the genuine article. The 'undead' variety? You know, going on for centuries, turning into bats and mist and stuff, scared of crosses . . . the whole nine yards."

Shannon didn't say anything.

He looked over at her. On this stretch of road, there were no streetlights. She seemed to be made of black and a few shades of gray.

"What if I told you *I'm* one?" she asked.

Jeff suddenly felt a squirmy chill inside. "You're not," he said.

"Are you sure?"

"Pretty sure.

Her hand returned to his thigh. Her fingernails dug in. He groaned and squirmed.

"*How* sure?" she asked.

"I'm sure I've seen you in daylight. And I've seen you in mirrors a couple of times. I've *definitely* seen you eat real food. Who's ever heard of vampires eating popcorn and Milk Duds?"

"Hmm. Good points. You must be right. I must *not* be a vampire."

He said, "You're not."

"Apparently not."

"Hey, come on. You're making me nervous."

"You'd better slow down," she said. "The turnoff's just around the next bend."

He took his foot off the gas pedal. "Are you really sure you want to do this?" he asked. "Go to a cemetery at this hour?"

"I spooked you, didn't I?"

"I *know* you're not a vampire."

"If you say so."

"There *isn't* any such thing."

"Of course there isn't."

"And even if they *do* exist, which I doubt, *you* can't possibly be one. Hell, you've got a *suntan*."

"But is my suntan *real?*"

"Come on, cut it out."

"Here it is."

Jeff stepped on the brakes and swung onto the side road. The old strip of asphalt looked gray in the moonlight. Nothing remained of its center line, if there had ever been one. The surface was potted and cracked. Weeds grew in the fissures. Though Jeff drove slowly, the car shook and bounced.

"Kill the headlights," Shannon said.

"I thought you didn't want to end up in the hospital."

"There's plenty of moonlight."

He shut off the headlights. "Jesus," he muttered, and slowed almost to a stop.

"It's all right. There's not much to hit, anyway."

"Hope not." He could see almost nothing in front of his car. "This is weird."

"I think it's neat," Shannon said, her voice hushed.

"Well . . . it *is,* sort of."

"It's like we're invisible." She was a dim silhouette in the passenger seat, her features shrouded by darkness.

Jeff grinned at her and said, "Maybe we can sneak up on the vampires."

"Nah. They'll hear us coming."

"We could park here and walk in."

"What if we need to make a quick getaway?" Shannon asked.

"I thought you *wanted* to run into some vampires."

"Vampires, yes; perverts and murderers, no."

"Ah. Okay."

"Let's park right up close to the graveyard," Shannon suggested.

Jeff realized that he could now *see* it.

When he'd shut his headlights off, the night had been infiltrated by moonlight.

The moonlight seemed to wash everything with a dim, pale mist: the cracked and pitted road ahead; the weeds growing through the asphalt; the thickets and scattered trees on both sides of the road; the old wooden church, with its boarded windows and broken steeple; the desolate, flat, weed-cluttered landscape of the parking lot in front of the church; and the graveyard off to the right.

As he drove into the parking lot, Jeff said, "At least we're the only car."

"So far, so good," Shannon said.

He steered toward the cemetery: a field of tombstones, burial vaults and statues, stunted trees, thickets, and long, dry grass.

"I don't see anybody," Shannon said.

"Me neither."

"This is *so* cool."

"Yeah." Jeff's voice sounded steady, though he felt as if his entire body was being shaken by quick, tight tremors. "I'll turn us around," he said.

"Good idea."

He made a U-turn, then backed up, swinging the wheel until the front of his car pointed to the entry road. Then he looked at Shannon. "Now I suppose we have to get out."

"Of course."

"Fun and games."

She reached over and rubbed his shoulder. "It'll be great," she said.

They unfastened their seat belts. When Jeff opened his door, the overhead light came on. He muttered, "Shit!" and scampered out.

Shannon hurried out the passenger side.

They both shut their doors quickly, silently. The light in the car went dark.

Standing by his door, Jeff watched Shannon stride around the front of the car. In the moonlight, her white blouse and white jeans looked as bright as a field of snow. Her blond hair, her face and hands were much darker, and hard to see.

"So much for the element of surprise," she said. She was smiling. Her teeth were white.

"I forgot all about the interior light."

"Well, nobody's here anyway."

"Maybe."

Side by side, they faced the cemetery.

Jeff saw many figures that looked to him like people. Some were apparently statues, while others were formed by combinations of bushes, crosses, shadows. . . .

"I don't see anyone," Shannon said. "Do you?"

"No. But there must be a thousand places to hide."

"You aren't going to chicken out on me, are you?" As she asked, she moved slightly sideways.

Their arms touched.

"Not me," Jeff said. Then he added, "You wouldn't happen to have a gun?"

"No, but I've got this." Her arm went away from his. As she turned to face him, she shoved a hand into a front pocket of her white jeans. She pulled out a folding knife. Using both hands, she pried open its blade. "See?" The three-inch blade glinted like silver.

"Hey, cool."

"I'm a dangerous woman."

"So I see. You wouldn't happen to have a cross or two?"

She shook her head. "I used to wear a cross all the time. You know, on a gold necklace? Never took it off. Not even in the shower. I figured the minute I took it off, I'd get nailed by a vampire. But then, a couple of years ago, I sort of started to think I might *like* it."

"Getting nailed by a vampire?"

"Yeah. You know? I *wanted* it to happen, so I ditched the cross."

"You really *are* a believer."

"A hoper."

"But no luck so far?"

"Maybe tonight," she said. "Let's take a look around."

"Okay."

Shannon folded her knife shut. Instead of returning it to her pocket, she held it in her right hand.

They walked toward the cemetery.

"If there's trouble," Jeff whispered, "make a run for the car. The keys are in the ignition . . . in case I don't make it."

"If there's trouble," Shannon said, "I'll stick with you. Like I told you, I'm a dangerous woman." She took Jeff's hand in hers.

This was the first time they'd ever held hands.

The feel of it sapped his strength, quickened his heartbeat, numbed his mind.

It's no big deal, he told himself. It's just her hand. Calm down.

Just her hand.

He gave it a gentle squeeze. She squeezed back, and turned her head and smiled at him.

"My heart's pounding like crazy," she whispered.

"Mine, too."

"This is *so* creepy."

"Me?" he asked.

"Not you, *this*. The *bone orchard*."

"Oh. Yeah." He saw now that they were standing among the graves. It came as no great surprise; after all, this was where they'd been heading when Shannon took his hand. But he had no memory of actually *entering* the cemetery.

Must've been on automatic pilot, he told himself.

He looked over his shoulder. They hadn't gone far. The rear of his car was probably no more than twenty feet away. But they'd already waded through the tall grass past several tombstones.

Shannon whispered, "This is better than any old movie, isn't it?"

"You can say that again."

"This is *real*. We're actually sneaking around in a *graveyard*."

Pulling him by the hand, she led the way. They walked slowly, trudging through the dry grass, ducking under low branches, stepping around stone monuments, sometimes pausing to stare at human figures—and to make sure they were seeing statues, not people.

They wandered deeper and deeper into the cemetery.

Soon, the car was out of sight.

They kept walking.

And found themselves in a moonlit clearing surrounded by burial vaults. The pale, stone buildings, all the same size and evenly spaced, looked as if they'd been carefully positioned to form a large circle. In the center of the circle, perhaps forty feet away from the chambers that surrounded it, was something that looked like a large block of stone.

"What is this?" Jeff asked.

"Who knows? I didn't even know it was here. You can't see it from the road." Shannon turned her head slowly. At first, Jeff thought she was admiring the vaults. Then he realized she was counting them. "Thirteen," she said. "Creepy."

"You like creepy, right?"

"Love it," Shannon whispered. "Come on, let's see what this thing is."

Still holding hands, they walked toward the strange, blocky object at the hub of the thirteen vaults. It was about the height of Jeff's shoulders, flat on top, apparently round in shape, and ten or twelve feet in diameter.

"What do you think it is?" Shannon asked.

"I don't think it's a fountain. Looks like nothing . . . a platform, a stage?"

"An altar?" Shannon suggested, and squeezed his hand.

"Could be."

They stopped a few paces away from it.

"This must be where they perform their human sacrifices," Shannon said.

"More than likely."

She bumped against Jeff's side. He bumped back.

"There're thirteen vampires, and they all come out to watch," she said. "The king of the vampires actually does the killing."

"They've got a king? What's his name?"

"Pete."

Jeff burst out laughing.

"It's blasphemy to laugh at King Pete."

"Oh. Okay. Sorry."

"So then, after King Pete opens the throat of the victim . . . and drinks his fill . . . he leaves her there for the others. They swarm in and scamper up and have at her. They're ravenous. They plant their mouths everywhere on her. Thirteen mouths, all of them *sucking* on her."

"Wow," Jeff said. He felt shaky and a little breathless.

"She's naked, of course."

"Of course."

"Come on." Shannon let go of his hand. She stuffed the knife into her pocket, then stepped forward, placed her hands on the stone, leaped, and thrust herself up. She swung a knee over the edge. Jeff thought maybe he should help her. But she might take it wrong, he told himself, so he kept his arms at his sides.

She crawled forward. When she was safely away from the edge, she got to her feet. She turned around. "Hey, this is great. Come on up."

"Okay." Jeff placed his hands on top of the stone, then just stood still and gazed at Shannon.

She looked wonderful standing up there in the moonlight, feet parted, hands on hips.

"You know what I think this might've been?" he asked.

"You mean *really?*"

"Yeah. A pedestal for some sort of statue."

"What makes you think so?"

"Seeing you up there."

"Yeah?" She suddenly raised her right leg, planted an elbow on its knee, and rested her chin on her fist.

"Exactly."

"So where'd the statue go?" she asked.

"They must've gotten rid of it."

"Maybe because it represented hideous, unspeakable evil. The thirteen worshiped it." She turned around slowly, arms raised. "Thirteen vampires. They built their tombs around the statue of their king. But the villagers grew wise to this foul sect of bloodsucking fiends and attacked in the night. They slew them all, then tore down the statue and destroyed it."

Jeff grinned. "That's probably just what happened."

"But they couldn't destroy the *evil.*"

"Which is with us always."

"Right."

He boosted himself up, scurried over the edge, and got to his feet. "I think it must've been a statue of King Pete."

"Hail to King Pete!" Shannon called out.

Jeff cringed.

"The blood is the life!"

"Shhh!"

"What's wrong?"

"You don't have to yell."

"Scared?"

"Want to get us kicked out?"

"By who?" Shannon asked.

Jeff shrugged. "I don't know, but . . . "

"I think you're afraid I'll bring out the vampires," she said.

"They were slain by the villagers, remember?"

"That was just a story. Don't you know a story when you hear one?

Come here." Standing on the center of the pedestal, Shannon gestured for Jeff to approach.

When he stopped in front of her, she put her hands on his hips. "If there *are* any vampires around here . . . real ones . . . they must've heard me. Don't you think so?"

He swallowed hard. "You were loud enough to wake the undead," he assured her.

"So they know we're here."

"I guess so."

"They'll be coming for us."

"Any moment."

"They'll come and suck our necks," she whispered. Easing forward, she slid her arms around Jeff and pressed herself against him. Stunned, confused, he wrapped his arms around her. He had never held a girl this way before. He could feel the warmth of her thighs. He could feel the rise and fall of her chest. And the push of her breasts. And the tickle of her breath on the side of his neck. Her hair, soft against his cheek, carried a mild scent so fresh and clean that it made him ache.

He moved his hands up and down her back. Through the cloth of her blouse, he felt smooth slopes and curves and no straps.

She kissed the side of his neck.

It gave him a sudden rush of goose bumps and made him squirm.

"That's where they'll get us," Shannon whispered. And licked him there.

He shuddered. "Gives me goose pimples," he said.

"Do it to me, okay?"

Shannon released him, so he loosened his hold on her. She took a small step backward. Head down, she unfastened a button of her blouse. Then another. Then she slipped the left side of her blouse off her shoulder. It fell and hung against her upper arm. With a fling of her hand, she swept her hair out of the way.

She was bare skin from her ear down the side of her neck, bare skin along her shoulder and down her arm halfway to the elbow.

And bare down her front to where a button held the blouse together.

Her left breast was only half-covered, the nipple just out of sight, shrouded by white cloth.

If that button goes . . .

Shannon curled a hand around the back of his head. Fingers in his hair, she drew his head down to the curve at the base of her neck. He kissed her gently there. Her skin felt smooth and warm.

"Harder," she whispered.

He opened his mouth, pushed with it, slid his tongue back and forth.

She moaned and squirmed.

While her left hand clutched Jeff's head, her right hand rubbed up and down his side from his hip to his armpit. His own left hand, he realized, was gripping her shoulder as if to hold her in place. His right was locked on her upper arm—but not where it was bare.

He moved it higher.

Up to where her skin was.

Shannon didn't protest.

So he caressed the smooth, naked skin of her arm and shoulder while he licked and sucked her neck.

Shannon writhed and trembled.

Jeff thought about the half-bare breast only a few inches below his hand.

But he stayed away from it.

"Bite," she gasped.

He pressed the edges of his teeth against her skin. It felt firm and springy. He squeezed a little harder.

"Make me bleed," she gasped. "Break my skin and suck my blood."

"I don't . . . "

"No! Wait!" She suddenly jerked his head back by the hair. Gazing into his eyes, she shook her head and muttered, "Wait," again. Then, "No good. Stupid." She released Jeff's hair and dropped her hands away from him.

In the moonlight, Jeff saw a silvery slick of spittle on the left side of her neck.

"You all right?" he asked.

"Yeah."

"Did I hurt you?"

"It was great," she said. "We've just gotta take our clothes off."

"*What?*"

She unfastened the next button of her blouse. The left side fell and hung below her breast.

Jeff gazed at her bare breast, stunned. He'd never seen a real one before. He felt as if his breath was being sucked out. His heart thudded. His penis, growing stiff, shoved at the front of his pants.

Finished with her buttons, Shannon pulled her blouse off.

Jeff gaped at her.

She was naked above her white jeans.

"Get yours off, too," she said, and tossed her blouse toward the edge of the pedestal.

"I . . . what's going on?"

"We don't wanta get blood on our clothes."

"Huh?"

Balancing on one leg, she brought up the other and pulled her sneaker off.

"What blood?" Jeff asked.

"*Our* blood." She tossed the sneaker aside. It landed near her blouse, but bounced and fell off the edge of the pedestal. "Don't just stand there." She tugged off her sock and gave it a fling.

Jeff began to unbutton his shirt. "What's going on?" he asked.

"We're gonna *do* it." She worked on her other sneaker and sock.

"Do what?"

"You see any vampires around here?" Shannon asked, and opened the button at the waist of her jeans.

"No."

"Me neither." She pulled the zipper down. "I don't think they're coming."

"Probably not."

"Never a vampire around when you need one." With that, she bent over, sliding her jeans down. She stepped out of them. Then she dropped to a crouch. Holding the jeans up between her knees, she dug into a pocket. "We'll have to do this ourselves," she said, and took out her knife. "Come on, take your clothes off."

"What's the knife for?" Jeff asked, and tossed his shirt out of the way.

"All the better to cut ourselves with."

Shannon stood up. Turning aside, she threw her jeans. They tumbled and flapped. In midair, her panties drifted free and fell toward her blouse. Her jeans disappeared over the edge of the pedestal. "Pooey," she said. Then she turned toward Jeff.

Pale moonlight dusted her hair, her face, her shoulders and breasts. Each breast cast a shadow below it.

So many shadows.

So many hidden hollows.

But her belly was brushed with light. So were her hips. And a tongue of moonlight found its way to a wispy tuft of hair between her legs.

Groaning, Jeff looked away from her.

"I'll help," Shannon said. She stepped up to him. "Here, you hold the knife."

She gave it to him. Then she unfastened his jeans. She crouched and tugged. His briefs went down with the jeans and his erection leaped at her face. "Holy mackerel!" she gasped.

"Sorry."

"Just, uh . . . keep it to yourself, okay?"

He swallowed hard. "Sure."

She finished pulling his pants down, then stood up and said, "I mean, we're not here to . . . you know, screw around."

"Maybe we should've kept our clothes on."

"And get them all bloody? My parents'll probably be up and waiting when I get home. They'll go apeshit if I walk in drenched with blood. Sit down. We have to get these off you."

Jeff eased himself down. The cool, stone surface of the pedestal felt rough and grainy against his buttocks. Leaning back, he stretched out his legs and braced himself with his arms.

Shannon squatted in front of him. She removed his shoes and socks, his jeans and shorts. Then she picked them up, twisted around, and snatched up his shirt. Holding them all, she stood and walked toward the edge of the pedestal.

Her hips swept slightly from side to side. Her buttocks looked creamy in the moonlight. Jeff watched how they moved with each step. And he stared at the shadowed cleft between them.

Instead of avoiding her clothes and the sneaker scattered in front of her, Shannon swept them together with her feet. Then swept them off the edge of the pedestal.

"What're you doing?" Jeff asked.

"Clearing the deck." She opened her arms. Jeff's clothes and shoes fell over the side. She turned around. "They'll be fine down there."

"Fine," he said.

"This way, there's no chance they'll get bloody." She came toward him.

Look at her, look at her, look at her. My God!

Jeff was dry-mouthed, trembling, hard—and a little embarrassed about the way his penis was sticking straight up out of his lap.

Shannon stopped at his feet. "Maybe we should do it standing up," she said.

Jeff licked his lips and said, "Fine with me."

He got to his feet.

It felt very strange to be standing up, this high above the ground, with no clothes on. In the middle of the night. In front of beautiful, naked Shannon. In a graveyard. Surrounded by thirteen burial vaults.

He turned around slowly, looking at the moonlit chambers, at the shadows between them, and at the pale, grassy clearing.

With a glance at Shannon, he saw that she was looking, too.

"Oh, my God!" she suddenly blurted. "Who's that?"

Jeff's heart slammed. He whirled around. "Where?"

"Gotcha!"

"Jeez!" He turned to her. "Real nice."

Laughing softly, she stepped over to him and put her hands on his hips. "Did I scare you?"

"Yeah. A little."

"I didn't really see anyone," she said.

"I know."

"But I *do* have this sneaky feeling we're being watched."

"Terrific," Jeff muttered.

"I'm all shivery."

"You and me both."

"Yeah?" She slid her hands behind Jeff and scraped her fingernails lightly up his back. Goose bumps scurried over him. He trembled. Her hands stopped at his shoulder blades. Holding him there, she eased forward. Her belly pushed at his penis. Her nipples touched his chest. Her wet, open lips caressed the side of his neck.

She kissed him, licked him.

Jeff moaned.

Her mouth went away. "Let me have the knife," she whispered.

The knife felt hot and slick in his grip. He kept his hand shut. "I don't know."

"You're not gonna chicken out, are you?"

"Might be dangerous."

"Of *course* it's dangerous. But not very. Not if we're careful. It won't even *hurt* much if we use the knife."

"What about . . . diseases?"

"What've you got?"

"Nothing, I don't think, but . . . "

"Me, neither. Come on, you want to do it, don't you?"

He didn't much care for the idea of playing vampire, but he very much wanted to have Shannon touching him again. And if it meant losing a little blood, fine.

"Sure," he said.

"You don't *sound* very sure."

"It's just . . . what if you hit my jugular vein or something?"

"That's why we got our clothes out of the way, silly."

With that, she had him laughing. She laughed along with him.

Then she said, "You're pretty nervous about this."

"A little."

"I'll tell you what. Why don't *you* go first?"

"I thought that was what we were talking about."

"I mean, you go first and suck *me.* I loved how it felt when you were doing it before. I wanted it to keep on going, but then I started to worry about our clothes. And I remembered about the knife—so now you can get to my blood without mauling me. Just a neat little slit or two. It'll be great."

"I don't want to *cut* you."

"I'll do it. Let me have the knife."

He gave the knife to her. Holding it in front of her belly, she looked down and tried to pry open the blade. She seemed to have some trouble with it. "My hands are shaking," she murmured.

Jeff stared at her breasts. They were only inches from his chest. The dark nipples jutted out as if reaching for him.

"There we go," Shannon said, swinging the blade out of the handle. It locked into place with a soft click. "You want the left side?" she asked. She tilted her head to the right.

"I guess so."

"Good." With her left hand, she fingered the side of her neck. "About here?" she asked.

"That'd be fine."

"You don't sound too thrilled."

"I'm thrilled, all right. Just nervous. I've never . . . drunk blood before. Just my own a few times. You know, when I've had a cut. Never someone else's."

"Same here. Now we'll find out what all the fuss is about."

"Yeah."

Keeping her fingers against her neck to mark the place, she brought up her right arm. Elbow high, she swung her forearm across the front of her neck and touched the point of her knife to the area in front of her middle finger.

"How's this?" she asked.

She's really going to do it!

"Fine, I guess."

"Ready?"

Jeff lowered his gaze from her hands, from the knife poised at her neck, and stared at her left breast. She was breathing hard. The breast was lifted by her expanding rib cage, then lowered, then lifted again.

"Jeff? Are you ready?"

"When you are," he said, and raised his eyes.

"Here goes." Her skin dented under the point, then enveloped it. The blade went in no more than a quarter of an inch, maybe less. When she pulled it out, a dot of blood grew and began crawling downward. "How's that?" she asked.

"Fine."

"No, wait. One more. Gotta make it official." She poked the point into her neck again—cutting a fresh wound an inch from the other. Then she ducked, set the knife by her feet, and rose up again in front of Jeff. "Okay," she said.

By then, blood from the first cut had spilled over her collarbone and was sliding down her chest.

Jeff put one hand on her right shoulder, the other on her left side—just below her rib cage.

Shannon soon had two strips of blood rolling down her chest.

Jeff stared at them.

"Are you gonna do it?"

Trying to sound like Bela Lugosi, he said, "Your blood, it is so beautiful to watch."

"You wanta taste it, don't you?" Shannon asked, her voice trembling.

Jeff watched the narrow, dark trails slide out onto her left breast.

Shannon squirmed. "It tickles," she said.

One stream curved off to the side of her breast, while the other trickled to its very tip.

Jeff crouched slightly, leaned in, and licked the blood off her nipple.

Shannon flinched.

He sucked her nipple into his mouth, swirled his tongue around it, and tested it with his teeth, relishing its stiff, rubbery feel.

"Hey." She pulled his hair. "Don't."

He took his mouth away. "The blood," he gasped.

"But no funny stuff."

"Sorry."

She let go of his hair.

He expected her to grab it again as he lapped the blood off the side of her breast, but she didn't. He licked the side and the bottom, and up from underneath to the front, briefly running his tongue over her nipple. She stiffened and moaned, but made no attempt to stop him.

Though he ached to suck on her nipple again, he figured it might be pressing his luck.

So he abandoned her breast and licked his way up her chest, following the strips of blood.

He followed them over the smooth curve of her collarbone, followed them to their source. As he latched his mouth against the wounds, he wrapped his arms around her and drew her tightly to his body. Her breasts pushed against his chest: the right was dry and warm; the left was moist and clammy. His rigid penis shoved against her belly and glided upward on slippery juices until its whole underside was snug against her.

He squirmed, rubbing her.

And he sucked.

Sucking, he felt her blood come into his mouth.

He wondered if he could make it *squirt.*

The harder he sucked, the more blood poured into his mouth. And the more Shannon groaned and gasped and writhed against him.

She's going *nuts,* Jeff thought. She *loves* it.

Bet she won't stop me now.

Keeping his right arm clamped against her back, he brought his left arm forward, turned himself slightly to make room for his hand to fit between their bodies, then slipped it in and took hold of her right breast.

It filled his hand.

The nipple pushed against his palm.

"Don't," she gasped, still writhing.

She loves it.

He squeezed the breast. It felt soft, firm, springy, incredible. He sucked harder on her neck. Blood flooded his mouth. Shannon shuddered and panted.

"Stop it," she gasped.

Okay, okay. Better do what she says.

He let go of her breast and put his hand behind her. Eased it downward. When he curled it over the smooth hump of her right buttock, she whimpered and squirmed against him.

Yes! This she likes!

"Jeff!" she blurted.

He slid his other hand down. He clutched her buttocks with both hands, digging his fingers in, pulling her more tightly against his body, rubbing himself against her, digging his teeth into her neck, sucking, swallowing.

"No!" she squealed. "Stop! It hurts!"

Of course it hurts, I'm biting your neck.

I AM biting her neck!

SHIT!

He opened his mouth and pulled his head back. Above and below the tiny knife cuts on the curve of her neck were crescent rows of tooth-holes. Deep, distinct impressions, as if he'd sunk his teeth into a block of cheese.

In the blink of an eye, they filled with blood.

He yelled, "SHIT!"

And then Shannon chomped the side of *his* neck.

Pain blasted through his body. He cried out, flinched rigid, then lost his footing as Shannon wrapped her legs around him. He stumbled backward, clutching her tight against him by her buttocks.

Then he fell.

His back slammed the stone. His head, past the pedestal's edge, hit only air. He let it hang, too stunned to raise it.

He had lost his hold on Shannon's buttocks. His arms lay by his sides.

But she hadn't lost her hold on his neck.

She was on top of him, squirming as she sucked.

Grunting as she sucked.

He could feel her teeth buried in his flesh, feel the force of her suction, feel his blood squirting out.

Hear the sloppy wet sounds as she sucked and swallowed.

Then her teeth released him. Her mouth went away.

"No. Shannon. Don't. Don't stop."

"Like it?"

"Christ. Yes. Please."

"No more blood. Not tonight."

"Please!"

"No, no, no. No more blood."

On elbows and knees, she glided backward, lightly sliding her nipples against his chest and belly and thighs.

And kissed his rigid penis.

Slid her lips around it.

Sucked it deep into the tight, wet hole of her mouth.

Squirmed and grunted, licked, sucked, stroked the hard length of it up and down with the slick O of her lips . . . and finally swallowed.

Later, they licked each other clean. Then they jumped off the pedestal and hunted for their clothes. Wearing their shoes but carrying everything else, they hiked back to Jeff's car. There, they patched their necks with gauze pads from Shannon's purse. Then they checked themselves for blood in the car's overhead light. After removing the last traces, they hurried into their clothes and sped for Shannon's home.

"I'm afraid you're going to be late," Jeff said.

"Who cares?" Shannon asked. "This was the greatest."

"Not only that," Jeff said, "but the vampires didn't get us."

Shannon grinned at him. "Think not?"

To Have You with Me

Randy Fox

—∞—

"Wake up, Lisa."

"Huh? . . . Mr. Hoyt? What are you doing here?"

"Shh, it's Andy, always Andy. Be quiet and get your stuff together. We're leaving tonight."

"What's going on?"

"No questions right now. We've got to get out of here."

I walked to the door and checked out the hall. There was nobody in sight. We were going to make it—if we were lucky. Turning away, I watched Lisa getting dressed. Her pale skin looked ghostly white in the dim light. Long, bed-disheveled hair hung over her face as she leaned over to pull her jeans on, the small mounds of her breasts pressing against her T-shirt.

A wave of revulsion struck me—*pedophile, child molester, pervert.* Was I becoming everything I detested? I found myself unable to look away.

Lisa finished dressing. There was little that she owned or wanted to take with her. "I'm ready."

I checked out the hallway again. There was only a minimum of security. The kids who ended up here were not the hard cases. Troubled, confused, the results of abuse, but not the ones that fought back; more the ones that were beaten down.

"Follow me and stay quiet. I'll explain everything when we get outside." We made it down the hallway and I used my passkey to get us out the back exit. If someone caught us, I could explain that . . . I had no explanation. I had no earthly idea what I would say.

Outside, the security lights were buzzing gently in the night air, filling the parking lot with a sickly yellow illumination. Insects looped and swirled around the glow, throwing their bodies against the glass separating them from the electric flame.

Lisa said in a whisper, "Why are we doing this? Where are we going?"

"Quiet! We're not out of here yet." We walked across the parking lot like we belonged there, watched over by silent video cameras. There was no way around them. But I knew how "attentive" Duane, the night guard, was, and if we didn't act suspicious . . .

"Get in the back and stay down," I said when we reached the car. Lisa followed my orders, but I could tell she was scared. She looked at me with uncertainty and fear. "I'm not going to hurt you like the others have. You trust me, don't you?"

"Yeah."

"Just stay out of sight."

I was right about Duane. When I drove though the gate, he gave me a glance and waved, yawning the whole time. Pulling out onto the main road, my heart hammered away with a staccato beat. The headache crept up on me. Starting at the base of my skull, it crawled over my head until it enveloped me with its dull ache. I pulled over at a convenience store near the interstate.

"Lisa," I said.

"Yeah."

"You can sit up now. Get up front." I reached over and opened the passenger door.

"I'm sorry I kept asking questions, but I don't know what's going on. Where are you taking me?"

I put my hand on the girl's shoulder. She was now in the seat beside me. "It's okay. I know you're scared, but that was the only way I could get you out of there." The headache had settled behind my eyes now. I kept blinking and rubbing at one eye as I spoke. "You're not going to another foster home or another facility. *I'm* going to take care of you. We've got to get away from here, though."

"Do you really mean that?"

"Yes." The pain seemed all-consuming. My eyes felt like they were going to explode.

"I can't believe it." Lisa was crying now. I slipped one arm around her, and she fell against me, laughing through her tears. "I love you, Andy," she said.

The pain in my head retreated, holding back and gently prodding at me. I hugged Lisa, closing my eyes and trying to ignore both the pain and my erection.

Eight aspirin and several miles down the interstate, the headache had retreated to the back of my head, probing with exploratory pains. The shock had worn off enough for Lisa to begin asking questions.

"Where are we going?"

"I told you, away from here. We've got to get out of the state. They're going to be looking for us, and we're going to have to hide out for a while."

"You could go to jail, couldn't you?"

"That's not going to happen."

"What about your job?"

"That doesn't matter. My *job* would have been to send you on to some other place where someone could abuse you. That, or another facility."

"The nuthouse."

"That's not what you're supposed to call it. We want to help kids like you, but the whole system just makes it worse. I couldn't take it anymore."

"But why me?"

I sat for a long time in silence. "Because you're special."

"Do you love me?"

"Of course I do."

I had known Lisa was special the first time I saw her. I'd been working with kids for years, and I was the perfect state-employed psychologist/social worker. I cared about my cases, but never forgot that they were just that, cases.

Lisa was something different. She was . . .

Wait a minute, who am I kidding? That's a lie. She was *nothing* special.

Just one more in the endless supply of children with the bad luck to be born to monsters masquerading as parents. Her case may have been a little worse than most, but it was still nothing I hadn't seen before. It wasn't until later that I realized she had that special quality. That special something.

"My daddy used to say he loved me."

"He lied."

"He would always say it when he did . . . you know."

I knew it wasn't so simple. I knew how an abuser's mind worked—love, manipulation, selfish desire. "He didn't love you, or else he wouldn't have used you like that. Your aunt Katherine didn't love you either."

"I know that. She was always mean to me—like she blamed me for what happened to Momma and Daddy. Sometimes I used to dream about Momma, but it was always a nightmare. We'd be in this little room and she wouldn't look at me. All she could do is scream. I wonder if she would've loved me?"

"I don't know. She was probably no different. She married your father, after all. You're better off with them all dead. I'm the first person who's really loved you."

Lisa pondered this a while. She said, "Billy Bowers told me that he loved me one time."

"Bowers—that was one of the foster homes, wasn't it?"

"Yeah, the second one I went to, I think. They're hard to keep track of."

"Was Bowers your foster father?"

"No! He was an old man, almost fifty." She looked at me. "Not like you. Billy was his oldest son, his real son. He was in college."

"Did he tell you after you had sex with him?"

"Well, yeah. It was right before Mr. Bowers caught us, and I had to leave."

"He was lying, too. That's what people have been doing to you your entire life. Did any of the other boys you've been with say that?"

". . . No."

"But you thought they did, even though they didn't say it."

She stared out the window, obviously not wanting to talk about it. She said, "I don't know."

I reached over to touch her, my hand quivering slightly with excitement. "I do love you."

She slid into my outstretched arm and cuddled against me. The pleasure jolted through me, competing with the pain in my head. I breathed in the smell of her hair while my eyes darted between the road and her dark, soft form.

We rode like that for a long time—Lisa, happy with her newfound sense of security, and me, intoxicated by my lust. I couldn't keep my eyes off her, and the thoughts of what I wanted to do kept playing through my imagination.

You want to have sex with her. You want to screw her, and you'll do anything for it.

I love her, there's nothing wrong with feeling physical desire for the woman you love, or any woman for that matter.

Woman? She's fifteen. She can't even drive a car, legally. When you get tired of her, what's next? A ten-year-old? How about five—they're really sexy at that age.

It's not that way at all! Lisa's had a hard life. She's very mature for her age. That's why she's so special!

Sure she's mature. Not every girl gets to lose their virginity to their father when they're four. Good thing you're around to replace him.

Stop it! I'm not forcing her to do anything!

Oh, no! You're not forcing her at all. You're much too clever for that. "I'm the first person who's really loved you." Lisa's father was an amateur compared to you.

I didn't want to hear any more, but the prosecutor would not relent. *Child molester, manipulator, monster! So high and mighty and pure—fighting for the rights of kids. The real Andrew Hoyt has finally been revealed!* My head pounded on like a lopsided wheel, the pain beating out a steady rhythm. I tore my arm from Lisa and placed it on the steering wheel. I tried not to look at her.

The sign in front of us read, "Welcome to Kentucky." *Congratulations, Mr. Hoyt, you're an interstate felon,* the voice said. A mental picture of Lisa's and my mug shots on posters spread across the country appeared. Her voice blew that image away.

"Where are we?"

"We just crossed the state line."

"I was asleep," she said, yawning.

"I know."

"I was dreaming about Kim again. It was just like all the other ones. You know, we talked about those in therapy."

"Yeah."

"We were back at the Nelsons' house, like just before her accident, but she wouldn't get up or talk. She just lay there and stared at me. I knew she *could* talk, though. She just didn't want to. I got angry at her and started screaming, but she still wouldn't talk. That's pretty lousy, isn't it?"

"What do you mean?"

"That I'd dream about Kim like that and get angry. You know what she's like now. She was my best friend. It's not her fault that she's in a coma."

"But you think it's your fault."

". . . No."

The anger rose out of me fast and sharp. "Look, we've talked about this before. It's not your fault that Kim had the accident, and it's not your fault that your mother or your father or your aunt are dead. You didn't kill any of them."

"I'm sorry."

"DON'T BE SORRY!"

She was crying now. The headache was back, squeezing harder than ever. Loops and swirls of light shot through my vision, blinding me. I pulled over quickly, loose gravel from the shoulder ricocheting off the bottom of the car.

I opened the door and leapt from the seat, running into weeds off the shoulder of the road. I had to get away. I was going to kill her or myself if it didn't stop. What was I going to do? Where could I go? The pressure in my head felt like it was splitting me in two.

I kneeled in the weeds, tears filling my eyes, and suddenly, I was struck with a moment of absolute clarity.

What did Lisa have to look forward to? Another three years, maybe, of being bounced around from foster home to state facility to foster home.

More boys taking advantage of her, figuring her for an easy lay—all the while despising her as a slut and a whore. Her losing the gamble and ending up pregnant, or worse, with AIDS, followed by an early death from disease or at the hands of some psychotic, abusive man—leaving an unwanted child to live through the same cycle.

I had devoted my entire career to helping kids, and for the first time I was actually doing something about it. I could provide a better life for Lisa than that. If I was manipulating her at all, it was for her own good. Everything I'd said to her had been the truth. As long as I didn't lie, how could that be manipulation?

I stood up and walked back to the car. The pressure on my head let up some. Lisa was huddled in the seat, sobbing, watching me with fearful eyes.

"I'm sorry," I said, getting back in the car. "I've got a headache and I'm tired. I'm sorry." I pulled her to me. "Everything's going to be okay." I held her close until her sobbing slowed.

"You're not going to leave me?" she said between sobs.

"No, I just panicked for a moment." My lips found hers, my head pulsing as I became more excited.

"I just want to be what you want," she whispered as I kissed my way down her neck.

"I know." I wanted her right then, more than I've ever wanted any woman, but I forced myself away and grasped the steering wheel. "We need to get going."

When we were back on the road, Lisa said, "Do you ever dream?" She was trying to be cheerful and make conversation.

A variety of images flashed through my mind: the churning dark skies; the swirling, crazy lighting, like overcharged fireflies; the little girl on the steps of the old house.

"No," I said, lying.

"Aren't you married?"

We had been riding in silence for a long time. It was about 3 A.M., but I wanted to get out of Kentucky before we stopped. "I still am, but that's over." I looked down at the smooth ring of skin on my finger where the wedding band had been for fifteen years.

"I'm sorry."

I let it pass.

"Did you leave her for me?"

"No. It was over anyway." For three weeks—and it *was* because of Lisa, but there was no reason for her to know that. Admitting to it would have only made the betrayal worse.

"Do you have any kids?"

"Yeah, a daughter."

"How old is she?"

"Twelve."

"Is she anything like me?"

Karen was already taller than Lisa, even though she was three years younger. She had long, straight brown hair like her mother, not blonde and curly like Lisa's. She was quick, outgoing, loved sports, and I had never once felt the desire to—"No," I said.

"I'd like to meet her someday."

"Sure."

"I'm really glad you already have a kid."

"Why's that?"

"'Cause I'm not sure I ever want to have any, and it wouldn't be right for me to feel that way if you didn't already have one. Now, we won't have to worry about that when we're married. You didn't want any more, did you?"

"No."

"What kind of house do you like?"

"I don't know."

"I'd kinda like to have one in the mountains. I've never been to any real mountains like they have out west. Do you think we could live there maybe?"

"Maybe."

"Colorado. That would be cool. You know they call Denver the Mile-High City, 'cause it's so high up in the mountains."

"Yeah, I knew that."

"Have you ever been there?"

"No."

"We could walk out our front door and play in the snow and go skiing and stuff. You could get me some cute little ski outfits to wear, and we could have a big fireplace that we'd cuddle in front of at night. Pretty cool, huh?"

"Yeah, that sounds great." A green sign appeared in my headlights, advertising the next exit. "We're going to have to get some gas."

"Okay."

The exit led onto a county two-lane that crossed over the interstate, passed a truck stop, and disappeared into the black countryside. We were in the proverbial middle of nowhere.

"I'm going into the store to get something to drink," Lisa said.

"Sure."

She walked away, swaying her hips in a little girl's imitation of a woman. I got out and started the pump. My headache had almost vanished completely, but my eyes ached from fatigue as I watched the numbers flicker around. *You disgusting pervert,* I thought. *You've thrown away everything—your career, your marriage, every moral and ethic you ever had—and for what? A stupid, skinny little girl with a bunch of pipe dreams.*

A truck pulled around on the far side of the station and parked with a whoosh of air brakes. In the silence that followed, I heard a "clop, clop, clop" sliding out of the night toward me.

A light emerged from the darkness of the highway. The burning eye and the accompanying clopping grew in intensity. It passed me and I saw a black carriage being pulled by a solitary horse. A straight-backed man, dressed completely in black and wearing a broad-brimmed hat, drove the assembly. He was sporting a full beard. Behind him, two women, also dressed in black, huddled next to each other. Their eyes met mine as I watched their progress, and they looked away quickly. In a minute, they faded back into the night, leaving only an orange and red safety reflector and two red, battery-driven taillights to be seen moving on down the road.

The gas pump handle clicked off in my hand, startling me. The headache returned, gaining intensity with each beat of my pulse. I returned the handle to the pump and closed the tank cover. I was foolish. Nothing changed the fact that I loved Lisa, and she loved me. The guilt and the doubts were brought on by the false standards I allowed society to place on me. So what if I was forty-three and Lisa was fifteen? Just because our relationship wasn't normal by the majority's standards didn't make it wrong, did it?

I walked to the store to pay and look for Lisa. I couldn't see her inside.

The clerk took my money through the slot in the Plexiglas booth. He couldn't help noticing my unease.

"Can I help you with something?"

"There was a girl that came in here. She was with me. Did you see where she went?"

"I think she went out the other door."

I managed to walk out the door instead of running. Looking around, I didn't see Lisa anywhere. The headache turned itself up a notch. The truck driver filling up his tank noticed me. I ignored him and headed for the back of the building. Lisa was there, a battered, black and white alley cat weaving figure eights between her legs. She bent over and let it push its head against her hand.

"What the hell do you think you're doing!" I grabbed her by the arm and jerked her up. My head felt like an explosion.

"I was just—"

"You scared the hell out of me!"

"I'm sorry!"

"C'mon!" Pulling her behind me, I hurried away. I knew the trucker was watching us, and the clerk, too. Stumbling to the car, I strained to find my way through the neon fireworks exploding before my eyes.

"I'm sorry, I just saw the cat and—"

"Get in!" I released her with a shove. Inside, she tried to continue with her excuses.

"I didn't mean to scare you. I wasn't going anywhere. I just wanted to pet the cat. It looked like one I used to have."

I leaned against the steering wheel and squeezed at the sides of my head. Lisa's excuses petered out, and she sat watching me.

"Andy?"

"I'm sorry," I said at last, my head still down. "I just got scared. Don't go off like that again."

"Okay."

Looking up, I saw the clerk watching me. I started the car and headed back for the interstate.

It was almost noon when we stopped at the motel. Kentucky was several hours behind us and we were zigzagging our way through Missouri. I didn't want to leave an easy trail to follow, and I still didn't know where we were going—maybe the Rockies.

The motel was a cheap, chain place. The Indian at the desk seemed more than happy to accept cash for the room. He asked no questions and didn't even glance at the fake tag number I wrote on the registration card. I had cleaned out all of my bank accounts before leaving. I knew credit cards would be useless—just a trail of paper to reveal our whereabouts.

I wasn't sleepy. I had passed the point where I desired rest. My fatigue was feeding on itself—buzzing on a diet of sleeplessness and caffeine. The pain was doing its part, too. The constant ache was a well I drew from to keep me moving forward.

Despite this, I knew I needed sleep, and daylight seemed the best time. Lisa was waiting for me when I returned to the car. She had tidied up, wadding fast-food bags, candy wrappers, and discarded coffee cups into a garbage ball, ready for disposal. I grabbed our bags, and we headed for the room.

Inside, Lisa wanted to clean up. She showered while I lay on the bed—curtains closed, lights out—watching the dancing patterns of my headache on the ceiling. I didn't hear the water shut off.

"Andy?"

Sitting up, I saw Lisa standing at the foot of the bed, caught between the cheap, pulpish light of the bathroom and the thin sliver of sunlight making its way past the curtains. Her wet hair looked darker than normal. It clung to her scalp and flowed down onto her shoulders in straight, ropy strands. She was holding a towel in front of her. She swallowed, nervously, like a child waiting for a parent's approval. There was little about her that could be called seductive, but I found myself moving toward her—consumed by my pain and desire.

I tore the towel away from her and kissed her body. A deafening roar filled my head as we fumbled onto the bed. She gasped and cried out in a mixture of pleasure and uncertainty. The lights and patterns churned before my closed eyes as I thrust away inside her.

All at once, the agony ceased. It was like a switch had suddenly clicked over to the "No Pain" position. I opened my eyes and looked up to see my own face hanging before my vision—eyes closed, breath puffing out between parted lips. An instant later, the dam broke and I was torn apart by the twin storms of pain and orgasm.

When I opened my eyes again, I was in the dream. As always, the skies above churned with dark patterns—constantly flowing and changing, like oil slicks in a murky puddle. The landscape was lit by great swirls and loops of lightning, flashing a hyperkinetic neon light show.

Something was different, though. Before, the dream always had this weird, unreal paranoiac feeling about it. Like the only reality was what I could view, and if I could just turn around fast enough, I would see nothing—a void, waiting to be filled with a world created by my perceptions.

This time, the feeling did not surround me. This *was* reality. It had always been here, and always would be. I turned around, looking for something in the blank landscape. When I completed my revolution, the house was before me—a slanting tar-paper shack with a corroded metal roof. The little girl sat on the front steps of the house. She was about six years old, with curly red hair and a smattering of light freckles across her nose and cheeks. She waved at me as she always did. I walked toward her.

"I've seen you before," she said. She had never spoken, and I had never been this close to the house. "What's your name?"

"Andy."

"Hi." She stood up. "My name's Katy. Are you going to stay here?"

"Where am I?"

She shrugged her shoulders. "Just here. It's where we live. I'd really like for you to stay. I get lonely a lot. None of the others are much fun."

"What others? What are you talking about?"

She took my hand and led me up the steps. "I'll show you, but I don't think they'll play with you, either."

Inside the house, the first room obviously belonged to Katy. A few old, broken toys were scattered on the floor. The walls were covered with a child's drawings of the adult world: scenes of traffic, figures working, what might have been people dancing in a bar, a couple having sex.

"I don't get to go outside much. I used to be locked up in a room like Charlie, until I realized I could be a little girl again. I still have to stay in the house most of the time. Sometimes I get out. I saw back outside one time."

"Who are you talking about? Who locks you up in here?"

"I used to be really bad. She hates me." Katy led me down the hallway. The sound of a woman screaming and crying in pain came from behind the first door we passed. "She's having a baby."

I pushed on the door; it refused to open. "Shouldn't we help her?"

"She never has the baby. She just keeps having it. That's why she won't let us in." Tugging on my hand, Katy led me away.

Farther down the hallway, I felt something brush my leg. Looking down, I saw a black and white cat pushing its head against my shoe. It purred loudly, with a rough, halting quality.

"That's Tomboy," Katy said. She picked the cat up, his body drooping across her small arms. "He's been here almost as long as I have."

We walked on to the next room. Inside, there was a hospital bed. Between the cracked and broken tiles of the floor, carpet and grass sprouted, growing in thick clumps. The girl in the bed lay still, eyes open, staring straight up at nothing.

"She hasn't been here that long. She's been like that the whole time. She comes and talks to her, but she never says anything. She won't talk to me, either."

"Who comes and talks to her?" I recognized the girl in the bed.

"You know. *Her.*" Dropping the cat, Katy backed away from me with her arms crossed, head down, not wanting to say more.

A roar suddenly shook the house and the walls quivered. I stumbled and tried to keep my balance.

"Charlie's mad," Katy said.

I left the room. At the end of the hallway was a locked door that shook and rattled with the next roar.

"Don't worry, mister," Katy said from behind me. "Charlie gets mad, but he never gets out. She won't let him."

The roar shook the house again. I grabbed Katy by the shoulders. "Who are you talking about?"

"You know. *Her.* You can stay and be my friend. She likes you. You won't be locked in a room."

Panicking, I ran for the front door.

"You'll be back, mister. Nobody's just a visitor here. We're all hers now."

I awoke to darkness and pain. My headache still throbbed against my eyes and temples. Lisa was beside me in the bed, breathing softly—her hair spread out on the pillow like a halo.

I stood up and stumbled for the bathroom, flashes of light filling my eyes. In the mirror, I examined the wounded visage that stared back at me. Who was I? What was I? What was I becoming? Did I even know this stranger that mimicked my every motion? Scattered stubble covered my pale, sallow face, and one eye had hemorrhaged a bright crimson.

I stand here and think about the people whose lives have intersected with Lisa's: her mother dying during childbirth; her father, dead from a brain aneurysm; her aunt, killed by a stroke at the age of twenty-nine; Kim Nelson, a mental vegetable at the age of fifteen. I'm too well educated to believe in curses, and besides, I'm different from all the others.

I love her.

Dusting the Flowers

David J. Schow

It tends to rain a lot in Louisiana, and the closer you get to the rivers, the harder you feel the rain. When downpours spill inches of flood in scant hours, news crews flock, drawn by the magnetism of disaster, hoping for a share of its bounty. Rowboating refugees regard the omnipresent camera lenses with resigned scorn. They mumble blankly about loss, or point out the roofs of their former homes, or press on with the search for lost pets, presumed drowned. It gets grim.

Mr. Gaines is of the carefully considered opinion that such people know little of true loss. They are uneducated and foggy with rage; when it comes to the romantic, they are easy, swift and shallow.

Media never come this far upriver to crank out their livings. No matter how fiercely the rains lash down—floating away automobiles, sluicing corpses smack out of their final resting places, magically vanishing the lower floors of houses, and forcing trillions more insects to gestate and take wing—there are more significant stories to be stumbled across in the place where Mr. Gaines make *his* living.

There was a time when the Hand held in its grasp no human remains. Mr. Gaines remembers this, and accepts his responsibilities. He is an adult.

Mr. Gaines is stocky and bald, with long watchmaker's fingers tapering from thick, wrestler's hands—an anomaly, like slim bamboo growing from the middle of a boulder. He generally keeps these double-duty hands near the center of his body. This gives him the thumbnail appearance of a compact, upright dinosaur, expression suspended in contemplation of a forthcoming live meal. He rarely blinks in front of people. The bit with his hands is an affection, a guard before the center of his being, the anatomical location Mr. Gaines fancies is the seat of his *ka,* which, according to the Egyptians, houses the essence of who he is, but is wily and quite able to enjoy an existence apart from his own day-to-day. Mr. Gaines does not want his *ka* to escape to inhabit some unworthy vessel.

He is actually much stronger than he looks.

He dislikes warm, organic tones, despite the fact that they imbue his existence—greens, browns, rusts, ochres, the tints of metal decay and the spoilage of life. If black is an absence of color, then Mr. Gaines's preferred color is gray.

Right now, the sky is massy, metallic, laden, and stinking of rain. Mr. Gaines lives on a tugboat, and never wastes time worrying about water that comes from the sky.

The last woman is a near-total phony, her flesh the mealy texture of a diet addict, her blue eyes crisscrossed with blown capillaries.

The propane torch accepts a variety of nozzles; the soldering tip has just cooled from an angry crimson glow. Mr. Gaines touches the tip to the woman's flank and she stiffens—purely a reflex jolt, very dull.

She is tall and painfully uncoordinated, her horsy body a compromise between cellulite and the scar tissue of elective surgeries—proof that her war had been not to burn fat, but bore it into submission. Her big Irish titties have been suctioned down to pendant bags, the nipples resectioned to nerve-dead medallions as appealing as raw calves' liver. Her sagging, almost marsupial pouch suggests vast indiscipline, neurosis, a mean mommy, a vapid life squandered in an empty search for her most colorless inner child. Under normal circumstances, her system would be swimming in prescription antidepressants. Her whole body is shaped like a lead sap.

Naturally, she seeks solace in a church of pain. Her boutique rags are stovetop-dyed in Black 15 and reek of clove cigarette smoke. *Make your face a shroud, and your eyes punctures,* thinks Mr. Gaines, as he plans to recreate her.

Beneath the pouch Mr. Gaines has exposed a stingy, puckered little snatch, dry and less like an orchid than the lips of a grouper. The listless smear of pubic hair is redolent of urine. *She probably wipes back to front,* he thinks. Her asshole is more appetizing . . . not that there is all that much visible or tactile difference.

The intaglio of her scars at first fools Mr. Gaines into thinking that this one might possess fiber or substance. Now he realizes—too late—the shiny islets of healing scab dotting her legs are the result of nothing more than sloppy shaving. Her scalp bears chemical burn patches from too much hair coloring.

Her mouth is nasty, downturned, with an underbite of disapproval. She looks better with all her teeth knocked out. Less smug.

Perhaps inspired by some supermarket magazine on borderline culture, this creature has found her way here, on the seek for vicarious danger. No matter, now. She is poised to eat the humiliation she has been begging all of her superior, wretched non-life.

"I suppose you've never heard the story of Phocas?" Mr. Gaines says. "He was a saint." The woman's apex of visual focus is centered somewhere behind him, glazed and flat, her eyes cognizant on a galvanic level only. She flinches at the touch of the blowtorch, pupils contracting, and that's about it.

"Phocas dug his own grave before his executioners killed him, in order that he might feed the soil after his death." Mr. Gaines leans closer with the torch, smiling, his eyes scanning the woman for some hint of texture, of fear, or resolve, or anything interesting. He finds nothing to engage him. Without control-top panty hose, sneaky tailoring, and an arsenal of cosmetics, she is nothing physical, and spiritually she is just as much of a lie. He has acted impulsively and chosen her badly. Now he sees she has worth only as protein or crude phosphorous.

Bound, ball-gagged with duct tape and lamp cord, hopelessly brimming over with fright appropriate to her true echo-boomer class, her teeth extracted by pliers, this one is stupid enough to still be fretting about rape. Mr. Gaines shakes his head sadly, for her to see.

"No, I am not going to fuck you," he tells her. "At least, not in any fashion you understand, and certainly not while you're alive. I have no wish to fight with you, or listen to you carrying on." He removes his glasses. After polishing the lenses, he gives the bridge of his nose a sinus-relieving pinch. "Forgive me. It's just that I am distressed because I cannot use you, you see. You're too vapid, too empty, too self-deluded for my needs."

At the porthole side of the flared cabin there is a flared vase of cut onyx, arranged dramatically with a spray of flowers in vivid, melted-crayon colors. It is an intentional incongruity in this otherwise monochromatic world. Mr. Gaines mists them, using a plastic bottle of biodegradable cleaner, and wipes off the leaves and petals, one at a time, with a paper towel folded into quarters. He holds up the towel so the woman can see the smudges it has picked up.

"You see? Gray—but invisible." He cleans a few more of the flowers, not gently, but with thoroughness. "I don't suppose you've heard of the butternut canker? No?" He shakes his head again. This is *really* sad.

Near the flowers, beneath a drop-down utility seat, a circular steel purifier quietly filters the air they both breathe. Condensation hangs on the grille. Outside, the humidity is a lethal, plotting thing.

"How about the anthracnose? It kills dogwood trees."

There is no comprehension at all in the eyes that return his gaze, then persist in darting, frantically, to the limits of the boat's cabin.

"Dammit," he mutters. "Thought not."

He resumes work with the torch, careful not to make a mess on the deck. Topside, a forty-gallon drum is already prepared to receive her . . . even if dumping her, along with all the rest, does little to further his cause tonight.

Visualized as tree roots, branches of the Mississippi web out by the thousands. Most terminate in irreclaimable swampland, in dead-end lagoons and bayou mud the color of iron. Tributaries are gnarled and treacherous; many open or close on the whim of faraway tides or nearby rainfall, and, like the secret nooks of a Chinese puzzle box, reveal themselves only to the faithful, the dogged, or the damned—and then, only during special ticks of the clock.

Most of the marshland is shallow and lethal; often, simply greedy, teeming with predators and laced with booby traps, snakes and gators, quicksand and suckholes, and deadly brain fevers that can expand the cranium like bread dough in the time it takes coffee to cool.

Below the Thirtieth Parallel, the state of Louisiana degenerates to the consistency of cheesecloth, punctured relentlessly by lake after pond after mudhollow. The water table went insane there a few centuries back, and the Delta resembles nothing so much as a burst organ, not just on maps, but from as far a vantage as synchronous Earth orbit. "Delta rhythm" suggests seductive backwoods music; when applied to brain waves, it alerts to damage, or disorder. Natives razz the Delta as the Colon of America and they aren't far wrong; whenever some bonehead pisses in Lake Erie, it eventually spews out here thanks to groundwater, fault lines, subterranean seepage, other mutagenic factors never deduced by cartographers. From outer space, it all looks quite innocent.

Incoming air passengers to New Orleans can peer through portholes, when they are low enough, in mid-approach, and sometimes spot Mr. Gaines's tugboat, shoving garbage barges upriver against the sluggish tide. That is about as noteworthy as Mr. Gaines ever becomes to the world outside his Hand.

Earlier in the evening, a news hog had captured Curta KIA sneaking out the loading dock door of Spasmodique. Of his tribe of hunter-gatherers of information, this reporter had been the only one hunger-crazed enough to accurately plot Curta's movements. By next dusk, there would be five cameras on her if she surfaced to grocery-shop; by the weekend, she'd rate an in-depth bloc, national. Five minutes on the evening news, she thought. She'd watched five minutes of film roll through a Moviola once and knew that this amount of time, under the right circumstances, could be an eternity. Five minutes, nationwide, on art. Consider that.

Curta KIA felt challenged and pure. She was skating the cutting edge at last.

The only reason the dolt from Channel 9 had been able to capture her video image was that she brooked no one's personal guarantee her truck would be padlocked; she'd gone to check it herself. For the viewing public that bit of tape would be frozen and digitally enhanced and repeated numberless times while critics and attackers ran their speculations. The pixels would become exhausted while her infamy, to get basic about it, would swing heftier publicity value.

Inside Spasmodique, she was alone. Her section of the main gallery was now bare. She chose which lights still blazed. Everything had been crated in one night—miraculous enough by itself. She had left behind a single piece, for the gallery's front show window—evidence that Curta KIA had been here—and another free piece of tape for the truly enterprising, or truly despicable, journalists. Evidence at the scene, for those who sweet-talked outrage and wanted to lap up scandal.

She had chosen which lights still blazed in the display areas. Privately, unobserved, she could appreciate all the time Madsur invested in his lines. Publicly, she could not suffer Abstractionists wrestling with themes of collision. She examined the impossibly huge canvas, the size of some studio apartments, and thought (kneejerk, and selfishly) of the attention she concentrated into a mere cubic inch. Still, Madsur's new work, titled *Eidolons*, soothed her in a way she would most likely never have time to investigate further. Her inner dialogue with this painting would end tonight. It would remain a secret.

Curta KIA was short, round, and blonde. She had a large crescent moon tattooed on the nape of her neck; a heavenly body of earthbound inks, gnawed by many lovers. She had kicked Prozac two years ago because she felt it was leavening her creativity. Now she held steady at mildly alcoholic, and had slashed back to five Gauloises per day. She no longer smoked them all the way down to the filter. She had extremely responsive nipples, to compensate for almost zero bosom, and enjoyed claiming she was French as an excuse for being flat-chested. It was her habit to shave her pubic hair into a landing strip of stubble just abrasive enough to pink whoever fucked her. Called "sturdy" in her youth, her body type was beginning to assume control of her metabolism. Overall, her portrait was fading, but gently. She suffered the crying jags less often.

She cultivated "sharp" as a personal adjective—a sharp appearance incorporating sharp industrial jewelry, sharp heels, sharp nails, very sharp gray eyes behind sharp-edged shades. These last had been a gift lacking weight or commitment, as were most of her accoutrements—offerings from merchants and wannabes, costly tokens from pushy fans, god, you could just *smell* the hunger on these people, the despair of being unspecial and untalented, as they tried to own her, be seen with her, piss-mark her.

And today, at last, she could flush all the hangers-on, because she was on her way to becoming truly famous.

After her own art-o-nym, Curta had named her show *Killed Inaction.* Some butt-scratching little dog-eaters in Korea had recently burdened the automotive market with a roller-skate car also dubbed a "Kia"; J. C. Christ, Esquire, didn't their advertising idiots do *anything* to justify their dole?

On the other hand, perhaps they were being market-smart . . . subtly, gruesomely.

Curta KIA's work was based on a synergy between organic decay and inorganic decomposition, her design schema wholly motivated by the dictates of found art. *Hardwired,* for example, first manifested itself as a spit-and-paste of bones and rust. In essence, it was half a skull, a puzzle-piece of a face, from the superciliary ridge where the eyebrow would be to the buccinator shelf, just above the upper canines. It was split right through the center of the nose hole. Other bones included were a few weathered ribs, a handful of vertebrae, and most of a pelvic saddle. Curta mirrored the missing portion of the skull in machine parts solidified to rust. Dozens of oxidized copper threads emitted from gaps in the skull, in bunches, to flare out and travel to different plug-in destinations on the bonework. Imprinted iron tubes and scabbed fixtures provided a superstructure that was not whole, at best, truncated, that tapered from top to bottom like an angular crosscut view of a robot woman, supporting itself upright on impossibly spidery wisps of rotten cable. The trick of the assemblage was in not utilizing clunky junk parts that evoked the doodads from some plumber's truck; the effect had a mantis elegance, flowing from the stark cyber-skull above to the spindly trifles of wire below, in mandarin curls like odd new forms of antennae.

The unofficial story went that Curta KIA scavenged in cemeteries for her raw material, particularly after floods liberated inadequate crypts and buoyed forth their entombed prizes. The notion was the stuff of urban legends; given Curta's tendency to spin-doctor her own image, it was a gentle untruth worth perpetuating—the kind that sometimes brought home checks to cash.

The disillusioning fact was that she purchased her bones and skulls mostly from junkies, who mainlined in the nooks and crannies of St Louis Number One, or from clueless Goth kids who thought coyoting around graveyards was cool. She had a file on cash disbursements invoiced to names like DiSang or Nepenthe or Mr. Lucarda, when a name was left at all. Whatever.

You could bleed into your paints in public, but if you painted nothing significant, who would ever give a shit beyond the carefully crafted, sensational rep? An artist was a vendor of illusion. The craft part was in Curta's use of solvents and stain, carpet beetles and oxyacetylene. She was fond of the deep, penetrative textures of heavy, vintage rust, and never burnished away such deposits unless she was shooting for some specific editorial point. She called one style "erosion strata," an impasto technique that went beyond the limitations of mere oil paint.

She had lost out on a show at Galerie to a pair of urban primitives from Queens whose idea of art was a dysfunctional hearse covered in coal tar, below a suspended mass of old sofa cushions, their interstices caulked up with cake and frosting. It took up a lot of room, just as its barely articulate creators had taken too much energy to dislike. Not the scene Curta sought, at all.

The opening at Spasmodique had been fairly sparkly. Many cameras, many eyes looking. Then, in the time it took to run a byte of libel on *News at 11,* Curta KIA saw her much-craved artistic notoriety become the tripe of tabloid TV.

The piece from which they could not deter their unblinking lizard notice was titled *Hidebound.* It was Curta's retrofit of the papery bones of a child, swaddled in mote-thin NASA instrument packet foil that boldly declared every wrinkle and contour. A big triangular piece in the contour of a widow's peak had been missing from the skull, so Curta had laced it back to wholeness with hundreds of microfine braids of lightly rusted wire, first joining strands, then marrying braids, then twining braid groups, in seemingly bottomless recombination.

Curta KIA had made the *Hidebound* orphan whole, and now the Great

Unlaid wanted her to burn at the stake. Fittingly, she had chosen *Hidebound* as the piece to leave for the gallery. She was already charting a new generation of the design in her head, to cheese off more strangers to come, and all their upstanding spouses, too.

Lawsuits and scorn and the concept of guilt had never much worried her. They did not bother her tonight. Disappointment was something she always anticipated, even invited. She was calmly impressed by the speed with which the societal relays had clicked over, and, in an instant, made her a ghoul.

Here is the lifework of Curta KIA. She robs graves. Maybe the graves of people you know. To blaspheme its sanctity, to dishonor its memory, and to callously convert your dead relatives into works of so-called "art" unfathomable by the likes of you.

Oh, it was a media hot button, all right.

Her most knifing concern amidst the abundant hype was that the mouth-breathing legions might get it into their collective brainpan, somehow, that Curta KIA *did not do all her own work.* Even if the professional world never heard her name again, she had fielded enough inquiries in the past twenty-four hours to support herself on the coin of trend-humpers for the next decade . . . which was more security than she had experienced in her entire life, so far. If this Curta KIA was really plundering the bones of the dead, then there was a world full of bored "new collars" and ex–Gen X execs with ready cash to exploit. But if she only *bought* her ingredients, if she did not procure them personally, and at risk, well, then . . . the price might have to go down.

Some painters, like Artaud Sphinx—another big prizewinner at the Galerie fiasco—let it leak that they farmed out washes and backgrounds to apprentices, who generally paid for the privilege. Artaud's brush and palette only came in for the detail work. His time was too valuable, what with parties in Monaco and photo shoots with anorexic supermodels on the beaches of Ibiza. After all, the imagination was still his, *n'est-ce pas?*

Okay. On some cosmic plane it had already been decided: Curta KIA was destined to sell uncompromised, real pieces. If she could hang on to her artistic integrity under moral duress, she would be rewarded with expensive attorneys who could vet all the small print.

To this end, tonight, she had arranged a rendezvous with some entity named Hraban, whose promise was to conduct her to an undisclosed location he called Final Rest, where she could prove to the universe that Curta KIA was for real.

Mr. Gaines is neither dead nor alive—at least, not on paper. He has never received a paycheck, nor paid taxes. No records detail his comings or goings. He has no credit cards; no database recognizes him.

The shit he is hired to dump upriver, in the region he has taken the liberty of naming the Hand, is so poisonous that it can fizz through lead and blind you for just thinking about it. Talk of hazardous waste of such caliber would parch your throat and raw your breath; you'd want to mask your face and close your eyes so stray molecules might be denied the chance to sneak into your body. Drum upon drum at forty-plus gallons each, decades of disposal, year in and out, trillions of tumors, quadrillions of amok cells, all itching for a shot at your metabolism. You would vacate the premises posthaste, without a backward look, never to return, hoping never to remember.

Mr. Gaines enjoys the implied threat of his environment. It makes his work seem larger and more important. It makes his job easier when everyone stays far away by choice.

He thinks frequently about waste. There is more every day to add to the mental cumulate, thus more time to invest in thought about the ways such waste might change the trajectory of his life, or that of others, overtly or not.

Just now, Mr. Gaines's sink zone is an anguineous backwater of the Hand, so named because he is the only person ever to explore and map the region. By his reckoning, the Hand is comprised of five tributaries that vaguely resemble an open left hand, palm up, with the thumb cocked at the top. His drawing depicted a sort of cartoon hand that had been squished in a doorjamb, the topmost digits all wobbly and crooked, the bottom ones trisected by bits of "land" untraversable by foot or boat. They looked like skeleton finger bones. The terminus of the index finger was a very deep lagoon. There had once been a sixth finger, below the pinky. Mr. Gaines had spent three years filling in that deformity with illicit garbage, and then a curious, almost miraculous thing occurred. The inlet grew shut, like a healing wound, in the space of five days. When it ceased to exist, he had begun deep-sixing his cargo in the farthest extreme of the pinky finger. Riverbanks amending their own topography was something Mr. Gaines understood and admired as part of the symbiosis between water and earth.

In Mr. Gaines's knowledge of the river and its ways, however, this particular branch had closed up unnaturally fast. It was like a hint for him to move on. He complied effortlessly. He was not a man burdened by *things*.

Mr. Gaines never keeps trophies. He permits himself few possessions and the most meager supplies. The weight of *things* could age you. *Things* collected dust, and forced you to buy or collect more *things*.

What Mr. Gaines knows about his victims, he learns directly, usually as they are begging to be spared.

He prefers the nonorganic. One of the reasons he lives on his boat is that there are set limits to the amount of space that may be absorbed by *things*. Less space means fewer items to dust. Where he usually anchors, there *is* no dust.

As a symbol of the control he wields over his life, Mr. Gaines maintains his vase of vibrantly colored flowers. All of these are cunning replicas configured of fabric and lace and plastic. There is not one genuine bloom in the bouquet, and certainly nothing to require the messy imprecision of organic activity.

Last night, the barge wrangler had warned Mr. Gaines to wear eye protection when handling the most recent load—seventy drums of some sort of bio-toxic runoff that was now happily deconstructing in the embrace of the Hand's stinkfinger. Chugging quietly toward his rendezvous, Mr. Gaines had seen something that had been there by the riverbank for months, but which he had never noticed. A half-sunken ferry, its stern submerged to the quarterdeck rail, the floating equivalent of a condemned tenement. Against the abandoned dock on an overcast and starless night, it offered absolutely no reason to be seen.

Now it had been strung with electric lights and torches, the latter indicating that those aboard were no demolition or scrap crew. Squatters? Certainly not on a tub like that one. No one in full command of his or her senses had any business being there, so dangerously close to the secret shallows that might lead to the Hand.

For Mr. Gaines, life had always been a succession of lists of problems. The process of living, more or less, was not in solving the problems so much as profitably trading them upward for a new and more complex set to figure out. That ferry seemed like a new problem, as well as another hint.

But not a threat. Not yet. And certainly nothing that could not remain in abeyance until his return from the city.

"Hraban" turned out to be an entry-level graveboy in a skirt, as thick and empty as a British music magazine.

"It's Old High German for 'raven,' actually," he grinned loosely. He had on too much eye kohl, in mimic of some singer who had impressed him, and whenever Curta KIA met his gaze, he lowered his eyes like a dog.

"What are you talking about?" Lingering near this submissive child made Curta crave a cigarette, a drink, something grown-up, to demarcate them.

"My name. You know, 'Hraban.'"

She couldn't believe this. "We'll pretend that's really interesting, okay, Huh-raben? Now, shall we?" He was too perfect: guileless, fatuous, desperately in search of a personality he thought he could acquire osmotically, given the correct peer group—thus, Final Rest. He could front and she could steer, and when he had ejaculated the information she required, she could fold him up and dispose of him, the ideal zipless entree.

It occurred to her that Huh-raben might have read the papers, seen the news. That would explain his slack-jawed silences and the awe of worship that radiated from his pores. If dog he was, he definitely wanted to rub his glands against something more famous than himself. Curta KIA had not decided yet whether she would fuck him. Too bad she could not stretch a condom over his brain.

"So, it's, like, nothing extreme," he said as he squinted through a flat, smudgy windscreen and did his best to pilot his Volkswagen along Canal. After crossing the river they would pick up the 23, southbound. "Should be like an hour to drive, and we got to go a little ways on a boat. But it's a recline; I think you might like it, whatever. There aren't any, you know, pressure people; everybody can just be into whatever they're into."

She had to find some way to tune him out or she might strangle him before they got another ten miles. Solution: autopilot. "So how long have you been into the Goth scene here?" she asked, just languidly enough. It was the only time during the trip she bothered to make direct eye contact.

As he began to prattle about being alienated, yet tragic, and how nobody else back in Wilmington seemed to be like him, Curta KIA settled in against the crook of her arm and the door. About the time he began to extol Chartreuse and tick off bands by name, she was comfortably courting nap rhythm.

Mr. Gaines maintains his seat by the rail at the Café du Monde, quietly sucking the foam from the head of a *café au lait* brewed from local tap water, which, according to the EPA baselines, contains particulate matter that is 40 percent recycled toilet paper. Watching an overweight quartet of tourists in bizarre white shorts herd toward the seductions of the T-shirt and tchotchke emporiums of Jackson Square, he reflects upon one small, good thing in his world—the local zoning ordinances which still disallow fast-food franchises in the Quarter, though a variance has let a Pizza Hut sneak in on Decatur Street.

It is not the beginning of the end, it was *the* end; why bother to tilt against it?

The bovine foursome is still within view, diminishing, listing tidally, a mountain range on the hoof. The absence of familiar brand-name food logos will make them moo and panic. In the Quarter, it is gumbo, jambalaya, shrimp creole, po-boys, or nothing. Jackson Square has a food court now. Mr. Gaines wonders whether their eagerness to wolf down meat pucks would wane if they knew the burger bore a 2 percent minimum of undifferentiated "bug filth," in compliance with USDA regs, or that on a per-patty basis, those same government standards permitted this so-called "beef" to contain up to one-fifth sterilized mealworm protein as filler. They are on their way to pound down grub, all right.

Sitting here in the city, speaking to no one, gliding among citizens and locals and visitors, Mr. Gaines feels like a secret agent, afoot in a foreign port—swap "exotic" for "befouled" and the picture is framed.

Mr. Gaines has already searched for the French Quarter on the Rue Royale, and found it long gone. He sees lemminglike tourists and drunken frat-house loudmouths. He sees dusty boutiques transmitting a desperate, yet noncommittal hunger. He searches for it in the Old Absinthe House, and finds only trendoids and yupsters and assorted necrophiles of consumer culture too boring to categorize. When, in the dead center of night, when the streets and alleys cleared, he tries to inhale the atmosphere—a treasured memory of the Quarter, for him—he smells only the reeking garbage of countless restaurants, all with the same six items on the menu, the compost of a cuisine long in its grave.

Unknown poets, apologetic alcoholics, and boatloads of other identityless romantics persist in inflicting their delusional architecture on the town—a distorted impression of a time long past and an era that had never been. Mr. Gaines tries to be forgiving and finds he feels empty, burglarized. Logic cannot elevate him from this profound sense of loss.

The Quarter has been devoid of ghosts for many years, yet no one has bothered to hold a wake to honor its death. No phantoms haunt the antique masonry or wrought iron, and those who seek the supernatural will find only key chains at Marie Laveau's, where the modern corporate mojo of Visa and MasterCard are accepted. The old design schemata that remain here can still engage the eye, but falsely, as relics—no sensuality teems from them; they no longer seethe. Tourists have helped the economy but driven away the fragile ha'ants that once lent the area depth. Bourbon Street is no more than a neon cutout, two-dimensional, a whole lot of nothing behind a flashy facade. Here, for ghosts, there is no sustenance and no foothold, no anchor, and no imperative to stay. Like many places once alive, the Quarter continues to exist by cannibalizing its own past, since any hope for a future was consumed and exhausted long ago.

This offends Mr. Gaines beyond words. What he had lost had been too loamy and rich, too layered in suffocatingly humid resonances of Spanish moss and the ghosts of murdered slaves, of pirate gold and the toxic kick of absinthe. It was a world in which bayou gators with gnawed-off limbs regurgitated a stew of lost travelers into the fervid bouillabaisse of the swamp, by the fire of lightning bugs, to the plaints of loons and mating amphibians, where the mulch of the dead percolated in quickmud shot through with creepers and kudzu and legend, and formed new voodoo life-forms.

Somebody should write a zydeco song about the weight of it all; the responsibility of myth that is being ignored here.

Even the House of Death has degenerated into a tourist trap. People swill Hurricanes and phony mint juleps and the whole place has the appeal of a prostitute with facial hair and a limp. Panhandlers impose. Street singers burden their walking dead audience with banal litanies. The songs change but the envy and sloth and hate that drove them remain at an unchanging level of dull animal contempt.

Mr. Gaines has searched in the narrow, cobblestoned alleyways, and found children spoiling for trouble—but not real trouble. He courts the consolation of crypts in St Louis Number One, and is crowded out by the crackheads lurking there after nightfall, come to pipe, work commerce, or bust the heads of the junkies who mainline behind this grave marker or that. Other creatures arrive later, to scavenge the discarded needles that pile up near the gates.

Being an alcoholic or a drug addict is one of the few things that makes sense, here.

For Mr. Gaines, there are no lurking specters of romance. Whatever he had once held in his heart about the notion of romance and romantic places is long gone, replaced inadequately by a clinical need to test his own limits in terms of the people he kills, and the toxic waste he dumps.

He thinks of roach parts in food, of rat shit and bug legs and fly dung—but no more than 2 percent. It makes an adequate comparison to his nocturnal sinkage. So much poison no one will ever notice. Eat it with a smile if it is sold by a jolly clown.

Mr. Gaines drops by Jean Lafitte's Blacksmith Shop, a place he has not had much use for since the idiosyncratic staff all got fired and the drink menu boiled down to six kinds of diet beer. Once mythologized as the darkest bar in New Orleans, it, too, has been scarified by entropy. The interlopers and eccentrics who corrupt Bourbon Street with their consumer-friendly flatline stumble in, slam down a few brewskis, and stagger out. A distinct tone problem enwraps the place like a winding sheet.

Mr. Gaines is just taking his leave when the fight starts. Some lizardy Goths strike a few sparks against some punk has-beens, and Mr. Gaines wants to be around to sweep up the mess.

Lawrence is a de facto leader type for his subphylum—neurasthenic, lucent-skinned, with fine birdlike bones. He fits comfortably into the class of maitre d' or undertaker, one of which he had probably been prior to his stylish bent for velvet, gloom 'n' doom, and all things Halloweenish.

His opponent, Needle, is so obscure that no one really cares where his rebirth name came from. To be an aging punk and alpha wolf, one has to own all the right markings and mileage, and Needle has enough tracks and injuries to guarantee his doubtful masthead qualities for at least another month.

Lawrence and Needle tread on each other's macho just beyond the darkness of Jean Lafitte's. Combat is mandated. There isn't a hell of a lot else to do.

While the Quarter easily contains the fluid lunacy of Mardi Gras or backstreet muggings aplenty, it refuses to sanction the fight, which is taken to the docks. Mr. Gaines follows it. In the end, the casualties number seven. He thinks that soon enough, he might kill Lawrence or Needle personally. Amazing, how the leaders never suffer directly in such little flashfire spats.

Later in the evening, Mr. Gaines searches for something to externalize the way he feels, and finds the art of someone named Curta KIA.

They heard the lawnmower chug of the generator first, followed by a powerful, deep, almost subaural bass line of such power that it rattled iron plating and rippled the filthy water with its metronomic pulse.

"There's no power," said Hraban, unnecessarily. "So we make our own." That "we," the neediness to cleave to some group or surrogate family, was stronger than the thumping bass, and struck Curta KIA in much the same way as the smell of the river she could no longer see. It was that dark.

They made their way, in the darkness, from the steel-hulled rowboat (surely stolen, she thought) up a makeshift gangplank composed of rotting hemp and shipping pallets knotted together, secured between two smoldering oil torches. The jerry-rigged ramp yawed drunkenly as they ascended.

Curta KIA abruptly recognized the thudding tune as an electronic dirge that had enjoyed some popularity and resonance more than a decade ago. Unidentified moist crap from the rope came free into the palm of her hand, slick and granular.

"It's a trap," she said. It was a joke until Hraban asked her if she was really afraid.

Turn around, she mentally commanded him, *and keep climbing. Don't speak to me unless you suffer the passage of a thought first.* She kept a clamp on her acid. Two drinks in her and things would have been different.

The former passenger ferry was sunken stern-down in the black water, its prow jutting weakly up like the nose of a dead badger. The lower decks, once used for automobiles, were probably all flooded. The portable generator was stationed outside the main passenger cabin, theoretically high, dry, and ventilated. It smelled the way a hot car engine smells when gaskets are frying.

"Welcome to Final Rest," Hraban said, taking pains to point out that FINAL REST had been smeared in all-weather paint near the forward passenger hatch.

Curta KIA entered a tilted chamber containing more than hundred people in black. Tepid light waned from strung bulbs as the generator yielded to the sound system; dozens of candles were burning. Cold pockets of light exuded chemical scents—vanilla, jasmine, licorice. The vast passenger cabin had been cleared of bolted-in factory issue and was parceled into countless little corners and circles of dim illumination. She smelled beer but did not see much being drunk from bottles or cans; everyone present seemed to have wineglasses or crude pottery mugs that looked home-turned.

Already, white faces were looking and white fingers with ebony or blood-red nails were pointing. Hraban pressed a long-stemmed glass of something into her hand.

"It's mead, I think," he said over the music, exaggeratedly forming the words by stretching his mouth to and fro, presumably so she could lip-read. He came off so funny, like a remedial dope whose medication was kicking his ass, that Curta KIA almost blurted out a laugh. The drink in her hand smelled like urine. Instead of screaming back, she draped her free arm around him and drew him closer, shushing him conspiratorially so she could scope the talent of the room.

Oh-so-tragic, easily cynical, fashionably aloof—Curta saw pale little deather girls and boys, flaunting a caustic disdain for life and each other through the practiced, hooded glance of the faux-aesthete or the defocused fixation of the lotus-eater; their eyes, like Hraban's, kohled with makeup filched from drugstores. Curta had been prepared for a parade of homeless disaffiliates, squatter kids and layabouts, runaways and black-clad bums sucking on clove cigarettes. Every once in a while, she met one of these poseurs who actually housed a shred of substance or a mote of genuine tragedy. So far, the prospects, like vampires, not only bit, but sucked.

A lot of them affected the expected dull uniformity: the scuffed boots with needle toes, the threadbare denim butts, the rail-lean, chicken-wing physiques with concave stomachs and hairless, larva-white flesh over sunken ribs. More often than not you could pat them down and come up with at least one or two sets of actual handcuffs or a demo cassette.

The fat ones were a hoot. They looked the most like the "witches" and "vampires" trotted onto talk shows every Halloween, always clutching the overweight pop novels that formed their gospel and yammering on about the dark romance of human blood. They were perpetually Becoming some new genus they fantasized would make them less dreary—essentially, a sort of jumped-up marsh leech with a groovy, depressing wardrobe, for whom mere human life was just parasite boot camp. Perhaps that was why they were all so hideously bloated with carbohydrates and saturated fat: practice, practice, practice. Or maybe they just ate all those big, fat best-sellers.

At least the older ones had stories to tell, thought Curta, weighing curse against blessing. This phylum generally exuded the stink of glitter rockers two decades out of step with the planet. They still mourned Ozzy's leavetaking from Black Sabbath, and performed sink-dye jobs on their thinning hair not so much to stay stylish as to mask the bald spots and encampments of gray. Where the fat ones looked perpetually gorged (not vampiric at all, unless they had vampirized the nearest Der Wienerschnitzel), the old ones secreted needy hopelessness as a communicable toxin. Yes, they were tragic . . . but it was the low-budget tragedy of a mental case pushing a shopping cart, not the tonier sculpture of a refined, doomed immortal.

Then there were the Others. Genuinely odd or cantankerous, but never turned up high enough. Faint suggestions of the true Gothic, where bold declamations were needed. If they had elegance, it was squandered or overdrugged; if style, it was borrowed from those with an equal poverty of the imagination; if mystery, it was ostentatiously spotlit. Real mysteries left such as these impatient and whiny. Some were young, trapped in the grip of a transient fragility they would spend the rest of their lives fighting to perpetuate. Some were older, with all the right piercings and scars, the ones with fading tattoos who could feed off you by unspooling the endless saga of the thwarted love or ambition that imprisoned them forever on a giant slide-ride to doom.

They came down here from Manhattan, blinded by mascara and shunning the cancerous sun, from the Carolinas, from Texas, from Seattle, from Iowa, they made hadj, scent-tracking on the blood brotherhood of those they thought to be like themselves—a scatter of outcasts, each the local weirdo of his or her birth town, iconoclasts and mutants, wild individualists sniffing for tribal unity. From Los Angeles they came, armed with propaganda from the Center for Vampire Studies in Pasadena (which documented the frigid, rock-hard fact that more genuine *nosferatu* resided in L.A. than anywhere else), too stunned or jaded to notice how the cutting edge had sliced them in two long ago. Sooner or later, they all wound up at Final Rest, or someplace like it. "Are you angel, beast, or elder?" they would ask each other, like dogs doing the butt-sniff.

What did they all want? Bands, books and magazines, where to dance, to see live shows, to get inked or pierced. Crash space for travelers. Knowledge for making plastic fangs and fake IDs for big-city clubbing, their righteousness so predictable, their edge theory making them all easy meat.

Hraban left her. More correctly, he was drawn away to be swallowed in the darkness by an intruder who had moved him as effortlessly as sliding a barstool.

"Fuck off, Raven," said the stranger. "Go fill your hole or I'll fill it for you."

Hraban was clearly jazzed by this abuse, rushing to make some sort of point-scoring intro. "Wow, Lawrence, I was just looking around for you, you know? This is—"

"I know who this is," the taller man said, laying a basilisk gaze on Curta KIA and compelling Hraban into retreat gear with a curl of his thin upper lip. Curta's hand was arrested in a warm, firm grasp. "Please pardon the Raven. He's a bit of an idiot."

Curta squeezed right back. "And you're Lawrence and you're *really different*, right?"

"You have the grip of an artisan. That's the only common thing about you." He took the untried drink in Curta's hand and dashed it to the floor, handing the empty wineglass to Hraban and replacing it, by seeming sleight of hand, with a smaller taste in what looked like a Soviet vodka glass.

Curta sipped the pungent, herbal stuff, politely, her eyes and mouth catching a surprise. Chartreuse, made by someone who knew the right tricks. "You haven't said anything fascinating yet."

He ran his index finger across his closed lips. If he repeated the gesture later, it would be to transfer his buzz to Curta's lips, with her indulgence. "Like many of these"—he indicated the others anonymously present—"I enjoy the beautiful and the disturbing. The ethereal is often the pulse to a darker passion. Unlike them, I won't bore you by going on about Morpheus's warm embrace, or how Death is my sanctuary. Most of the campy vampires and fashion roadkill standing around us are too hung up on seeking the coolest death, or, lacking that, the most public melancholy."

"Some of them are only seeking the right bands to like," Curta said.

"Point."

"Meanwhile, you're bleeding," Curta pointed out. His cheek on the right side was scraped redly back into his ear.

"A disagreement in the Quarter earlier. No consequence."

"You'd better avail yourself of a Kleenex unless you want one of these supplicants to lick your face. Might be unhygienic."

"They're really not so bad, all in." The worry-line dividing his brow told her that he already felt he was wasting time with the blah-blah. "I was at your show, at Spasmodique. I wonder if you noticed me."

"No."

"That's not surprising. You spent nearly the whole show staring at everyone *else's* work. Madsur shows promise, if not as an Abstractionist, then as a Minimalist."

"You're dating yourself."

"Sorry; I liked the painting too. But not as much as *Hidebound.* The orphan. The braided orphan, forsaken, yet important in death."

"Thanks." She had a Gauloise in her hand and before she could display it, Lawrence snicked an old-fashioned hard-case Zippo one-handed, striking the flint on the way up. She held his hand to steady the fire. "What does it say on your lighter?"

He handed it to her. The inscription was crudely hand-stamped, not a job done for beauty. The words were polished smooth by the passage of years, nearly as illegible as the inscription on a forgotten tombstone:

ONE HAS NEVER
LIVED TILL HE HAS
ALMOST DIED LIFE
HAS A FLAVOR THE
PROTECTED WILL
NEVER KNOW

66–69
PLEIKU

She was silent for nearly a full minute, then said, "You seem very well-preserved."

"Maybe I'm Undead." He pocketed the lighter. "Maybe I just eat right."

"Fighting in public isn't very self-preservational."

He smiled his first real smile of the evening. "I enjoy it. Can't help it, really. I won. I always win. Come with me. I presume you have a purpose for actually being here, and you don't seem to have the disposition for slumming."

He offered her his arm and she looked at it. This made him smile again, and he appropriated a candelabra and led her out of the ferry's main cabin.

"This thing is half-underwater," said Curta as the echo of their footsteps along the corridor became apparent against the fading music. "What's holding it up?"

"Cars, I think. Industrial junk. Toxic waste. The odd corpse or two with feet eternally shod in quick-dry cement. That sort of thing. But mostly, cars. The automobile hold was full of scrap from chop shops when this thing was scuttled. Turns out so much junk had been dumped in this bend of the river that she sank so far, and no more." With a glint of malice he added, "Which means the pile of garbage upon which this ferry is reefed may settle or shift at any moment. Think of that in terms of risk."

"And you've got the explanation as to why this place became Final Rest?"

He stopped walking to answer. That lent weight to the reply, whether Curta KIA cared to notice or not. "It serves them as a Modernist reliquiae, to help them carry out their enactment of places and sensibilities long dead. I really don't know; moreover, I don't care. The old cars, the dead bodies—that's the story. It serves. Alfalfa and the Little Rapscallions back there buy it—as local myth, it's potent enough and serves the purposes of fear/belief systems, so who am I to say it's not true? Why did you come with me, a stranger, away from the crowd just now?"

"You said you liked my sculpture, and you sounded like you knew what you were talking about when you said it." She treated herself to a long pull of her cigarette; the cherry glowed as if sexually stimulated.

"It touched me. I meant what I said. I saw things like it, a very long time ago. Those things were not attractive."

She reached out to touch the wall. It was oozing foul-smelling liquid, like the nitred bricks of a catacomb. Sometimes bacteria could oxidize forsaken metal into forms of acid or cyanide. "Careful," she said.

"But your work took all the ugliness out of those images for me." He raised the candelabra. There was less ambient light at this end of the ship.

"Where are we?"

"Upper aft passenger deck. If you could see the back wall, you'd notice it was rounded off."

Curta KIA could not see the far bulkhead, because it was underwater.

They stood in a hatchless passage staring down a decline of nearly twenty degrees. Scant feet away, the decomposed deck slid beneath dark, still water like the deep end of a dirty swimming pool. The rank air was alive with mildew and sporulative microbes. Bleached, unidentifiable litter floated without ripples beyond their reach; other sodden castoffs were no doubt stacked up amid mud and swampy decay in the butt end of the boat. The wavering firelight sought to trick the eye and make every shadow seem engorged with virulent life.

"Sometimes they come here to shoot up," said Lawrence. "Sometimes, they die." He extended his open hand toward the biliously cloaked mysteries of the far side of the cabin, beyond the reach of the light. "I think you may find something you need in this room."

She fought to stay wry. "I think you're nuts if you think I'm wading in there alone, with no light and no antibiotics, groping maggoty corpses and grabbing water moccasins by mistake and getting annelids in my boots . . . Lawrence."

He chocked the candelabra against the remains of a folding deck chair, which leaned back against the nearby wall on two legs. The candles flickered in protest against the pestilential air they were forced to burn. "You wonder if you are for real, in your art," he said, solemnly folding his arms. "You judge others without having to prove yourself. I don't want a treasure hunt. Do I look like some groupie who would wallow in the mud for a chance to fetch you a skull?"

Her body wanted to backtrack, but her ego denied easy fear. "What, then?"

That snaky smile was back. "I want one dance. Dance with me. Show me you are who I think you are." With that, he held out his arms, and he could not have been more alluring: clean-shaven, clad in black, and smelling faintly of Osiris oil.

Suddenly Curta KIA was notably wet; crimson rose in her like heated mercury and her heart compelled her blood to speed. Maybe Lawrence had hypnotized her. She wanted to ride him hard, grind him to obeisance with her pussy and make him scream when he came. With her excellent grip, she caught the back of his neck and pulled him to her level. Her mouth ferociously pried past his closed lips. He drew a deep nasal breath in surprise, his pupils dilating in the candlelight. She would rape him orally, first; spiritually, last.

And they locked bodies, more collision than embrace, grinding, then caressing, probing hands not removing clothing so much as gathering and redistributing it. They circled, moving away from the hatch, toward the water. It had become like a dare, now, and neither of them had to ask stupid questions about commitment. She pulled his sleek dark hair and forced him to kiss her, the same way she would make him hard and plunge him inside her, but only at the right moment, and only if he gave up the control.

They spiraled together, in a cobra's mating tango. Now they were knee-deep in the fetid water, feeling semisolid, subsurface items fumble invisibly beneath their footing. Black bubbles coughed up. Any second now, Curta KIA would plunge her spike heel through the rib cage or eye socket of some putrescent, long-deceased grave waver, to sprawl without grace and punch through a bladder of gelid tissue—so much ennui, turned into so much fertilizer.

"There are bodies beneath us, right now," he said, and she shivered, thinking of age-old chandeliers still hanging in the dark ballrooms of the Titanic. The murky tideline lapped at the floor like a wavering, demi-phantasmic demarcation between nondeath and afterlife.

Lawrence jerked stiff, his hair whipping forward as speckles of his blood dotted Curta KIA's face. She had to catch him as he slouched, deepening their embrace. As they tipped over backward, she saw the blade of the folding Army shovel that had felled him. She did not see their assailant, only that edge of olive-drab metal swinging back for her as Lawrence's body bore her down, as surely as any schooled rapist, into the liquid corruption she had feared. She splashed, was held submerged by a hand on her throat and a hand on her forehead as her body fought to flee, to respirate.

Her fingertips seemed two thousand miles away. The septic, black water roared like Niagara. She heard it filling her ears and then there was nothing else.

"About ten years ago, in the Northeast, spruce trees in the higher elevations began to die in uncommon numbers. People blamed acid rain and the scientists didn't disagree with them. That, and all those coal-burning smokestacks in the middle of winter. But the poisonous rain didn't just burn the trees as it fell. It liberated the aluminum in the soil, which was then carried into the trees, killing the roots. Now the trees had a much harder time acquiring phosphates and calcium and magnesium from the soil, which was itself depleted by the acid rain. The pH of the air was somewhere between that of lemon juice and battery acid. The forest became a field of gray skeletons. Ever hear of the beech blister?"

Mr. Gaines shakes his head. The thing in front of him is too busy bleeding and lolling in and out of cognizance to fake any interest. He stares into dulled gray eyes, seeking to peel back the thoughts of his prey. Inside that damaged head, nerve endings are blowing out like popcorn.

"No? How about the woolly adelgid? It attacks hemlock?"

Mr. Gaines touches the blowtorch to Lawrence's left nipple and pushes until the blunt soldering tip sinks into the flesh with a sizzle. Bound to the riveted seat, the taller man arches in muffled agony against his duct-tape restraints. His face turns red, his eyes bug out, and he lapses, twitching. Vent flames from the tip barbecue wispy hairs surrounding the spot where his tit used to be.

"I hate that smell, young man."

Oh, god, how it is boiling up inside of him, the rage, threatening to percussively deploy the cap of his skull and spray the room with the electric fallout of his anger.

"You know how maggots wriggle inside a carcass, making it appear to move? I saw you infesting the Quarter earlier tonight. You come as a carrion eater, to feed off the corpse of something I once loved. You rape its remains and desecrate its memory. Do you want to know what a vampire is? A vampire is the street bum of the supernatural. Do you want to know about death? I'll show it to you."

Mr. Gaines flips the pressure cover off a fifty-gallon drum that has been painted over at least fifty times, its logos and warning stencils long buried. The drum is half full of greenish muck like algae, faintly luminescent. It stinks the way acetone does, but filigreed with corruption, an odor which mentally damaged serial killers often claim to smell—an olfactory illusion particular to their dysfunction. Vapors from the slush sting Lawrence's bleeding eyes. It is a color not found in nature.

Mr. Gaines spends the next two hours skinning Lawrence, then loads him into the drum and seals it for tonight's dump. He notices that Lawrence has been castrated. The amputation scars are decades old. Lawrence is incapable of entertaining an interview on this matter. Then Mr. Gaines discovers Lawrence's cigarette lighter, which intrigues him one more degree. Perhaps he should not have been so quick with this one.

Maybe the other one can answer some questions.

Curta KIA understands pain; she just isn't very good at it.

She is firmly bound up, nearly immobile, yet not gagged as she had seen Lawrence to be, before her. There must be some reason.

It seems as though a year has passed since she swam up from unconsciousness. There is no clock to be seen, and outside it is still the darkest part of the night. Her watch is gone, along with her sharp jewelry and sharp clothing. Except for the duct tape, she is naked. On a boat; she can hear the water and feel the subtle port-to-starboard sway. The stench of what befell Lawrence still hangs in the air.

She recalls being blindsided by a bike messenger once, in New York City, and actually seeing flashbulb-style stars, only noticing an eternity later that she was still sitting, spread-legged, in the middle of traffic. What she feels now is much the same. Gray water is leaking out of her ears. For the first time she notices the air purifier in a corner, minding its task, changing their atmosphere.

She can see Lawrence's blood on the deck, stretching out to lazily parallel the seams of the wood as it dries.

"Trees sequester a great deal of carbon. Remember your basic houseplant care? Plants absorb carbon dioxide and give us oxygen. But if the trees die, that carbon is liberated into the air, where it joins the carbon from smokestacks and exhaust pipes to accelerate the greenhouse effect. Instead of soaking up excess carbon, the dead forests now release it. Do you know what CFCs are?"

"Chlorofluorocarbons. The stuff that eats the ozone layer. I usually charge for tutoring, and I goddamned well know I didn't get paid for this little strip-and-torture show."

Mr. Gaines replaces the blowtorch on a shallow tabletop and turns to face Curta KIA with one eyebrow cocked. More important, he puts down the torch without lighting it.

"Do we know each other?" Mr. Gaines has never before made this kind of mistake. "Surely not."

"I don't care who you are." Curta's voice does not quaver; rather than basking in terror, she realizes with a giddy sort of contact shock that she is *angry*. She is going to die right on the brink of savoring victory, success, revenge, all professional. The prices for her pieces will shoot up a thousandfold. Her loss will be considered a modern tragedy in the arts. Books will examine her oeuvre. No dolt will remain uninterviewed. And when that orgasm is done, she'll own a piece of history, comprise the stuff of legends, and be the recipient of something like love. But posthumously—hence, the anger, blue-hot and sterilizing.

She also sees what Lawrence's yelling and screaming had gotten him. She doesn't add anything. She waits to see. Helpless, she waits.

The bloodstained bald man regards Curta KIA from the edge of his gaze, his round, bespectacled head cocked in the manner of a praying mantis. He still hasn't picked up the torch.

With a sickening lurch, Hraban pitched headfirst, arms outflung, smashing his face into the port bulkhead. Making a bellows groan like Industrial Revolution iron reluctantly changing shape in a forge, Final Rest's hull listed, almost as though Hraban's impact was enough to rock her.

Hraban could feel the cartilage in his nose crunch and sunder, but all he could hear was three or four people yelling and the rest screaming as turbid water gushed in to join them with amazing speed. By the time he tried to push himself up from the deck, it had tilted by forty degrees. He slipped and banged his chin against an ancient fire extinguisher mount, feeling an abrupt wet gout of blood before his head submerged. The crowd panic went all muffled and bubbly in his brain.

His eyes were wide open but saw only lightless flat black. He drew a deep lungful of fouled sludge which his muscles immediately attempted to expel. Turning; he was revolving now, like a weightless astronaut, thudding into unseen objects as he spun, feeling his damage accumulate too fast to track. No candles. No generator. All the hatchways were stuck open forever. A hand grasped his calf, scratching for purchase, and then let go.

Hraban inhaled his own blood, and that didn't work either. *Up* no longer existed.

The ridge of discarded automobiles and seafill gave way, and the derelict ferry rechristened Final Rest slid off its cloven perch and capsized like a fat lady rolling over in a saggy bed. It sank in less than ninety seconds. When it went down, most of its occupants were trapped against the inverted decks. Air pockets burped free and made the surface of the water shudder as seismic information was dispatched. Within the hour, the lower life-forms of the swamplands moved in, to feed.

"I was in love once, a long time ago," says Mr. Gaines. He trails off on the verge of a revelation, disinclined to the inelegance of baldly littering the air with the castoffs of his personal past. "I don't like what happened to the corpse. Have you ever loved something that died?"

Curta KIA, still restrained and naked, says nothing in the hope it will win her more moments of life than the unfortunate (and late) Lawrence. A stormy expression of disappointment momentarily crosses Mr. Gaines's brow, then is as gone as a squirt of steam. He smiles to himself, and scratches thoughtfully behind one ear. Then he uses a box cutter containing a single-edge razor blade to open up Curta KIA's exposed right thigh, lengthwise. Now she yowls, high and loud, like the girl she is determined not to be.

"Please don't make me repeat myself."

"Everyone loves things that die, you piece of shit!" Breath husks out of her; she knows about blood but is not accustomed to seeing so much of her own.

"I'm not interested in everyone. You. Yes or no?"

When she looks at him, he is cleaning the box cutter on her clothing. Bitterly, she plays: "Of course I have."

"Better." Mr. Gaines steps back to her and she cringes. He tapes down a swath of bandage over her thigh, then steps back to his workbench without looking into her eyes at all. He toys with tools and (apparently, since she cannot see from her disadvantaged angle) scribbles or sketches on a tablet, with his back turned to her. By the time she looks down at her injured leg, the gauze has gone deep scarlet even though the incision is a shallow one, mostly for drama.

"I thought there was nothing good left in the bosom of my dead love," says Mr. Gaines. "All I see anymore are people like you, and more people worse than you. But I keep checking, and hoping, because I cannot quit. I just can't let go, it seems, which is a handicap when you love too much."

There comes a distant rumbling, like the aural aftershock of an earthquake or bomb test. Mr. Gaines interrupts his benchwork to glance toward the southeast. Loons and herons are taking wing, scattering.

"The Earth is about to meet its own twilight," he says. "I know something of the Earth—what we take from it and what we put back. Sometimes the quality of what we thieve away is not compensated. Look at my flowers."

Mr. Gaines indicates the cut vase of artificial flowers, the ones fed only by cleaning fluid. Curta KIA is lagging too far behind his peculiar train of thought, wasting time trying to guess how she needs to beg for her life.

"Please," she says. "I'm just very afraid." It is at least an attempt. No urban macha, no attitude, no religion or guilt or accusation. Nothing left except a human appeal—the sort of thing this madman might judge too messy.

Mr. Gaines is holding his finger to his lips. Curta KIA does not continue to speak.

"These have a kind of purity," he says of the flowers. "They represent life, but with the durability of a manufactured device. They bespeak a sort of permanence, in the face of the decay of all things earthly, don't you think? Nod your head, now."

Curta KIA nods her head, sensing an "opening." When she tries to speak, to say *what are you going to do to me,* Mr. Gaines slices open her other leg, and when she screams, he pours stale lime juice concentrate from his galley fridge into the "opening." At last, he gags her, so she will not repeat the offense or interrupt him again.

Mr. Gaines sips distilled water from a glass bottle. "Now this"—he holds up the bottle—"is recyclable. Earlier tonight, for the first time in a very long time, I saw something that was as attractive as these flowers, something that makes as much sense to me as this glass bottle. It was a work of art in the window of one of those galleries. An assembly of bone and steel, of ganglia and wire, foil and flesh, contrasting new and old with youth and age, obsolescence with utility." A rapturous look skims across his features. "I cannot express to you how that piece of art made me feel. It was from the soul. It was pure. It made me understand that I was not alone."

There are tears in Mr. Gaines's eyes as he says this.

There are tears, too, in the sharp, gray eyes of Curta KIA. Now she fights her bonds. Now she tries to kick and thrash herself free. At least she has listened to the things Mr. Gaines has had to say.

As her brain begins to black out from hypoxia, Mr. Gaines attempts to be reassuring. "Don't worry. You're going back where you might do some good. Carrying the knowledge you now have, the story I've just told you, you'll certainly do more good than your friend out there."

Topside, her open drum awaits her.

The next night, after dumping thirty-seven drums in the Hand, Mr. Gaines cruises past the spot where the ferry sank. The dock is engirded by hazard tape and police cars. The cops are suffering because the planking and joists are so rotten, and more than a couple of uniforms get unceremoniously drenched in standing water the texture of chum bucket slop. Efforts are encumbered by the rain, busily bucketing down like a cruel joke. Floods are coming, and to Mr. Gaines, floods mean more space in which to hide things. He never worries about water that comes from the sky.

There are bones hugging the pillars of the submerged pier. Human remains litter a slip of oil-blackened jetty. The water tonight is dangerously full of predators. Mr. Gaines sees officers collecting body parts in plastic trash bags, and wonders how this mop-up will be explained.

No question, really. Mr. Gaines does not have to check to see whether the small charge planted on the ferry's hull detonated correctly. The passengers of Final Rest now share a cosmopolitan community, down in the silt, among the bottom-feeders, their ornaments settling in the sunken crypts of the automobiles of those who preceded them. Death is an efficient leveler, and enough rain can rinse away any unpleasantness.

His behavior tonight is the same simple curiosity that caused him to pause at the art gallery window the previous night. One can always learn new things.

On the way home, Mr. Gaines spies a skull, perched like a headlamp atop some waterlogged flotsam, bobbing wildly in the downpour. He rescues this castaway. Later, he thinks, he might clean it, perhaps saw away parts of it and replace them with wire or metal, emulating the artwork that so impressed him.

Perhaps, tomorrow, he won't even kill anybody.

Bloodlight

Stephen Mark Rainey

S he moaned softly as Perez thrust the last of himself into her and withdrew slowly, teasing her by giving a final half-pump before his erection withered. He buried his face in the silky blonde hair gathered at her throat, breathing a sigh into her ear that told her he was satisfied. Which he was . . . but only partly. He let one hand slide tenderly over one soft breast, down her abdomen. She turned her head so she could look into his eyes. He closed them.

"You're wonderful," she said.

"So are you," he whispered, not insincere.

"What's wrong?"

"Nothing's wrong."

Elizabeth sat up, forcing him to shift position. "I wish you'd talk to me. I thought we could share things, Tom. You do this with me and then shut me out. I saw it coming. Damn it."

"I'm sorry," he said. She tried to find his eyes, but he hid them. "It's not you. Please believe that."

"I'm not sure I can." Elizabeth squeezed his shoulder, then kissed his cheek before sliding off the bed. "Call me later. Okay?"

"You're leaving, then."

"I must."

He nodded. "I'll call."

She disappeared into the bathroom, turned on the water. A few minutes later she emerged, dressed. Picked up her pocketbook. Leaned down to kiss him once, then slipped out the door without a word.

Perez hadn't moved. Sweating, but numb from top to bottom. He didn't want to hurt her. She loved him, he sometimes loved her. If he could love at all . . .

So many women he'd had. Done everything there was to do with them. He thought Elizabeth would be the one to tame him; she almost had been. Her sex was the sweetest he'd ever known. But after so many, what thrill was left? His was an obsession, a drive that gave him no peace. How many had he hurt without qualm? Did they even care, these women? He'd tried it with men, seeking that crucial new sensation. Pleasure, for a short time, then . . .

The numbness.

Perpetually wending its way through his body and soul, snuffing every fire he managed to kindle. Turning the finest wine sour. It was killing him.

Absently, he rose and went to the bathroom, relieved himself. Glanced in the mirror. A dark shadow around his jaw, heavy pouches under his eyes. Creases in his forehead, and a wisp of gray that wasn't there yesterday marring sienna temples.

He soaked his face with steaming hot water, savoring the heat until it dissipated, like the thrill of making love to Elizabeth. She should have been the one. He wanted her to be the one. His heart thumped hard once in his chest before settling into a slow, steady rhythm.

Lifting his razor, he swiped at the whiskers, roughly, without cream. A tingle, and then a spot of red. He let it pool and run slowly down his cheek, where it spread among the bristles of his night-grown beard.

He wished for pain. Anything. Anything but the numbness.

Plain, double-edge razor blades weren't so easy to find anymore. Everything was disposable, bendable, pivotable, or Teflon-coated. But he found a pack of twelve Wilkinson blades and carried them home with senses suddenly keened: an anticipation such as he knew before he went to bed with a woman. In his bedroom, he stripped off his clothes and stood before the mirror, studied his firm, well-toned pectoral muscles, the finely angled bones of his cheeks and jaw, the well-defined network of veins in his slim forearms. His biceps were not large, but they were hard. He cared for this body, pushed it to its limit often. No scars except for a thin white line in the crook of his right elbow where he'd been cut by glass when he was twelve—a baseball from the game next door, exploding through the picture window of his parents' living room where he sat.

He lay down on his bed, eyeing the silver blade clenched between thumb and forefinger. Pain glinted in its keen edge, waited eagerly for him. He didn't want to damage his body; only to feel. To see the blood. To *taste* the blood.

Ever so gently, he touched the narrow blade to his right palm, pressed one steel corner into the flesh. A tiny crimson stain appeared on the metal. A minute flash of fire in his palm, stinging his nerves all the way to his wrist. He winced, wondering now if he was doing the right thing. Was this not madness? Dementia?

No, it was the killer of numbness. The murder of creeping death.

He drew the blade slowly across the heel of his hand, barely biting into the skin. Didn't want to cut too deep. Not to damage, only to feel.

There. A stream of watery blood, running down his palm to his wrist. An almost sexual delight, yes. And pain. A small, insignificant pain, but it was alive and true. A method to feed the flames and banish the sensual darkness within him?

Dementia?

He sighed, watched the blood run a little farther, then gathered his nerve and lowered his hand to his mouth. He tasted salt and spice, in a sticky but satisfying draft. He realized then that his penis was throbbing, struggling against his jeans. With a shudder of excitement and disgust, he unzipped his fly and began to stroke his hardening cock with his bloody hand. He watched the red drip from his palm and run down his swollen member to his groin. It hurt, just a little. But the color of blood: so rich, so pretty. He felt its warmth, all the way to his heart.

By God, he *felt* it.

He climaxed so hard he almost feared he'd ruptured something inside. And when he drew his hand away, his penis was awash with bright blood, and his palm still leaked the crimson water of life. His racing heart kept going, going, didn't want to slow down.

The thrill . . .

"Dinner at my place tonight?" Elizabeth asked. "I'll cook. You bring wine. Red."

"Yeah, sure," Perez said into the receiver. "Sounds nice."

"Seven?"

"I'll come."

"Good." A long pause. "I love you, Tom."

"You're sweet. I'll see you tonight." He hung up, exhaled deeply. He'd bandaged his hand, and it no longer hurt. He was glad, though, because a little fire still smoldered inside, and he didn't want to have to hurt constantly to keep the numbness at bay. It was nearly five o'clock, and the sun had crept behind the trees on its way to the horizon. He went to the window to stare at the golden beams cutting through the pine boughs that surrounded his house. His thoughts were of Elizabeth, of her delicate beauty, her soft, radiant hair the color of those beams. *Something* had touched him inside, something he hadn't felt in so long he'd forgotten it. But it was beautiful. An almost romantic dreaminess. A treasure.

Brought by the blood, he knew.

What if, before he went to her, he drew a little more? Would it heighten the pleasure when they went to bed, as they inevitably would have to? What if . . .

The idea chilled him, sent streamers of cold fire through his veins. But with that seed now planted in his brain, it could only bear fruit; if not, he would not be able to function with her, with the unfulfilled fantasy draped over him like a veil.

He went for the blade.

Again, he lay naked on his bed, holding the razor's edge against his palm. Drew it slowly along the old cut, opening it to a new pain that jangled through his nerves. The beautiful blood came, and this time he cut just a little deeper, knowing it was the wrong thing to do, but driven—as he was sometimes driven to masturbate until his cock was raw and stinging. The blood was a deeper color now, ruby-red, catching the sunbeams and sparkling like priceless jewels as it ran unchecked down his wrist.

He then lowered the blade to his erect penis; stared at the potentially deadly instrument with horrible fascination. He could still stop. He remained in control. He could prevent himself from succumbing to dementia.

But all it would take was the slightest touch.

He pressed the corner of the blade softly into the spongy dorsal surface of his penis. Hot agony flared there—from such a tiny wound! Just a nick . . . and that was as far as he dared go. A crimson dot grew where he'd cut himself, pooled and ran into his thick pubic hairs. Now—how would it feel when he entered Elizabeth, the tension of his erection reopening the little cut? A pain that would enable him to cross the threshold into divine pleasure?

He lay there for a long time, until the sun's last rays disappeared and the room became a ghostly cavity filled only with shadow. His naked body stood out pale against the dark bedspread. The blood that had coagulated at his groin burned black.

Something tinkled outside, so he thought; a little tuneless wind chime that barely pricked his consciousness. Turning his head, he saw the nearest trees slightly illuminated, perhaps by moonlight, he thought, until he realized the glow was tinted orange-pink. And it wavered amid the foliage, as if someone were approaching through the woods carrying a blood-colored lantern. He put away the little pain in his groin and sat up, wondering what the hell this might be. There was a path through the woods that led toward his nearest neighbor's house, half a mile up Sylvan Road, but who would be using it now, and for what purpose?

The tinkling sound became more pronounced, but it seemed to have no source—as if it echoed only through the chambers of his own skull. The light brightened as it drew nearer, and then he saw the little pinpoint of ruby fire, floating through the darkness toward his window. Like a crimson firefly, the point of light came to rest directly beyond the glass pane, holding him hypnotized by its gentle swaying. And a moment later, the light began to fade.

No, not fade. *Transform.*

Something pale took shape against the black backdrop: a floating white wisp of smoke, perhaps, or a diaphanous sheet suspended in the air. Then, the strangest thing. . . .

He saw features. A face peering in at him. Something so thin, so bone-white. Inhuman. A tremor of terror seized him, but he could not move from his place. The eyes were black, hollow; it was like looking into a pair of bottomless pits gouged in chalky stone. White silk fluttered behind it as the wraith floated outside the glass, watching him, beckoning him with empty eyes.

"What the hell are you?" he whispered, unsure if he could even trust his senses.

No response. Only the dead, empty stare that burned all the way to his heart. Perez didn't know if it was by his own will that he lifted a bloody hand and waved at the thing—inviting it to enter.

A moment later, as if no glass separated the bedroom from the out-of-doors, the thing appeared in the air over the bed, hovering as silently as the breath of the dead. The air grew cold around him, and while he knew dread, his heart thrilled at the sight of this apparition. There was no numbness within him. Only piping-hot blood, carrying fire to all his extremities—to his once-again erect penis, an arrow of flesh pointing obscenely at the floating shape.

A thin, bone-white arm—emerged from the fluttering white raiments and reached for his wrist. Frigid, skeletal fingers closed gently on his lacerated hand, lifting it up to the deep-set eyes. The touch of the thing—like ice—counteracted the fire in his veins, creating such a stirring mix that Perez gasped in shock, exhaling a lungful of air into the ivory face shimmering just above his. He saw a thin black slit widen slightly, and within the opening, he glimpsed silvery sharpness, quickly hidden as the thing swallowed his breath. It raised his injured hand to that slit, and a moment later, he felt the chill of its thin lips on his skin; the gentle pressure as it drew blood from the razor cut. A quick gleam somewhere in the twin pits in the skull. And then, slowly, a seething, feathery mass tumbled down around its head, a soft mane of pure white hair that tickled his uplifted arm.

The shape drifted toward the foot of the bed. And Perez saw the narrow skull lower toward his bleeding penis. He trembled in anticipation, then felt the cold touch of its lips. He closed his eyes and, willingly, let the thing take from him. The sensation horrified him, but held him in thrall, and most important, drove any remaining vestiges of numbness from his body. Surely, this was insanity. But such beautiful madness! He felt himself coming to orgasm, and still the coldness gripped him, tugging at him, harder, stronger. Every muscle in his body constricted as he prepared to eject his seed into the consuming maw of the thing that was stealing his life.

His entire body exploded, so fiercely that he screamed. A wave of coldness overtook his consciousness, and for several moments, everything went completely dark. He lost his grip on himself utterly then, and slipped into a place he'd never seen or felt; someplace that existed between night and day, a land where one might venture only in dreams. And here he lay until the morning sun peeked above the trees and warmed the autumn air to the temperature of blood.

He awoke to a pounding at the door; frantic, relentless. Groggily, he sat up, noted with little care that he was still naked and that crusted blood smeared the bedspread beneath him. It hurt to walk, but he managed to grab his bathrobe, stagger down the hall through the living room to the front door. Leaning against it, he called weakly, "Who is it?"

"Tom? It's Elizabeth. Let me in."

"Wait a minute," he said, fumbling at the lock. When he pulled the door open, brilliant sunbeams fired into his eyes and burned him. He turned his head, holding up a hand as if to ward away the evil spirit of daylight.

"My God, what's wrong with you?" Elizabeth asked, rushing inside. "What happened to you last night?"

He stared vacantly at her, shook his head. "Nothing. Nothing happened. I fell asleep. I'm sorry."

"Like hell," she snapped, standing before him with eyes of contempt—that a moment later turned to worry. "Look at you. Tom, there's blood on your face."

"It's okay. I'm okay."

He let her lead him to the bathroom, where she stood him in front of the full-length mirror. He almost gasped at the sight of himself. His face had gone the color of ash, and his eyes peered from deep, dark-ringed sockets. A long smear of dark blood decorated one cheek. And when he looked at his right hand, he saw the jagged gash, now caked with clotted blood. He felt no pain. Only numbness. Numbness, everywhere.

"Did someone hurt you?"

"No. I just felt bad. Went to sleep. Must have cut myself somehow."

Elizabeth opened his robe, confirmed he was wearing nothing underneath. But then she noticed his groin and recoiled with a sharp cry. "Jesus Christ, what's happened to you?"

He looked down. Saw his blood-coated, shriveled member, the tangle of pubic hairs matted against chalk-white flesh. "I don't remember," he muttered. "I don't know what happened."

Not quite true.

He remembered a crimson light at the window. The white wraith floating above him. The touch of freezing lips against his skin. The pressure of his blood being drained.

Black, hollow eyes, glaring into his.

"Come lie down. You need a doctor."

"No. No doctor."

But he did not resist as she led him to the bed and helped him lie back. She cringed at the sight of the blood on the bedspread, but said nothing more. Instead, she went back to the bathroom, returning moments later with a wet washcloth. She wiped away the dried blood as much as possible, and set about cleaning the cut in his hand. He felt nothing.

After she had washed him, she sat down on the edge of the bed, leaning over him with tears in her eyes. "Please talk to me. Tell me what's going on here."

He turned away from her. His eyes then fell upon the bloodied razor blade on the nightstand next to the bed. She saw it at the same time. Her eyes went to the stain on the bedspread.

"You did this, Tom. You did, didn't you? Oh, God . . . you must be sick.

You're sick." She broke down and wept then, her tears pouring through clenched fingers.

He lifted his good hand and touched her hair. So soft and lustrous. But she withdrew, and when she looked at him, her eyes were red with anger and revulsion. "Don't touch me. Goddamn it! I loved you. How could you do this?"

"I didn't . . . "

His voice failed him; only because his brain could not find the words.

"You need help, Tom. I'll call a doctor if you want. But I'm getting out of here. Stay away. Please, just stay away from me."

He nodded, closing his eyes against the daylight outside the window. He heard her footsteps retreating down the hall, the front door slamming. And then a long silence.

Sometime later, when he opened his eyes again, a bit of his strength had returned. He sat up, examined himself, felt a new disgust at what he'd done to himself—and what he'd allowed to be done. Still, he felt no fear of the thing that had visited him. No; more a fascination, a curiosity that overcame all other emotions. He rose, went to the shower and washed himself thoroughly, scrubbing himself so hard he opened the cut in his hand again. This time he felt it, but the pain was dull and distant, and only served to remind him that the numbness was returning, and that he really didn't care whether Elizabeth came again or stayed away for good.

"No," he groaned. "That's not right."

She had to come back. He loved her.

He knew how to love. He could never forget that.

The phone had rung three times, but he hadn't answered it. He spent the rest of the afternoon staring out the window, wondering why the daylight bothered his eyes so, but determined to face it. It seemed the answers lay up there, in that golden ball making its way across the sky. He remembered some far-off place he'd been during the night, a place of blood and dreams. In that place, there had been no sunlight. There was color, but always muted by darkness. *Why?* he asked the sun. *Why weren't you there?*

Sometime late in the afternoon, he realized it was Sunday. Tomorrow he'd have to go back to work. The idea sickened him: long days of mindlessly producing campaigns designed to sell other companies' products. A nightmarish place, it seemed now, full of false, fluorescent sunlight and one tedious assignment after another. Sometimes he wondered if the numbness had not been born there, where everything but heart existed in the work they created.

And as the day waned, he began to feel a subtle heat rushing through his bloodstream. Anticipation. A growing intensity of sensation, like he'd felt last night. God, he wanted Elizabeth so. Wanted her body. To touch her, kiss her, enter her. To come inside her. To share his blood with her.

"You see, I *can* love you, Elizabeth."

Spoken to the dusk settling around the house. An owl called back to him. And the crickets began to sing.

Once the stars began to sparkle overhead, Perez went to his nightstand and took up his razor blade, staring at its cold edge with the thrill of rapture. And it was no longer just Elizabeth he thought of. Somewhere, out there in the darkness, *something* waited, perhaps even watching him as he stood framed in the window.

He pressed the sharp edge of the blade into the flesh of his bare chest. Cut deeply. And pain exploded through his body, pain so severe he almost fell. But by strength of will he dragged the blade down the length of his sternum, mesmerized at the sight of his lifeblood pouring freely from the cut. It ran down his stomach to his crotch, again puddling in his curly pubic hairs. He gasped hoarsely as a new jolt of pain shook him and he dropped the blade from his trembling fingers. God, it hurt. It hurt so bad.

He stepped forward and pressed himself against the window, staring deeply into the pitch-black canopy of trees. His heart raced in anticipation. And, thank God, his wait was not a long one.

The little fire appeared in the distance, weaving slowly between the shadowed pillars of the woods. It made its way steadily toward him, casting its bloodlight upon the tall trunks along its path. He heard the tinkling of chimes in his head: a lyrical, inhuman voice singing to him, he thought. And the pinpoint of light drifted to a spot just outside the window, where it hovered motionlessly for a moment before beginning to dim, as it had the night before.

Then, the thing floated in front of him, just beyond the windowpane. The incredibly narrow, smooth white skull with gaping eyes, its flowing, featherlike shroud fluttering in the breeze. Its hair fell around its face, waving slowly as if possessing a life of its own. When Perez backed away, beckoning it to follow, a smear of blood remained on the glass.

The thing reappeared just in front of him, advancing slowly, forcing him to willingly retreat to the bed. He lay back as the wraith smothered him with its icy chill, consuming his every exhalation through the slit beneath the tiny knob of its nose. The pair of empty sockets burned at him, and he lifted his arms to invite it down upon him.

The skull-face lowered to his bleeding chest, and he experienced the familiar pressure once again—this time with such force that he momentarily felt dread wash through his body. But it didn't last long; no, he surrendered himself to his visitor, realizing the consequences, but no longer caring. This was indeed the ultimate thrill, was it not? A purity of sensation, the pinnacle of his every desire. Truly, the experience of a lifetime—death.

The thing gazed at him, as if seeking permission to continue. Peering back at it, without fear, he nodded.

"Take me all the way."

Sensation began to slowly return. He opened his eyes and saw the featureless ceiling, the midnight blue beyond the window. The blood that remained on his chest was cold, black against his milky skin. He lifted one arm, effortlessly, for it seemed as light as a feather. And bone-thin, as if the very tissue within had been drained away. Lifting his head, he saw that his entire frame had withered. What remained was skeletal, frail. Yet power seemed to burn throughout his body, and, even greater, the desire for sensation ached in the pit of his stomach.

He rose. Drifted above the bed, as light as smoke, his naked body gleaming in the moonlight that seeped through the window. He floated in front of the mirror—yet there was nothing there. Nothing at all! Only the reflection of his vacant room. The blood, now cold and dead, lingering on the bedspread.

Power! He could feel it coursing through him. One quick thrust of his mind sent him floating toward the window—and then through it, as if the solid panes were no more than clear mist. He rose into the night, his eyes black pools beneath the brilliant moon. His house, the woods around it, all shrank into the darkness as he ascended and drifted purposefully toward the town in the distance, where he would find Elizabeth and sate his burning hunger. She would know him, he thought; know his longing and submit to his will. He would have her blood, savor her essence, as he'd so desired in life.

He felt his way to her—smelled her, tasted the air where she'd passed. He appeared at her window, saw her sleeping in the darkness, her gold hair spilling over her pillow. The hunger was almost maddening now; so sweet it would be to take of her blood.

He willed her to awaken. She stirred restlessly, and moments later opened her eyes. For a time, she seemed not to register his presence, but when her eyes at last regarded him, she drew back with a gasp. He raised his cut hand, which no longer dripped blood, and waved at her. She shook her head, her face taut with fear. But he soothed her, transmitting reassurance to her with his all-seeing eyes.

At last, she nodded to him.

He passed through the window, floated toward her—and nearly cried out as the sharpest pain he'd ever known flared in his gut. He had to have her. Now! Now!

Her blood tasted wonderful . . . like honey and cinnamon, so sweet he wanted to weep. He drank deeply from her throat, ignoring the tears in her eyes that begged him not to kill her. Holding the power of her life and death in his hands, he felt compelled to laugh. To sing out in joy, to exclaim that, finally, he felt everything he had ever wanted to feel in his daylight years. At last, he pulled away from her, and she sank to the pillow, still alive, breathing shallowly. He had no desire to destroy her.

But now, his thirst momentarily quenched, something stung him—like the prick of a needle injecting Novocaine into his still-living bloodstream.

"No," he whispered, realizing what was happening to him. "No, please."

Just as when he'd had sex with her, the satisfaction of his feeding slowly drained away, leaving him totally unfulfilled. An empty shell.

Numb.

This, he realized, was the ultimate numbness of life beyond death. An eternity of craving awaited him, he now knew; endless eons of searching for satiation, only to be cheated at each scarlet fountain from which he drank. Horrified, he stared at Elizabeth, at the blood pouring from her beautiful neck. With his skeletal fingers, he touched her warm skin.

His had once been so warm.

If only he could have been satisfied then.

Elizabeth stirred and opened her eyes, looked at him without comprehending what she saw. He retreated now, floated through her window and away into the sky, a captive of the silvery moon above. Even his power of motivation meant nothing now—less than nothing. Every sensation, every nerve, dead.

In desperation, he searched the night for the thing that had visited him, the thing drawn by his need and the shedding of his blood. He called to it, peered into the woods for some sign of its telltale bloodlight.

But it was gone, its purpose served.

Elizabeth hovered between sleep and wakefulness, dimly registering a pain at her throat. But its meaning eluded her, for she could not remember what had happened in the night.

All she could recall was the sound of weeping. A familiar, bitter weeping, fading away into the distance.

The Privilege of the Dead

Thomas S. Roche

S he wore a black silk robe and thong slippers. Her black hair hung in a curtain across one side of her face, just down to the high cheekbone, leaving one black eye to stare at me. The curve and pucker of her lips was accented by the black lipstick. Her flesh was alabaster. Her cigarette was unfiltered.

She was outlined in the streaming light from the church windows overhead. I regarded her sadly, as I always had. Inhaling the smoke from the braziers, I recalled the taste of her lips as they'd tasted on Valentine's Day, two dozen years ago. She had given herself to me, and I to her.

She stretched on the black velvet bedcover, her hair falling back, revealing her white face. As she stretched the black robe shifted, revealing the vale between her breasts. The cigarette jutted rakishly from her dark lips, and she opened her arms in a beckoning gesture. Then the cigarette disappeared into a wisp of smoke as her lips parted and she began to sing. Her voice was clear, high, beautiful, the seductive wail of the siren.

She pronounced her prayer of damnation like subtle caresses, enticements, seductions, for she was and had always been the only living poet of despair, the sole architect of the gates of Hell, the suicidal chanteuse of the apocalypse. She sang out the opening line of her tortured erotic death-poem, uttering mournfully the long wailing agony of life after death: "I am only waiting . . . for my razorblade . . . valentine . . . "

She laughed, the sound of broken glass.

It was a song that Sasha had made into her own masterpiece. Her mournful wail somehow brought out the agonies in the song, somehow chilled the blood while arousing the senses. She was the premier singer of her time. Her music was unclassifiable; she was a movement of one artist, because only she could master the style. Her work encompassed opera, jazz, industrial, goth, Gregorian chant, and of course every period of classical music. And yet it transcended them all. She was the only member of the avant garde in the final years of civilization—at this, the very end of the world, as the years racked closer to triple zeroes. She was just about the only genius left. She represented the culmination of centuries of development in vocal music—she echoed Bessie Smith, Siouxsie Sioux, Diamanda Galas, Lena Horne, Lydia Lunch, Maria Callas. She broke my heart nightly. Her records brought me to tears. She was the vision of the feminine, the tortured anima of a civilization in decline. She was, as well, the very essence of dark sensuality. She could have any woman or man or androgyne she wanted. Sasha was the goddess of desire, and loss.

Perhaps that was why I went with her. Perhaps that was why I succumbed to her charms, when I sat there in the front row watching her sing the song for the very last time.

I had received an invitation directly from her agent. It was flattering to be contacted by a representative of the great Sasha Nobody, who had redefined music for the next millennium—or, more accurately, redesigned the art previously known as "music." My live-work space at the top of the Babylon Tower was graced with several coffee-table books, most notably the Rosencrantz book which showcased Sasha in all her beauty, mixed with fragments of her poetry and lyrics and pieces of cutup art. Some of the art, particularly the collages in the centerpiece, had been created out of patterns computer-designed to evoke certain neuroauditory responses in the viewer, triggering memories, visions, dreams which would otherwise have remained dormant.

In particular, these neuroresponses were mated to certain subliminals implanted on the twenty-fourth Nobody album, most notably in her vocal adaptation of the Little Fugue and in the operatic version of "Razorblade

Valentine." The original version of the song, on her first album, had been a moving pop anthem, an antiballad that demonstrated flawlessly the minimalist tendencies of Sasha's early career. But the later Sasha Nobody, a broken thirty-four years old and incarcerated in a Bern psychiatric hospital after the public suicide of her demoness-lover and sometime collaborator Anna Cecilia Misfortune, had something new and not entirely favorable to say about "valentines." The shattered postbreakdown Sasha had recorded a new version of that song from the inside of her padded cell, the sound crew working entirely by remote. In the agony of her madness, Sasha had taken that song and made it entirely her own, made it a thing of lush terror and razor blade decadence, of tragic overacting and subtle, understated dreamdance, of hunger and seduction and hypnotic high-tech apocalypse to mirror the agonies she had suffered in this, the cruelest of all possible worlds.

The night after the recording session, Sasha was erroneously administered an experimental microseizure-inducing psychiatric drug and witnessed a conjuration of phantoms, visions, and demons, torments she was, she said in interviews, unable to describe even in song. In the morning the physician on call prescribed Sasha a rescue-dose cocktail of Thorazine, Catharohalt, methotrexamazine, and v6t, which caused irreparable neural damage that, Sasha feared, might interfere with the future utilization of her image and likeness in subliminal form. Sasha, of course, brought suit, and won a healthy sum, but the award was kept to six figures by the fact that Sasha's lawyers were unable to convince an international jury of the loss of future earnings due to this malpractice. The lawyers' hints at an EEC conspiracy were denounced in the government-controlled presses, but the leagues of Sasha's faithful knew that anything was possible. Even so, her lawyers were not able to prove anything, and a trail of mysterious suicides halted the requested Interpol investigation before it began.

The neural damage, and most certainly this whole experience, had shattered Sasha, whose performances lost their rage and terror but gained something infinitely more heartbreaking. Sasha's spirit seemed to draw ever deeper into her fragile form, until she seemed a ghost of marble. Her eyes grew otherworldly, as if her night in the spirit-world had caused her to see beyond the veil of death. Her voice, growing steadily more beautiful as her agony increased, became, more than ever, an implement of despair. She wailed her requiem to Anna Cecilia and to her own brutalized millenium. Sasha, divorced forever from her beloved Misfortune, drove her work ever onward toward new heights of pain. Sasha drew her razor-sadness across the throat of humankind and wept as her white dress became soaked with civilization's blood.

But the height of that agony had been reached in the stirring two-minutes-twelve-seconds in that psychiatric hospital, when Sasha had uttered the definitive version of "Razorblade Valentine."

And so it was, a singular moment of pain never to be superseded. "Razorblade Valentine" was, without a doubt, Sasha's *Meisterstück.* Critics, whether or not they acknowledged the artistic validity of the implanted subliminals, unanimously voted the new version Sasha's definitive anthem to pain.

I, as the most accomplished and multipublished critic of Sasha Nobody's work, agreed with them, and had published a controversial article in the important Vienna arts magazine *Das Ende* which summed up my views of Sasha's own personal erotic apocalypse, despite the fact that she and I had never, at that point, met.

In particular, I thought it interesting that the themes of subliminal suggestion in "postmusic," as I was fond of calling the new avant garde, which was mostly theoretical at that point, had figured prominently in my earlier book *Nyet,* an academic treatise on neonihilism and theoretic manipulation.

Sasha and her collaborator Anna Cecilia, I heard through the international grapevine, had read and enjoyed *Nyet.* The book had, supposedly, been a great influence on the singer.

That, in and of itself, seemed to justify my early career.

It pleased me just knowing that a creature of deathlike beauty as delicious as Sasha Nobody could enjoy my work even to a small degree. But to know that I had influenced her—that changed things entirely. It made me part of the process, rather than just another hyperintellectual critic.

And so when I listened to Sasha's singing, I felt there was a special bond. I felt I had, in some small way, contributed to her art—perhaps as much as or more than even Misfortune. I felt I was part of *Niemand Vierunswanzig.* My soul was in the album, and particularly in "Razorblade Valentine."

The song was Sasha's tour de force. The subliminals were buried so deep that no human could possibly be independently aware of the magicks being worked on her or his mind. That was what made them insidious, and impossible to control, both legally and philosophically speaking. That was what made Sasha Nobody such a master, or mistress, of the art form.

The subliminals, linked as they were between the Rosencrantz book and the twenty-fourth album, would cause any person viewing the collages in the book to be slowly seduced and overwhelmed by the memory of Sasha's "Razorblade Valentine." The song would start to play in your head. It would be almost silent at first, gradually seducing you, and would finally become a raging crescendo, up to several hours later if you viewed the collages for more than a few minutes.

But, more important, the version of the song that would play in the viewer/listener's head was an entirely different version of the song—even more Sasha's masterpiece, since it would be colored by the mental perceptions and brain chemistry of the listener. And there were lines in the song that Sasha had never, to my knowledge, sung in public or in the recorded performances of "Razorblade Valentine." Lines that alluded to the relationship she had had with the six-foot androgyne angel Anna Cecilia Misfortune, whom she had worshiped like a goddess. And whose death had rendered Sasha a prisoner in her own hellish isolation. The psychobiologically recorded version of the song was phenomenally chilling. A document of the apocalypse. A record of madness. The distillation of pain in a digital hypodermic needle. At times, astonishingly, Anna Cecilia's wailing dirge could be heard wandering in and out of Sasha's vocals aimlessly, like a little girl seeking solace. It was impossible to hear this ghostly keening without tasting the agony Sasha had endured in Bern.

Those who hadn't heard the song experienced nothing out of the ordinary when viewing the collage.

I heard only rumors concerning the Misfortune vocals in the psychobiological construct. It was whispered that Anna Cecilia's keening was not inserted from earlier recordings, but was rather the sound of a highly developed construct, an artificial intelligence Misfortune had programmed before her death, programmed in preparation for the collaborative psychobiological postopera, *Dirge,* which Sasha and Anna Cecilia had dreamed of for many years. Sadly, the program was incomplete, and incapable of reason or independent thought. Its existence had been truncated by its creator's premature suicide. The Misfortune-construct's personality was, apparently, nonexistent, though it did possess something that could be considered sentience, as a true artificial intelligence. It possessed all the necessary capacities to speak, think, communicate—but its "intellectual" abilities, and most of what would be called "emotion," were not a functioning part of its gestalt. The construct, in its solitary existence, could only feel pain and loneliness, and there its emotions ended; it could only whisper its terrified agonies of damned silicon eternity into psychobiological constructs for the lonely torment and ostensible entertainment of the living. Misfortune's ghost could only mourn, and sing backup vocals.

There had been some controversy—medical, philosophical, theological—concerning this technique of implantation, and a consumer warning label was finally affixed to both the album and the book. The copyright and licensing issues involved in the use of a construct were merely a pleasant diversion for international legal analysts—never mind the labor laws. On the other hand, the issue of implantation seemed, to me, absolutely central to the consideration of artistic viability in the preapocalyse era. My article in *Das Ende* summed up my feelings on the subject, and it seems I hit a nerve. Shortly after the publication of the article, I was dismissed from my teaching position at the university. It still pains me to think about it, but it has ever been the fate of the radical thinker to receive the disdain and hatred of the untalented sloth.

The article, apparently, was considered blasphemous to the scientific, artistic, and theological sensibilities of the world's community of thinkers.

In this article, titled simply "*nichts,*" I went on for some time concerning the philosophical ramifications of visual arts being married psychobiologically with postmusic. After some soul-searching, I had included in the article my theory—call it a hypothesis, rather—about the origin of the psychobiological link. Sasha Nobody claimed, in press releases and interviews, that the subliminals, in both the collage and the music, were inserted in the studio—*after* Sasha's recovery from the mad doctor's "cocktail"—through high-tech splicing and cybernetic neural-construct implantation.

I imagined that might be the case, but rather than accept the scientifically plausible, I wryly posited something much more insidious.

I imagined that this was Sasha's natural talent, possibly awakened by her night on her padded-cell vision quest: her skill, to take over the minds of her listeners, to overwhelm them with her presence even when she was not present. I suspected that Sasha was nothing less than a succubus, draining the souls of her listeners.

For only I, I suspected, had subjected myself to the experience of playing Sasha's "Razorblade Valentine" over, and over, and over again, one hundred times, while simultaneously viewing the Rosencrantz collage.

And it was during this experience that I tasted Sasha's lips for the first time. When I awoke, my seed had been spilt across my belly and I knew, in my heart, the texture of her flesh.

And so it was that, unemployed but solvent, finally having achieved the hostility of the academic establishment, I came to be in the City, to attend my first Sasha Nobody concert, her Valentine's Day performance at the Club Orphanage. Celebrating the coming of the year of the three zeros. They were charging five hundred dollars a seat for the exclusive performance on Violet Street. But I'd found myself, quite unexpectedly, with a free ticket.

While sitting in a café, contemplating my fate, I had been approached by a representative of the singer, who introduced himself as Sainte. He wore a black suit and a black tie, and spoke excellent English. It was not my habit to attend live music performances—I'm something of an eccentric, or a purist, that way. I believe that the experience of live music unnecessarily pollutes the art, whereas digital sound purifies.

But it was such a thrill to be invited by Sasha. It was a validation of all I had sought to achieve.

My seat was front row center.

She was a goddess. Her beauty was that of a thousand divas, yet a million times more sublime than any, ten million times more true. She emanated the stuff of apocalypse.

I will not try to describe her work; it would be blasphemy. Those unfamiliar with Sasha's art quite simply cannot understand its beauty. But I will say that in her live performance, Sasha Nobody was unequaled. I drank in the wonder of her singing, the beauty of the knowledge that I was giving myself completely to her. I knew it was hopeless to search for subliminals in her voice, but some small part of me did so, dreaming that I could taste the reality of her seduction in the performance.

The performance of "Razorblade Valentine" was an almost perfect echo of the song I had heard inside my head, the definitive death-anthem.

I felt she was singing to me. She looked into my eyes from across six feet of empty space.

She sang the entire song staring at me, staring deep into my eyes. I remembered the taste of her body from my dream-nightmare, from the vision I'd had while viewing the collage and listening to her song. I tasted her lips and smelled her scent. I was on the very verge of tears when Sasha whispered the final syllables of the song. *"I am nothing if not a razorblade valentine."*

The black curtain fell, and I was lost in the explosion of applause and fanatic screaming in a dozen languages for an encore. I sat there weeping, overcome. It was during this moment that the man in the black suit and black tie, Mr. Sainte, approached me again, and asked me if I would accompany him backstage.

Sasha's dressing room was up four flights of stairs, in a breathtaking steeple warehouse at the top of the Orphanage, dominated by an enormous stained-glass window. The Orphanage was housed in an ancient church that had been converted to a performance space. The lavish dressing room was legendary.

Windows, floor-to-ceiling, displayed to us the entire range of the city's lights.

In the stained-glass shadows of the room, Sasha was stretched on a black velvet canopied bed. I realized her intentions without hesitation. It seemed natural, in some fashion. But it was still more of an honor than I ever would have hoped for. It was like the whisper of the goddess, to hear the invitation echoing through the enormous room. She was inviting me into her bed, and was doing it without a word. For the communication between Sasha and myself was beyond language.

She wore a black robe. Her beauty was radiant, her flesh alabaster. I removed my black clothes soundlessly and she stretched back on the bed, parting the robe. The flash of her white flesh was nothing if not divine. As I climbed, nude, onto the bed, I heard the slight hum of electric motors and was enveloped in darkness as the black velvet curtains of the canopy pulled themselves closed. In darkness I tasted Sasha's lips, as her slender ivory fingers took my wrist and guided my hand to her breast. She reclined into the pillows of velvet, her white arms cast abandoned over her head, her body displayed to me. My fingers traced a path, reverently, up to her high white cheeks, and I took her face in my hands and kissed her deeply, pressing my tongue against hers, feeling the seething warmth of her desire and tasting the salt of her kiss. She was upon me, but without moving her body or touching me. She was a goddess to be worshiped and revered and devoured. Sasha drank deeply of me, and I of her. We came together four times that night, each of us dreaming in silence, our flesh pressing into each other's, our ecstasies explosive in darkness. It was as I kissed Sasha in the last moments of our final devourment that I realized her lips had grown cold and her breast still. Her heartbeat had been the pulse of art, the drumbeat of postmusic, the throb of my salvation, and now that pulse, that drumbeat, that throb, had stopped all of a sudden in a lush and violent finale. With me as the only encore.

I had never before made love to a woman, though I had been with many men, in the United States and in Europe. I was not particularly inclined toward heterosexual behavior—but Sasha was (need I say it?) a special case.

In a sense, perhaps, I had been saving myself for Sasha. And perhaps she, in a more esoteric sense, had saved herself for me.

There was the necessary autopsy, of course. Sasha's suicide note was an interactive virtual-reality CD-ROM of an unreleased work, which spoke explicitly of her death, her cremation, and the terms of her will. The performance, needless to say, was brilliant. The terms of the will were extremely strange, but they were nonetheless legally binding, and thus there was little to do but to accept them. It seemed particularly odd to me that someone as devoted to Gothic representation in postmusic as Sasha had been would desire her body to be cremated rather than buried, though the Arctic Ocean seemed an appropriate site for the scattering of her ashes. Sasha also explained, in Italian and German and Latin and Czech, what she had planned to do that night. I stumbled some over the Czech. She had taken a slow-acting poison, an incredibly expensive designer drug she'd had custom-made, doubtless in one of the exclusive Dutch cafés—but which one? The police, always suspicious where art is involved, investigated my background extensively. My career was tumultuous for a short while after that, but eventually I became something of a cult legend . . . as if I were the man who had fucked Sasha Nobody to death. In academic circles, the fact that I was accused of murdering the artist I had studied brought me very close to divine status.

I was immediately offered a position as lecturer in Postmusic Studies at a nearby institution of higher learning, and had accepted it just as quickly.

I wept at her funeral, to be sure, for this was the greatest and only voice of postmusic, forever silenced. Of course, I knew now that I had been more of an influence on Sasha than I had recognized—why else would she have chosen me to share her final climax, her final encore? And why else would she have given me the keys to her Orphanage?

I had composed my own death-poem years before in my introduction to *Nyet*, and Sasha had been an astute student:

> "Suicide is the rage-scream of the disenfranchised, the only weapon left to take full control of one's life, the last avenue of expression for those who either are not allowed to or are unable to express. It is only through the act of noble suicide that we can reach out from beyond the grave and touch the flesh of the living. It is the privilege of the dead to have pronounced their final curse, and to punctuate that statement with oblivion. . . ."

So much pseudointellectual bullshit, I was later to decide. And yet, when one publishes, she or he cannot retract that information, cannot change his or her mind, cannot clarify a theory or qualify a statement. And so Sasha kindly took me at my word. And fed me my own bullshit—a spoonful at a time.

For that is what Anna Cecilia had done, years before. She had plunged to her death holding a copy of *Nyet* bearing my inscription on the inside cover: "To Anna Cecilia." I found it curious that I could not recall ever having met the girl, or seen her at a lecture. And surely I would have remembered such a divine androgyne. . . .

Sasha, for all her embracement of death, could not live without her Misfortune. It seems logical that she would have had to blame somebody.

It seems logical, and obvious, and perhaps even justified. I had not forgotten that final chilling sentence of Sasha's interactive CD-ROM will, which summed up her entire career, life, and love. Sasha delivered the curse herself, her black lips moving precisely, with red tongue dancing between them as she pronounced what came to be my death sentence. The statement, a subtle parody of my own words, was also scrawled in Sasha's hand in what appeared to be playful verse on the liner notes:

"It is the privilege
of the dead
to exact
a most
exquisite
form
of revenge."

LOVE IN VEIN II

My first indication that something was out of the ordinary was in the vivid dream that caused me to sleepwalk, singing what must have been a very flat version of "Razorblade Valentine" as I walked, nightshirt-clad, down the street in the general direction of the Orphanage. That experience was not repeated, but I began to experience other, more insidious, dreams. This was a few months after Sasha's suicide, as the public furor was beginning to die down. These dreams progressed to vivid memories. Except that they were memories of things that had never happened. Oh, to be sure, they were similar to events that had actually occurred. But they were subtly different. And yet they had the sensuous intensity of actual memories, brought to full flower in dream. Not unlike my death-dream of Sasha.

The dreams grew in substance, until my nights were filled with the witnessing of complicated erotic postmusic nonoperas starring Sasha and myself. Our midnight couplings were punctuated with the most extreme forms of blasphemy, in which the ghostly Sasha seemed to delight. She whispered many times that she would devour my soul, and devour it she did—deliciously.

It was thus that I began to understand that Sasha was coming for me. I began to realize that these tastes, these smells—these sensations and textures and experiences—were, in fact, being born spontaneously, as much as anything in the "physical" world. They were really happening, somewhere deep in my mind. Sasha was after to me, a ghost come to take me and drain my soul. After a time, she came to me every night, and then eventually during the day. It became impossible for me to produce anything in writing except highly visual representations of Sasha's lovemaking with me. Surprisingly, these sold very well. . . .

Our trysts were violent. Occasionally when she climaxed she would laugh. The sound of breaking glass.

I would hear Anna Cecilia's plaintive keening in the distance while Sasha and I made love, moving counterpoint to the poetry of heavy breathing.

Sometimes in the dreams, Sasha would talk to me, give me directions for my lectures, tell me things. She whispered to me that I was to meet her that first Valentine's Day. In the top story of the Church of the Orphanage. Where we had made love the first and only time while Sasha was on this side of the grave.

This had been the greatest oddity in the terms of Sasha's interactive will, you see. She had been the phantom benefactor of the Orphanage, had purchased the old church anonymously, through an untraceable series of international business connections, and had it turned into a performance venue. It had seemed impossible at first. But now it all made sense to me. That I should be given ownership of the building where her rather erotic death had occurred, and thus have access forevermore to reenact it.

Whether or not Sasha is able to enjoy her revenge—I can't know this. But I do know that she comes to me, now, and whispers her poetic seductions, wet Valentine's Day liturgies framed black-lipped against my flesh. It is Sasha's form of prayer, I suppose. It is, after all, the privilege of the dead to torment the living.

Perhaps it is the only form of prayer allowed in Hell.

The years reset themselves, numerologically speaking, long ago. After all the theorizing about apocalypse, postmillennialism, and *fin-de-siècle* decadence, the taste of despair passed, for most, and the sun dawned bloody across a bleached sky, illuminating the bones of the fallen. Ragnarok had ended, and the survivors just kind of put their swords away, not really giving a shit anymore—not that they ever did.

Only the goddesses and gods and giants remained on the battlefield—broken, and weeping.

After two dozen years, I still do not know, and I suppose I shall never know, whether Sasha's ghost is a psychobiological construct of a chemical that was implanted in her sweat, her saliva, her lipstick, her juices; perhaps a carefully designed side effect of the designer drug that killed her, whose invention she commissioned and sponsored. Or possibly just a ghost. Sasha was a brilliant artist, and this was her greatest work of art. She destroyed every fragment of evidence—and I looked. The autopsy had discovered nothing, and so the body had eventually been released for destruction per Sasha's will. This was probably the logic behind the delay of the onset of my symptoms. After all, Sasha's ashes had been scattered across the Arctic Ocean near Tuktoyaktuk by the time I tasted her again.

I am trapped, it seems, for all eternity.

But it is time for the cycle to turn. And even eternity is at an end.

She wears a black silk robe and thong slippers. Her black hair hangs in a curtain across one side of her face, just down to the high cheekbone, leaving one black eye to stare at me. The curve and pucker of her lips is accented by the black lipstick. Her flesh is alabaster. Her cigarette is unfiltered.

She stretches on the black velvet bedcover, her hair falling back, revealing her white face. As she stretches the black robe shifts, revealing the vale between her breasts. Her lips part and she begins to sing. Her voice is clear, high, beautiful, the seductive wail of the banshee, the agony of the disenfranchised.

She sings out her tortured erotic death-poem, the long agony of post-mortem eternity: "I am nothing . . . if not a razorblade . . . valentine. . . ."

From under my leather jacket I take the revolver, .44 magnum, short-barreled, an archaic weapon without neurotransmitter-stimulating capability, but with its own simple, yet rather definitive, effect on brain-wave patterns. I raise the pistol, part my lips.

I laugh, the sound of broken glass.

Copyrights